The Sword Of Aether

The Sword Of Aether

ANIA BO

Copyright © 2023 Ania Bo
All rights reserved.
This is a work of fiction. Names, characters, places and incidents either are the product of the author's imagination or are used fictitiously. Any resemblance to actual persons, living or dead, events or locales is entirely coincidental.

Edited by Jorge J. Pérez
Cover design by Zana Arnautovic
Typesetting by N2JD Localization Services

No part of this book may be reproduced, transmitted or utilized in any form or by any means, mechanical, printed or electronic form without permission.

*to my twin daughters, my sweet loves
who encourage me to be who I am
and nourish me with endless love
I am proud to be your mother.*

CHAPTER 1

THE CHAMPION OF THE KOLLEKS

The smell of beer, mixed with that of urine and sweat, burnt Hugo's nostrils and throat as he made his way through the tables. The howling of so many drunk men made the young boy, barely a teenager, dizzy and nauseous, more so due to his particular condition. The louts all around him felt like wolves; howling, laughing and swearing to Aether, the god of all the races of Siran, the great continent. The boy moved through the rowdy crowd as best as his weak, addled body allowed him to, hoping to deliver the pork stew on the tray in his hands over to table six without bumping into any of the customers, or the half-naked wenches walking towards them all over the barroom floor. When he reached the table, Hugo paused for a second to smell the meat before serving it. He salivated, his limbs weak and trembling, and his stomach churning in tight knots. He was grateful for the darkness of the room—the only light coming from the few, strategically placed candles atop the tables, glowing in fuzzy circles among the haze. Hugo placed the tray on the table, using the darkness to sneak a last look and whiff of the delicious-smelling stew, when a rough voice boomed from behind him.

"Boy." A strong, bald man called from the counter. Hugo didn't hear him, fixated on the stew, and the pain in his stomach.

"Boy!" The man repeated, louder, almost a bark. Hugo started, aware, and the knot in his stomach grew worse—but not because of hunger. The edge to the voice shook him, and he grabbed the money on the table and limped back to the bar as fast as he could.

"Yes, sir. Sorry s—" Before he could finish, a large, meaty hand swept clear across his malformed face, stinging his flesh like a hundred bees.

"Respond to me when I call you, you useless hunchback. I don't pay you to stand around. Here, bring these to table three." The man said, nodding to a tray holding five mugs of beer.

"Yes, Jack, sir." Hugo said, bowing, his cheek throbbing.

"What's that now? That's not my name, little pig—not for *you*."

"Sorry, sir."

"What's my name?"

"Kind Jackie, sir."

The beefy man crossed his arms and smirked, looking down at Hugo with his one good eye, a dried pink scar like a thunderbolt crossing down his other one, white as a corpse's.

"Good. Now get going, little pig. Before I lose my patience again."

Hugo bowed and hurried out of "Kind" Jack's way, zigzagging through the mazelike floorplan of the infamous alehouse once more, tray in hand. A few seconds into it his arms started to shake, not only due to the weight of the tray and its mugs of beer, but also because of the fact he hadn't had anything to eat after a meager breakfast of bread and cheese... eight hours ago. Hugo slowed down to gather his strength, and to not spill any beer, but the slower he walked, the more the wenches stumbled into him, forcing him to almost dance around the tables to avoid them. He finally arrived at table three and set the heavy tray down, immediately noticing the intense stench of unwashed bodies in the air and stifling a retch. The men had long, unkempt hair, and wore dirty animal pelts on their backs, like those who came from *outside* the city walls... The worst and most dangerous kind of people around, Hugo knew. Hugo hurriedly took the silver coins from the table and made his way back towards the bar.

His stomach hurt something fierce, and suddenly the mixed stench of smoke, sweat, urine and meat, combined with the pit in his stomach, became too much for him to handle. He hurried to the kitchen room, right behind the counter, and vomited what little he had in him into an empty spit pot.

Before he could even take another breath, Jack's hand was on his collar, pulling him up and tossing him clear across the kitchen and against the wall, knocking the wind from his lungs.

"You disgusting, useless pig! I take you off the streets, give you a job to feed your miserable family, and this is how you repay me? By puking all over my kitchen? Clean that mess up *now*, or so help me, I'll have you skinned alive. You hear me, you useless invalid?"

"Y-yes Mr. Jackie, sir. I'm sorry, sir… I'm s-so sorry." Hugo said, wiping his mouth with the sleeve of his dirty tunic.

The young boy stood up, shaking, almost convulsing, and grabbed a clean rag from a nearby bucket. He hurried over to the pot and pulled it up, moving towards a tub of clean water nearby.

"And hurry it up!" Jack said. "I need you back on the floor immediately. Take too long, and I'll send Bull back here to fetch you—understand?"

"Yes, sir." The boy replied, his face growing paler, and went to work on the pot as fast as he could. As he exited the kitchen, he saw Bull sitting on a table next to the bar, eyeing the room carefully. The giant of a man was all muscle, his head as bald as Jack's, but his features chiseled from pure steel. He dressed differently from most of the men at the tables—cleaner, more sophisticated. There was a clear air of danger about the man, and the large sax knife on his belt drove the message home. He turned his deep-set eyes on Hugo, like a bird of prey looking down at a helpless rabbit, and the young man turned away, a shiver and a chill rippling up his bent spine.

Bull, Hugo knew, was the butcher of the Edgetown Cutters—one of the most notorious gangs in town, and "Kind Jackie" was one of his best employers. He paid the Cutters good money to keep Bull around his bar—the Beggar's End, and Hugo knew the big brute was a big part of why the alehouse remained as trusted and reliable a place of business as it did.

Hugo felt that familiar hand smack the back of his head, nearly knocking him over.

"New order. Table nine. Now." Jack said, putting the last mug of ale on another tray. Hugo did as told, nodding his head, his whole body aching. He made his way to the table, trying his best to ignore the stench surrounding him as best as he could. Once there, he noticed the men at the table were fully occupied with a group of whores—some of Jack's finest, he knew, and paid him very little mind. He placed the tray on the table, picked up the silver, then headed back, fearing another smack to the head, when suddenly, a strong hand grabbed his forearm and stopped him.

"Two more, boy." A tall, hooded man ordered. He was sitting across another one, also hooded. Both of them looked dangerous—more so than any of the other patrons in the house tonight, and Hugo's pulse quickened. These men were different from the rest: they weren't drunk, or smelled like vomit and sweat mixed together—on the contrary, they were clean, quiet and discreet. Hugo quickly nodded, then hurried back to the counter.

"Two more beers. Table one." He said to Jack as he placed the coins in the earnings box behind the counter. Jack grunted, giving the men at the table a sidelong, distasteful look, then got to work pouring the beers.

Hugo gave the two men another look—they didn't look like they belonged to the Cutters, nor any other gang he knew from the area. Who were they, and what were they doing here? As he was having this thought, he caught Jack's eye. The man gave him a subtle nod, and Hugo nodded back.

There was a reason why Jack had chosen Hugo for this job, and it certainly wasn't for his capacity to do it well. No one spared a small, miserable invalid like Hugo a second look. He could blend into the background as easy as he went, and that afforded Jack other... opportunities.

Hugo placed the beers on the men's tables and moved to the next one over, a cleaning rag in his small hand. He started cleaning the top, all the while his ears pricked towards the men's hushed tones and shrouded lips.

"The load will leave from Savior's Gate," one of them said.

"With the lady?" The other one asked.

"No. With the old man."

"Alright. The payment shall be delivered to him, then."

"No. I'll collect the money. Here and now."

"We always see the goods first."

Hugo tried to get a good look at the "buyer," so he could report the man's features to Jack, and maybe, just maybe, get a bit more food at the end of his shift as thanks… but as he did, he noticed something strange. The buyer reached out his gloved hand to shake the other man's, and in the uncertain light, Hugo noticed how unnaturally large it was.

His heart skipped a beat, and he rushed back to Jack, eager to pass on the information, barely able to draw a full draft of air.

"The Sons… why are the Sons here, of all places?!" He murmured to himself. While he limped back to Jack in a near-panic, the door to the Beggar's End burst open. A tall man in a black cloak was standing at the door, framed by the burning orange light of the setting sun behind him. Hugo, already in a panic, felt himself almost lose control of his senses upon the terrifying sight. He stumbled right onto another serving wench, making her spill all the mugs and ale she was carrying onto the alehouse floor as she came out from behind the counter.

"You clumsy, useless shit!" Jack said between gritted teeth, storming towards him. Hugo cringed, pressed his eyes shut, then braced for what was coming. "I'm going to flail the skin off from your deformed back, then throw you out to the gutter!"

Hugo dropped down on his knees, raised his arms, expecting the worst… but the worst didn't come. He dared open his good eye and saw something that his brain just couldn't understand. The black-robed man stood over him, grabbing Jack's thick, meaty arm in a solid vice grip. Jack, on the other hand, was dumbstruck, staring the newcomer in clear shock.

"Leave the boy be." The black-cloaked man said, his voice sharp and certain. Suddenly, all conversation and hubbub in the alehouse waned down to a thick, palpable silence.

Jack snapped right out of it and, eyes wide, addressed the man.

"Do you have any idea who the fuck I am, stranger? Let go of my hand now—or you'll surely lose it."

Bull pushed a wench off his lap, sending her sprawling to the floor, and strode coolly over to the counter.

"You may want to do as the good man says, stranger. Now."

The black-cloaked newcomer did as told, releasing Jack's hand.

"Good," Bull said. "Now turn on your heels, and leave. You're not welcome here."

"I'm afraid I can't do that."

"And why the fuck not?" Jack said. "This is my fine establishment, and we don't tolerate troublemakers like you here."

"But… good sir, I'm making no trouble. I just didn't want the boy harmed." The man said, very calmly and coolly, almost with a hint of humor to his voice.

"You're not—then what do you call this?" Jack said, spreading his arms wide. "Coming into my establishment? Touching and then *ordering* me like you own the place? Just who in all the blazes do you think you are? The king of the Kolleks?"

"Maybe he thinks he's the Sword of Aether—come to save the poor and the oppressed." Bull joked, and the whole alehouse broke out in malicious chuckles.

To everyone's surprise, the black-robed man joined in on the chuckling.

"Maybe I am." He said.

Then, with a snap of his fingers, he conjured up a living flame over his hand, tearing sharp gasps from every throat in the alehouse. Murmurs filled the darkness of the room.

The man then opened his entire palm, and a roaring flame burst up from it: a small pillar of dancing fire, briefly illuminating everything in the dark, hazy room like a small hearth—revealing the reality of the dregs and filth that filled Beggar's End that night. The pillar of fire died down to a small flame once more, drawing the deep darkness back in.

"Do you know who I am now?" The cloaked man said.

Jack—and everyone else in the room, bowed. Some even knelt.

"M-my lord Odmund, Champion of Aether! Forgive this old, blind fool…"

Hugo's eyes grew wide as an owl's, his entire body frozen as he lay on the floor, staring up at his savior.

"Stand up, son." The man said, and Hugo did so, the room spinning slightly around him. He looked around the alehouse, noticing how everyone was looking at them. He also noticed that the two suspicious men from table one had vanished—slinked away during the commotion, no doubt.

"Are you Hugo Sondors?" Odmund asked.

The boy didn't speak at first, his face a mixture of fear and awe.

"Yes, my lord, he…" Jack began.

"I asked the boy." The champion cut him off in a stern voice, then looked at Hugo… and offered an easy smile.

"Y-yes, my lord. I am."

"Do you know who I am?"

The boy nodded. "Yes, my lord."

"You don't need to fear me, Hugo. And call me Odmund, alright?"

Hugo nodded again, and a smirk appeared on Odmund's face.

"I am a friend of your brother, Tudor."

Odmund saw the recognition in Hugo's eyes—and the pain.

"I am here to pay the blood-debt I owe him. I… was with him when he died." Odmund said, and his eyes filled with a similar pain to Hugo's. The boy just nodded, not fully understanding what the Champion of the Kollek meant by that.

"Tell me, Hugo… Do you like working here?" Odmund asked and looked around the room coolly. Hugo felt his heart leap to his throat, his eyes as wide as a barn. He looked back to Jack, who looked down at him with a look that spoke of fire and brimstone.

The man seemed as if frozen solid, staring at him from behind a thick sheet of ice.

"Don't look at him, Hugo. Look at me." Odmund said, a smirk on his face. "And speak honestly." He looked over to Jack, then Bull, then everyone else in the room. "None of them can hurt you now."

Hugo stared at his shoes—ragged, torn and patched in so many places, they were more sack than leather. The silence in the room became so thick, one could cut it with a knife.

Hugo built up his courage in a way he never had before. This could turn out incredibly bad for him… or…

"No." He finally spoke, very clearly, despite his lisp fully showing. "No, I don't."

Odmund nodded. "Then… how would you like to live and work with me in the castle instead?"

Hugo's eyes darted up now, his face stricken with shock, his mouth agape. Jack stifled a small whimper.

"T-the castle? C-castle Kellum?"

Odmund nodded. "The very same. How about it?"

"B-but… my lord…"

"Odmund."

"S-sorry… Lord Odmund… I am an… invalid. What help can I be in a castle? How can I possibly serve you?"

"It's true…" Jack began. "He can barely serve drinks in this place and—"

"Silence!" Odmund said, looking up at Jack with a look of cold steel in his eyes. The owner of the house froze and flinched, and his skin grew so pale, he looked like he could have a heart attack at any moment.

Odmund looked back down at Hugo. "There's always work to be done in the kitchens and washrooms, son. I'm sure we'll find something you can do well, and good people to teach you. So, what'll it be?"

Hugo didn't have to think it over for long. After a fleeting moment of pondering, he smiled ear to ear and nodded vigorously, his green eyes beaming with joy.

"Yes, my lord… Um, Odmund. I accept!"

Odmund smiled back at him. "Excellent! Then run back to your mother and get clothed and washed. I expect you in the castle tomorrow at dawn. I'll introduce you to the servant's master, Radolf, and he will teach you everything you need to know to start your new life."

Odmund then looked up at Jack—the look of a lion sizing down a jackal. "If the boy doesn't make it to the castle tomorrow, dressed, washed, fed and in great condition—I'm personally making another visit to this shithole, Jack… and I won't temper my flames then. Are we clear?"

The proprietor nodded, his eyes a mix of fear and hate.

Odmund didn't like that. "I said, am I clear?!"

"Yes sir, Champion!" Kind Jackie squealed.

"Good. Oh, and before I leave—the boy will need coin for his new clothes and food. Give him everything he's made today."

"E-every last coin?"

"Every last coin."

Jack turned even paler than he was, if such a thing was possible. He shambled behind the counter, stiff as a tree, pulled out the box of silver coins Hugo had been slowly filling up all night, and put most of them on a small leather bag. Then, without looking at the boy, he dropped it into his cupped hands, trembling something fierce.

"Good." Odmund said. "Now let's go, Hugo. You have no reason to stay here anymore."

Hugo bowed deeply.

"Thank you, my lord!"

The Champion of the Kollek turned around and the boy joined him, not even sparing Jack one last look.

"It's just Odmund to you, Hugo. Just Odmund."

***

Odmund got back on his horse, tended to by his armed escort, and made his way back to the castle as the rising sun lit the labyrinthine streets of Kellum in complex ways—casting deep shadows from the buildings and walls, while lighting the cobbled roofs with a golden glow. Fitting, he thought, as Kellum was, at heart, a complex city, just like Odmund's inner world. As the king had once told him, complexity was good for both the protection of the capital and the heart of a man.

The champion quickened his pace through the waking streets, as he didn't want to be late for a very important occasion today—the graduation of the Chosen cadets, the elite special forces of Kellum and all the Kollek people of Siran.

On his way to the barracks, Odmund remembered his own graduation day, and how excited he'd been all those years back. That was the day he'd finally get to wear the Chosen Corps uniform for the first time: that legendary black vest with red-striped shoulder paddings that every man and woman around the kingdom knew, feared and respected. He touched the Corps' insignia on his breast—shaped as an infinity symbol—and sighed with honor and pride.

The Chosen cadets' barracks was a huge stone building nestled on a corner of the castle grounds, and sporting many small dormitories, a mess hall, classrooms, and of course, a training yard. The cadets' dormitories were plain, but functional: they only had two beds and two small dressers in each. The dressers, Odmund remembered fondly, held the same exact uniforms for all the cadets, regardless of gender: Two pairs of pants, long-sleeved cotton shirts dyed in black, and a pair of thin leather shoes—as well as some simple bedclothes for sleeping. This was all the cadets were permitted to wear until they graduated from their training at age 16—as they were made to earn their individuality through their service and effort. Remembering life as a recruit of the Corps made Odmund smile for a moment.

As he arrived at the training yards, Odmund heard the voices of the academy drill sergeants, barking at the cadets to gather in neat rows, amidst bright, flickering torches. As they saw him walking towards them, the sergeants got even more excited and pressured, realizing their commanding officer had already arrived.

"Hurry up now! Lord Odmund is already here, seedlings—get into your rows, now!" The sergeant ordered as loud as she could, her eyes darting between Odmund and the young soldiers.

The cadets did as told, scrambling to form neat rows of varying numbers, (according to each Corp), across the wide yard, facing their sergeants.

Odmund stood to the side of the large, raised podium at one end of the yard, and watched the Chosen seedlings settle into their rows, as younger cadets who were not yet of age watched from the windows lining the yard. He could see the glint in the cadets' eyes—a spark and a fire behind each of them. They were the future soldiers of the strongest army the continent had ever known—the future of the Kollek race, and they knew it. Seeing that fire in them lit something inside of Odmund as well, reinvigorating him and refreshing his own strength in a way few things could.

As he stepped up into the podium, he looked over the group of congregated cadets—each divided into its house or "Corps," based on the unique abilities that each individual possessed.

First in line were the Scals—those with the ability to see things from far away, even behind solid objects, with their special eyes.

Behind them were the Veruters—those who wielded their voices as weapons and could use them to manipulate the wills of others, with the proper training and experience.

Then there were the Acris—cousins to the Veruters, Acris Chosen could hear sounds for hundreds of meters around them. Some of the best could even pick up sounds from miles away.

Behind them stood the cocky and impulsive Fetears—who could move like blurs, as fast as the wind, and were known for getting in and out of places they shouldn't be in in a flash.

Then there were the few, mysterious and often mistrusted Cauda—Chosen with the power to read other's thoughts, after long and arduous years of training, and even make people feel nauseous, dizzy or even fall unconscious with just a touch. Because this type of Chosen was so rare, there were only two graduates this year—the first in over five years.

Then, finally, at the back stood the Musal—the more feared among the Chosen: those with the physical strength to lift one hundred times their own weight, and the bodies and muscles to prove it.

"No Odons this year," said a feminine voice next to Odmund, catching him by surprise. He knew the voice, of course; to him, it was like silk and honey, like warm sunlight turned into sound. He turned with a smile and beheld his beloved: a blonde lieutenant in her dark uniform, like him, with long, knotted, blonde hair and green, sparkling eyes, glistening brightly in the early morning light. Her warm smile made Odmund feel safe and relaxed—like everything wrong with the world suddenly didn't matter. Like everything was and would always be ok.

"Efilia," he said, nodding to her. "I didn't hear you come up."

"That's because I didn't want you to," she teased.

It took all his self-control not to embrace her and greet her in their usual way—with a passionate kiss to her soft lips—but they were both ranking officers in the Kollek army, and it would've been grossly inappropriate for the occasion. So, he smiled at her quip, and his eyes told her everything he'd do to her later.

Efilia couldn't help but return the smile, then nodded towards the congregated seedlings.

It seems like you'll be the only Odon again this year, my love." She said.

"So it does," Odmund sighed. He shook his head. "If we had more Lords of Fire, we'd stand more of a chance against the Pentaghast and their Night Judges."

Efilia looked at the gathered crowds as the sergeants finished organizing them and passing them the tools they'd need for the ceremony.

"Are the Judges really only afraid of fire?" Efilia asked Odmund, without looking at him.

"Appears so," he said. "No one else—not even other Chosen, seem to faze them."

A shiver went up Efilia's spine then. "Good thing there are only five then…"

"Indeed," Odmund finished. "And yet... if the king allowed me to join the Holy Expeditions—I could use my flames to keep them safe. To drive the Judges away... if not kill them entirely. We wouldn't have to deal with so much death, and..."

Efilia put her hand on Odmund's back and ran her fingers down his spine, cutting off his words. She then spoke softly, but very clearly.

"Our king knows what's best for our people, Od... You need to trust his wisdom."

Odmund sighed.

"Yes. I know he does." Odmund said. "Thank you." He took a deep breath, but Efilia could see the hollowness in his eyes, the lines in his brow and his set jaw.

"Besides," she added. "You're too important to risk like that, love. To him... to the Kollek... and to me."

Odmund was just about to say something else when the sergeant in charge of the ceremony barked an order from below.

"Seedlings, at attention!"

The cadets stood up straight and began to stomp their right feet in unison, creating a steady beat. The chief sergeant then turned to face Odmund, and they all waited for him.

The rhythm stopped as soon as Odmund raised a hand, stepping forward in the podium.

"Faithful seedlings of the Chosen army!" He began, speaking at the top of his lungs. Today, your lives change in ways you cannot imagine. You've worked hard, suffered and made great personal sacrifices to get here, even though the choice was not your own. Not all of you made it either—those unfit among you fell prey to the very gift Aether has given you." He turned to another section of the group.

"You have seen friends die. Others go mad, unable to control their power... and you've all grown without traditional families, groomed for this calling from birth. It is not fair, but neither is this world. We've groomed you out of necessity, to ensure the survival of our species, our people. And now, by your own grit and merit, you have ascended your training. You have bloomed to the point of earning the title of Chosen, the privilege of becoming the loyal soldiers of our Maker, Aether, and called to serve His faithful people. *Your* people... the Kollek. You've been chosen by divinity to serve King Ulor, our god's hand in this world. From this day forward, you will bear all the duties of a Chosen soldier, assigned to a squad, and reborn as anointed servants of the king's army!"

He paced from one side of the podium to the other, hands laced behind his back, his black uniform glistening in the torchlight as if it were itself catching fire.

"You worked hard to survive, hard to control your powers and minds. Never forget we were all sent to this world to protect it from the heathens that would corrupt it: the dreaded Pentaghast and their magic-born abominations, the Night Judges, created from their own flesh to hunt us all down. We were also sent to fight the dark Nor, cursed by Aether long ago for their pagan ways and arrogance. And let us not forget the other enemies of our kingdom and Aether's will: the so-called 'Sons of Forest', rebels against His will and our king's wise vision for all of us. All of them enemies of the Kollek spirit, and darkest threats to our very way of life!"

He stopped at the center of the podium and looked straight ahead.

"The Kollek were weak once... long ago. Looked down upon, used by the other races as they saw fit... until the day Aether decided to honor us by letting a faithful Kollek woman give birth to the first Chosen. The destiny of our nation and race was written then, that we would rule the world in peace and wealth! Your abilities are a gift to help us serve this great nation and protect it. You are the Chosen of Aether! A Chosen never betrays, never lies, never fears... and never stops fighting. We are born to fight... and we *die* in the fight."

The crowd shouted in one voice.

"We're born to fight, and we die in the fight!"

Odmund saluted them by pounding his gloved fist on his heart. Then he pulled his dagger from his belt and took off his glove from one hand.

The chief sergeant signed the seedlings to follow suit, so they too took out the small knives they were given and held them in their left hand.

"Until the coming of the Savior—the Sword of Aether himself, we are *all* that stands between the proud Kollek peoples of the Siran and the darkness. Now... do you, Chosen of Aether, take the oath of serving our god, and His servant, King Ulor, as His right hand... even at the cost of your life?" Odmund asked, holding the knife over his open hand.

The cadets all swore in unison, as they'd been taught. "I do! My oath is my blood."

"Then seal your oath with your blood, and may Aether bless your sacrifice!"

Odmund then sliced the dagger over his palm and spilled the fresh blood onto the grass before him.

The seedlings then followed suit all at once, while the sergeants kept a careful eye on them. They raised and clenched their fists and made their blood fall with Odmund's, drunk by the earth of the Academy. Two Scal sergeants carefully assessed the scene with their special eyes, ensuring everyone did as told.

"Do you, the Chosen of Aether, take the oath of using the power given to you by your god *only* for the service of this nation?"

"I do! As blood is my oath!" They all shouted as strong as they could again, and clenched their hands to spill a second drop... Then put their knives back in their scabbards.

Odmund put his own dagger back in its sheath, and raised his palm, showing the blood leaking from the cut he'd made.

"Then, by the authority given to me by the Hand of Aether, High King Ulor of the Kollek, I accept your oath, which has been sealed with your blood, as I seal it with my own. Your oath is now bound, and I proudly announce you all as King Ulor's holy soldiers. Long live the king!" Odmund shouted, raising his fist and conjuring up a powerful flame on it, which lit up the entire courtyard as bright as midday. The crowds cheered and echoed his words.

"Long live the king!" The seedlings said as loud as they could and hit their fists on their chest along with Odmund. And once again, Odmund, his chest swelling with pride, beheld the future of his people.

CHAPTER 2

THE MADMAN AND THE HUNTRESS

As the first rays of the sun appeared beyond the sharp, distant mountains, the sweet smell of blood rode the wind down the Golden River, wetting the two jackals' appetites. They paid the utmost attention while watching the old, half-naked villager in the distance, throatily eating uncooked rabbits and drinking their blood.

"Do you see the jackals watching us behind those trees? On the other side of the river?" Axel asked to no one in particular, while drinking the blood of the dead rabbit.

"So what?" He replied to himself, looking at the jackals with his one good eye, blood dripping from his bushy, unkempt beard. His short hair was a mess and showed signs of the struggle he'd recently endured while catching his crude breakfast.

"They don't even blink! I hope they don't find a way to cross the river!" He said, his voice afraid.

"Don't worry… They can't do anything to us." He replied, the voice now stable and calm. "And besides… I have you, right?" He took another bite from the other rabbit's flesh, finishing it.

As the old man realized there were no more pieces left to eat, he threw the bony, mangled carcass aside.

"Hey—BE CAREFUL! You'll stain our clothes, you damn fool!" He said.

His old, weathered body stood up with effort. He then walked over to the river's edge and washed his hands, beard and mouth, making his way over to his discarded clothes. He scanned them, ensuring that there was no blood on them. Aside from some dirt from his journey to the woods, his linen pants, patched cotton shirt and brown overcoat were somehow perfectly clean. Were it not for the mess of blood on his beard, he could've even passed as a decent member of society.

"I don't understand why you're so worried about these rags." He shrugged, looking sidelong at the four dead rabbits on the ground, an expression of guilty desire clear in his eyes.

His face suddenly changed, becoming more serious and focused. "Because they're all I—*we*, have!"

"Who cares?" The other him said, shrugging again. "I'm handsome even if I'm naked, old man. My body would sweep all the wenches of Halstead off their feet!" The other him parroted, flexing his lanky arms.

"Enough!" He shouted, then donned his old, brown shirt and patched trousers.

"You are no fun." His other voice complained with a disappointed face as he tidied himself back up. He looked at the jackals watching him from the other side of the river, nine meters away. With a quick move, he picked up the rabbits from their tails.

"Wait... what are you doing? Wait a moment—no, I say! We should take those back and save them for a stew or something!" The other him begged, but his arm was getting ready to throw the rabbits to the other side of the river all the same.

"It won't do to have people see us carrying half-eaten animals like that. And it won't do for them to rot here, while hungry eyes watch from across the river."

With a good throw, he lunged the first rabbit across the surging waters. As soon as it fell on the other side, the jackals twitched and started to move, very cautiously at first, then faster. Their eyes darted between the old man and the free meal he'd just hurled near them. With the arrival of the second and third rabbit, they threw themselves at the carcasses, fighting each other for the bigger pieces of raw flesh.

"Please… at least save one for me!" Axel begged.

"Shut up! You've already eaten enough! Your mouth smells like a butcher's table! The girl will be up soon, too. We have to go back."

He threw the last rabbit across the river, angry at his other self for being so stupid and nonsensical. Axel walked away from the riverside and into the far-off woods, leaving the jackals to enjoy their small feast, tearing the remains of the rabbits to shreds with yellowed fangs, bone and all. The old man's eyes stared back at the jackals from time to time with regret and longing, until the trees took them out of sight.

Axel enjoyed the rays of the sun as they leaked and danced through the colorful leaves of the trees; cast in shades of yellow, orange and light greens still. The fresh fruit hanging on them shook lazily in the calm breeze of the dawn, while falling drops of morning dew pretended to be like light summer rain, despite it being early fall. The calming song they made upon the leaves and forest floor made it seem like they enjoyed being something they were not.

"You wasted a perfectly good meal!" Blurted the other Axel, breaking the perfect moment. "You were a killjoy when you were a kid, and you're still one now. Why is it that you can't loosen up at least a little bit? No wonder you look like an old, ragged sack!" He said in a rough, angry voice.

"I wasn't a killjoy. I was responsible and level-headed. One of us had to be. So, if anyone's to blame for us looking like a wet rag, it's you." The other him stayed silent. Then, pressing the advantage, he added: "Shut up now. We're almost at the village. I don't want you to talk once we're there. You make me look like I'm mad."

"Aren't we?" The other him laughed, just before his right hand slapped his left one.

"Okay, okay! I'll hold my—*our*, tongue…"

"Thank you." He said, standing on the top of the hill near the village.

"The glorious border village of Halstead... a precious, unspoiled hamlet full of bright souls—far-removed from the cares of the world, isn't it?" The other him said inside his mind, the sarcasm heavy in his voice. As Axel clenched his fists, the other part in him stepped back.

"Okay, okay... You do know you'd be hurting yourself too, right?"

Axel grimaced. "They are family to us. They saved us when we were wounded, fed us, and sheltered us. We owe these people a debt. Do *not* make light of them." He sternly said.

His inner voice hushed as there was nothing left to be said.

The village was currently celebrating the coming of autumn, as was shown by the colorless clouds emanating from chimneys on the thatching of small, wooden cottages, and the orange-leafed decorations on the portals of the mud and thatch huts that lined its streets. Pumpkins, barley and wheat also adorned gardens and windowsills, giving the town a picturesque look.

The quiet village, built originally by hunters and woodcutters in the middle of the Redwood Forest, was surrounded by tall trees. Its narrow stone roads seemed like paths of ants, showing the way in and out of the labyrinth of mud houses, wood and thatch cottages that made up the bulk of the buildings. Although the village could in no way be called a town, there was still a huge square with a large statue of King Ulor in the middle, just like on every other sanctioned settlement throughout the Kollek kingdom, facing a special building: a small, almost ruined Aetheliour, the home of the god Aether. There was a sun emblem on the king's forehead and star figures on his fingers. Underneath the statue, a metal plate read: "Long Live The King, The Right Hand of Our God Aether."

Apart from the statue, it wasn't hard to see the village wasn't home to any rich people. The only outstanding building was a huge, mistreated barn, belonging to the village's appointed ealdorman, "Rapid" George, called such for how fleet of foot he used to be long ago, during his prime hunting days.

From his vantage point in the hill above the village, Axel could see that the townsfolk were already awake, most of them on their way to start their daily routines. Staring at the golden-lit village and the bright dawn rising behind it, Axel breathed in the cold, fresh air of the autumn morning into his lungs, allowing himself to enjoy the stillness of the view in front of him, if for just a moment…

A moment that, sadly, wouldn't last, as Axel was suddenly startled by the image of galloping horses through the forest. He rubbed his eyes just to be sure he was seeing right.

"Oh no…"

He walked left and right in a building panic, hoping to get a better view, but the image remained partly shrouded by branches. Eventually, climbing a bit higher, he managed to see them clearly. The soldiers wore grey riding cloaks: the advanced forces of King Ulor.

"They are here earlier than we expected…"

"Oh no no…" His inner voice panicked. *"What will we do? What will you do?"*

"Calm yourself, you fool. I'll find a way." Axel took control and ran down the hill as fast as he could, hoping to reach Halstead before the soldiers. Although he was just several hundred yards away, and much closer to the village, the road seemed impossibly long. His old lungs couldn't cope with the speed his mind was demanding of him, and he tumbled down the hill, rolling like a ragged sack of potatoes, cursing every important name he knew. He landed on his back, the wind knocked out of him and the trees overhead spinning all over. Somehow, despite his old age and frailty, he found himself to be just fine, if a little sore.

"Damn this old body!" Axel complained as he tried to get up.

He could feel the other him roaring in laughter inside him. He considered smacking his own face good—then the ache running through his whole body warned him against it. The old man stood up, gingerly, rubbing his lower back, and took a moment to let some of the sting pass, then slowly started running again.

Thanks to the shortcut provided by his long fall, Axel managed to reach the village before the soldiers. Right before he entered old Shelly's backyard, he wiped his clothes as best as he could, brushing away leaves, sticks and dirt, then did the same for his hair—which by now looked more like some kind of bird's nest. While passing through her garden window, he came eye to eye with her as she washed her vegetables in the kitchen. Her surprised look was met by a kind smile from Axel.

"Mornin,' Shelly!" He said.

The old woman hesitated for a second, then waved her own hand as well. "Morning."

Axel nodded, then promptly continued on his way to town.

"Why do you do that?" The other him asked.

"Do what?"

"You know you're too old and… dysfunctional, for any of that, right?"

"Shut up."

"But… it's true."

"I said *shut up*. She… feeds us every now and then."

The other him just shrugged. "Fair enough."

Once at the square, Axel stopped and checked to see if the soldiers were already there, which thankfully, they weren't. Nodding to himself, the old man picked up his pace and walked towards a peculiar-looking cottage on one side of the square: the one belonging to the young village hunter, Merki—the last proper hunter in Halstead.

Her cottage was the oldest one in town, and even from a distance, it was clear just how weathered it was. She had done many repairs throughout the years, like boarding up on the holes of the walls with wooden planks, but she was no carpenter and the age still showed. Although the cottage was old, its garden, however, was well-cared for, with well-pruned apple trees and bushes, (which Axel helped himself to every once in a while).

Axel entered though the front yard and knocked on her door, a little harder than he meant. To his surprise, nobody answered. He looked around the square, where she could often be found helping some of the villagers in the morning, or selling some of her latest catch, but she wasn't anywhere to be seen.

He knocked again. Still no answer, so he knocked one more time, faster now. "C'mon, Merki… not today, of all days… you *must* be home."

"Who is it?" A young woman's voice yelled from the cottage's backyard.

"It's Axel!" He shouted back as he walked through the right side of the house.

Upon hearing the sound of his voice, Rage, Merki's hunting dog, barked and ran over to him. He was not the least bit happy or excited to see him. On the contrary, Rage growled at him with the hatred of ten dogs, all stuffed together into a single mass of muscles, teeth and claws. He gave Axel his customary greeting of bared, yellowed fangs and low growls. Axel replied to him with his customary scowl.

"Down, boy!" Merki sharply commanded. Rage stood down, but his eyes never left Axel.

"What do you want, Axel?" She asked him, sharpening her hunting knife in her hand with a small stone. "I'm setting out on a hunt soon, so make it quick."

Her brown hair shone under the golden morning light. The autumn colors of the forest glittered in harmony with it, and with her pure white skin. Her eyes were like a play of light: one day the old man could swear they were green, the other day brown or amber. Today they were amber, just like the dried leaves of fall rustling all around them.

"What will you say old man? What will you say?" Axel's inner voice wondered.

He cleared his throat. "That's perfect, Merki. You know how you've always said you'll teach me to hunt one of these days? I think I'll join you today, hmm?"

"Really?" Merki asked.

"Really. This town could use another hunter, don't you think? Even if it's one as old as I."

Merki thought about it for a moment while she assessed Axel.

"However, there's a catch. We need to go *now*." He finally said.

"Why now?"

"Because I'm starving." Axel cut in. "That is, ahh, I haven't eaten in so long. I'd very much appreciate it if you could help me catch something for breakfast."

Merki gave him a look, raised an eyebrow, then pointed with her knife to her orchard. "Just eat an apple or two, old man. We'll set out in an hour or so. I have a few things to do before we set out, you know. Equipment to maintain, for one."

"No!" Axel said, more abruptly than he meant. Merki's eyes widened, and she stopped sharpening the knife. "I mean… I'm *really*, really hungry, old friend… and I heard from Shelly that a large herd of deer passed by her house not too long before sunrise. If we wait, they could give us the slip." He lied.

"A herd? This close to town?"

He nodded.

Merki mulled over it, touching the tip of the knife to her chin. Then she said, "Alright. Let's go. Just wait here till I get my stuff." She walked past Axel, and went inside the cottage. Despite how it looked from the outside, the inside of the house was so tidy and well-organized, it seemed as if it didn't belong in Halstead.

"Come on boy." She ordered Rage, who was waiting for her outside of the door next to Axel. "You too, old man. And you *better* be right about that herd."

Axel simply nodded, doing everything he could not to let his anxiety show. "Yes, yes… let's hurry along, then."

They made their way through the square and back down the southern street, leading out to the wild woodland beyond—and away from the soldiers and their horses. A sliver of calm and relief came over Axel as he realized that they were far enough now, and would soon enter the embrace of the forest, blocking all sound.

However, he miscalculated a single fact—Merki's senses weren't like his or any other person in the village. She had refined them to near-inhuman levels during her years as a huntress, fending by herself in the wilds, and now, almost by the edge of the village… she suddenly stopped.

"What? What's wrong? Let's keep going! My breakfast is getting away!"

"Do you hear that?" She asked.

"Hear what?"

"Horses… Many of them. Riding at a gallop towards town!"

The villagers began to spill out onto the streets to see what the ruckus was all about, and a murmur of excited and fearful voices started to spread through town. Merki turned back towards the village square at a leisurely jog.

"Hunting will have to wait, old man! C'mon! It's got to be the king's soldiers!"

Axel pursed his lips. *"Almost, old man. Almost. I guess we were too late after all."* His inner voice sighed. "It's all because of *you*. You just had to waste the morning chasing after rabbits, didn't you?" He shot back, wordlessly. *"Well, we had to eat! Plus, they were early! We weren't expecting the soldiers to be here yet…"* Axel took a deep breath to calm himself, then followed the villagers' voices to the square.

"The king sent his men! He remembers us!" Some were saying.

"Are we in trouble? Did somebody do something wrong?" Others murmured.

"We paid our taxes… why would the king send soldiers here?"

The man leading the group was a good-looking man: a captain, by the looks of it, bearing three stars on his shoulders. He stopped his horse in the middle of the square, right in front of King Ulor's statue. Although he wasn't the oldest, being in his late twenties, he was clearly the leader of the soldiers. An older soldier with a grizzled beard and short, graying hair, stopped his horse a few feet behind him, to his right. He, Axel saw, had two stars on his shoulders. Aside from them, there were three younger-looking men—recently drafted villagers, by the look of them.

"A drafting party…" Merki murmured to Axel under her breath.

Although the two soldiers seemed well-cared for, the villagers were young and clearly very, very green under their gills. One of them, a youth with thin black hair and pale skin, looked so frail, that Merki thought a strong wind might blow him from his horse at any moment. He had big, startled eyes that popped out of his bony, sharp face. Another one with brown eyes and greasy hair couldn't be older than seventeen, and yet he held his young head high, as if he were a decorated soldier of the king's high command. His hand kept on fixing his brown hair while his eyes looked around the villagers as if they were the lowliest of dregs. The last of the recruits was bulky and more soldier-like than the rest, but the look in his empty eyes and half-open mouth told Merki the poor sod couldn't be trusted to light a fire without burning his house down, let alone use a sword properly.

The captain, however, looked bright and awake—his eyes darting around the village, assessing the people and the lands. His eyes rested over the old Aetheliour and a look of concern, and even disgust, passed over his eyes. He pursed his lips and looked over the people of Halstead once more, this time a flicker of religious zealotry overcoming his features. Once he surmised every villager in town had gathered, he began his announcements—without bothering to dismount his armored steed.

"Citizens of Halstead. I am Captain Locke, of the king's twenty-third battalion. I am… honored, to salute you as a captain of respected Kollek army, under the command of our King Ulor, Right Hand of our God, Aether. By King Ulor's command, the Kollek army is looking for brave, patriotic men to join the advance forces in our fight against the evil, godless Koartiz."

Seeing the villagers' vacant expressions, he sighed, then clarified.

"The race of heathen magic-users from the east—the sworn enemies of our people. Aether's mercy, how much of a backwater is this place anyways?" He whispered the last bit to the grizzled, older man next to him, barely audible, but Merki picked it up clear as day. The older man just shrugged; his features clad in stone.

"For forty-five years now," Captain Locke continued, "We've managed to hold them back from our lands—especially after our victory at the battle of Rainbow Falls—but we still need brave, young men to keep them and…" He hesitated, and Merki could see the unease in his features plain as a book.

"Go on…" The older soldier next to him whispered.

"And their unholy monsters… the Night Judges, from our borders. Each brave man who enlists will be awarded with the right to great spoils and bounty. All patriotic and courageous men of Halstead—step forward!"

The villagers exchanged looks. A young man wanted to step forward, but his mother held him by the arm and shook her head. Everyone in the kingdom, even this far back in the middle of nowhere, knew just what happened to soldiers who signed onto the advance forces.

"They became live fodder, sent to be ripped apart by the Night Judges, or the Koartiz warriors, while the real soldiers carry out their missions." Axel's inner voice told him as he watched the proceedings. "Just mere distractions of flesh and blood—that's all they are." Axel added to his other self.

The lieutenant, however, was right about something. King Ulor had always paid the families of dead soldiers well. And then again… every once in a while, one of or two of them *did* survive. But it was often the exception. Definitely not the rule.

The males were looking at each other in the confused crowd. None of the women wanted to send their boy or man away; they already had a hard time making ends meet as it was, and sending their men to war would only likely mean receiving a measly payment in return. In such an out-of-the-way village, men were the only protection they had against prowling bandits and other potential scums lurking among to roads, waiting to steal their food. Not to mention, the flesh-eating savages that lived beyond the river, in the forbidden woods beyond Kollek lands…

"Once more…. By King Ulor's command, the Kollek army is looking for brave, patriotic men to join the advanced forces. Each brave soul who enlists will be awarded with the right to spoils and bounty. All ambitious and courageous men of Halstead, step forward!" The captain repeated. However, as he looked at the assembled, all he could see was the fear in their eyes.

"I know you think there's little chance of survival, and little spoils, in joining the advance forces… But what you don't know, is that we are *very* close to winning this war and destroying our enemy for good. We all have to sacrifice for our country and our children. As men of the Kollek kingdom, we are responsible for them—for their future. But the truth is, if we don't defeat these wretches and their foul stain off our lands, we won't have a future. We will lose our country, our lands, our sons and daughters—and we will never get them back. We have to stick together to end this tyranny, which our ancestors had fought against for centuries. There is light at the end of this tunnel. However, we only prevail if we act now, and deliver the decisive blow to the enemy while we can!"

The men of the crowd looked at each other. The captain's speech seemed to have stirred up a fire in some of them, and a few looked ready to step forward… but before they could, and to Axel's deep dismay, Merki ran over to the center of the square.

"I… I want to join the king's advance forces!" She clearly said.

Rage, her dog, ran behind her, sitting by her side, watching intently. The captain looked her way and his eyes widened. He quickly corrected himself and noticed the bow and arrows, the knives at her belt, and the confident demeanor of someone who knew combat. He also noticed her breasts.

"That's… really brave of you, miss…"

"Merki. Huntress and skilled archer of Halstead."

"Yes… Merki. However, I'm afraid, we are under strict order to only enlist *men* to the advance forces. Maybe you can join one of the local garrisons as a ranger, or help around the halls?" Locke said in as kind a tone as he could muster, while the older soldier beside him looked away in clear disgust.

Merki took a step closer towards the captain, with her hunting hound behind her, and repeated: "I want to join the *army*, sir. Believe me—I've probably killed more than all these children combined," she nodded her head at the three recruits, to offended stares from the greasy-haired one and confused ones from the other two. "Even if it's just deer and wolves." She said in a lower tone. Her eyes, however, pierced into the man with cold steel. Rage, sensing her tone and energy, padded softly next to her, his belly rumbling with a low growl at the taller, armored creature atop the horse.

The captain bent forward to look Merki in the eyes.

"By King Ulor's command, the advanced forces is only to look for men, miss. The brave women of the Kollek race are welcome to give birth to Chosen children if they can, or serve in some other capacity—but the men need their women home to return to—they *can't* join the army."

"That's nonsense." Merki said, eliciting gasps from many of the villagers, and drawing a baleful look from the old man next to Locke. The captain, however, held his fist up, signaling him to stand down.

"I didn't make the rules Merki, huntress of Halstead. Your king and Right Hand of Our God Aether did. If I show up at one of the garrisons with a damsel wanting to see war, it's my head on a pike. I'm sorry."

Merki shuffled on her feet, weighting her options.

Locke looked up at the crowds once more. "Anyone else? Does anybody here have more stones than this girl? C'mon, men! Show your wives what you're made of!"

"How about a guide, then? A hunter for your travels?" Merki said, drawing Locke's attention back to her.

"By Aether's sake, Locke, put a boot to this wench already." The older soldier said, rolling his eyes, but Locke immediately held his hand up again. "Hold, Gerard. I want to hear what she has to say." He turned to Merki. "I'm sorry… a hunter? A guide? Why would we need such a thing? We're fully armored soldiers of the king!"

Merki fixed her eyes on him, and against all odds, he could've sworn they turned green under the shifting light.

"We are at war, brave captain of the Kollek. Halstead and its surrounding lands spread for miles… and are quite dangerous for *men of the king* such as yourself."

Gerard, Locke's second in command, drew his sword. "You're threatening us now, little wench? Why don't I show you how to speak to a king's soldier then, if you're so eager to be a part of the military?"

"Gerard, *hold*, I said!" Locke's crisp command ringed through the village square, eliciting a near complete silence.

"The young huntress didn't mean anything by that. Did you?" He eyed Merki very carefully, the message clear in his eyes.

"Of course not," she bowed. "I only meant to say that I can guide you all safely out of these parts. And I can hunt great game while we're at it. You'll eat like kings on the way back to the garrisons... and eventually Kellum, my lords."

"Dammit, Merki..." Axel cursed under his breath.

"Locke... She could be dangerous. One of them damned rebels..." Gerard warned him.

But the captain was looking at Merki with different eyes now. There was curiosity in them, yes... but also something more.

"Tell you what, Merki. I like your spirit. And we could definitely use a hunter in our group for our journey back to the capital... If only for the food. If you can hunt and bring us a fully grown stag for tonight... maybe I'll let you join us on our way back. Show us how great of a huntress you really are... But only if you can bring it to us by tonight."

Merki held his gaze for a moment, then said: "You'll let me join the army if I bring you a stag?"

Locke smiled easily at her. "I didn't say that. I said I'll let you join our group... Travel with us. Maybe."

She took a deep breath and considered his words.

"Don't do it, Merki... Don't do it..." Axel uttered to himself.

"I'll do it." She said.

"Excellent. We'll dine like kings tonight, then. Now, anyone else?" He looked away from the young huntress, and focused on the crowds once more.

Merki nodded, and immediately broke into a heavy stride towards her house, followed by Rage and Axel.

"Merki, wait!" He rasped, following her back to her humble cottage.

"Sorry, Axel. I'm afraid you'll have to find someone else to teach you to hunt."

"What are you thinking? Are you mad? These men will ravage you, then leave you by the side of the road without a second thought! They're not going to honor their word."

Merki scoffed, then flashed Axel an easy smirk. "I'd like to see them try."

Axel shook his head. "That's beside the point! You're leaving Halstead? Everything you've built here? Everyone you know?"

Merki stopped in front of her home and turned to face Axel. "Everything I've got here, Axel? I have *nothing* here." She spread her arms in exasperation. "A run-down ruin of a house. A village of less than thirty old, tired faces. No men my age, no guild to join and make a name for myself, no future! Nothing! Now, because of this damn, seemingly endless war, and the fact that we live in the farthest possible reaches of our kingdom—*these* men are the only ticket I have out of here. The only shot I might get at a *real* life. And I'll be damned if I don't take it."

Axel stared at her for a good while, waited for her to calm down a little.

"A humble life in a backwater village might not be so bad, my dear girl… there are monster out there worse than any wolf or bear you've faced. Far worse. Trust me."

Oh, I know. Merki thought.

"I don't care," she told Axel. "I'm bringing that man a fat stag, and we're eating well tonight. Then, I'm leaving this place. You can keep my house if you want… if you're really that fond of Halstead and its people. I bet you're tired of sleeping in that little shed by the outskirts you call a home."

Axel shrugged. "There's no talking you out of this, is there?"

"No." She firmly said.

He sighed deeply. "Then… let me go with you."

She scoffed. "What? Are *you* mad, old man? You can't make such a journey!"

"You'd be surprised…" He told her, in a voice that, for just a moment, surprised her.

She looked him head to toe. The village hobo, to whom she'd given shelter and fed for the past few years. It would be good to have a familiar face on the long road to Kellum, the Holy City of the Kollek people… and yet… once they got there, what would she do with him? She couldn't move forward with her plans with an old, decrepit man hanging on her side. She just couldn't.

"I'll think about it." She lied. "Now excuse me while I go hunt that stag and secure our ticket out of here."

CHAPTER 3

THE SONGBIRD

The dense humidity in the basement level of the castle made it hard to breathe.

All the maids and servants of the royalty and high-ranking officers of Kellum were stuck in their smaller rooms, packed like canned shrimps through the long, humid corridors. And yet, they were the lucky ones, as the lesser servants were made to live in a small house a few hundred meters away from the castle; a place the inside folks called "the Bosom."

The first room near the stairs, only slightly bigger than the others, belonged to one of the most experienced servants in King Ulor's service, Mere. She was the loyal personal maid of Ifir, the Spymaster of the king and overseer of the Chosen army.

Mere, despite her old age, usually woke up before sunrise, quickly got dressed and prayed to Aether. She was getting older, having reached her mid-sixties a few weeks back, and had a harder time each day feeling comfortable in her work attire. She was always silent as a rock, but her niece, Loure was just the opposite: she enjoyed singing as she got ready for her day, instead of praying. Loure was almost seventeen years old. She had golden yellow hair, bright, white skin, and light-brown eyes. Her youth gave her a flawless body with a thin belly and tight hips… which she loved to show off. Mere watched her get ready, eyeing her silently.

"When will I be able to transfer to another duty?" Loure asked Mere.

"What do you mean?" Mere asked, a bit surprised.

"I really won't have to wash dirty clothes and emptying chamber pots for the rest of my life, will I?" She rolled her eyes.

"You arrived here just a few weeks ago, Loure, and only because your mother begged me to help you. You'd rather be working in the fields, out there in the cold, or worse? Be happy with what you got. Most girls your age would *kill* for a job at the castle." Mere said in a scolding tone, as she made her own bed.

Loure rolled her eyes again.

"I know aunt Mere, and I'm very grateful… However, I didn't come here to wash their dirty undergarments and clothes… I thought there'd be more, like serving food to the royals, or helping gallant Chosen knights dress up! I can do *so* much more than washing." Loure argued, while filling cottons in her bra to make her breasts seem bigger. If it wasn't clear in the tone of her voice, Mere could see her real intentions for getting a job here now… but it was too late. Loure was already in the castle.

"What are you here for, then? Come on. Out with it." The old woman asked, staring the young woman down with stern eyes.

"Well… I can give another son to the king." Loure answered with poise and feminine composure.

Her words pierced Mere's soul and fanned a panic in her bosom. She crossed over to her niece and grabbed her arm in a quick, sudden move, sinking her nails into her flesh.

"If you value your life, dear niece, or mine, you'll *never* say something like that again within these walls! If the queen ever hears you…Or worse, my lady Ifir… Oh dear, may Aether protect us!"

The young girl stepped back, pulling away from the sharp pain in her arm. And yet, even as she did, there was a rebellious shine of determination in her eyes that scared Mere even more.

"The king may have as many sons as he wants." She defiantly said. "And once I give him one… *I'll* be as strong as the queen, and I'll make Ifir pay for what she did to you!"

Mere's breath caught in her throat, and her eyes became so big, they looked as if they'd pop right out of her skull.

She opened her mouth to answer back to Loure, but the words got stuck halfway through. Her hand reached over to her right ear unconsciously, the one that could not hear anything. Seeing her aunt's confusion, Loure got closer to her left ear and whispered.

"You've been here for so long that you've even forgotten your real name. You are Meredith, of the forgotten noble house Huzen, not just "Mere the Maid." But I *will* make you remember who you really are, aunt. Trust me. I am ready. I've been getting ready for this *all* my life. Somehow… some way… I will restore the name of our house."

The young girl looked into her aunt's eyes and Mere's fear grew stronger. She was ambitious—but ambition alone wouldn't help her survive the horrors of this castle. She needed smarts as well, and those, Mere could see plain as day, she lacked in worrying amounts. The old maid pulled her hand back and slapped her niece across the face so savagely, she fell over her bed.

"You will never, *ever* leave this basement or your work here, or I'll be sure to send you straight back to your miserable family home myself! You hear me?" Mere shouted at her, then slammed the door behind her as she left in a fury.

Before she climbed up the stairs, however, she touched her deaf ear one more time… but then immediately shook her head, composed herself and tidied up. A deep breath of stale, but familiar humidity calmed her nerves and gave her the necessary courage to move on.

The effort of climbing the stairs brought out the usual pain in her knees again. She was getting old, and the humidity of the basement made everything worse for her old knees. Through the small window of the stairs, she saw a couple of little birds flying to a point higher in the keep. She did her best to speed up.

"The birds are already coming... damn you Loure—I'm late!" She whispered. "Ignorant peasant girl... but the fault is really mine. I was the one who brought her here. Stupid, Mere, stupid!"

She urged her knees to move forward as she prattled on to herself. Her pain was the best pill for her anger now, and she swallowed it dutifully, one step after the other. The more she focused on the pain in her legs, the less she would focus on her building rage at Loure.

She wiped her shoes before stepping on the silk red carpet in the corridor once she arrived at the top floor of the castle, which belonged to the king, the queen and Ifir. Then, doing her very best to compose herself as if nothing had happened, she rushed to knock on Ifir's bedroom door.

"Come in, Mere!" An almost angelically silky voice said from inside.

Her voice was unusually calm and peaceful today. Mere knew that wasn't a good sign. Unfortunately, she couldn't do anything else other than pray for her niece to not be heard by someone. The castle was, after all, full of eager ears and running mouths. Pushing her worries aside as best as she could, the old maid opened the ornate and incredibly detailed cedar doors to the Spymaster's chambers.

The room was as warm as a summer day.

The fireplace still had few burning logs in it from last night, and the soft light of candles accompanied its greatness. The polished wood flooring was covered with animal pelts that Ifir herself had hunted, and the lush silk quilt covering the massive, lush bed was the fanciest piece in the entire bedroom.

Mere found the owner of the room standing radiant and regal next to her bed, like a marble statue of the finest make. Ifir's long, black hair flowed down her shoulders and covered half of her naked body. Her green eyes held the most intense look in the entire kingdom. Mere, at least, had never seen a more powerful and hungry look—not in any of the lords, ladies, knights or dukes that walked the halls of the great keep. The old woman tried hard not to meet eye to eye with her mistress, as usual, so she walked briskly over to the Spymaster's closet and waited for the usual order.

"The emerald green one, I think… the one with the long sleeves." Ifir said.

Mere picked the silk dress among so many others and moved near to help dress her up. That was Ifir's favorite color, as it was a perfect fit with her eyes. After putting Ifir's shoes on her feet, Mere helped her to her makeup table.

"I see you're running a little late." Ifir said with a questioning tone, looking at Mere through the mirror standing in front of her as she worked on her hair. The old maid gave only the smallest fearful glance, meeting Ifir's eyes for just a second, before resuming all her focus on her hair.

"I am most sorry, Your Grace," she said. "My niece hasn't gotten used to the rules of the castle yet, being so new at her job, and so it falls to me to teach her." Mere's voice was tinged with fear as she combed Ifir's dark hair.

"Ah… I see. Well, I hope she gets used to them soon. It's never easy being a new face in an old place." Ifir said.

Mere didn't raise her eyes this time.

"Thank you, Songbird. I'm sure she will."

Once the maid had finished her work, Ifir stood up from the velvet-cushioned chair and Mere ran to open the balcony door for her. The sun was about to rise, its golden rays bathing the white marble surfaces in a golden, almost divine glow.

Ifir walked out to greet the new day, breathing in the fresh, cold air of her green lands—now turning shades of orange and yellow—and beheld the great city before her. Kellum was the crown jewel of the Kollek kingdom—spreading out as far as the eye could see.

Castle Kellum was the prime landmark of the great Kollek Kingdom, rising powerfully on top of Breezebound Hill, one of the fabled "singing mountains" of the kingdom, named as such because of the uncommon tendency for songbirds to flock around them at all times of the year. Below the hill, the city spread out in all directions. Ifir assessed the different districts of Kellum, built in rings emanating from the center, from closest to farthest—Aether's Path, which surrounded the Castle District, followed by Noble's Row, Merchant's Way, Hammer's Burg, Edgetown, and the last one, Outer Silence. Outside the city walls, Ifir beheld the Greenwood, spreading as far as the eye could see to the south.

Shortly thereafter, colorful little birds settled on her balcony parapet, standing out against the white and black of the marble railing. Their presence made Ifir smile. Like every other day, the birds waited for her singing. And just like every other day, Mere noticed, with a tinge of fear, there was something off about them. They did not look or act like birds normally would, but rather stood eerily in place, waiting on Ifir like little feathered servants.

When she started her song, the chorus of colorful birds accompanied her.

In just a few seconds, there were more birds in the balcony than members in the grand choir of the city's Aetheliour, and their melody was so joyful and unusually loud, it boasted enough power to wake every noble this side of the castle. Despite the sweet sounds, Mere couldn't help but feel a pang of terror every time she saw Ifir's gift at work.

The Songbird of the Kolleks could do terrible things with her voice. She could shift the way of the wind, persuade small-minded creatures like birds to do her bidding and, on occasion, even take a person's life. Her morning song was, more than anything else, a reminder to Mere and anyone else that heard it of that very power.

A very clear one.

Ifir kept singing a mournful, harmonic crescendo until all the birds in the hill around the castle found themselves flying around her balcony, covering the tower where she resided like a dark, living storm cloud of fluttering wings, chirps and caws – it was the Songcall, a ritual the people of Kellum had come to expect, fear and even venerate. It was a message for the Chosen of the castle, as well as the people of the great capital, of who really held the true power among the Kollek. Such a seemingly simple act helped keep the people of Kellum in line and remind the Chosen of their calling. It was overly theatrical, Ifir knew… but so very effective.

The Chosen and Kollek soldiers on duty turned to face the Songcall, and saluted her from down below, acknowledging the event and its significance. She responded to those within sight with a slight nod, finishing the somber song. Then, at the end of the song, most of the birds scattered like an explosion of tiny particles, flying away from the royal tower.

Ifir then moved over to a drawer and procured a bag of seeds, which she nonchalantly placed in a feeding bowl on her balcony. The few birds that remained immediately crowded over the seeds and began to peck away savagely. Ifir watched them, her eyes looking beyond the small, simple creatures before her… and left the balcony. As she stepped back into the room, her face suddenly became cold as an iceberg, as if she'd left her former herself on the balcony and someone else had ventured back inside the chambers. While Mere held Ifir's cloak ready for her, someone knocked on the door.

"Come in," Ifir ordered. A soldier respectfully walked in and saluted Ifir.

"Good morning, Songbird. The king summons you for breakfast in the Common Hall." Ifir smiled at the news.

"I'm coming." She replied. When the soldier left, she took a deep breath and looked at her image on the mirror one more time to be sure she looked well, then left her room and walked fast down the stairs, showing little regard for the old maid who seemed to struggle as she tried to keep up with her.

I'm too old for this, Mere thought. *But then… this is all I know. Where else would I go? This is nothing compared to what awaits me, should I be forced to seek work somewhere else… Nothing indeed.*

As soon as they reached the first floor, after a painfully long descent down the main tower, Ifir turned to the Common Hall. The walls of the corridors were full of windows that allowed the cool morning breeze into the castle. A cold chill blew past Ifir as she walked, which made Mere shiver in her serving garbs. The old maid could've used two furs coats, given how cold the wind could be already at this time of year, and this early in the day, but Ifir seemed to not even notice the bone-chilling cold, dressed only in her thin silk dress.

The Songbird | 39

Aether's mercy! Mere thought with amazement.

As they arrived at the tall, heavy doors of the hall, a pair of royal guards in ornate, golden armor opened the way for them. Ifir went in briskly, with Mere following close behind.

Inside the Common Hall was a long table, spread out in the middle of a huge stone room, half of which was currently shrouded in darkness. Every corner of the room was decorated with marble statues of past kings of Ulor's line—the dynasty which had been ruling the Kollek for centuries. As it were right now, however, most of them had their faces shrouded in darkness, looming eerily in the dark corners of the rooms like silent, brooding guardians. The ceiling was decorated with sun and moon frescos made by gold and silver, as the symbols of Aether. The huge windows were painted to tell the story of how Ulor's house became the chosen cradle of the Hand of Aether; from the wars they spearheaded, to the favor Aether poured on them like rain, and how the sun shone upon the men of Ulor's line, anointing them as kings. The rest of the room, on the other hand, was decorated with small trees, plants and colorful flowers; the way the queen preferred.

The breakfast table, in contrast, was near a massive fireplace, and as a result, gleamed as bright as a day; ready to receive its noble family and their guests. Beside it, a full regiment of servants waited to serve their lords at their stations.

As she walked to the table, Ifir noticed that she was neither the only one being invited nor the first one to arrive. At the right side of the king's chair, Queen Etheria already sat at her rightful seat; her golden yellow hair shinning as brightly as the flames of the fireplace. Her big, green eyes carefully examined Ifir, who hesitated for a second at the door before walking in. At the left side of the king sat young Prince Urail; Ifir's favorite. He was the king's eldest, at fifteen years old, and was named after King Ulor's grandfather, whose sharp eyes he'd inherited, Ifir knew. His looks were like arrows out of the bow, and his dark hair and upright posture was just like his father's. Seeing him reminded Ifir of the days she had with the king in the castle, once upon a time long past.

"Songbird," twelve-year old Princess Flora joyfully said. Her green eyes shone upon seeing the Songbird. The little girl's yellow hair and big eyes were just like her mother's. Her plait was decorated with flowers and her white dress gave her the appearance of a newly bloomed flower.

"Princess." Ifir saluted her with a smile. "My king, Queen Etheria…" She didn't look at the queen as she made a small bow of her head, instead immediately turning her eyes to Urail. "My prince." She finished.

The other members of the court were there as well, but Kollek custom didn't dictate Ifir, in her superior position, had to greet them. So, she didn't.

After saluting everyone, she calmly walked to her seat, next to the princess. Seeing every member of the court present at the table, Ifir looked at the king's eyes with concerned thoughts. Ulor slightly nodded at her, recognizing the meaning of the look, while the queen pretended like she was busy with her daughter, caressing her hair. Sitting next to the prince was Commander Siegen; whose grey hair fell on his deep scar and one blind eye. He saluted Ifir with an unpleasant smile.

"Good morning, Songbird." His deep voice rumbled, interrupting Ifir's eyes upon the king. She saluted him with a forced smile. The coin master, Fermand, was at the table too, his skinny body almost lost in the majestic chair. He rolled his eyes at Ifir, ignoring her just as she'd ignored him.

Odmund, champion of the Chosen army, stood behind the king's chair. His face was as cold as a stone, as always. A servant hurriedly moved to pull Ifir's chair, and she silently took her place at the crowded table. Mere, watching the proceedings with her owl-like eyes as always, took her place at her usual spot behind Ifir and stood still as rock, awaiting further orders.

"Good morning, faithful servants of Aether and the proud Kollek kingdom." King Ulor said. Everyone replied to him in differing tones and intervals: "Good morning, my king."

Queen Etheria looked at the head servant and nodded. There was a little bit of everything on display, from cooked ostrich eggs, vegetables, fresh bread and fruits, to cakes and other kinds of top-quality, mouth-watering artisan sweets.

After a few nervous bites of not knowing why Ulor had summoned everyone here, finally, he spoke.

"I have some important news to share today. However, before I begin, our Songbird here will share some information that has come to her notice. Ifir." He extended his hand at her. Etheria's eyes snapped to the king, who ignored her. She looked between Ulor and Ifir, then focused back on her plate, clearly upset by something. Ifir hesitated momentarily, gathering her thoughts. She looked uncomfortable and uncertain—something that was not typical for her at all. Everyone noticed this, and paid even closer attention: everyone but the queen, who was focused on her plate and continued to avoid eye contact with Ifir.

"I received some troubling news late last night," Ifir finally said while Ulor dug into his plate like a hungry wolf. Everyone at the table became all ears, especially Siegen and Fermand.

"A Head Sorcerer and his Night Judge attacked my forward scouts as they searched for the whereabouts of the Stone. As you all know, we'd heard a promising rumor that a Head Sorcerer had been seen around the Sleeping Mountains a fortnight ago. My spies went there to see if they could find any sign of the Stone, or learn about its location, when they were set upon by the Sorcerer." Ifir frowned, despite her best attempt to keep calm.

"I assume none of them survived." Siegen stated, knowing the answer already. He clenched his teeth. Ifir noticed he was holding his knife tighter.

She shook her head lightly, the annoyance clear in her eyes. "Unfortunately. They were ambushed by the Night Judge… almost like it knew they were coming."

"Father…" The prince began, not knowing whether he should continue or not. "Send me after the Stone… I'm ready."

Ifir's heart skipped a beat.

"Urail!" The queen interrupted without hesitation. The king, however, didn't look up as he fiddled with the food on his plate.

"Your time not arrived yet son." Ulor finally said, offering a smile. But Urail insisted: "I can go with Odmund. We will protect each other and bring the stone to its rightful king." He looked at Odmund standing behind his father. Then, seeing the look in his eyes, he turned his gaze back to his father.

"He is likely the Sword of Aether, my king, and I am your son." Everyone looked at each other in silence.

"Prince Urail." The queen warned him one last time. With a move of her hands, maids ran over to pull both the prince and princess' chairs. The children grimaced and rolled their eyes.

"I admire your passion, my son… But you're not yet ready for the horrors of war. These are the Night Judges we're talking about. Only Odmund here stands a chance against them—and we need him here, to protect our people."

Urail looked away in disgust. "You mean, to protect *you*…"

"What was that?" The king asked, his tone suddenly growing chillier than the morning air.

Urail didn't answer at first, but then hung his head and sighed. "Nothing, father."

"Indeed," Ulor said, watching him carefully. "Now do as you're told. Odmund is needed elsewhere today, in either case."

Ulor waited until his children had left the room and raised his hand, summoning Odmund forward.

"I need you to patrol the city with your men today. See how the people are getting ready for the Imperation Day celebrations. Put on a little show for the masses." The king looked into Odmund's eyes to make sure he was fully understood. "Be sure they are in the… ah, *right* spirits to celebrate."

"As you order, my king." Odmund said, though the look in his eyes belied his feelings for the order.

The king flicked his wrist. "You are dismissed, Champion."

Odmund saluted Ulor and left with his elite Chosen guard.

"Maybe Urail is right, my king… you *could* send Odmund to find the Stone." Queen Etheria said while gently touching Ulor's hand.

Ifir got very busy with her food. Fermand and Siegen both followed the conversation closely.

"I'm sorry, my queen, but that may not be the best move to make," Siegen said. "We can't afford to risk Lord Odmund—not now, with the state of the war. People see him as a beacon of hope and strength—the Sword of the Kollek. If we sent him on such a dangerous mission, and Aether forbid, something happens to him, morale would fall drastically across every front."

"Not to mention, taxes!" Fermand interjected in a high-pitched squeal.

"I'm... sorry?" The queen asked, a puzzled look on her face.

"So many of our lords and barons are having trouble paying taxes right now. The Champion here is the best tool we have use to keep them in line—him and his, what you call it, *fireworks*." Fermand caressed his long beard on his small face and added: "Fear's the best tool we have right now to keep them in line—not to mention, the people revere Odmund as a sign from Aether—if we lose him, they won't be so eager to pay their, ahem... *holy* shares."

The king nodded, stroking his chin, then Ifir joined the conversation. "He is the only Chosen that can conjure fire, my lord. The gift of the prophecy. He really could be the Sword of Aether. We can't take the risk of losing him *before* we find the Stone."

"If there even really *is* a stone, my dear Songbird." Etheria added. The commander nodded as their eyes met. "I have to agree with the queen here, Songbird—and I mean no disrespect by it. We've heard rumors of the Stone—the source of the enemy's power, and your spies have confirmed these rumors... but what if they're a diversion tactic from the enemy? A red herring, intended to distract us from the Holy Expeditions? We need to maintain that possibility."

Ifir looked down at her food and continued eating calmly as ever. "Do you doubt my information, commander?" She asked.

"No... I..."

"Or my capacity to fulfill my job?" She stuck a knife on a piece of ham and looked up at him, a cold, empty stare in her deep-green eyes.

"Of course not, Songbird."

"Good. Because, if I say that there is such a thing as the Stone—and that it's the source of the Pentaghast's power—then it's true. You know why?"

Siegen lowered his eyes, unresponsive.

"Because it is my *job* to know, with all certainty, everything that happens in this kingdom and outside of it. And I'd never bring something like this to the court if I wasn't sure there's at least a sliver of truth to it. So don't question me, commander. Keep to your tasks, and let me keep to mine."

Etheria, even though the words hadn't been directed at her, looked down as well, every bit as chastised as Siegen, then busied herself with her silverware. Her chest rose and fell in slow, huge breaths.

"We will assess another angle in our next meeting. Figure out what went wrong and make amends. We must know where the heathens keep their precious Stone—that could be the key to ending this whole war in one decisive move." Ulor said with a tone of finality, and took another bite from his meat. "However, we shall speak of this no more for now." His warning was clear enough in his tone, if not his words, and the members of the court returned to eating, sparing not a single glance at each other.

"Darling…" Etheria said after a moment. "This is all very important news, I'm sure… but that's not really why you brought us all together here today, is it?"

"Hmm? Ah, of course! And I even sent Odmund off already. No matter, I shall tell him later." He said, gesturing towards the queen. "We are very happy to announce that Etheria is with child! I will soon have another boy." He grinned at the queen as he spoke, and she held his hand on the table.

The members of the court looked at each other.

"What joyful news!" Fermand said. "May Aether protect you and your family, my king and queen." Etheria had a huge smile on her face, holding her belly, and clearly enjoying the atmosphere the news had evoked.

"May Aether bless you and your family, my king." Siegen said, nodding towards the monarchs.

The Songbird | 45

"May Aether abundantly bless the baby." Ifir said, nodding towards them, but not looking at either.

The king nodded and raised a hand. "Yes, thank you, thank you. We're very excited." He then immediately gestured towards his butler without looking at anyone. "Towels," he said.

The butler immediately moved his hand, summoning one of the servants. Soft steps echoed from the dark side of the room, and as the light of the fireplace fell upon her, a young girl's image appeared next to Ulor. As her features came into focus, Mere felt a lump in her throat and a stab of panic in her heart. The serving girl standing next to Ulor was no one else but Loure. And to make matters worse, she was currently wearing a maid's dress which was *definitely* too small for her. Mere suddenly lost her connection with the world. She felt her senses go numb; couldn't see or hear anything but her own mind as it asked her some very burning questions. *"Who helped her? How did she managed to arrange the butler? When did this happen?"*

The young girl, however, behaved just as if she'd been working in the castle for years. Her steps were sure and her composure total as she kindly extended a warm towel bowl to the king with a flourishing, coquette move. Her cheeks were red, and she wore a seductive smile on her plump lips, which she tried not to show anyone but the king himself.

Mere clenched her teeth.

Ifir and Queen Etheria laid careful, very interested eyes on Loure. Ifir, especially, looked at the queen just to enjoy the jealousy on her face, while the king's eyes, however, were now fixed on the young servant's fresh beauty.

"That'll be all for now." Ulor said, his attention clearly elsewhere.

As Loure walked back to her place, Ulor shot a look at Ifir. She was looking down at her plate, her face the very picture of concentration and focus as she sliced up a fat sausage with a sharp knife. Then she threw a short, sharp look at the king to remind him that their agreement didn't involve maids or other women. Seeing her look, Ulor turned his eyes away and nonchalantly resumed his breakfast. His eyes met with the butler's after a moment and the old man nodded, almost imperceptibly. He understood his king's command: this wasn't his first day at the royal dining table, after all.

Mere, always aware of her surroundings, knew the meaning of that move very well too. And she knew that, despite her little charade, Ifir and the queen were currently scanning every single move of Ulor's—every little twitch and breath. Even if luck was on Loure's side and Queen Etheria hadn't seen it, Ifir *had* seen the command, as very little escaped her. Mere took a deep, shuddering breath. A storm would rage through the dark corridors of the basements tonight one way or another—one that could very well mean her end, and undoubtedly, Loure's.

Suddenly, the doors to the hall opened once more, and a messenger walked in. He whispered something into the butler's ear, who stood closest to him, and the old man passed the message to Ifir.

"A carriage has arrived, Songbird." He whispered.

Ifir turned towards the people in the hall.

"My king, queen, commander, coin master." She saluted them and left the hall as fast as she could.

The show was over. Ifir's face turned to ice the moment she left the hall. She didn't reply to any greetings, nor stop for anyone in the castle on her way out. Something had sent her into the darkest of moods, and Mere had a gnawing suspicion of what it was. Her heart was pounding so fiercely in her chest, she felt like she'd pass out.

She was *definitely* too old for this kind of stress.

They eventually reached the door to the castle gardens, in the back of the keep, which were designed with colorful roses and accented by an elaborate, expensive fountain sculpted in the shape of a bird. They passed the gardens and went out the reinforced back gate, joined by two armed guards, before reaching a small cottage nearby. The black carriage was waiting in front of it. The driver opened the door as soon as he saw Ifir approaching.

"Ahh. Chosen babies." Ifir smiled, but the smile did not reach her eyes.

There were two young, lovely girls, known as nuns of Aether, who were tasked with traveling around the country and collecting Chosen newborns, them bringing them to Ifir.

"Newly born Chosen babies are the gift of Aether to our holy kingdom, Songbird. May Aether protect you and the light you bring to our kingdom." The nuns were so beautiful and lovely that Ifir forced herself to look happy. However, Mere knew better—she'd grown used to Ifir's charades and trembled at the storm brewing beneath the masks.

"May Aether protect you, sisters. Thank you." Ifir said and signaled for Mere to run and take the babies. Mere carried them two at a time to an ornate cabin built by the side of the road for Chosen babies; where it was common knowledge that Ifir assessed the babies using her own abilities, then assigned them to a specific Chosen clan or house, based on their powers. No one but Ifir was allowed inside during the process—and no one had ever seen her do it.

When she entered the cabin, Mere stumbled in fear upon seeing an old, decrepit-looking hag sitting near the fireplace. Mere hesitated for a moment, as always, but the old crone didn't move, nor acknowledged her presence. Naturally, she corrected herself, as the hag was blind, deaf and mute. The Fallen One, Ifir called her—another one of her secrets. Mere had seen the woman before but had no idea who she really was, or where she came from, only that she arrived and left in a similar black carriage as the one that brough the babies. Try as she may, she couldn't explain it herself, as she'd never seen it, but it gave her the feeling that something else was afoot. Something always was with Ifir.

Before Mere brought the fifth and sixth babies, Ifir walked in, so Mere ran to bring in the last couple of babies. As she returned, her job complete, she found Ifir caressing the first two. Her big, emerald-green eyes looked longingly at them, almost as if they were her own.

"How sweet you are, my precious. Are you a boy, handsome?" She spoke in a silky soft voice.

Mere put all the babies on a long table, covered by a fine, plush rug. The babies were all newborn, and recently collected from their mothers, she could see. As Mere came back with the last two babies, the others had started to get restless. Some had even started to cry… but Ifir, seeming unfazed by the noise, began to sing to them. They all stopped, falling into perfect silence moments after the sound left her lips. That was usually the end of Mere's duty. She had never witnessed the rest of Ifir's ceremony with the little lads. The old maid moved to leave the room, as usual, but all of a sudden, Ifir spoke.

"No. I want you to stay today." She said in a tone colder than snow-chilled steel.

Mere froze at her spot, then nodded and moved back inside. She looked at Fallen One, but the old woman clearly couldn't even notice them.

"Close the door." Ifir commanded.

Mere did as told.

"Do you ever wonder what I do with these children, Mere? You've been with me long enough. Always carried them in your arms. Aren't you the least bit curious?"

Mere lowered her gaze. "It's none of my business, my lady."

Ifir looked the old woman over, from top to bottom. There was pity in her eyes. Taking a deep breath, she continued. "True... but today, I *want* you to see. You've earned that much. And I'm sure that you, being one of the eldest servants in the keep, would never betray my trust, would you Mere?"

Mere froze on the spot but did her best not to show it.

"Never, my lady."

"Good. Because when you betray the people that respect and protect you, there's always a price to pay."

Mere saw that yawning darkness in Ifir's eyes again, just like in the Common Hall when Ulor looked at Loure, or when Etheria announced her new baby. Ifir resumed her singing, and the six babies fell into a deep sleep. Even Mere couldn't help but become drowsy at the Songbird's powerful, lyrical voice. It was as if the sound caressed one's mind, pulling one's senses inside a deep, black, velvety shroud. It felt like wind and water against the skin, slowly overcoming one's consciousness and willpower. Then, abruptly, Ifir stopped singing and stood up, holding one of the babies. Mere came out of the spell, back to full attention. She felt groggy and disoriented for a second.

Ifir then walked close to Mere, holding the baby gently in her arms. She caressed its head softly with the back of her hand, staring tenderly down at its sleeping face…

… and snapped his neck.

Mere flinched and yelped at the slight cracking sound. It was so sudden, so weak. She bit her lip and shut her eyes, looking away, swooning weakly despite her best efforts.

"You know why I prefer to do it this way, dear Mere? It's because I love this tiny, weak sound. It's so frail and lyrical, isn't it? Just like the weak begging of my enemies." Ifir asked, smiling with a wide, unsettling grin. Mere was in utter shock. She could only nod, breathless.

Ifir moved to pick up the second baby, and Mere stood, watching with horror, as she repeated the same heinous act.

One after the other.

Crack. Crack. Crack.

The tired old woman was sure she'd hear that sound in her nightmares every night until the day she died. After the last baby had been silenced forever, Ifir opened the door of the cabin. The Fallen One stood up with a huge, black sack in her hand, still as the grave, dressed in all-black tatters, somehow perceiving that the event was over. As soon as Ifir and Mere left, she started throwing the corpses inside the sack.

"My horse." Ifir called to her guards, whom she'd ordered to wait outside. While waiting for them, she smelled some of the roses from the garden. Mere, on the other hand, was trying to stop her body from shaking, doing her very best to keep herself from fainting as the creature in black threw the bodies of the babies into the large bag.

With the arrival of the guards, Ifir mounted her black, noble horse, which was taller and bigger than any of the others in the city save for Ulor's.

"I have important errands to run now," she told the guards. "Stay here and see to it that no one follows after me. As always, the babies are asleep, and I will be back for them later. Under no circumstance can anyone enter the cabin. Not even you. Understood?"

The men nodded.

With a sharp kick to the sides of her steed, Ifir then rode the beast to the outskirts of the castle, her silk green dress flapping like a gale behind her in the wind.

Mere nodded to the guards, barely maintaining an even stride as she walked back into the castle. As soon as she was out of sight and earshot, she ran to her room as fast as she could. She pounced down the stairs to the servant quarters, her heart pounding in her chest. She didn't notice the pain in her legs at all.

She reached her room, breathless, and opened the door—only to see Loure cleaning her naked body with clean towels. A sexy, silky nightgown was laying on her bed—one Mere had never seen before. Loure smiled as soon as their eyes met.

"I told you, aunt of mine… I am more than ready." Her voice had a melodious quality to it as she spoke, her eyes fluttering. Mere couldn't take it. It was all too much. Something snapped inside of her, and she shook her head in fear like a madwoman.

"No, no, NO!!!" She screamed at the top of her lungs, running out of the room.

Loure watched after her, shocked at her aunt's completely uncharacteristic outburst. She'd known her to be one of the most level-headed, if downright sour, people she knew. What in the world had happened to her? And where was she going in such a hurry?

The young, beautiful lass shrugged. Mere was old. Maybe her old nerves couldn't take Loure's proactive spirit. She'd most likely gone out to do some laundry or order another of the maids around to vent some steam.

Pity the next girl she storms into, she thought.

After carefully cleaning herself and applying some rose extract on her neck and body, Loure held the dress over her body, looking at herself on the mirror.

Suddenly the door slammed-open again. Mere was back, and she was looking at Loure with wild, violent eyes, like a madwoman. She was breathless again, but this time she was holding a small bottle with a pale, green liquid in her hand.

The Songbird | 51

"What's that?" Loure asked. She'd seen similar vials in the castle apothecary's office while doing her cleaning rounds, but had no idea what it was used for.

In an unexpected move, the old maid uncorked the vial and threw the green liquid onto to Loure's face.

It took her brain less than a second to register the burning pain of the searing acid, eating through her flesh.

Loure fell on her knees, screaming with a savage pain and patting her face—then pulling her hands back as they started burning too. She accidentally looked at herself in the mirror, and the creature that stared back at her, face bubbling in places and melting in others, nearly made her faint. She wailed like a woman giving birth.

"W-what... what have you done to me?!"

Mere kneeled next to her, tears in her big, wild eyes. Her hands shook as she pulled her close by the shoulders, before savagely whispering to her face.

"Save your *stupid* life!"

CHAPTER 4

THE FORBIDDEN FOREST

Merki and Rage walked silently through the depths of the Forbidden Forest, towing a borrowed horse from the village stables.

They had stumbled onto a deer pack's tracks not long after entering the deep part of the woods, to Merki's luck, and she'd noticed a stag among them. The tracks had led deeper and deeper into the woods, until they'd reached the Golden River, and disappeared. Merki had known what that meant. The pack had crossed over to the other side. The side that no one was supposed to enter… but Merki followed them all the same.

Now, the further she moved into the forest, the darker and damper it got. She could see the changes in nature—how the land seemed to get grimmer with each step. These, she knew, were the last secured lands before the mythical place known as the Antler Mountains, rumored to be the ruins of the Cursed Nor Temple, which was said to be hidden in a valley: the source of an ancient and dark evil. Merki knew just how dangerous being near there could be. Still, she was willing to risk anything for the chance to get out of Halstead and accomplish her deepest goal—that of getting to Kellum in one piece.

Rage walked ahead of Merki, following scents and scouting the area whenever she stopped for a second to check around.

He turned his head often from side to side, following the stag's trail all over the place, while making more noise than Merki would've wanted as he rustled through the leaves. The branches of the tall trees played shadow games with them, making the path shift and change depending on how the light fell on it, confusing Merki's senses.

Eventually, she stumbled across a fresh set of tracks, and her hunting instincts told her the stag was near. She gave Rage a signal to stay put, secured the horse to a nearby tree, then ghosted away alone after the tracks.

The trail led her deeper and deeper into the foreboding woods, but after half an hour of blending with the noises and movements of the forest, Merki finally reached her prey. She arrived at a watering hole, and on its banks, spied a group of deer… with a majestic stag among them.

"Got you…" She said to herself.

Careful as could be, hiding behind a series of bushes downwind of the pack, Merki drew a single arrow, knocked it on her bow, and aimed. She held her breath, waiting for the perfect moment amidst a flurry of falling leaves… Then clicked her tongue. The stag raised its head in alarm, and before it knew what had happened, an arrow had appeared on its long, glistening neck. The stag staggered forward several times, then its front legs failed it and it crumpled over.

Merki released her breath. The rest of the pack dashed out of the way, galloping for their lives. She moved closer to her mark, one of her knives drawn, and noticed it was still breathing. Bleeding out profusely, as she'd hit its carotid artery, but still alive. She quickly slit its throat and ended its suffering.

Immediately, she allowed herself a sigh of relief, and closed her eyes, ushering a silent prayer to Aether, or whatever god of the hunt was watching over her.

"This was too easy…" She wondered to herself with a scoff as she removed the arrow and moved towards the water to wash the blood off her knife. Then she corrected herself. "Hell, *something* had to go my way eventually. No, this is fate giving me a hand, surely."

She stood up and was just about to heft the stag across her back... when she heard them.

"Ha, ha, ha! You idiot!" A man's voice said.

Merki looked around and for a tree with thick branches. As soon as she found one, she hung her bow across her shoulder and ran towards the tree, making nearly no sound, climbing it as high as she could. From her new vantage point, she saw three well-equipped hunters on a nearby glade, standing over the carcass of a skinned bear. The man to the right of the bear walked over to another one and slapped his head. "You're too funny, Borun! You must've been dropped in the head twice when you were born, didn't you?" He held Borun's shoulder and shook him as much as he could. The man, in turn, just smiled like an idiot.

Even Merki could see that he wasn't the sharpest tool in the shed—but he was as huge as the bear they'd killed: the man was all muscles. They all were.

Zugans, Merki thought.

The animal pelts they wore, along with their wild demeanor, made them easy to identify. They were the savages of south, the only people crazy enough to live in the borders of the cursed lands. She'd never seen them this close to the Golden River before, though.

"We'll split the reward for the pelt this time. You both did good today." The third man, standing to the left of Borun, promised.

"*Akhal,* Jacqul, *Akhal!*" Borun shouted, raising his fist. *Akhal* meant "long live" in the language of the Zugans, Merki knew. They used the phrase for thanking, praying and even before setting out on a hunt: basically, for anything that was good. Zugans weren't really that complicated.

Seeing them so merry relieved Merki a little.

Good. They're just out hunting, and they're nearly done. They'll be gone soon. Maybe they won't notice the stag... She thought, holding onto the hope.

As the men walked away in the opposite direction, hauling the bear on ropes, Merki heaved a silent sigh of relief. She got ready to climb down... but then...

"By the Mother of the Wilds—what is *that*?" One of them shouted, pointing to a ditch in the earth behind an area of heavy undergrowth and fallen leaves.

"Is he dead?" Borun asked.

Merki stopped for a second, already knowing that her curiosity would cause her nothing but trouble. She climbed a bit higher to see anyway.

The three savages pulled a man out of the ditch, lying face-down on the ground. The man was taller than them and seemed to be wearing basic tattered clothing—a cotton shirt, linen pants and simple shoes. His hands and feet, however, were enormous compared to the other men…

Borun picked up an old leather bag from the ground, just a few meters away from the body.

"Borun. Don't touch it." Warned the oldest among them, Jacqul, in a stern voice. His tone urged Borun to throw the bag away immediately.

"Can he be from Halstead—that dirty little village on the other side of the river?" Kelph asked Jacqul.

"I don't think so." He said, eyes scanning the large body with care. "They know this is no place for their kind. We should be careful." The older man replied.

Merki watched the proceedings very carefully from atop her perch.

The one called Jacqul drew his dagger, urging the others to step back. "I'll check to see if he's dead." He carefully turned the large man over on the leafy bed of the forest. The man looked young, no older than twenty-five. His skin was cut and torn all over. Jacqul checked the man's pulse.

He couldn't feel one.

He waited for a moment longer, then looked back at his men.

"He's dead." He waved them forward. "Come. Search him thoroughly and take his things. He won't be needing them anymore, but we do."

They all did as told, walking over to the man and checking his body and bag for loot. The one called Kelph dug out an old, wooden flask from the bag and gave it to Borun to hold. He then procured a nasty-looking sandwich, if it could even be called that. It was only a piece of dirty bread with a few leaves of lettuce.

Borun wasn't really happy to see that the contents of the man's bag were as poor as his clothes. However, as he dug into the depths of the small bag, his fingers suddenly brushed something else. An idiotic smile appeared on his face, and the other two perked up, upon seeing his reaction. Even Merki couldn't help her curiosity, unconsciously edging forward in the tree branch.

"What is it? What did you find?" Asked Kelph with thinly veiled excitement.

Borun took his hand slowly out of the bag and opened his palm. There were four small amethyst stones gleaming under the filtered sunlight in his hand.

"*Akhal!*" Kelph shouted, raising his fists towards the sky. "We hit gold!"

Jacqul, despite himself, looked excited too. He tried to gauge the quality of stones. They were as clear as diamonds, which wasn't common in these parts. The only places in history to produce amethysts this pure were the fabled mines of the Nor, thought lost to time and war. Aside from this, amethysts were forbidden throughout the kingdom by order of the king himself, as they were the only known thing that could nullify a Chosen's powers. Only high-ranking Kollek soldiers could carry weapons or tools made of these, and then, use them *only* to hunt or fight off rogue Chosen.

That was, aside from the black market, which ravenously sought out amethysts to sell to the highest bidder in the richer parts of the kingdom, of course. However, as soon as they made the connection between the amethysts and the proportions of the man's hands and feet, their excitement turned into something else.

"He's... he's one of the Sons!" Said Borun, a look of building fear in his face.

"You mean a... rebel?" Kelph asked, looking at Jacqul. "But... what's a rebel doing this far south? Isn't the war way up north?"

Jacqul looked at the man with fierce eyes, then his own went wide in what Merki could only describe as full-blown fear.

"Stand back!" He shouted.

"What?"

"I said, stand back, you fools! This man's no rebel! He's…"

"He's moving!" Borun yelled.

***

Kade wasn't sure what was happening, but his aching, tired body was begging for relief. His body twitched a couple of times and his eyelids opened, almost in slow-motion, as if they were as heavy as mountains. He'd never felt so weak, so spent. Still, despite his utter exhaustion, he was still able to put together the troubling fact that he was surrounded by armed men… and he noticed that these men were currently holding his precious amethyst stones—the only thing keeping him alive and protected from the Curse, in their hands. For all he knew, it was these very stones that had prevented the Curse from taking complete hold over him before, allowing him to wake up now and giving him another chance…

… and now these strangers were taking them from him.

He extended his arm, weak, shaking, reaching towards the stones. He felt a rising heat building up inside of him…The Curse. He was running out of time.

The men looked at him with pale faces—they'd felt his cold, dead flesh—they *knew* he'd been dead. Suddenly, without being able to stop themselves, they stepped back in fear and drew their weapons. Borun put the stones in his pocket, and Kade felt his desperation, and the growing heat, rising inside of him. He could feel his blood starting to boil in his veins again… and then his muscles suddenly erupted in an indescribable pain.

"Shoot him… Now!" Jacqul ordered Kelph, who'd been holding his bow aimed at Kade, the knocked arrow quivering in fear. However, before the man could shoot him, Kade felt something overtake him. His mind blurred, and an unfamiliar strength took over his body.

Kelph shot him from just a few feet away—a sure shot, Merki knew, even for an amateur. And yet, when the arrow struck, it only found dirt. Kade was standing next to it, completely untouched. Merki hadn't even seen him move—but the bed of fallen leaves around him had exploded all around the clearing, as if hit by a sudden gust or gale.

How in the world could he manage to move that fast?

Another blink, and Kade was suddenly upon Kelph, raising him by the throat. He squeezed hard and the savage's head snapped to the side, like a stick broken between a giant's fingers.

Borun, half in shock and half berserk, jumped Kade from behind, axe held high. Kade heard the move before Borun made it, stepped to the side, and the axe swung through empty air. Borun stumbled and fell to the ground, tried to get up, but suddenly found Kade's foot at his throat before he was able to do anything. Kade twisted at the knee sharply, followed by a sickly crack, and Borun's eyes rolled into the back of his head. Jacqul had picked up Kelph's bow during the short span of time, and had another arrow knocked on the tip already, aimed at Kade.

"Stand back! You can take the stones! Just leave!" The old man said.

Kade, however, could not hear him. The Curse inside of him called out for blood, his mind encased in a deep shroud of thick fog. His wild eyes fell upon the tip of the arrow aimed at him... then back at the old man's eyes. He saw the fear there, but it meant nothing to him.

The old man shot.

Kade twisted his torso to the side and let the arrow whistle by, slamming into a tree behind him. He grabbed Borun's corpse by the leg as Jacqul knocked another arrow in a swift, trained motion, but just before he shot again, Kade brought the other man's corpse up like a shield.

The arrow struck the Borun's flesh, the bloody point coming out of his waist, spraying Kade's face in blood.

Jacqul froze, unable to move.

Merki watched in terror.

Everything was happening so quickly she didn't know *what* to do. Then, realizing the old man was going to die if she didn't do *something,* her fingers bristled the arrows on her quiver. She felt around, then procured a special one—its fletching black, instead of white. She knocked the arrow on her bow and looked down the length of the shaft. The amethyst point gleamed in the sunlight. She'd been saving this arrow for a special occasion… and this was as good a one as it'd ever be.

She held her breath, drew on the bowstring, then felt a cold hand clutch her heart as Kade just blinked out of where he was standing… and appeared in front of the old man.

His arm was coming out of the man's back, bathed in pure, glistening red, raising him into the air. The man stared at Kade with wide eyes, their faces awfully close to each other, while blood trickled down his mouth and dripped onto the young man's monstrous face.

Kade stared back, eyes glazed over, expression wild and berserk… then threw the man's corpse aside, leaving a gaping hole in his chest. Merki froze, unable to breath. The panic she felt in that moment was unlike any she'd ever felt before.

Kade pulled his arms back, stared at the sky and bellowed a yell of pure, unbridled rage—the howl of a wild animal; a sound that made it seem like he was almost in pain. Finished with the men, he then made his way to Borun's corpse and rummaged around his pockets for his amethyst stones, like a hungry beast, desperate for his fresh meal.

The moment his fingers touched the stones, a visible calmness reconquered Kade's body and soul. His muscles felt an intense relief and his burning pain disappeared. His mind was calm, at last… then a hot, sharp pain spread throughout his shoulder and he grunted, stumbling forward. He looked to the side and saw an arrow shaft coming out of his left deltoid. He stared at it, confused, as he saw it dripping with his blood…

… Then passed out cold once more on the forest floor.

CHAPTER 5

DREAMS AND DISAPPOINTMENTS

Odmund could see Hugo's eyes filling up with hope as he started his first lesson on castle conduct and etiquette.

They were in one of the cellar rooms of the castle, and across from Hugo stood an older man, his head bald, but his posture and form wise and regal. His name was Radolf, Odmund's head servant, and the man who had basically raised him. Radolf assessed the young hunchback with kind but firm eyes as he taught him what he needed to know to serve in the castle. Odmund knew Hugo was in good hands, as Radolf was one of the strongest minds he'd ever met. He trusted him implicitly.

"Now, now boy," Radolf began. "Being a hunchback isn't an excuse. You can do better. Straighten your step, like so." He was walking up and down the room with Hugo, fixing his posture and steps as he did.

"Serving one of the Chosen is almost like serving Aether Himself, Hugo. Do it like you mean it, son. You *do* want to serve to the champion someday, correct?"

"Yes, sir." Hugo replied.

Odmund could see the determination on the boy's face. His clenched teeth and narrowed eyes belied the pain and awkwardness he felt in his movements, but other than that, Hugo expressed no complaints.

When they made a turn in the room and walked to the other side, Radolf saw Odmund watching them from the corner, in the shadows. The champion nodded to him, and the old, dignified servant nodded back, letting him know everything was going well. Radolf then led Hugo back towards the other side again, and when he turned once more, Odmund was already gone.

***

Odmund exited the cellars and climbed up the stairs to the castle's main hall. As he did, he heard the swift gallop of a heavy horse back in the gardens and saw Mere, Ifir's personal maid, rushing into the keep, looking as tense as ever. She sped by him so fast, Odmund didn't even want to imagine what Ifir had put her trough this time.

The poor woman deserves a break, he thought.

He made his way out of the hall and onto the main grounds of the castle. His elite guards were already waiting there for him with his horse. One of them offered him the reins and he swiftly mounted his white steed—which was clad in gleaming golden armor. As soon as he did, two servants ran up to him to spruce up his red cloak. His guards got in line behind him on their own horses and they quickly left the castle grounds, intent on beginning their patrol of the streets of Kellum.

The fancy roads of Aether's Path, filled with colorful flowers and citrus trees, were so wide as to allow a whole army through them. Odmund, however, knew that the colorful, affluent road was not a true reflection of the city as a whole—not for the people, at least. The further one traveled from the castle, the starker the change, he knew. Wide, lush streets full of gardens and fountains, their roads sculpted out of the finest stone, quickly gave way to crumbling roads, dirt and decay. In the farthest district, known as the Outer Silence, he even often found it hard to breathe, due to the palpable desperation one could feel from the people who lived there—folk who struggled each day for a single meal, and for whom every day could be their last. The city, he mused, was a living reflection of Aether's eternal world—from Aether's Garden to the devil Luden's home, from wellness to malady, from affluence to absence. Odmund looked back up the hill towards the king's chambers, up high in one of the castle's tallest towers, from which he knew the whole of the city and all its shades of greatness and decay could be seen, as if it were Aether's own domain.

After a short ride from Aether's Path, Odmund's cavalcade entered the next district over—Noble's Row. This was where the affluent of the city made their home—the nobles, clearly, but also the captains, commanders, business magnates and wealthy merchants, among many others. The champion slowed his horse, then put on his best face, intent on getting this duty over with as quickly as possible.

It was all a show, he knew. He had the power to defeat the enemies of the Kollek—to bring true peace and prosperity to his people, and yet the king, in his infinite wisdom, had him putting on a show. Riding around the districts, reminding people of Ulor's protection and heart towards them... as well as the reach of his arm, he knew.

As he passed by the nobles' large mansions and manors; past their perfectly manicured gardens with tall columns and flowing fountains, he saw servants, as well as their masters, taking note of his passing. They stopped, staring in awe—and some of them a little fear, he noticed with a pang in his chest, as he slowly trotted his glistening horse through their streets, his group of fully armored men trailing close behind.

A message and a show, he thought. *That's all this is. All he thinks me worthy of these days.*

He waved at the nobles and their servants as he passed, acknowledging their stares and waves. As he rode further down the road, he passed a manor belonging to one of the most affluent families in the city. It belonged to a wealthy merchant... or was it a baron? He couldn't remember. From its garden, he heard a feminine screech of excitement, and soon saw a noble lass in an elaborate yellow dress rushing towards him from the manor gardens, her servants trailing behind her in a rush.

"Champion, champion!" She ran over to the side of the road and waved a red ribbon in greeting, as if they knew each other well.

Odmund nodded to her from his horse. "My lady," he called out, bowing his head slightly. The other girls surrounding the maiden giggled and saluted Odmund after her, throwing jealous looks at the girl in yellow.

He had no idea who the maiden, nor any of her friends, were.

Odmund smiled and waved, then continued his pace down the district. Seeing all the young, eager maidens of Kellum's upper class drove his thoughts back to the castle... to a certain blonde Chosen, who waited there for him at the end of the day. Suddenly, this whole task seemed like less of a burden, realizing he had something very good to come back to once it was all over. His Chosen guards, however, enjoyed the attention this posting gave them, and were not shy in the least when it came to flirting with all the girls they ran across.

The rest of the morning and afternoon passed by in the same slow, cantering drawl, with Odmund leading the way through the key streets and thoroughfares of the city's districts, barely taking the main road between them, and instead insisting on fulfilling Ulor's wishes as best and thoroughly as he could.

He passed down Merchant's Way, saluting the store and stall owners, and drawing whole crowds from the very busy streets, then through Hammer's Burg—the home of most of the middle-class laborers and workers of the city. Here, the distinction between the districts grew clearer, as the well-paved roads and streets with flowing creeks, flowers and trees, gave way to more humble roads of cracked stone—the posh homes and stone buildings turning into more modest wood and brick structures, their outsides weathered and worn. The citizens' clothes also reflected the change—going from brightly-colored dresses and suits to more simple clothing of cotton and linen, while also sporting more earthly, basic colors—or a lack thereof entirely.

However, it wasn't until Odmund reached the district known as Edgetown—the one before the Outer Silence, that things didn't take the starkest turn for the worse. Here, most streets aside from the main street, (which always looked nice and had a high guard count despite the district), were in clear disrepair—the roads cracked and uneven, showing more dirt than stone, and its people wearing more patches than clothing on their backs. He noticed how the folk's reactions to him and his men changed drastically too—from cheers and accolades to subtle, submissive nods, with some even outright cringing away in fear. Some folks, he noticed, watched him secretly from their dirty windows, quickly closing their stained curtains as he passed. Some still greeted him, bowing their heads and calling out to him by his ever-present title, but till their voices were low and weak, even wavering. Very few people here, all the way in Edgetown, had joy on their faces. They avoided the soldiers' gazes, most of them bowing humbly out of the way, the mothers pulling their children back and holding them close, as if Odmund would suddenly leap at them and try to devour them. The Champion of the Kollek suddenly wondered if his title also applied to these folk, all the way in Edgetown. Was he their champion too? Did these people see him as the beacon of hope, the symbol of victory, that some from the other districts considered him to be? If so, why not? What was going on here that made these people so scared of him, even the children, who had nothing to fear from someone like him?

A part of him, very deep inside, already knew the answer—but his dominant part pushed it down, pretended it wasn't there. He wanted other answers. Prettier, cleaner answers, to a truth he feared he wasn't strong or powerful enough to change. The very nature of the city, of this world—of his king's rule.

The citizens weren't the only ones acting differently, however. Odmund's guards were completely alert and silent here, their eyes darting from side to side, ready to spring to action at a moment's notice. They knew the kind of place they were in—what the people thought of them, and more importantly, of symbols of Ulor's rule like Odmund. They steeled themselves before the thought that, if they didn't get out of there fast enough, they'd have to bloody their blades before the sun went down on them.

Odmund continued the steady patrol, until they reached the last gate—the one leading to the Outer Silence.

"Sire… I think that's enough for today. We should go back." One of the elite guards said.

Odmund considered the question, then shook his head. "We've still got the Silence to patrol. Those are our people too—our citizens, and they deserve to know we remember them… or at the very least that we're still around."

The guards looked at one another. One of them unconsciously put a hand on his sword hilt.

"As you say, sire. We can go down the main road to the southern city gates, then turn back. We've still got just enough daylight." He said, looking back at the crimson sun, setting behind the sea of roofs and chimneys behind them.

But Odmund shook his head again.

"No. We shall patrol it properly… All the way to the harbor. We are Chosen. We do not fear our own people, men… Regardless of their disposition towards us."

The guards stayed silent, and eventually just nodded. Odmund spurred his horse into a canter and they made their way after him, all of them grasping the hilts of their weapons now.

Once they arrived at the Silence, and left the facade of its main road, the transformation of the city reached its final, grotesque form. Odmund knew this district very well—as he knew this was the heart of corruption and filth of his beloved Kellum. He even passed by Beggar's End—the hole he'd saved Hugo from just a few days back. Here, no one looked at them, let alone greet them. Everyone kept to themselves, either putting their heads down, or walking away from them in obvious attempts to put as much distance between them as possible.

Here, the city beyond the district walls gave way to a maze of foul-smelling slums, full of buildings in various stages of decay and ruin. The streets were mostly dirt and mud, and the alleyways reeked of vomit, feces and often, to Odmund's refined senses, blood. Most of the people here wore rags and covered their faces as he passed them by, hiding their illnesses or deformities. Those who didn't stared at him with vicious eyes—the criminal element of Kellum, he knew. This was their turf, and they wanted Odmund to know it. He stared back as they rode, but didn't make any attempts, one way or the other. He just rode on, letting his presence there be message enough.

Soon before reaching the gate to the harbor, (which spanned and connected several districts, as the sea cleaved a sort of bay into the western part of the wheel that was the city), they saw a couple of men running out of an alleyway in a mad dash. Odmund stopped his horse and signaled for his men to hold with his raised fist.

"Do we go after them, Champion?" One of them asked, his sword already half-drawn.

Odmund hesitated for a moment, his senses telling him there was something else to the scene—another detail… a sound, coming from the alleyway. A woman, groaning, weeping, her voice weak and choked.

"Two of you, cover the entrance to the alleyway. The other two, with me."

Odmund dismounted and rushed into the darkness between the buildings, two of his men hot on his heels. He opened his palm and conjured a flame, pushing the dark away. Immediately, his eyes saw the woman, lying on the ground, in a pool of blood. Odmund ordered his men to surround him, then ran over to her, lowering the intensity of his flame.

"What happened?" He asked her, a hand on her shoulder. "Are you alright?" But then, he saw the dark stain of blood coming from her waist, pouring down her meager, gray dress.

The woman could barely speak, her own blood choking her. She coughed and spat the blood on Odmund's shirt, grasping it weakly with a trembling hand.

"M-my… baby…" She croaked, pulling at Odmund's collar in a feeble attempt.

"S-slavers… don't let them…"

Dreams and Disappointments | 67

Odmund stared at her, eyes wide, his heart thundering inside his chest.

"Slavers? Here? Where are they going? Do you know?" He asked. But as he did, he saw they woman's eyes glaze over, her breath coming in short, weak gasps… then she went limp, letting go of his collar, and collapsed on her side.

Odmund stood up and stormed over to his men, waiting outside the alleyway. "The men who ran away—which direction did they go in?" He asked, his voice hard.

"They disappeared into the alleyways, sire. Do you want us to pursue?"

Odmund raced over to the alley his guards indicated and stopped cold at the entrance. Before him loomed a labyrinth of darkness and doors, of wooden plankways and rope stairs, full of hanging laundry and fabrics. There was no way for them to traverse those pathways as they were, clad in full ceremonial armor, especially with the growing darkness of dusk behind them, and no way to know which of the dozens of paths the killers had taken.

Odmund turned to a nearby beggar—a wretch of a man. "The men that ran past here—which way did they go?!" He demanded.

The beggar, a blind man, now that he took a closer look, started cackling. "They're long gone now, Chosen. Lost to you and your men." He said, then cackled some more. Odmund grabbed him by his scruffy collar and lifted him off the mud and grime. "Where do they go, then? Where can I find them?!"

The man sobered up a bit, but instead of fear, he offered Odmund a defiant look—a look that spoke of someone who had nothing to lose in this world. He spoke in serious tones.

"Nobody knows, Champion. They are like shadows—they come and go, and disappear as soon as they do, leaving no trace of their passing."

Odmund heard the honesty in the man's voice, saw his grim, serious expression. He let him go, then turned to his men, standing close behind, their weapons at the ready. "You will not speak a word of what you witnessed here. Not a word!" He shouted like a dragon, wanting to put out the fire in him.

Odmund then got on his horse and galloped like a storm out of the Silence, his guard following swiftly after him, leaving only shadows and death behind.

***

Back at the castle, near the Chosen barracks and training ground known as the Nest, Efilia walked up the stairs with the excitement of the announcement.

She could hear the other Chosen talking to each other: "I made it to the list this year." One of the second-year soldiers said to her friend.

"Ooh, so exciting," Her friend replied. "All the regional kings and queens will be watching this year. No pressure, huh?"

Efilia's steps became faster, but once she reached the fourth floor of the building, there was almost no place to stand. The place was so crowded that she had to push her way through to get to the wall where "the list" had been displayed.

"Argh... It's at times like this that I wish I was a Scal." She murmured while still halfway there.

"Efilia!" A male voice called from the other side of the room before she could reach the board with the list. She rose on the balls of her feet and saw a hand waving at her from the crowd of heads.

"Urk!" She shouted back, waving as well. A tall, handsome man with black hair and piercing eyes smiled at her from beyond the other Chosen, drawing some very jealous looks from a lot of the ladies around.

"Come here!" He said.

Efilia did, pushing through the gathered crowd and drawing straight-on venomous looks from some of the girls.

She smiled at her friend after finally catching up to him. "Have you checked? Is your name on the list?" She asked, nodding back at the board. Her eyes shone with hope. Urk, on the other hand, was lost in her smile. "Well... have you?" She insisted.

The smile disappeared from Urk's lips. "No, I didn't register this year. I don't understand why everyone is so excited about it, though… I mean, the winner is certain. We have one Odon… and he will win again, and again, and again." He looked away from her as he spoke, his demeanor completely changed. "Next time, however, once Odmund loses the right to attend due to his duties… that'll be another story. I'll finally be the champion." He smiled again, but the smile did not reach his eyes.

"So… if you don't care about the lists… why are you here then?" Efilia asked while trying hard to catch a glimpse of the list from where she was.

"Just passing by," Urk said, shrugging. I was giving a self-defense class on the next room over. You know how Gerun loves leaving me with kids while he goes off to enjoy warm sunlight and wine." His words made Efilia smile again.

"When you've served as long as Battlemaster Gerun, you earn a little break every once in a while," she said. "Besides, I know how much you love kids." She nudged his arm and smiled at him. He stared at her smile as if it was the only thing in the room… Then realized that he was indeed staring, and so quickly changed the topic.

"Come, let's see what section they put you in." Urk said, using his wide body to make a way towards the board of listings.

"You think I made it to the list this year…?" She asked, half to Urk, half to herself.

"Of course you did. You beat all the other Vertures during the eliminations. You have to be." He pulled her through to the wall. At long last, the list was in front of her. Her eyes scanned the first scroll with excitement… then the second… then the third. She stared at the board wordlessly, her mouth agape, her eyes wide as an owl.

"This is surely a jest…" Urk said in low voice. He looked down at Efilia and saw how pale she'd gotten. She was frozen on the spot, barely breathing, her eyes glued to the board, as if they could somehow make her name appear on one of the lists by sheer force of will.

"Efilia… Come with me." He held her by the wrist and took her away from the crowds, onto a nearby balcony at the end of the hall. She was still pale, her eyes lost in the distance, her lips moving, but no words coming out. Urk placed a gentle hand on her shoulder.

"I… I can't understand why." She finally said in a low voice. "I worked so hard." She looked at Urk's eyes, a look of genuine confusion and betrayal in her own. He could see the building anger in them, bubbling up like hot water in a kettle, about to spill over.

"If I'm not even worthy enough to participate in the Chosen Tourney, how will I ever rise to the rank of captain?! Dammit all!" The words exploded out of her mouth, and her cheeks flushed. Urk could see the line of her set jaw as she clenched her teeth, her nostrils flaring, a frown distorting her brow.

"Efilia…" Urk said, very gently.

"You fought with Od last time, Urk. You almost beat him. You tell me; am I really so far behind all of you?"

"Calm down Efilia. We will talk with the Board and figure it out."

"The Board?" She asked.

"Yes, Gerun is part of it, along with Ifir and some others. He's in the garden right now. We can just go and ask him. No problem. Maybe there was a mistake, and we can easily fix it. Come on, let's go." Urk said.

"A mistake… yes." She said, color returning to her cheeks. "That must've been it."

They ran down the stairs in haste and reached the garden a moment later. Urk smiled at her and let go of her hand. "Wait here. I'll be back soon." He walked over to a gray-haired Chosen in a high-ranking uniform and sat next to him.

Efilia noticed that the Battlemaster of the Chosen wouldn't return her gaze, though, making every effort to keep his eyes on Urk. The two men began to talk and Efilia pricked up her ears.

"I really don't know why Urk," Gerun said, and Efilia picked it up clearly, despite him trying to speak in hushed tones. "She was excellent during the eliminations, far outperforming the others… but the Songbird insisted that she isn't ready yet, and so forbid her from entering the list. I don't agree with the decision myself, but… you know how it is around here. What Ifir says goes, all else be damned."

Efilia turned pale again and felt the rising heat on her face once more.

Dreams and Disappointments | 71

"Thank you, Battlemaster." Urk said and saluted his superior before he left. However, when he looked back to the spot where he'd left Efilia… she wasn't there anymore. He looked around the garden and, upon realizing she was gone, cursed under his breath.

"Damn…"

The young Chosen lieutenant stormed out of the Nest and onto the castle proper. She flew up the stairs to Ifir's offices like a gale. She had no idea what to say, do or think, but she couldn't take such a humiliation standing down. She needed to know.

"Is Ifir in her office?" She asked one of the guards outside her rooms.

Clearly noticing Efilia's state, the soldiers looked at each other in fear and shook their heads.

"No lieutenant, she isn't." One of them said. "She's… out."

"Dammit… Did she leave any instructions of when to expect her back, or…"

The guards shook their head again.

"Damn!" She said, and walked away, heading back down the spiral stairs to the castle foyer. On her way down, she heard the unmistakable sound of Ifir's high-breed steed arriving at the back garden. She hurried down to the foyer and, with all the confidence she could muster, awaited her to enter the keep.

Ifir entered the castle from the back garden doors, looking tired and unhappy. She looked up at Efilia for a moment, then stared past her, barely recognizing the fact that she was even there. She walked past the young Chosen in a rush.

"Songbird," Efilia called out to her.

"Soldier," Ifir said, and kept walking.

"Commander Ifir!" Efilia said, raising her voice more than she meant to. Ifir suddenly stopped… and so did every servant in the room. The Songbird turned her neck back slowly, and very intentionally, a single eyebrow raised in question… and the question very clear.

Who in all the hells do you think you are?

"I'm… Sorry, Songbird. I didn't mean to shout. I, uh… I need to ask you something important." Efilia said, looking suitably chastised for her outburst, but still committed to her goal.

"Then ask... soldier." Her voice was smooth as silk, as if nothing had happened.

"I need to know why you took my name off the Tourney list. I won the eliminations... by a long shot." Efilia's voice was certain and headstrong.

Ifir looked Efilia from head to toe... then walked closer and closer, to the point where her chest was brushing with Efilia's. The young Chosen could smell the musk of Ifir's horse on her clothes. Her sweat. And something more... blood? Before she had time to ponder it further, Ifir extended her head past Efilia's face, and whispered to her right ear.

"Do you question my decisions, soldier?" Her voice had a unique ring to it—like it was coming from Ifir, but also from the very depths of the earth around them. Efilia felt the castle begin to shake, her hairs standing on their end, and she knew—she knew she was experiencing Ifir's dreaded *Voice*. Despite the feeling of power coming from it, however, Efilia noticed that it didn't really affect her as she would've imagined it to. There were horror stories surrounding Ifir's Voice... but to her, it seemed like a gentle tremor, rather than a skull-splitting screech of agony—as one of the castle's surviving victims had put it.

A look of sudden confusion, she noticed, briefly brushed past Ifir's features as she looked at her. She expected Efilia to react very differently, it seemed.

"... Y-yes, Songbird. In this instance, I do. I deserve the opportunity... I fought *very* hard for it." She looked down at her own feet, avoiding Ifir's steady gaze.

Ifir looked her up and down again, crossing her arms.

"You want to know why I pulled your name form the list, darling?"

"Yes... please. I need to know."

"Because are weak, Efilia." Songbird said.

Efilia's eyes widened. "I... am not!" She couldn't control herself. Her chest heaved, and her nostrils flared once more. "I defeated all the other Veruters in my group—I passed all of my tests. I earned this!"

The servants all around them seemed to shrink into the walls and floors of the castle. Coin Master Fermand came out of one door with

Dreams and Disappointments | 73

a book of records in one hand, saw the scene, then turned right back around, saying; "No, no, no, no… I've got too much on my plate today for this."

Ifir, in turn, came closer to Efilia's face, to where she was literally breathing on her nose, and a serpent-like smirk appeared on her lips. Her voice, however, when she spoke, was cold as ice.

"You may have outer strength, dear child… But inside, you're *weak*. So… very… weak. Like a little canary, hidden away on its cage. I see you for what you are, little canary. And so, I decree you *unfit* to proceed."

Efilia, despite her courage and anger, felt herself shrinking back at Ifir's words, trying but failing to hold her chilling stare.

"You will stay within your limits, little canary… or next time, you'll find yourself down in the dungeons, feeding the Nor. *That's* what someone as weak as you deserves." The threat in Ifir's voice left Efilia speechless.

Ifir stared her down one more time, then, with that same diabolical smirk, she turned and left the room. As soon as she did, the servants resumed their movements, and the foyer of the castle breathed again. Efilia stood still for few seconds, then shambled towards the back garden of Castle Kellum. She sat in one of the stone benches, among the flowers and hedges, her eyes glazed over, her breath coming in slow, shallow intakes.

And she wept.

CHAPTER 6

THE CHOSEN IN THE WOODS

Merki rode back to town in haste, a man tied on the back of her horse instead of a stag.

"Come on, old Lor…" She told the horse she'd borrowed. "We're almost home… just a bit more, old boy." She said, doing her best to encourage the lanky, pale creature. Her dog, Rage, ran happily and seemingly unfazed next to them, keeping up with the horse without any visible difficulty.

Merki, however, felt just as tired as the horse looked. Dragging the mysterious man's body through the forest, putting on top of the horse—as strong and fit as Merki was, that had been one hell of an effort. Still… her luck couldn't have been better. Here, she had set out to hunt a stag for the captain back in Halstead—her ticket out of this town in the middle of nowhere, and she'd found something much, much better.

A Chosen.

One of sacred warriors of the Kollek people. But not just any Chosen, she knew, for all of the king's Chosen lived and trained at the capital. A few were sent to strategic battles and war fronts to serve as special units—and a few more, mainly those who could see, hear or move fast, were sent as scouts to spy on the enemy forces.

Then there were those who rebelled against the king and their country and fled to join the Sons of the Forest, as they were known around these parts.

This Chosen, by the ragged looks of him, *had* to be one of these.

An honest to goodness rebel.

And Chosen rebels, she knew, carried with them the highest bounty in all the land. The payment for the delivery of one was… unimaginable. But for Merki, the best reward of all was that of the law of the King's Bounty—which said that anyone in possession of a rebel Chosen had to be granted escort and an audience to the king, directly, and commended publicly for the capture. Most bounty hunters perished in the most painful of ways when going after a rogue Chosen, of course, so the law of the King's Bounty wasn't invoked often—maybe only a handful of times since it'd been instated and spread throughout the kingdom.

And yet, here, Aether had placed one right under Merki's bow sights.

She looked at the Chosen man's body, bumping up and down as the horse did its best attempt at a "canter," and felt some relief at the fact that the man was still unconscious. If her limited knowledge on these matters held up, the amethyst arrow, piercing so deep into his flesh, into his *essence*, should keep him out of action for half a day or more.

All the same, she kicked the sides of the horse lightly, hoping to make it move faster. The last thing she wanted was for the man to wake up on the way to town, after what she'd seen him do to the savages back in the forest.

Half an hour later, and Merki had finally arrived at the outskirts of Halstead, revealed by the firelight among the trees. She steered Lord around the tree cover of the forest to a spot a few hundred yards behind her cottage—still far enough into the wood that nobody would notice her. It was the perfect place to stash her prize, at least for a while; a small clearing in the great forest that surrounded them which she knew well, easy enough to miss, but still close enough to return to—if one knew the way.

She dismounted, and despite the killer pain on her back and the merciless fire raging on her inner thighs, she managed to slowly lower the Chosen to the soft, grassy ground.

Damned Chosen... what do they feed these people that they grow so sodding large, anyways?

Once safely on the ground, she covered his large body by hiding it among some bushes and made sure that the binds on his hands and feet were tight enough. She then tied Lord to a tree and looked at Rage, who patiently awaited his next order.

"Wait here, boy. Bark at anything that approaches that isn't me," she gestured at Kade's hidden body, the tip of his boot poking out from the bush. "Don't let anyone near him." She gave the trained war dog the orders with a quick sequence of hand signs—a gift from her father that had come very handy since he'd left her Rage to care for. The dog barked once, letting her know he understood the order.

"I'll be right back, boy." She finished.

I hope.

She then disappeared into the nearby trees, leaving the two beasts and man in the calm quiet of the evening woods.

As she passed between the old cottages on the outskirts of town, the village slumbered in near-complete silence. The only sound muddling the otherwise peaceful, late-night countryside mood was the laughter and high voices of the soldiers, which Merki had all but expected. She wasn't a believer of any one faith, per se, but she'd silently prayed that they hadn't started drinking yet like other soldiers came before.

There was a huge bonfire in the garden of the Eriksons', the ruling family of Halstead, with a pig stuck on a spit in the middle, drops of fat dripping from it and sizzling on the coals below. The smell was mouth-watering. The three recruits Locke had brought with him ate and drank noisily around it, enjoying the "hospitality" of the richest family in town. The Eriksons' son was serving the soldiers along with his mother, both of them carrying plates full of fruits and pastries, which they'd prepared for the soldiers as a show of hospitality. (With a humble request for Locke to mention

Elder Erikson and said hospitality to his superiors back at the capital, of course.)

"Hope the food is to your liking, captain." Elder Erikson, who was standing next to the table and watching over his family's work, said to Locke, who was sitting at the table with Gerard and the rest of the men, enjoying the evening.

"It most certainly is kind sir." Locke replied. "Thank you so much for opening your house to us."

Elder Erikson smiled with joy. "It's our pleasure to serve to our king in every possible way we can."

Locke nodded right before he spooned up some of the piping-hot tomato soup they'd placed before him. The owner of the house stepped back, "Please let us know if you need anything else."

"Actually… I do." Locke said. "Can you point me to your hothouse?"

The recruits, already a few drinks in, chuckled at this.

Locke smiled at them. "Now boys—we all take shits, don't we? Gerard, cover these louts for me while I'm away. I'll rejoin our feast shortly. And don't let them drink too much, you hear? We have lots of riding to do tomorrow."

The old soldier grunted in reply, focused on his own bowl of soup and meat, and Locke disappeared towards the back of the house with Elder Erikson.

It was at that time that Merki finally arrived at the Erikson's front yard, panting, sweating, her heart drumming in her chest. She looked around for Locke in a rush, the bright light of the firepit making it difficult to focus her eyes, but she couldn't find him.

Dammit, where is he?

"Oi, it's the huntress!" One of the recruits said in a thick mountain accent, holding up his mug of ale. "Did you bring us that stag, then?"

Merki cursed under her breath, standing at the edge of the yard, unsure of what to do.

"Where is your captain, soldier?" She asked the young man.

The recruits looked at each other and chuckled. The young man walked over to her now, so they didn't have to speak in raised voices.

"He's, uh… indisposed right now. He'll be back shortly. I'm Jarrie, by the way. From Tuquan—a few days' ride northeast." He stretched out a greasy hand, which he wiped against his pants several time, to little effect.

Merki shook it all the same. "Merki. Huntress of Halstead."

"Merki! Such a pretty name. Say, you haven't met the other lads, have you?"

"I don't believe I had the pleasure, no."

"Well," Jarrie continued, clearly a little buzzed by the ale. "That sour-looking dreg over there by the fire is Leord."

"Fuck off, yodel." The recruit responded, carefully slicing into his slice of pork with the airs of one who wasn't used to eating outside like this. He was the one with the greasy hair, brown eyes and arrogant airs, Merki noticed.

"Charming lad," Jarrie continued. "Captain picked him up on one of the bigger towns. I think he comes from one of them posh families." He then pointed to the other recruit, eating an impossibly large piece of meat by the table. "That one's Ourg. He's a lot friendlier, if a little touched in the head, if you know what I'm saying." He whispered the last few words to Merki, getting closer to her. She grimaced a little at the smell of alcohol on his breath, as she nodded and forced a smile. "Say hi, Ourg!"

"Hiii…." The other young man said, raising a hand, then immediately went back to gorging on his meal.

"So, where's the stag?" Jarrie continued. "You did catch it, didn't you? Else why would you be here? Unless…"

"The stag is back at my place." Merki said. "I have a couple of details to iron out with the captain as to our agreement, in private, and so I need him to come with me. Is he coming back soon?"

"Yeah, he's just—"

"Not here right now." Gerard said, appearing behind Jarrie, seeming to have materialized out of the shadows cast by the ring of firelight.

Fuck, Merki swore.

"He left me in charge." The old soldier continued, looking Merki head to toe with eyes that did little to hide his disdain for the young

The Chosen in the Woods | 79

huntress. "And as you can see, we're already eating here, miss. You took too long with the... stag. Lost your chance. Now sod off."

Merki stared at the tall, well-built man. Despite his age, he still had the body of a warrior, and the airs of someone who had killed his fair share of people.

Maybe even enjoyed it, a voice told her.

"I'm sorry, lieutenant... but I can't do that. I brought captain Locke his gift, and I can't leave until he receives it."

The old man scoffed and grinned, showing his full set of teeth—a wolfish grin that did not reach his eyes. "Then where is it, lass? How come you pulled it all the way to your place, and not just bring it here? You want to get the captain alone in your cottage, is that it? Appeal to his more... male urges? Is that what this is all about?"

Merki's cheeks flushed. She frowned, but held the bigger man's stare.

"I..." She began, but was cut off.

"Or maybe you're one of them Sons of Bitches that likes to roll around in the mud and make trouble for our military? Maybe you're just looking to drive a knife between our good captain's ribs, once he's safe and comfortable under you, in the stack of hay you probably call a bed? Get you some favor with your rebel friends for killing a decorated officer. Is *that* it?"

Merki noticed that the other recruits had stopped eating. Jarrie, the thin, ferret-looking one that had talked to her, had walked back a couple of paces. He was looking at the proceedings with clear fear in his eyes, while Leord stared with unveiled interest, and even awe. Ourg looked both worried and sad, his mouth gaping. She also noticed, for the first time, that Gerard was in full armor, where everyone else had stripped down to more basic and comfortable clothes for the night. He wore a thick coat made out of fox fur, over a plate cuirass, gauntlets, and tall greaves. She also noticed there were at least six knives on his belt, with two larger dirks strapped in leather holsters under his arms... on top of the soldier's standard-issue longsword, hanging from its sheath on his belt. He was basically a walking armory.

Merki swallowed hard, despite herself. She pushed down the urge to *really* drive a knife into the foul old bastard in front of her—who'd not only accused her of being a harlot and a liar, but also a common criminal—a rebel: the worst of the worst. An irony, given that her gift to them was probably one of those very same people. She reminded herself of her mission, her goal and her focus, and swallowed her pride down—but it took every single bit effort she had in her to do so.

Although… despite her confidence as a hunter… even she had doubts over whether she could take on this particular man face to face like this.

"I am not a rebel… and I am not a wench… sir. I just want safe passage to the capital." She said, in a very careful, neutral tone. "And to do that, I brought captain Locke a gift, as I promised."

"A stag?"

Merki hesitated. "I…. ah…"

The old man inched closer, his eyes squinting.

"Gerard!" A familiar voice rang from the house. The old man closed his eyes and Merki could've sworn he uttered a curse under his breath. He turned around, revealing Locke, who was fixing his clothes and tightening his belt. "Is there a problem here?" Locke asked. "I mean, can't a man go relieve himself for a moment, without…" He saw Merki for the first time, standing out in the darkness, partly hidden because of the shadows cast by the firelight.

"Oh, it's… you." He spoke, his previous tone of jest all but gone. He recovered then and spoke again. "It's you—the Huntress of Halstead! So, where's my stag? You… did get me the stag you promised, right? I mean," he gestured around them with his arms. "Clearly, you didn't get it in time for dinner, but… I'm generous. I could still be convinced to let you come with us, if—"

"The stag is at my place. Come with me, and I'll show you." She said. The anxiety in her tone was so obvious, it made Locke hesitate before responding.

"Go back to your house, you say?" Locke said, giving her a sidelong look. The recruits all looked at each other and grinned.

"Yes."

"Captain," Gerard began, massaging the bridge of his nose with his fingers. "You can't really be considering…"

Locke held a hand up. "Hush, Gerard. I…"

"I… want to show you something." Merki said, the tone in her voice urgent, her eyes avoiding Gerard's icy stare. "Something… other than the stag."

"I fucking knew it…" Gerard said, walking back to the table. The recruits all started to laugh. Ourg even whistled at Locke.

Locke, on the other hand, frowned at Merki. "Really? I mean… sure. Ok."

Merki sighed. She hated herself so much at that moment, but she could see no other way to get him to come with her alone, especially with Gerard acting so suspicious of her. She couldn't risk the old bastard finding out about the Chosen before Locke; before she had a chance to explain.

"Good." Merki said, her jaw set. "Come with me then, captain."

Locke looked back at his recruits and raised his eyebrows. "I'll be back soon boys. Gerard…"

"I know. I'll keep the lot in line…" The old man grumbled, and bit into a piece of bread, looking as miserable as ever.

"Great. Follow me." Merki said, leading the captain through town and towards her cottage, completely aware of all they eyes upon her—the villagers, looking outside their windows, or from their porches as they sat smoking their pipes, Gerard, following them closely, making sure that Merki didn't take any wrong turns, and even old Axel, staring at Merki from the statue of the king, where he'd most likely spent the day sitting and begging.

Merki reached her front door, unlocked it, and beckoned Locke inside with a quick gesture of her arm. He entered the home, in total darkness, until Merki walked over to her hearth and lit a fire. She then moved around the small cottage, lighting candles, producing enough light… but not too much.

"Ok… so… this is the part where you show me the stag, but seeing as I'm not detecting one in this cozy cabin of yours… I take it we'll just get right into the good part?" Locke said, crossing his arms and arching an eyebrow.

Merki sighed deeply, her back to him, then turned.

"We're not having sex, captain. And there is no stag."

Locke's expression went through several phases—from excited, to confused, betrayed, then angry. "We're not… There isn't… Then why in the seven hells did you bring me here, woman? Do you enjoy wasting the time of the king's men? Is that it? Or do you—"

"Just… shut up for a second, and let me explain."

Locke stared at Merki with his words hanging from his mouth, eyes wide.

"I found something in the woods, captain. Something bigger and more important than any dumb stag."

"You… found something in the woods. What could you possibly find in these woods that could interest me, woman?"

Merki stared him down, her arms crossed. She hesitated for a moment.

You're in it all the way now, Merki. No backing out.

"A rebel."

Locke's eyes grew wide again.

"And not just any rebel… A *Chosen* one."

Locke's eyes grew wider. He gazed at her for a moment, looking her from top to bottom. "You… You found… and I assumed, *captured*, a rebel Chosen? Is that what you're saying?" Merki nodded. He frowned… then broke into laughter. "You expect me to believe that *you* took down a rogue Chosen? How desperate *are* you, lady? Not even a whole squadron of trained guards from the king's own castle can take down a Chosen!"

Merki took a deep breath… and let it go.

"He was badly wounded and hurt. He seemed… lost. Killed a few savages who tried to take his belongings, who thought he was dead. I was up on a tree, watching it all happen."

"So, you, what? Poked him full of arrows until he passed out? You know that's not enough to suppress a Chosen, right? Are you trying to take me for a fool, huntress of Halstead?"

"My father was a soldier, captain. Like you. Before he… Before I… He left me arrows. Special ones, tipped with amethysts. For my protection. I'd never used them until today."

"I don't believe you."

"You don't have to," Merki said. "He's a couple of minutes away from here, bound and asleep. Come see for yourself."

Locke's face suddenly flushed of any blood it could possibly hold, went as pale as a full moon.

"Y-you brought a rogue, feral Chosen near the village?! Are you mad, or just plain stupid?!"

Merki allowed herself a small grin.

"I thought you didn't believe me."

"I don't! But that's beside the point! God above, woman! They require continuous contact with amethysts when they're feral, or else they can't be controlled!"

"He's still got the arrow in his shoulder. You should have one of those special cuffs, don't you?"

"Yeah, I do, but…"

"Then I suggest you stop whimpering and come with me before he wakes up, then."

Merki walked over to a back door and opened it, revealing her back yard. "Your war dog won't see us slipping out this way." She gestured toward the Erikson's house with her head. Towards Gerard. Locke just stared at her with a mixed look of confusion, renewed respect and terror.

"Come with me, captain. Secure the Chosen rebel—and honor the Law of the King's Bounty." Merki said, her tone brooking no further argument.

"You'll take me *directly* to the capital."

Chapter 7

A Duel Under Lamplight

Locke stood in the woods behind Merki's cabin, eyeing the bound, unconscious body in the grass, a single lantern lighting the clearing.

"By Aether's mercy... You really did find a Chosen." He said, the awe clear in his voice. He walked carefully over to Kade, his sword drawn, and knelt beside him, giving Merki a quick look. Her dog looked between the two of them, wondering just what in the world was going on.

"I swear, if this is some kind of trick..."

She rolled her eyes to heaven. "It's not. Go on. Look for yourself."

Locke nodded, then proceeded to check the size of the Chosen's hand. Rage began to growl in protest, but a few clicks from Merki's tongue brought him right back to her side, tame as a puppy. Merki patted his head and mouthed the words "good boy to him," winking.

With the dog out of the way, it didn't take long for Locke to notice the amethyst arrow on the man's shoulder. He immediately took out the amethyst cuffs that only captains like him were issued and proceeded to put them around the Chosen's wrists. Immediately, the man's irregular breathing stabilized, and he seemed to drift into a deep sleep.

Locke stood up, looking at the man in tattered clothes before him, seeking, studying him.

"Well, that's a Chosen alright. And he looks like a rebel, too. Unless he got lost from his unit on a mission and went feral in the wilds… then stole some poor farmer's clothes. But that seems very unlikely."

"How so?" Merki asked.

Locke crossed his arms and kept his eyes on the man. "The frontlines are far from here. Nothing of interest to be sending Chosen squads for either. This… isn't good."

He gave Merki a look.

"Are you certain he was alone when you shot him?"

"Aside from the men he killed… yes. Why?"

"Well…" Locke bit his lip. "If he *is* a rebel, then chances are his group isn't far away. There may be more rogue Chosen like him out there. And even if there aren't—the Sons of the Forest aren't a threat to take lightly either. They're most likely looking for him as we speak."

Merki didn't need to see Locke's expression to understand the gravity of the situation.

"Shit." She whispered.

"Indeed. And now he's here. What do you think will happen if the Sons find him?"

"They'll burn down Halstead. Kill everyone in it." She said under her breath, her words trembling.

"Correct. We need to move him out of here as soon as we're able—get him to the nearest garrison."

Merki considered it for a moment. "The one near Rockpour?"

Locke nodded. "That's the closest one, Waterval. We can set up a proper armed escort for him there to Kellum. I guess you're getting your wish after all."

Merki nodded. "So, you'll honor the Law of the King's Bounty?"

"Of course," Locke said. "Besides… I'll get some of the praise for this little miracle here as well. Might even have a shot at getting out of this shit recruitment detail, closer to the frontlines, perhaps…"

"You really want to be closer to the war?" Merki asked, frowning. "Why?"

Locke frowned right back, but not with any kind of malice. "Why not? I want to fight for my country—not haul ass around the mountains convincing yodels to throw themselves at the enemy." He looked away from Merki. "There's no honor in that."

The young huntress nodded in understanding. "Alright. Well, we've got to get the arrow out, and get him ready to move, then."

Locke held up his hands. "Hold your horses, lass. My men are in no condition to ride right now. And besides, if the rebels do attack, we stand much more of a chance in a defensible position like Halstead rather than out there in the wild. We'll move out tomorrow, once we're rested and refitted for such a journey… and once I find a way to explain this… mess to my men."

Merki was about to say something else when the bushes behind them rustled.

"What… mess, exactly, captain?" A bassy, familiar voice asked.

Fuck, Merki thought, closing her eyes. *Fuck, fuck and fuck.*

"Gerard…" Locke said. "What are you doing here? I told you to watch after the men!"

The older man grinned, baring his fangs. "Oh, they're alright. Passed out from all the food and drink. But *you*…are here. Not at the cabin, getting all dirty with the lady." He pointed a finger at Merki.

"How did you…" Merki began.

"You think I wasn't paying attention? That I wouldn't see you two scamper off into the woods?" He advanced on Merki, getting awfully close to her. "I have half a mind to gut you right here and now, lassie. That is, if you can't explain why you've dragged a captain of the Kollek royal army out to the woods in the middle of the night. Are you waiting for your rebel friends? Is that it?" He shoved Merki hard, causing her to stumble onto the grass. Rage immediately barked at the old soldier, baring his fangs, and he almost jumped at him too, had Merki not given him a sharp command to stand down.

Merki took a deep breath, stilled the raging fire that churned within her.

A Duel Under Lamplight | 87

"Gerard, stop! It's al—" Locke began, but it was too late. The old man's face had grown pale, his hand reaching for his longsword and pulling it halfway free of its scabbard. Rage looked carefully at the soldier from Merki's side, hunching on its forelegs, growling, its fangs showing clearly in the lamplight. If Gerard even tried to swing his sword the heavy hunting dog would pounce on him like a hungry wolf in a heartbeat, as he'd been trained to do… and Merki wouldn't stop him this time.

"Is that… A Chosen? A *rogue* Chosen?" He said, stammering, staring at the man in the grass, who'd been shrouded by the darkness so far.

"Gerard… it's all under control. Sheathe your blade—*now*."

"The hell it is! The bloody harlot *is* a rebel! What is going on here?" He looked between Merki and Locke. Merki stared back defiantly at him from the grass, her hand awfully close to the knife she kept in her boot. Rage growled, acting almost like an extension of her, his muscles coiled for action.

"Gerard—stand down!" Locke growled. "*Now*, soldier!"

The familiar tone and command activated the old dog's military training, and he snapped back to his senses, slowly sheathing the sword back into its hilt, blinking furiously. Merki waited a moment then clicked her tongue again, setting Rage at ease… while pulling her hand away from the hilt of her own knife.

"Our huntress stumbled onto a miracle while out in the woods. It's a sign from Aether, Gerard. An answer to our prayers. She bagged us a lost Chosen… and has invoked the Law of the King's Bounty."

A moment passed in the clearing before understanding slowly dawned on Gerard's face.

"*What?*"

Locke walked over to him, his hands raised in a gesture of placation. "I'll explain it all soon. We need to move the body somewhere else, hide it, till the morning. Our mission just changed, old friend." He said, placing a hand on Gerard's shoulder. The old man still looked stunned, confused and angry, all at once. "We're going back home—to Kellum. With a rogue *Chosen* for the king."

"A rogue..." Gerard whispered, shaking his head, his mind racing. "But... what about other rebels. They'll be... shit. By Luden's balls..."

"Yes..." Locke said, his hand still firm on Gerard's shoulder. "We need to move fast. No more recruiting. Straight to..."

"Rockpour," the tall man said. "He'll need a proper escort."

Locke nodded.

"And until then..."

"Yes. We'll have a massive target on our back for his rebel friends, wherever they are."

Gerard considered the situation, his breaths steadying. He looked between Merki, Locke and the sleeping Chosen—a creature of unimaginable power and carnage, he knew. He looked back at Locke... and shook his head slowly.

"What if it's all a trap, Locke? I've been in situations like this before... Chosen don't just fall out of the sky, boy! What if your little fox there is in league with the Chosen, their friends just waiting for us out on the road, to gut us while we sleep? No..." He shook his head with more vigor. "This isn't the way the world works, Locke. This all smells rotten through and through."

Locke considered his veteran lieutenant's words. He looked back at Merki, still on the ground. She looked between the two of them, understanding dawning in her eyes, and shook her head frantically.

"Just let me fix this here and now, captain." Gerard said, his sword hissing as it slid halfway out of its scabbard. "I'll kill the two of them, and we'll just keep going—move away from all of this."

"No," Merki interrupted. "NO! I am *not* a rebel! I know it seems too convenient, but I found this man out there in the woods, near the Forbidden Lands! Rebels don't tread there—only savages! You have to believe me!"

Locke looked back at the Chosen and sighed. He then looked back at Gerard, a look of placation in his eyes.

"We need this, Gerard. This man's our way out of this thankless job detail."

A Duel Under Lamplight | 89

Gerard's set his jaw hard. "You would put us in mortal danger… just on the off chance that this yodel's telling you the truth? You would risk all of our lives?"

Locke shook his head, frowning. "We'll tie her, then. We'll tie them both. Make sure they can't wander around when we make camp."

Gerard scoffed, rolling his eyes. "God above, captain…"

"It'll be fine, Gerard. We *need* this."

The old man looked down at Locke with poison in his eyes. "You mean, *you* need this."

Locke frowned. "…and so do you. Maybe more than me."

Gerard held the captain's stare, his hand still gripping the hilt of his sword. Merki put her hand firmly over the hilt of her small knife as well, ready to pull it out in a heartbeat; her muscles coiled, ready to spring to action at a moment's notice. Her hound had started to tense up as well.

"Don't challenge me, Gerard. You are older, wiser… but still under my command."

The old man looked down at his captain, and a look of pure disgust passed over his features. Merki held her breath.

"Ahem…" A new voice sounded in the clearing. "If I may, gentlemen."

Merki recognized the voice. She couldn't believe it.

From the shadows of the trees emerged an old, harmless-looking man in simple, but well-groomed clothes. Axel.

We're dead, Merki thought. *Oh, we're fucking dead.* Rage, upon noticing the old man, greeted him by baring his yellowed fangs almost soundlessly, as usual.

"And just who the fuck are you?" Gerard asked the newcomer.

"My name is Axel," the old man said, ignoring the dog and focusing on the soldier. "And I am a caretaker to the young lady here."

Locke and Gerard exchanged glances.

"I've been… ahh… listening to your conversation, yes. I assure you that I mean you no harm. And neither does the girl—she's no rebel. She was born and raised right here, in Halstead."

"And why should I believe you, old man? You have the stink of a rebel to me—hiding in the trees, following us, eavesdropping."

"Yes... I can see how you may come to that conclusion. But you see, I was charged with keeping an eye on our friend here a long time ago. Wherever she goes, I go... even if she doesn't want me to."

Merki frowned. Axel's words struck her, but also his demeanor, his tone and sure posture. This wasn't the village hobo she'd learned to tolerate anymore, but someone else.

"Charged by whom?" Merki asked him. Axel gave her a knowing, sidelong look.

"By your father, Halidor. Before he passed."

"And how did my father know you?" Merki asked, despite herself, a lump in her throat.

"We met in the capital back when he was posted there. He's the reason I came to Halstead in the first place. I owed him."

Locke and Gerard watched the exchange with curious eyes, but Gerard's hand was still on the hilt of his sword.

"I served as a caretaker in Kellum for many years... at a place called the Nest."

"The Chosen training grounds..." Locke whispered.

"Indeed," Axel replied. "I studied the Chosen there, served them, and helped them in their training. Your father was posted as a guard there for a while, young Merki. This was, of course, before you were born. Before he moved to Halstead."

Merki's eyes were wide as a barn, her chest rising and falling, her mouth agape.

"Is that why you were always hovering around me? Why did you never say anything, old man?" She asked him. "All these years I thought I... Why didn't you tell me?"

Axel smiled at her. "Your father's wishes. He didn't want you to think he thought you incapable. I was only to watch—and help, if needed, from afar."

Locke sighed, then took a couple of steps away from Gerard.

"Satisfied?" He asked him.

Gerard looked between Axel and Merki. The girl looked suitably flustered, but it could all be an act. He knew how committed these rebels could be to their cause.

"To hell with this. I still think this is a mistake, Locke… but you'll do as you deem best. You're the captain."

Merki let out the breath she didn't realize she'd been holding, and slowly got up to her feet. Gerard stood to the side of the clearing, arms crossed, and gave her a stern look.

"Don't think you're off the hook that easy though, lassie. I'll be keeping an eye on you… One wrong move… one bad mistake… and I'll lop off your head, just like *that*. You hear?" He made a quick motion with his thumb across his throat.

Merki didn't answer. Instead, after sharing Gerard's frown for a moment, she walked over to Axel.

"What are you doing here?" She asked him.

"Keeping the promise I made to your father, my dear. Now," He turned to Locke and Gerard. "I suggest you pull that arrow out of our Chosen friend there before you move him for the night. I assume none of you know how to remove amethyst from a Chosen properly?"

The soldiers looked at each other. Axel nodded to himself. "Allow me, then. I'll need some Marigold and water. Merki?"

"On it." She said, and began to search around the clearing for the common plant.

"Now… as soon as she comes back, I'll pull the arrow and apply a poultice of Marigold to the wound. That'll keep it from getting infected. However…"

"The Chosen will wake up." Gerard said.

"Correct. He can't harm us with the amethyst binds on… but I'd still advise against riling him up too much. He'll be disoriented and scared. We need him calm. Agreed?"

Both Axel and Locke looked at Gerard. He looked back at the two of them, confused for a moment, the grunted his approval and moved away to lean against a tree.

"I'll need you to hold him down once I pull the arrow, captain. Are you up for the task?"

Locke nodded, though he didn't even try to hide the fear in his eyes.

Merki came back with the plants and some water she'd taken from a nearby creek. Axel took the plant and crushed it in his palm, adding water and making a small ball with it. He passed the ball of soggy plant matter to Merki. "Apply it to the wound as soon as I pull the arrow."

Merki nodded. She'd treated wounds on her own body several times before. She knew what to do.

"Ok, here it goes." Axel said. He laid the Chosen on his back against the grass and gripped the arrow's shaft tightly… then, with one firm pull, he pulled the arrow out of the man's shoulder, in a light spray of blood. Merki immediately pressed the Marigold to his wound while Locke held the man steady against the grass by his arms.

The Chosen's eyes shot open and he immediately jerked forward, gasping in pain, his eyes wild and his face contorted. He started to convulse, thrashing left and right like a large fish out of water.

"Hold him!" Axel told Locke, and the soldier complied. Merki staggered back, falling on her bum against the grass. Axel quickly put a hand over Kade's forehead and muttered some words.

"Shh… You're alright… You're alright… You see the sun, and the sun is with you…" Something about the words worked, because as soon as he finished speaking, the Chosen stopped trashing and grunting. Instead, he laid on the grass, sweating, panting for dear life, shutting his eyes tightly from the pain.

Locke stared at Axel with wide-open eyes of his own, while Gerard watched from afar, his knuckles white on the hilt of his sword. Merki watched from a few feet away with bated breath. They all waited for the Chosen to calm down, watching him take one massive breath after the other, slowly going back to a normal rhythm.

Eventually, the Chosen opened his eyes, weakly at first, his mouth still agape, drawing long breaths.

"W-where… where am I?" He asked.

"In a safe place, friend." Axel cooed. "How are you feeling?"

"I… It hurts. My shoulder. My head."

"It'll all be alright soon. We're treating your wounds. We found you in the woods, nearly dead."

"The woods..." The man said, only half-awake. "The woods... The Curse! The Curse!" He started thrashing again, trying to get up, and Locke held him down once more.

"Calm down... Calm..." Axel spoke to him, in the same nurturing tone, as if speaking to a child. "There is no curse here. You are safe, Chosen."

Locke and Gerard exchanged confused glances. Locke looked at Merki and she just shrugged.

"I... No Curse? Are you sure... I, ahh... Good. Good." He seemed to relax.

"What is your name, young Chosen?" Axel asked him after giving him a moment.

"My... name? My name... is Kade." He finally said.

"Well, Kade..." Axel began. "Welcome back to the land of the living."

"Where am I? Who are you?" He asked the old man.

"We're asking the questions here, Chosen." Locke said. "What happened to you? Why were you out in the forest all alone?"

The man grimaced, then tried to sit up. He noticed the cuffs and binds for the first time, then his eyes widened once more. He shot a damning look at Axel.

"It's for your own protection. They will come off once we're sure you're not a danger to us." Axel said.

"Like hell they will..." Gerard whispered from afar.

"Now answer the man's questions, Chosen." Axel finished, throwing Gerard a sour look.

"Chosen? I don't know what... What's a Chosen?" He said.

Locke, Merki and Axel exchanged looks.

"Why have you bound me? What is going on?"

"Kade, you... killed three men out in the woods. Don't you remember?" Axel said.

"I... did?" He frowned. "I remember heat. Lots of it, all over my body. Then... figures. And... blood."

He looked at his hands and clothes. Saw the stains of dried blood on them.

"Did I really do that? That... wasn't a dream?"

"I'm afraid not." Merki said. "I saw you do it... Kade."

He saw Merki for the first time, and flinched, as if he'd never seen a woman before. He stared at her for longer than was proper, making her look away.

"Kade... Chosen." Locke said, drawing his attention back to the moment. "What do you remember before killing the men? Why where you out there alone in the woods?"

"I... can't remember."

"He can't remember..." Gerard said under his breath.

"Lieutenant..." Locke said, a warning in his eyes. The older man looked away.

"Try, Kade. You have to remember." Axel told him.

The young man frowned. "Can I get some water?"

Locke looked at Merki. She handed him her water skin, and he drank it all greedily.

"Thanks," Kade said, handing the skin back to Merki. She took it gingerly and quickly, looking at his large hands with caution.

"Speak, Chosen. Where did you come from?" Locke asked, once more.

"I... I only remember the forest. I was running from it... The Curse. And it caught me." He looked at the people around him. "How am I still alive?"

"As I said, Kade, there is no "curse" in these lands... You made it through the woods and collapsed. Why were you there?" Axel repeated... but Merki noticed something in his eyes, in his look—something that she'd never seen before. Was it a message? A warning? His eyes looked... different.

Kade shook his head. "I can't remember."

"Then... what do you remember?" Asked Locke, crossing his arms.

"I... my brother. I remember my brother."

"You have a brother?" Axel asked him.

A Duel Under Lamplight | 95

"Yes... I was looking for my brother. I need to find him... to bring him back, but..."

"The Curse got to you?" Axel said.

Kade nodded, looking entirely defeated.

"And where is your brother, Chosen?" Locke asked him.

"Don't call me that!" The man erupted. Then, seeing the shocked expressions around him, his features softened. "I'm sorry... just... my name is Kade. I don't know what a "Chosen" is. And I don't know where my brother is, either. All I can remember is that I'm supposed to find him. Bring him back."

"Back where?" Locke asked, crouching on his haunches, looking Kade eye to eye.

"Home," Kade said, as if the words were new and foreign to him.

"And where's home?" Locke insisted, his eyes fixed on Kade's.

The Chosen man frowned, then shook his head. "I... I don't recall. Where are we?"

"Goddammit." Said Gerard, and he stormed across the clearing, drawing his sword and pointing it at Kade's throat, causing him to shrink back against the grass.

"Where the hell did you come from, and why are you here?! Answer! Now!"

"Gerard, for fuck's sake!" Locke screeched, scrambling back from them.

"Soldier!" Axel pleaded, pushed to the side.

"No more games, you traitor. Tell us why you're out here, or by Luden's Horns, I'm slicing your head clean off!"

The Chosen man looked up at the soldier standing over him with sheer terror in his eyes. He started hyperventilating, trembling... then broke into tears.

"I don't know, I don't know!" He said, between sobs. "Where am I? Who are you all? What do you want from me?!" His voice was almost a squeal.

Gerard stared at the helpless looking thing below him with a look of pure confusion, and more than a little disgust. "What in the hells is *this*? A lily-livered Chosen?" He sheathed his blade and started to walk away, pinching the bridge of his nose. "Now I've seen it all."

Merki, despite her better judgment, scrambled towards Kade, who was lying prone on the floor in a panic, and put her arms around his head, raising him up. Rage joined her and started to lick the Chosen's fingers, which still smelled of fresh blood.

"There, there… it's ok. It's alright. We're not going to hurt you." Merki said to him. Then to Geralt: "Do you threaten to chop off the heads of everyone you meet? Does that get you off, you old, sick bastard?"

He looked at her over her shoulder, took another look at Kade, and scoffed. "For Aether's sake." He shook his head and left the clearing.

Locke and Axel moved closer to Kade once more. "I'm… sorry about that," Locke said to Kade. "What's wrong with him?" He asked Axel. The old man frowned, shaking his head. "It could've been the amethyst, or the blood loss… or whatever this "curse" he speaks off might be. This boy has lost his memories."

"Aether… amnesia?" Locked said.

Axel nodded. "Looks like it."

"Then what do we do?" Locke asked.

"We do what we said we'd do," Merki said, her voice suddenly firm once more. "We take him to the king. Rebel or not, he's clearly a Chosen. They'll know what to do with him. Besides… you agreed to honor the Law. You are bound to take me, and him, to Kellum." She said in a tone that brooked no further argument.

"And I as well." Axel added.

Locke gave him a look, and was about to complain, when Axel added: "I'm the only one here with firsthand experience working with Chosen. I can be of help. Besides, where she goes, I go." He looked at Merki, eyes wide, and she nodded.

"Where I go, he goes." She said.

"Well…" Locke muttered. "I guess that's that, isn't it?" He looked at the two of them with a bewildered expression. Neither of them back down.

"What's… Kellum? Why are you taking me there?" Kade asked.

A Duel Under Lamplight | 97

"It's the capital of the Kollek. Your people, remember?" Merki said. "You said you're looking for your brother?"

Kade nodded.

"Then that's where you'll find him… or someone who can take you to him. It's the largest city in all the land; the greatest gathering of people from all corners of the known world. If you can't find your brother there—he simply can't be found." She finished.

Kade looked at Axel, and the old man nodded.

"It's your best hope." He said.

"And where all Chosen, like you, belong." Locke said, gesturing to Kade's hands. "That's what we call folk like you around these parts—big hands, big feet. They all go to Kellum. If your brother came this way… then that's likely where he ended up as well."

Kade looked around him. He still had so many questions, and he wasn't sure what to think of any of this… But he couldn't see a better alternative. Out there, alone… he might never find his brother, he knew. Not in time.

He nodded to them.

"To Kellum, then."

CHAPTER 8

THE MISSION

King Ulor paced back and forth within the war council chambers with the fury of a gale.

The weak light of the setting sun filtering from the small windows played illusions on the marble statues in the chamber. His velvet cloak hung and trailed behind him as heavy as if carrying the burdens of his entire race. A young servant, desperate to prove himself, stoked the fires in the grand fireplace of the chamber as Ulor strode about. Unnerved by the king's foul pacing and occasional angry mumblings, he accidentally dropped the tongs he was holding, causing a loud, clanking sound that grated on Ulor's ears. The king stopped pacing, then slowly looked at the feeble young man, kneeling near the fireplace, his hand half-stretched to recover the blackened tool. He grimaced, staring the boy in the eyes, and the servant nearly died there and then, frozen to the spot. Ulor then gave his personal butler a long, hard look, then slowly pointed a finger at the young servant.

"Why the hell is he still in my service?" He hissed.

His obvious anger rumbled within the stone walls of the cold, damp room. The poor servant's legs shook in fear and, upon a nod from the butler, he walked out of the chamber as fast as he could, keeping his eyes strictly fixed on the old, cold stones which paved the floor.

"Apologies, sire." The butler answered, bowing to the king. "I'll be sure to find a suitable replacement immediately." The king's eyes searched the dark room, regretting the lack of bigger windows. However, the sensitive purpose of the room demanded it. King Ulor decided to fix his eyes on the massive table dominating the center of the chamber, and at the detailed map of the continent sprawled on top of it. The king signed for his butler to leave, and the man obediently and silently left the room.

On the map, there were figures representing Kollek soldiers and others representing Koartiz—the main enemies of the Kolleks, spread across the different lands. The large map contained an incredible level of detail. Ulor could see every corner of the Kollek kingdom on it—from Halstead in the south, closer to the Nor lands than most people knew, to the mountains to the north to the wide-open plains of the east, all bordering the crescent-shaped Koartiz lands.

To the south of Halstead one could see the Golden River, bordering the infamous savage lands, known locally as the reaches of Zuthar, home of Zugan tribe. Then, further south from these, Ulor located the chain of mountains known as the Antlers. Beyond these, a dark spot on the map marked the fabled Cursed Lands of the Nor race, Norzou. The Kollek held the largest swath of lands on the continent of Siran. These were widely known as the Land of the Gods. There were three big continents on the map, aside from Siran: one was called Arram, which was the dead continent, cursed by the Alerian sorcerers of the Koartiz race during the War of the Cursed King. Siran was all marked in black, due to there being nothing there but death and desolation.

The other continent was named Pesus. This one had three major kingdoms on it: Kolis on the west, a Kollek kingdom belonging to King Suran from the noble house of Freiz; Rekon, which belonged to the Kollek king Dlearin, and Yairn, which belonged to a Koartiz tribe which had no magic powers, unlike the Alerian Koartiz. Between Siran and Pesus were eight more islands, ruled by the lesser kings and queens of the Kollek kingdom.

After the War of the Cursed King, the only land left to the Nor was Norzou, the old temple city at the center of the Nor civilization, which was thought lost to modern history somewhere in the Antler Mountains. Nowadays, it was more commonly known as the Cursed Lands, and stood pressed between the lands of the Kollek, to the north, and the infamous, secretive Koartiz, to the south. It was strange to see how much fear such a small land could spread in people's hearts. On the other hand, the Koartiz, who'd branded themselves as the keepers of heaven and hell in their religion, had been forced out of their lands by the Kolleks; their remaining lands forming a crescent strip on the east of the continent, running from the north to the east, and finally ending below the Nor lands to the south.

Ulor had spent much time and effort sending countless attacks to conquer the eastern sections of land belonging to the Koartiz, hoping to acquire the fruitful resources, such as their amethyst mines, fertile lands and long shores with well-developed harbors, but the sorcerer race never let the east fall, as they fiercely believed these lands were the bridge between heaven and hell… And, as Ulor had learned time and again, defeating an army set on belief, especially one with such powerful war tools and abilities as the Koartiz, was near-impossible. The Koartiz had proven experts in disguise, using the lay of their lands to their advantage, and employing fighting techniques which had become the nightmare of Kollek troops all over the kingdom.

As Ulor pondered all of this, a knock was heard from the door of the war room.

"Come in," he ordered. Commander Siegen appeared at the door, saluted the king and walked in. As soon as the door closed, he moved to a space on the other side of the war table, and was about to speak, when Ulor cut him off.

"Where in the seven hells of Douren is Ifir, Siegen?" He asked. Siegen knew he could give him a straight answer, but it would only make Ulor angrier, so he chose to keep silent, lowering his eyes to the map.

"Well? Do you know where she went?" The king roared at him.

"No, my king." Siegen finally said. She never tells anyone where she goes or what she does… as is her way." The tone of complaint in his voice was easily noticed by the king.

As the king's eyes burnt in anger, the chamber's doors suddenly opened again and Ifir walked in as graceful as ever, her face the very picture calm. She saluted her king.

"Apologies, my king. I was tied up with official duties." She hovered over to the table with the map on it. "Have we begun already, then?" The king looked back at her with clear anger in his eyes. Ifir looked into the depths of the Ulor's eyes, and offered him a challenge with her own. Ulor eventually looked down and his semblance relaxed a little.

"It is quite alright… we were just starting anyways." Ulor shook his head, and Ifir smirked a knowing smile. It was a scene that Siegen was quite familiar with—Ulor forgiving Ifir as always.

"Now… Show me." The king ordered to her in a more even tone. "Show me exactly where our men were found."

The king bent towards the map with a serious look in his eyes, waiting for Ifir's to point the location out to them. She put her index finger to a spot between the Carmeuse Lagoon and Mareec, amidst a forest surrounded by hills.

"It wasn't even close to the Sleeping Mountains?" The king squinted at the spot Ifir had shown.

"But at least a six-day ride from there… hmm." Siegen said in amazement.

"I know," Ifir said. "There must be something we're missing here." She spoke, her eyes still on the map. Ulor looked at her. Seeing that she was biting her inner lip, he didn't ask the question in his mind. He knew the Songbird well enough to know she hated not having answers.

Siegen stepped in, noticing the tension in the room. "Those bastards… The Pentaghast, work for the Lord of Darkness, Douren, my king. But you are the Hand of Our God Aether. No dark force can stand against your light. We will soon hunt them down."

"Naturally, Siegen… Aether is with us in these troubling times, just like He was with my forefathers when the last king of the Nor was cursed and cast down. Soon, He will smile upon us again and our troops in the north will surely prevail. The Alerians will have their day of reckoning."

Siegen nodded, but Ifir seemed to be listening. Her mind was clearly somewhere else, her eyes still on the spot she'd shown them.

"As you say, sire… so it shall be done." Siegen said, clenching his fist and holding it to his breast. The honor in his tone and determination in his eyes were stronger than the steel he bore.

"We will win this war, Siegen." Ulor said. "And when the Sword of Aether reveals himself to us—I will break all the curses in these lands, conquer the continents as their rightful king, and the Hand of Our God. I will break the spell over Siran, and stake my claim to the treasures of the heathen Nor, so every man and woman living on my lands may taste the bounty of Aether in this world."

Suddenly, however, Ulor's smile disappeared, and a deep frown overtook his features. Even uttering the name of Siran sent shivers up his spine. The huge continent was entirely ruined, unable to hold or produce any sort of life, after the terrible spell that the Alerian sorcerers cast when they created their supposed magical stone and punished the Nor.

Dozens of envoys had been sent to Siran after the conflict, hoping to plunder its riches, or at least bring back news of its fate… but none ever returned. All who were sent to the cursed continent either died on the way, or disappeared, never to be seen again. Future envoys reported dark skies and foul, unnatural weather surrounding the shores of the continent—and the land was believed to have fallen to a terrible curse ever since.

"But before we can claim that future, we have to push past a few more obstacles…" Ulor continued, regaining his wit. "Like last week's incident."

His commander nodded. He grimaced, pondering over the mess they currently found themselves in. "Have you had any offer on a course of action?" He asked Ifir. She raised her eyebrows, as if completely out of the conversation, then nodded.

"I always have a plan." She firmly said.

"As we previously discussed at breakfast, the unit carrying the Sacred Manuscript our agents discovered near Lake Groum was hit by Night Judges in the dead of night. Fifteen Kollek soldiers' dead bodies were found there." She looked at Siegen who nodded in approval. "However, five of our Chosen's corpses were found in a spot between Carmeuse and Mareec, which is a day's ride from where the regular soldiers were found. Our surviving scout said our Chosen had had the Manuscript, and that they saw one of the five Pentaghast in the Sleeping Mountains." Ifir summarized the situation by moving the soldier figures on the map and showing the position of all the key players in relation to one another.

Siegen looked at the grey and red soldier figures which were near the Lake Groum, to the north of Kellum.

"Those damned abominations snuck into our lands, passed right under our noses, and as usual, we had no idea, nor even a warning. No matter how many troops we send—it never makes a difference when it comes to them." Ulor said through gritted teeth, barely containing his explosive anger.

"Maybe they were rebels, sire… and not Night Judges," Siegen proposed. "How are we so sure it was them? The Sons of the Forest might've staged the scene to look like a Judge encounter."

"No…" Ifir said. "My scout checked the bodies thoroughly. The cuts were too precise to have been made by normal hands. Only Judges cause death with such precision. The Judge must've passed through Lossen's Forest. It's highly likely that it then moved through this area here—the Whispers of Death." Ifir traced a finger over a nearby mountain range known for its sheer drops and perilous cliffs. "It must've been traveling in its accursed animal form—which explains why my other agents weren't able to pick up the trail."

"Damn sorcerers and their unholy animals! They can try as hard as they want, but they will never prevail. I have the Sword of Aether in my service. Odmund is destined to be the one to release the power in the Stone, and he *will* eventually rise to his calling. It's only a matter of time until we find the Manuscript telling me how to unlock the power in him."

Ulor walked back to his desk in anger and slammed his fists on its surface, knocking down several items.

"Dammit!" He roared. His anger hushed the others in the room.

"I swear to Aether that, as soon as I have the power of the Alerian's Stone, I will complete the job that the Nor's Cursed King could not. I will conquer the entire world... and set it free."

Ulor's eyes stared at the Nor lands in the map. The determination in his tone was enough to scare Siegen and Ifir for a moment. He walked back to the map and cast his eyes upon it. Siegen watched him carefully, thinking back to what he'd just said...

As the legends went, hundreds of years ago, Luden, the Cursed King of the Nor, had raised the largest army the world had ever seen, in a bid to kill the Five Head Sorcerers of the Alerian and claim their vast power. He almost succeeded too, but during the decisive battle of the invasion, when the Alerian's defeat was almost certain, the sorcerers foiled his plans by creating the Stone of Eternity—a supposed magical relic that houses all the magic power in the world in a central focal point. The creation of the stone cast a spell that obliterated Luden's forces and the Cursed King himself, sparing the Koartiz, and the Kollek of that time, from a terrible fate.

The act of doing so, however, had sent the world spiraling into chaos. The Grand Cataclysm, as it became known, was unleashed upon the creation of the Stone, changing the natural order of the world, and unleashing widespread devastation over distant lands. And yet, this was still a better outcome over the fate of the races, had they not acted in time as they did, as Luden and his unholy army of immortal soldiers would've destroyed all life in their bid for power and dominion. If the Stone hadn't been formed, there'd be no one left today to complain about it.

Or so the story went. There was no way of confirming the fact as history now—only myth and legend from a time long since passed.

The fact that Ulor seemed to be putting so much stock in it, and the Stone, concerned Siegen. Ifir, on the other hand, seemed perfectly fine with the idea of Ulor completing the Cursed King's unfinished business and seeking after the Stone.

"May you live long to see the day, my king." Ifir said, encouraged by Ulor's zeal.

Suddenly, someone knocked at the door and both men looked up from the map.

"Come in!" Ulor ordered.

As the doors opened, a fat, bald man walked in. His whole body was covered in tattoos, and he wore an outfit similar to that of the sorcerer figures on the map. Even his eyelids had tattoos of signs and letters in the old language. The old man carried a rolled map and a bottle filled with blood.

"Gobent, you're finally here," Ifir said. She walked to him and welcomed him as if he was an important guest. King Ulor nodded upon seeing him, then to Ifir. A look of acknowledgment passed between the two.

The portly man nodded to Ifir, then moved towards the table, his frail legs buckling under him. His pupils were like small dots in the middle of two cups of milk. The rest of his face, however, was darkened by tattoos, like all other senior Koartiz warriors.

It was immediately clear that the old turncoat sorcerer wasn't Siegen's favorite company. The man flinched and froze the moment he saw the old man standing at the door, and even as the Koartiz looked at him, he barely nodded back, as if hesitating in welcoming him. If Gobent gave a single care of Siegen's treatment, however, he didn't show it one bit. He instead tried his best to avoid any eye contact with the commander. In fact, he tried to avoid eye contact with the king, too. There was no doubt, however, that he was Ifir's favorite. Bringing him to the castle alive and willing to cooperate had been a huge success for her, after all—a crowning achievement as the kingdom's Spymaster.

"Now that you're here, Gobent, perhaps you can help us make some sense out of all this." Ifir pulled the man around the war map and showed him the triangle of death that the Judges had created.

"Kourtin le-peam, leum. Kourtin le-selem kelum!" Gobent said as soon as he saw the map. Nobody really understood the words, but Ifir knew enough of ancient languages to know they were a prayer.

"The N-night Judges…" he stuttered. "They walked in your lands in their corporeal form… not as animals." He looked at Ifir with his bugging eyes. "They never do that." He shook his head and looked into the King's eyes. "Unless…"

"Unless what?" Siegen said, impatiently.

"Unless they were summoned."

"But… they can only be summoned by the Five, no?" Ulor asked. The old sorcerer nodded, feebly. The three members of the court exchanged worried glances.

"So, we have one of the Pentaghast here… in our lands." Siegen said, voicing everyone's concerns.

"How can they move right under our noses without us noticing them?" Ifir asked at Gobent in anger. The fat man shrugged his shoulders.

"Where did they take the Manuscript, then?" Ifir asked.

Gobent looked at the map for a second, thought on it, then put his finger on a spot near the north border, around the Forgespire area, which consisted of small caves that looked like spires made from mudstone, and bellowed smoke as if hiding forges underneath them. The place resided in the southern boundaries of the Koartiz lands.

Gobent finally looked into Ulor's eyes.

"It must already be in the Koartiz lands, King Ulor. The Manuscript, I mean." The old man's eyes pointed to the map on the table as he spoke.

"In only two days?" Ulor asked, incredulously. "They crossed all this distance in only two days? Damn …" Ulor whispered. "Those accursed magic heathens move too fast."

"They do." Gobent replied. "Though they're not themselves the owners of their magic, sire. It belongs to the Sword of Aether, who came before. It's his magic they channel… my lord." Gobent said, matter-of-factly.

Ulor dismissed the fact impatiently.

"I know, Gobent. I know. You don't need to explain every technicality."

Gobent opened his mouth to say something but, following a sudden instinct, decided to desist. Commander Siegen, however, noticed Gobent's reaction and his confusion. That old traitor had to know more than he was telling... How could, after all, a man who'd betrayed his own race be trusted to tell the whole truth?

"This is magic, King Ulor. There is always a weak spot. We just haven't been able to discern it yet." Gobent said with a calm and certain voice.

"For centuries we've tried everything and have accomplished little, aside from the butchering of our men. Once we find the Stone of Eternity, and Odmund is able to unlock and deliver the knowledge hidden inside to our king... He'll then handle the Judges and the Pentaghast." Siegen said, turning to Gobent.

His words flattered the king, but not the old man.

"Can't you do magic to locate the Stone, old man?" Siegen asked Gobent with a stern look. Ifir sighed, knowing well how little Siegen liked the old man, and what he was trying to accomplish here. Ulor could read her annoyance as well, his eyes keeping careful stock of her throughout the meeting. Gobent shook his head, not even deigning to give a spoken answer. He then noticed the king's curious eyes on him, so he unwillingly and tiredly elaborated.

"I can't do magic, Lord Commander. None of the Alerians can, except for the Five Head Sorcerers, the, uh…. Pentaghast, as you call them." Gobent's thinly masked annoyance was clear in his voice.

Siegen wasn't convinced though. He was about to add something else to that, but the king interrupted him.

"Yes, that's all fascinating Gobent, but I only care about results. We need to make a plan to get the lost Manuscript back—it could hold the key to awakening Odmund's powers. We can't let it disappear again."

"You can't get it back, sire." Gobent answered.

"Actually… if we take the northern path around the Forgespire area…" Siegen began.

"… then every man you send will die one by one. It's a death sentence, commander. The Forgespire area is impassable. It is one of the best protected areas in all of the Koartiz lands. You should know that. The landscape is full of underground cities and hidden ambush points—there is no place to hide or traverse safely." Gobent enjoyed humiliating the commander with his ignorance this time.

"Well, do you have a better suggestion, Gobent?" Siegen asked, clearly angry now. "We're painfully low on options here!"

King Ulor stared at the old sorcerer. Ifir smiled, enjoying the way her man humiliated the commander in front of the king. Everyone in the room was aware that the old man knew he had to be useful if he really wanted to stay near the king or Ifir and further his own plans... so, in interest of proving his worth to them, he walked closer to the map and tapped a finger over Forgespire City.

"I am not from Forgespire City, mind you," Gobent said. "But I know there are secret passages that run under the spires that dot the land. These could provide a route to the stolen Manuscript page. It's said that around this area lies a temple that once belonged to one of the Five, in which he protects the sacred remains of the Sword of Aether. Nobody has ever seen the actual temple, however, and most treat it as a myth. However, there's an entrance to this passage on our side... though I do not know where it is, exactly. The Manuscript might've passed through there to get to the temple, if it really exists."

King Ulor raised his eyes from the map and nodded at Siegen. The commander nodded back.

"That's more like it, Gobent. This information will be more than helpful. Is there anything else we should know about Forgespire City, aside from the spires or these secret passages? Any other hidden dangers?"

"Aside from the usual Koartiz patrols... no, sire. None that I can think of. The real danger would lie in the temple itself, if you can find it."

"Excellent. Thank you for the information, Gobent. You can now return to your work." Ifir said.

Gobent bowed his head and walked out of the room without looking up. His old legs buckled every step of the way in his haste.

As the door shut behind him, Ifir looked at the commander.

"I know you don't trust him Siegen, but I need you two to work together. That attitude you have against him is grating on my patience." She warned him.

"Apologies, Songbird. I just... can't abide someone who betrays his own people." The man replied.

"I share the sentiment... but the enemy of my enemy is my friend, Siegen. That's the way it's always been." Ulor said.

Siegen nodded. "But... he's one of them, Your Majesty. A Koartiz sorcerer, in our castle, close to our secrets!"

"No. He *was* one of them... but not anymore. He's a wounded member of their herd. Trust me on this, Siegen... that man has more reason to hate the Pentaghast, and everything they stand for, than we do. He'd rather die before giving them any sort of advantage." The king smirked as he spoke, instilling confidence in the commander. Ifir allowed herself a smile, seeing how quickly Ulor jumped to her defense.

"As you say, my king. I trust your judgment." Siegen replied, though his eyes still betrayed his doubt. He wished he could have known what the king knew.

Ulor looked into Siegen's eyes one more time. "Right, then. Onto the matter at hand, dear Songbird. Do you have any suitable candidates in mind for this crucial mission? Mind you, we'll need someone strong... but also willing to die. This may be one of our riskiest attempts yet."

Ifir looked at the map one more time, then smirked.

"Yes..." She said. "I believe I do."

CHAPTER 9

THE JOURNEY BEGINS

The road from Halstead to Rockpour takes about two weeks... Locke mused, looking at his map. *Reaching the Carp River and passing the Imperial Valley will take another day. If we follow the Carp River...*

The road plan was still occupying Locke's mind when his thoughts were interrupted with a slapping sound.

"Wake up rookie!" Gerard shook Ourg, who had dozed off under a tree near Merki's house. The old wolf walked back to Locke then, standing a few meters away from the garden with his eyes on Merki's cabin, in front of which Jarrie stood guard.

"This is the last chance, Locke. Are you sure we're going through with this?" Gerard asked him. Locke understood the old war dog's concerns very well, but he nodded all the same.

"The bigger the risk, the greater the reward, Gerard." He said, then turned his eyes back to the map.

Gerard edged closer and put a hand on the map. "Listen to me, captain... I know how rebels operate. I've crossed their paths before, and they're cunning and deceitful. But above all, they're loyal. They never leave a man behind."

Gerard was so close, Locke could feel his breath on his neck. He moved back a little.

"They may come for him any moment. Are you sure we want to risk that? The girl and the old coot—they'll just be a burden. They might get us killed." He turned his gaze to the men and the girl in front of the old cabin.

"She invoked the Law of the King's Bounty, Gerard. We're bound to honor it or it's our heads on a pike—if word gets back to our superiors. Besides, they seem capable. The girl took down the Chosen all on her own… and the old man seems to have a way with words, as well as knowledge on the Chosen. They'll be helpful to us. We just have to take him to the garrison in Waterval, that's it. Can you keep a tied man alive for few days Gerard?" Locke's voice had an impatient edge to it now. Seeing no hope in talking with him, Gerard nodded briskly, then walked away.

Locke could hear him murmuring to himself and shaking his head in anger.

Soon, Elder Erikson and his son came along with two bags of provisions for the road. They gave the bags to Gerard.

"Here's food for the road, lieutenant." Elder Erikson said. "Bread and potato patties, sire, as well as all the leftover cured meat we had, some fruit, and cheese."

Gerard nodded in thanks. "You're a good man, Erikson. Our superiors will hear of how well the people of Halstead and its elder treat the king's soldiers."

"Thank you, sire. Thank you so much." Elder Erikson said, bowing.

Gerard saluted them and passed the bags to Leord. "Put them on the horses." The young soldier nodded and did as told, while Axel appeared with two brown horses and a small horse wagon for the rebel.

"You must be kidding me…" Gerard said, seeing the rickety wagon, which looked like it'd fall apart at any moment.

Seeing him arrive, Locke stood up and tidied his map.

"Alright, that's everything. Let's go, everyone—sun's already up and we've got a long road ahead of us."

The soldiers got on their horses after carrying a sleeping Kade to the wagon, who elicited fearful and awe-struck looks from the villagers gathered to see the soldier's off. Merki and Axel got in the front wagon seat, (and Rage, on Merki's lap), with Axel holding the reigns of the horses, and soon they were all off, trotting the small convoy away from the rural village to the farewells of the village folk.

Merki looked back at Halstead one last time... at her cabin, and everything she'd known so far in her life. She took a long, shaking breath. Axel, gently coaxing the horses along beside her, smiled at her.

"It's going to be ok, young Merki." He said.

Merki nodded. "I know... I'm ready."

A few moments later the town disappeared from view, devoured by trees on all sides. Merki settled in her seat, looked at the sleeping man in the wagon behind them, next to most of their bags and belongings for the trip, and Rage, who looked out the side of the wagon with his tongue out and his tail wagging. She patted her eager partner on his head, then carefully took out a small wooden horse from her travel bag. She coddled it in her hands as she looked at it, and her breath caught in her throat.

It's finally happening, dad. I'm finally fulfilling my promise, she said to herself, then stowed the horse back in her luggage, just as carefully.

***

About three hours into the roads, and through the interminable sea of bronze, red and yellow trees, the soldiers were getting restless. This was the perfect kind of country for rebels to set up an ambush—plenty of cover and places to hide.

Before setting out with Locke and Gerard, each recruit had brought the best armor and weapons they could from their respective towns, as they would only receive proper military equipment—and training, once they reached their assigned garrison, which, due to the change of plans, was now Waterval. Jarrie had brought a spear with him that had belonged to his father, as well as a small buckler shield, and a basic gambeson that looked like it'd been patched and repaired several times. Ourg had brought a hammer with him—the kind one would see in a forge, and a helmet made of tanned leather, reinforced with strips of iron. It was clear the boy had worked as a blacksmith or born to a family that owned one. Finally, Leord, clearly the more affluent of the three, wore a full chainmail vest over his shirt with a gleaming iron helmet. He wore a short sword at his hip, and a crossbow at his back, with a pouch full of short, dart-like arrows. It wasn't military-standard equipment by any means, but far ahead than what the other two had. They'd all been lucky enough to secure a horse for their journey each, however, even though Jarrie's was little more than a pony.

The three of them had been gripping their weapons tight for the majority of the ride, keeping watch over the surrounding woods. They rode to the sides of the wagon, with Leord riding at the back with Gerard, while Locke rode at the front, leading the convoy.

Locke looked back for a moment to see how everyone was doing. He noted their tense expressions, especially in the recruits' eyes. Merki, he noticed, while also on guard and holding her bow at the ready in case of an attack, seemed much more relaxed and composed.

Gerard saw him look back and nodded, looking then at the others as well, and catching Leord's eyes. The young recruit nodded, crossbow in hand as he rode.

"You think he'll wake up any time soon, lieutenant?" He asked Gerard.

The older man turned his head towards the road. "We'll see," he said.

Axel looked back at the young soldier and smiled. "Not to worry, young man. The Chosen sleeps deeply. I gave him a mixture that would put even the strongest man under for a whole day."

Everyone seemed to breathe a sigh of relief at the news.

"Who would've thought we'd end up escorting a Chosen, and to the capital itself, no less?" Jarrie said. Leord, to his surprised, nodded. Ourg smiled at him quite stupidly, but innocently. "I've never been to the capital before. Bet it's pretty." He said.

"Oh, quite pretty." Axel added. "Full of gardens and spires and tall buildings everywhere. You'll see for yourself soon enough."

"It's also full of whores and shit, especially in the lower districts." Leord added with a cocky smirk.

Jarrie turned back to look at him. "You've been to Kellum then?"

The young man smirked even prouder. "Once. When I was a child. My father had business with one of the barons there, in the so-called "Nobles' Row.""

"Wow…" Ourg said. "Did you sleep with any of them whores?"

"Eyes forward, men." Locke gently prodded them, bringing them back to attention. "There'll be enough time for talk once we set camp for the night."

"Yessir." They said.

Their banter reminded Gerard of his time serving in the capital of the Kollek. He resented the memory.

Everyone there knew how the chain of power worked in these lands. They knew that Night Judges were the apex force in the continent—the thing that not even Chosen could kill. Chosen, on their part, were the next rung in the ladder—easily able to kill regular Kollek troops unless they were smart enough to avoid them… or run from a hopeless battle at the right time, like Gerard had done.

A deserter and a coward, his superiors had called him. For running away from rebel Chosen. For trying to save his men.

He'd almost been court-martialed, had it not been for the fact that he alone survived that impossible situation—his men torn to pieces before his eyes, by both Chosen and rebels. He survived, yes… but not without a reminder. He was taken prisoner for information and tortured for days on end. In the ends, he managed to escape, and make his way back to Kellum.

And yet, instead of a hero's welcome, he'd been stripped of his rank as part of the elite guard and sent to do time like a common criminal on this thankless job detail.

Damn you, Siegen, he thought to himself.

Retirement, proper retirement, seemed like a dream for him now. The old wolf still remembered the days he served directly under Siegen on the battlefield.

"Running away from battle, and not only once." Siegen had said, looking deep into Gerard's soul through his eyes. "You know the penalty of such a behavior Gerard."

"The battle was lost, sir. I did what I had to do to save my men."

"Hah…" Siegen laughed aloud. "Saving your men? Your men serve the army to die, not to run Gerard. If you teach them there is such an option, then we won't find soldiers willing to fight the fights we need them to." He stood up and walked to the window.

"There is no such thing as a war without casualties, soldier. Sometimes men die—are *sent* to die, as part of a bigger strategy. Your retreat order cost us greatly, soldier. We had another group ready after yours, but lost it, and the valley, due to your cowardice."

Gerard remembered the rage he'd felt that day. How he'd wanted to throttle the commander out the nice window behind him, send him tumbling down his nice office in the nice castle grounds.

"However, I am aware of your caliber as a soldier, and I realize it'd be a shame to just strip you of rank and send you to work in one of the mines." Siegen's words were ironic, and he had sarcastic smile on his face.

"Thank you, sir." Gerard's trembling voice said.

"This morning, a young, unexperienced man became a captain of the Kollek army—by his rich father's graces, you see. I am in a good mood today, so I offer you an option: you can be assigned to this man's squad; teach him and protect him… or you can go serve in the mines until your back gives in of old age, and they carry your dead body out in a wheel cart."

"My teaching is even better than my soldiery, sir." Gerard said.

That day was the last day that Gerard and Locke saw Kellum. Since then, they'd been travelling around the lands as part of the recruiting forces, enlisting men for the advanced forces. It was an important job—but a thankless, and relatively safe one. Gerard hated every second of it. He knew he'd never regain his status and honor here, serving as a glorified babysitter on the edges of the kingdom… but what else was he supposed to do? Until opportunity showed itself, he was stuck.

He let out a long sigh atop his horse and continued his due vigilance. Maybe Locke was right… and taking this Chosen to the capital would revoke his punishment? Give him another chance? If only life were that simple, however…

Meanwhile, Axel and Merki rode on in silence, but they secretly kept careful stock of the group's mood. Merki looked at the road while Rage nudged her hand with his black, wet nose, asking for a petting… in-between staring and growling at Axel, of course. The old man tried to ignore him, but occasionally spared him a quick scowl, before looking back at the road. On one of these times he caught Merki's eyes, staring out at the road ahead of them, and noticed how strong and firm they were—how she looked more the warrior than any of the other young men around them.

As Axel pondered this, Rage suddenly began to growl again… but not at him. The strong, fuzzy mutt threw himself over Merki's shoulder and stared towards the back of the cart.

"Hey… hey! The Chosen is moving!" Leord shouted.

Kade opened his eyes and saw the light filtering and flickering above through the canopy of trees. He realized he was moving and, startled by the feeling, squirmed in the hold of the wagon. Rage barked at him, right in his ear, startling him further.

"Hey, down boy! Down!" Merki said, grabbing Rage and putting him on her lap.

Gerard had already drawn his sword, his eyes fixed on Kade for any wrong movements.

"Calm, Chosen. Calm." Axel said above the din. "We're on the road. You're in a wagon. You were asleep. Everything is alright."

"Gerard, report! What is happening back there?" Locke asked.

"The Chosen's awoken."

"What is he doing?"

Gerard looked down at Kade, who, upon Axel's words, had calmed down a bit. "Nothing… yet." He said.

"Did you sleep well?" Axel asked Kade.

"I… I guess."

The Journey Begins | 117

"Any nightmares? You were tossing and turning around all night yesterday. The herbs should've prevented that."

Kade hesitated for a moment. "Some, yes."

"Any of those remind you of who you are, Chosen?" Gerard asked him. "Or where you came from?"

Kade looked into Gerard's eyes long and hard. He didn't like the man very much and could tell he was trouble. "None," he said. "I keep dreaming of a woman in the woods. Red hair. The sun behind her. Do you know anyone like that in your village?" He asked Merki.

The young woman shook her head.

"What about your brother, Kade? Do you remember anything?" Axel asked.

"Only that I need to find him. That it's… vital." He said.

"Aether's mercy…" Gerard said, then scoffed. "Well, you best behave, boy. Keep your voice down and help us keep a lookout while you're back there."

"A… lookout?"

"For rebels."

"… Rebels?"

"Fuck… Men and women in hoods and rags, riding horses, probably holding bows or knives. Anyone who isn't us, you simpleton."

Kade took a deep breath. "Got it."

"Here," said Merki, passing him an apple and some cheese. "Eat up. We've got a long road ahead of us."

Kade took the food gratefully and started to nibble on it, casting the occasional look towards the young soldiers, who seemed as scared with him as they were fascinated, while trying to avoid Gerard, who kept staring at him like a dog sizing up his next meal.

"Try to keep quiet while we're on the road." Merki told Kade over her shoulder in hushed tones, as he ate. "And don't move too much back there."

"Ok." He murmured back.

The rest of the day's ride went on in relative silence, as no one uttered a word for hours. In the mountain roads, only the clip clops and deep breaths of the horses were heard. Merki, despite her cool demeanor, kept a firm eye on Kade throughout the entire trip, her right hand never leaving the hilt of her dagger, just in case. Rage stayed with her all the time, enjoying the fresh autumn breezes and passing scenery with his tongue out. Locke, on the other hand was lost in his thoughts, the silence surrounding him letting his fear gnaw at him more and more. The recruits tried to keep watch around them, but often snuck looks at Kade, who mostly looked up at the trees, and occasionally went back to sleep—or at least pretended that he was. He grimaced often, looking down at the shoddily bandaged shoulder where Merki's arrow had struck.

They crossed deep ravines and valleys, clambered over lush, amber-colored mountains, and next to babbling creeks. At one point, they crossed a ford of cold water and stopped for a moment at the riverbank to give the horses a brief rest and eat lunch. Kade was allowed to get up and stretch his legs, although his hands and feet were still bound. (Merki had changed the length and style of the knots so that he could walk a little, but not run.)

They then entered another seemingly eternal forest and trudged along at a steady canter. A couple of hours after that, as the light of the setting sun started to blaze red through the thick trunks of the trees, Locke gave an order.

"Let's stop here. We're just outside the boundaries of Dearun Forest. It's best if we make camp here, before night falls upon us." The soldiers heartily agreed. They made their way out of the main road and found a perfect spot to make camp inside the tree line, then dismounted.

Locke immediately gave orders to set up camp. One of the recruits hurried to set down the supplies, another to get water, and so on. Locke, along with Axel and Merki, helped Kade out of the wagon, and tied a long, thick length of rope to his waist, which he then fastened to a large oak tree.

Once again, Axel reassured the young Chosen with the words: "It's for your own good." Kade begrudgingly accepted it. He knew his options in this situation were few, and at least, until an opportunity arose, it'd be best to play by these people's rules. Gerard watched him from the shadows of the trees with the eyes of an eagle, the message in his eyes clear.

Just one move out of line. Just try it.

Kade sighed and sat down among the roots of the trees, stretching his sore, stiff legs.

After setting camp, the group sat down to eat a simple dinner: bread, fruit and some of the cured meat from Halstead. Gerard stood away from the group, keeping watch for any possible rebel movement around camp. They didn't dare risk a fire, for fear of it giving away their position to any possible pursuers.

Despite tensions still being high due to the danger of an attack at any moment, the recruits relaxed somewhat, and spoke of their homes and villages, enjoying the opportunity to rest. Merki brought Kade some food, but quickly went back to the main group. Locke kept his eyes on Kade most of the time.

Axel watched the mood of the individual members closely. He was the calmest among all of them, despite being the oldest and frailest. As he ate a piece of meat, his other voice suddenly rose inside him.

"*We should take this opportunity tonight, old man,*" it said.

Opportunity to do what? Axel asked it.

"*Kill them all in their sleep. They suspect the girl, but not you. Kill them, then take the Chosen for yourself. You can do it. It'd be easy.*"

You really are mad, aren't you? Axel said.

"*Don't you mean, we?*"

No, just you. Shut up and let me eat in peace. We need these people, fool. Despite our original plans, we've fallen in with them, and must now see things through along with them. Besides... I would never lay a finger on Merki. And neither will you. Are we clear?

Silence in his mind. *Good.* Axel nodded to himself and finished his meal.

"Captain," he then spoke. Locked looked his way, looking as if he'd been startled from a daydream.

"Yes?"

"I'll see to the Chosen now. Give him another herb infusion for tomorrow. Is that alright?"

Locke nodded. "Please do." Axel prepared the infusion of special herbs with some water, which, due to the lack of a fire, he was unable to boil. He knew it should still be potent enough to knock Kade out for the night, at least... but he'd be awake most of the day tomorrow, however. He didn't tell Locke that, though.

He walked over to Kade, who had just finished eating his share of the rations.

"Chosen Kade," Axel spoke in hushed tones. The young man flinched at the sound all the same, startled for a moment.

"You... Axel, is it?" He replied in a lowered voice as well.

The old man nodded. "Here's your drink for tonight."

Kade took it and smelled it. He looked back up to Axel. "It'll put me to sleep again, won't it?"

The old man nodded. "For the night, at least."

"It's for my own good?"

Axel hesitated for a moment, then nodded again.

Kade sighed, looking down at the basic wooden cup filled with green, grass-smelling liquid... then gulped it down.

"Good," Axel said. "You'll sleep better tonight, hopefully."

Kade nodded, then stared at the old man. "Hey... Axel."

"Hmm?"

"Are you sure these people will help me? That I'll be able to find my brother?"

"Do you remember anything?" Axel asked, his tone suddenly more serious and alert. "Where you're from? What you were doing in the woods?"

Kade hesitated for a moment... then nodded.

"I do. I..."

He noticed that Locke had walked closer. Gerard was also looking his way, despite being quite far away. Everyone in the camp had stopped talking, their ears now tuned to his voice—even Merki and the recruits.

"Well, go on." Locke said, hands on his hips. "Talk."

Kade took a deep breath. "I remember running away from my people. Running through the forest, as fast as I could, hoping to escape the Curse. The forest was angry. It cut me, hurt me, pulled me back… as if it didn't want me to leave. Then there was this massive chasm—a giant cleft in the earth."

Axel nodded, encouraging him to continue.

"I thought that was it, that I wouldn't be able to continue. I remember feeling so much fear… but then I remembered my brother. I remembered how crucial it was that I found him and brought him back… and I jumped."

"Brought him back where?" Locke asked.

"Back home, to my people."

"And who are your people, Kade?" Locke asked. "Where is your home?"

"I… It's not clear yet. I only see shapes, blurs… impressions. I know it's somewhere in the forest. Somewhere back there, beyond the chasm."

"Continue," Axel urged him. "What happened next?"

"I barely made it across the chasm. It must've been a hundred feet wide or more."

The Edge, Axel thought. *Then that means… it really is him.*

"I landed on the other side… battered and very hurt… but alive. Then, the Curse caught up to me. I remember heat… all over my body. Then the forest disappeared all around me, the trees sinking into the ground, a rush of wind like a storm. I thought I was dead, or dying. But a moment later, it was all gone. The trees were back, and the wind was gone… but things were different."

"How so?" Locke asked him.

"I could… well… It sounds like madness."

"Go on. Tell us all the same." Locke insisted.

"I found that… I could hear everything. Everything around me, for nearly a mile, even. The rustle of leaves off in the distance, like tremors. The babbling of a faraway creek like a downpour. The movements of animals in the trees, like thunder. Everything was so… loud. And clear."

Locke looked at Axel. "He's an Acris, then… isn't he?"

Axel nodded. "It seems so."

"An... Acris?"

"Your Chosen gift. It revolves around your perception of sound. That means you're an Acris."

"An... Acris? But... that was the Curse, playing tricks on me."

Locke shook his head. "No. Those were your powers... don't you remember? You should've experienced them before at your age. Most Chosen first feel their abilities as children."

Kade blinked and frowned. "I... I don't understand."

Locke threw Axel a questioning look, looking more than a bit confused himself.

"Must be the memory loss... Or something in the forest. I can't say for certain." Then he turned towards Kade. "However, this is progress. You remembered more."

"Not enough," said Gerard, who'd moved closer to the group almost without notice.

Locke looked up at him, crouching near Kade as he was. "It'll come back to him. Give him time."

Gerard scoffed. "Of course it will. It'll all come rushing back right after he's standing over our dead bodies, with his rebel friends prying our valuables out of our cold, stiff hands." He gestured for Locke to follow him, and the captain did so. The two men walked away from earshot, and Gerard let out a long, deep sigh.

"Locke... can't you see this Chosen is just playing you for a fool? All of you? He doesn't have 'memory loss'—he got separated from his scouting party, or maybe ran into a patrol somewhere up north and ran away from a losing fight. He's a *rebel*, Locke. And he's playing us for time. When we least expect it, his friends will catch up to us and slit all of our throats—mark my words. Plus... there are old and fell things in these ancient mountains, Locke... Things worse than rebels. I, for one, don't want to stumble into any of them while carrying a fucking *rogue Chosen* on the back of a rickety wagon. Do you?"

Locke took a deep breath. "I understand, Gerard... but we need to bring him alive to get the benefits of the Bounty. I know we're taking a risk—many risks, but... What other choice do we have? We *need* this."

The Journey Begins | 123

The old man shook his head. "I was placed in this detail to advice you... captain. If you will not heed my words, then do as you wish. But count on it... there *will* be consequences."

Locke flinched at that, and took a step back.

"Are you... threatening me, lieutenant?" He asked, his hand easily moving to the hilt of his sword.

Gerard saw it, even in the darkness of the night. The moonlight filtering through the trees glowed brightly over Locke's plated gauntlets, and his sword's pommel. He looked back up at Locke's eyes, and said: "Of course not, captain. Just offering some prudent advice. I'll keep first watch tonight. You can relieve me for second watch later. You should get some rest." He nodded back to camp.

Locke stared at him for a moment, then turned around without saying a word. He went back to camp looking like nothing had happened, finished his meal and gave orders for the recruits to rest while Gerard keeping an eye on Kade. He seemed the very picture of the responsible, composed leader—a seasoned captain.

And yet, when he laid down in his bedroll, he couldn't fall asleep. He tossed and turned, hoping to get some rest for his watch later in the night... But he couldn't. Gerard's words were like a hot coal in his skull, sizzling and turning, weighing on him, denying him any kind of restful sleep. He turned one last time and finally allowed his mind to hover over the question at the center of his unrest.

What if he's right?

CHAPTER 10

LIGHT AND SHADOW

Queen Etheria caressed her belly, eyeing herself on an elaborate mirror in her dressing room and enjoying the image that greeted her. Her maids were busy opening well-engraved chests full of dresses in every color imaginable. From the mirror, Etheria saw a blue silk dress with chiffon details on it.

"That one. The blue one." She told the closest maid, looking at her through the mirror. "Make it ready for tomorrow."

The maid nodded and carefully took the dress out from the chest.

"Have you summoned Fermand?" She asked to her head maid, Kareen, who was the oldest and largest of the maids. She usually just stood by the side, silently directing the other girls. When Etheria spoke, all the maids paused their work, along with the old maid, who bent her head before answering.

"Yes, my queen. The messenger was sent already."

"Good."

With the queen's approval everyone went back to their duties.

Etheria decided to sit in a large, ornate couch on the side of the room and work on a piece she was knitting for her new soon-to-be-born baby, while she waited for the coin master. As she worked with the large needless, a yell of frustration was heard from the next room over.

Flora. The queen sighed.

"I hate old languages..." She heard her say. All the ink and papers on the princess' desk toppled over as she swiped them off in a rage. Her governess pushed her chair back in fear.

"My princess!" She said.

Etheria looked at Kareen, who ran to check on Flora. Then, considering that it might take more than her maid to calm her daughter, Etheria slowly got up and followed the maid.

"I hate it!" Flora insisted.

Her governess was about to say something else when she saw Etheria enter the chamber. She bent her head towards her. Flora's eyes widened upon seeing her mother.

"Flora?" Her mother's calm voice echoed among the walls of the study room.

"Yes, mother?" Flora looked at her as if nothing had happened and smiled.

Etheria raised her hand, signaling for the maids and governess to leave the room. They all did as told, bowing at her on their way out. Etheria then walked to a sofa placed behind Flora's chair. Her eyes caught the stain of the ink on the silk carpet and she rolled her eyes, took a deep breath, and sat down.

"Come here, my girl." She said, and the princess sat on her lap.

Etheria caressed her cheek, parting the hair on her shoulder, then raised her head up by gently cupping her chin.

"Listen to me, my Flora. You'll be a woman in few years... and I think it's time we... talk about a very important thing you need to know. An important secret of life. Would you like that?" Her eyes looked deep into the princess'. The little girl nodded excitedly, clearly happy that she wasn't being punished, but rewarded instead.

"This is a secret which can only be passed from mother to daughter," Etheria said in a whimsical tone. "Just as my mother passed it to me, long ago. Do you want to know what it is?" Flora nodded and got closer to her mother, so that she could hear better.

"Women… are the brain of existence, my child." The queen said with her eyes on the princess. She saw that Flora didn't quite understand what she meant, so she elaborated.

"Imagine that the whole world is a body, Flora, like yours, or mine." Etheria said, and the child nodded. "Your father is the king, right?" She nodded again. "He can do whatever he wants; have anything he wants, correct?" More nodding. "Well… that's because he is like the muscles of our body. He has all the power. But if the king is the muscle, then what is the queen?" Etheria asked.

"Hmmm…" Princess Flora hummed, thinking for a moment. Then her eyes grew bigger, and Etheria nodded.

"Flora, men rule the world with their bravery and power; women, on the other hand, rule the world with their wisdom. Always remember that the muscle needs a *brain* to control it."

A huge smile appeared on Flora's round, immaculate face. Etheria smiled back with a grin of her own.

"Now tell me, my little queen, who are you?" She asked her daughter.

"I am the brain." The princess wisely answered.

"That's right. Then, as the brain, you should learn to love your studies, my princess. You should learn as much as you can, know everything you can. Because your wisdom will shape the world in the future. To control the… *muscles*, you will need every last bit of information, of wisdom and knowledge, that you can acquire. Because muscles without a wise brain only damage the world. Power without control only causes harm, like a mad dog, tearing other everything in its path apart."

Flora's eyes grew bigger again, her back straightened.

"Like the Cursed King?" She asked in fear. Queen Etheria nodded, with a sad expression in her face.

"Like the Cursed King, my child." She said, approving. "See? Knowing even a little about history has already made you wise enough to see the danger."

"Yes, mother." Flora said and hugged her mother tight. "I'll be the best brain I can be." She said. Her little arms tightened her mother as much as they could. Feeling the pure love of her child put a smile on Etheria's face.

"That's my girl," Etheria said, as she caressed the princess' hair and put a kiss on her head "Now, I will call Teresa back, and you will learn as much as you can—even if it's not very fun. Right?" She stood up with confident and a kind smile. Flora nodded and stood up.

"Teresa, you can come back in." Etheria called out, and the governess walked back in. Etheria walked out of the room and blew one last kiss at her daughter, who smiled and blew one too in return.

Back in her chamber, Etheria stood near the window and gazed over the most beautiful rose garden in the whole city—her private gardens at the back of the castle. Then, her eyes hovered over the dark doors at the end of the garden, standing out in stark contrast to everything else. That… was the entrance to the Direhalls. One of the darkest and vilest of places in all of Kellum—and perhaps the entire kingdom. The things Ulor and Ifir kept down there… Etheria shuddered just thinking about it.

The irony was not lost on her. One that seemed to permeate every aspect of life in this castle, she knew.

***

Down at the gardens, Efilia stood alone amidst the flower bushes.

To any onlooker from afar, she was just another Chosen on a break, enjoying some alone time. However, a closer inspection revealed a different story. The Chosen lieutenant was paler than usual, her eyes red and her demeanor sickly. She stared right at the black door in the gardens—the gate to the Direhalls.

"I'm not weak." Efilia said to herself. "I'll prove to that witch that I'm not weak." She hadn't been able to control herself though. After Ifir shut her down in the foyer, she'd retired to the gardens, and let her feelings stream lose. How could she say she was weak? What did she have against her? Ever since Efilia could remember, Ifir had always driven her harder than the other Chosen, expected more, punished her more harshly. And now, she wouldn't let her compete in the Chosen Tourney? Was she trying to keep her as a lowly lieutenant for the rest of her life? Just who did she think she was?

She'd even threatened to send her to feed the abominations in the Direhalls, no less—a tasks only given to those meant for execution, or the harshest of punishments. Aside from the worst criminals of Kellum—the lowest of the low, only highly trained people cared for the Nor monsters under the castle (without being torn limb from limb). Even then, they couldn't be Chosen, as the Devourers, as they were called, posed a higher danger to people like Efilia than anything else… save one of the Night Judges, perhaps. To threaten her with that was the same as saying she had the value of a condemned murderer or rapist—the worst of Kellum society. Those were the types usually sent to feed the creatures… and often in a public manner, so all the nobles and dignitaries of the city could come and watch them be ripped apart.

Is that what Efilia meant to her? How much she was worth in her eyes? Surely, there had to be another reason—something other than her effort, duties and performance. Everyone else commended her for her hard work. Efilia decided then and there that she would just have to prove herself to Ifir. She would show her that she was stronger than she thought—and in the process, get the truth out of her.

She walked over to the black door and stood before it. Its darkness seemed to draw her in, to invite her, seduce her to enter. Suddenly, she felt nauseous.

She was about to knock on it—to enter the dark void inside and show Ifir just how strong she could be, when she heard Odmund's voice behind her.

"Lia!" He said. She looked back to meet him. "What are you doing here?"

Efilia considered telling him about her encounter with Ifir… but he'd hear of it around the castle eventually. Every Chosen would. Rumors and gossip spread fast in Kellum, she knew. She also didn't want to have to explain herself right now. Seeing as Odmund brought her a measure of comfort and joy—things that she needed now more than anything.

"Just admiring the door, love. It really stands out in such a lush garden, doesn't it?"

Odmund looked at it for a moment. He didn't pay these sorts of things much mind, but now that she mentioned it, he noticed how strange it was to have the entrance to such a dangerous place in such a public and relaxing part of the castle.

"I guess it does, yeah. Now tell me, what's wrong? You look like you've seen a ghost." He led her to a nearby marble bench in the gardens, and they both sat down.

"I… didn't make it to the list." Efilia said.

Odmund blinked. Then he frowned, deeply. "What do you mean you didn't make it to the list? You were the most qualified among all the Veruters this year!"

Efilia shrugged. "Apparently I ruffled some feathers and got disqualified."

Odmund scoffed, his cheeks flushed. "Whose feathers? Tell me, and I'll go speak to them right now. I am the Champion of the Kollek—they will have to listen to me or face the king's wrath."

"Not this one." Efilia said, staring at the grass.

"Wait… you don't mean…"

"Yeah. I ruffled the feathers of a Songbird."

"Ifir… Well, shit."

"Yeah."

"I don't understand… Why's she always been so tough on you? Maybe I can talk to her… or Ulor. I don't know, there must be something I can do."

Efilia was already shaking her head before he finished. "And get blacklisted by Ifir? No, my love. Let it go. I'll figure out Ifir's problem with me on my own. You can't fight everyone's battles."

"But… I can go talk to…"

"Ulor? You know how he'll react if you bring Ifir up. Just let it be, Od. I don't want you to get in trouble on my account. Plus… you may get me into more trouble by trying to help."

"More trouble? What do you mean?"

"I… sort of confronted Ifir. In the foyer. In front of everyone."

Odmund took a deep breath, then slowly let it go, looking at the gardens. "Oh…"

"Yeah."

They sat in silence for a moment, contemplating the beautiful scenery around them—the butterflies, flying over the flowers, and the chirping birds, hoping from one bush to the other.

"I'll still find a way to help you, Lia." Odmund said. "I have to. Otherwise, what's the point of this title and position? I won't go to Ulor or Ifir, but… I'll keep my eyes open for any opportunities."

Efilia sighed, then grabbed Odmund's hand, taking comfort in its warmth. "Thank you." She rested her head upon his shoulder. "Now tell me—what about you? I can tell something's been troubling you recently, but you keep acting like it's not there… Is everything alright?"

"It is… yes." Odmund said, his eyes facing forward. "Well… A lot has happened in the last few days. There's been a couple of new, umm… developments. I've been processing them, that's all." Efilia could hear the hesitation in his voice. It wasn't like him to keep things from her.

"What do you mean?" She asked.

"For starters, something new is happening in the Silence." He informed her.

"The… Silence? You mean, Outer Silence?" Efilia straightened up, her eyes filled with concern. "Od… Why did you go there? What were you thinking?" Suddenly, she forgot all about her own troubles and woes.

Odmund smiled and shook his head slightly, as if he weren't sure he should have said anything.

"Tell me, Odmund. You can't just say something like that and not follow through."

"Ulor sent me to patrol the districts—in full regalia. Just a show, as usual. We went into the Silence and… I'm pretty sure we stumbled into a human smuggling operation."

Efilia's eyes filled with horror. "Here… in Kellum?"

Odmund nodded. "They killed a woman and took her son. We chased after the men but couldn't pick up their trail. The Silence is… well, it's a different world from ours."

"What will you do?"

Odmund shrugged. "What can I do? I'm the Champion of the Kollek, protector of our king and queen, but I can't order our forces around. That's Siegen's job… or Ifir's. I only have that authority under special circumstances. I'll request an audience with our commander later and see if he can spare some men to investigate the Silence—see if they can root out the source of the smuggling operations down there… if they're even willing to head that way at all."

"You think he'll listen?"

Odmund shrugged. "I hope so. If not…"

"Odmund… What? You're not thinking of…"

"No, no… forget it. It's nothing."

Efilia took a deep breath. "Well… just don't do anything reckless, alright?"

Odmund smiled at her. "When do I do anything reckless?"

She smiled back and nudged him with her elbow. "*Always,*" she said. "Now, what was the other thing you were going to say."

"Hmm?"

"You said a 'couple' of things. That's two, last I checked."

Odmund sighed.

"I took the boy as my servant the other night." He finally said.

"Which… oh, Od… oh no, you didn't." She pulled her hand back from his. Her voice was somewhere between anger and shock.

Odmund was serious now. "I had to, Lia. I owed him, and his family. Besides, you should've seen the conditions the poor kid was working in… they were inhuman. He's just a 14-year-old, barely more than a kid."

"There's lots of 14-year-old kids in the slums, Od. Why not take any other one? I mean, I feel for the poor kid, but… Aether's grace, Odmund."

The champion sighed.

"I have to face up to what I did, Lia. I can't keep running from it. Pretending it didn't happen. If I don't…" He shook his head. "I'll never escape the ghosts that haunt me." Efilia noticed how Odmund had started to hyperventilate, the line of his set jaw, and the veins in his forehead. She put her hand back on top of his.

"It wasn't your fault, my love. It was an accident. We were learning the limits of our potential back then... and besides, they forced you to do so. You didn't even want to." Efilia spoke with tenderness and compassion, but Odmund's features remained set in stone. He grimaced, looking away from her.

"That's not true, Lia. I wasn't forced that day to do anything. I *wanted* to do it, to feel my power run loose.... I wanted to show it to the whole world. To be something *more*. It was all my fault."

Efilia clenched her teeth, and suddenly, without warning, she felt the sting of tears in her eyes. Something rose up inside her chest—a familiar fire, and it threatened to consume her.

"Never say that, Od. None of this was our fault." She said, louder than she meant. She stood up, clearly upset. "We've never had a choice about *any* of this. We were taken from our families, trained to be weapons for the kingdom since birth—even forced to push past our limits all the time, for Aether's sake! And it's never enough—not for Ulor, nor Ifir. They'll *never* stop."

Odmund stared up at her in near shock and looked around the garden, hoping no one had heard the treason Efilia, a Chosen lieutenant sworn to the very king, had just spoken. "Lia!" He hushed, looking at her with wide eyes.

Efilia shook her head and crossed her arms. She wiped a quick tear with the heel of her hand and looked down at her boots. "I'm sorry. It's just... It hasn't been an easy day."

"... It's ok," Odmund said. "I understand."

"But that doesn't mean bringing the boy here was a good idea, Od. Seeing him every day will only torture to you, not change your past. Nothing can change our pasts."

"I don't know..." Odmund shrugged. "At least I can give him a better life and honor his pain this way. I owe them that much."

Efilia sat back down and held Odmund's hands tighter, looking out into the gardens.

"Don't you worry what'll happen when Ifir learns who he is?"

"She won't." Odmund said, but his tone betrayed his fear.

"You have to send him away before it's too late."

"Back to that misery of a life, Lia? It's my fault they're in those circumstances. His brother was the main provider of his household. When he… When I… no, I can't send him back to that suffering."

"She will kill him, Od. If she finds out who he is, she will kill him, and everyone in his family. Just like that." She snapped her fingers.

Odmund shook his head. "Ifir is strict and radical… but she's not a murderer, Lia. She wouldn't do that to a poor family that has nothing. What would she get out of it?"

"You give her too much credit, Od. She's a sadistic monster who enjoys other people's suffering, is what she is."

Odmund realized there was more to her words than she was letting on.

"What are you talking about?" He asked.

Efilia realized she'd let things get too far and sighed. She didn't want to tell Od, but now, quite frankly, she didn't care. She had to make her point.

"She threatened me with assigning me to feed the Nor. She said that I was weak, and that *that's* what I deserved. After all my effort and sacrifice, she treats me like I'm worth the same as a lowly criminal."

Odmund stared at her, unblinking, his face the picture of shock. "Lia… did she really say that?"

"Yes. Why would I lie to you about something like that?"

"Aether…"

"That's your fair but strict Songbird, love."

It took Odmund a few moments to recover. Then, he said: "You're one of the strongest people I know, Lia! How could she say something like that? Ifir can't… I mean." He clenched his fist hard, and Efilia saw sparks coming out of it. "I have to tell Ulor, Efilia. Ifir can't just go around threatening Chosen like that! Especially not in front of servants and commoners!"

Efilia knew she was at the point of no return. No matter how much she regretted letting Odmund know about her assignment, she also felt relief in being cared for so much. She placed her head on his shoulder once more.

"You won't tell Ulor, my love. You'll do it for me. I have to fight this one on my own."

Odmund's chest rose and fell like the bellows of a forge, his fist starting to sputter with small flames. But then, Efilia placed her hand over it, and the flames died out. "I won't let Ifir tear me—us, down, love. I'm stronger than she thinks."

She allowed Odmund some time to calm down. Eventually, his breathing stabilized.

"Ok," he said. "But I'll be here if you need me. If Ifir threatens you like that again, you let me know. Or if, Aether forbid, she makes any kind of move against you…"

"I know," Efilia said. "I will."

Odmund looked at her now, their faces so close their noses were almost touching.

"I'd gladly risk my life for my king and kingdom, Lia. I'd risk my men's too, if it came to that. But not you."

Efilia allowed herself a slight smile, staring right into Odmund's eyes. "Nor I you." She said, and kissed him. Odmund embraced her in his strong arms and they kissed, as brightly and passionately as the sun that shone over them, forgetting all the cares of the world in a moment that seemed to last forever.

***

Loure sat in a dark room in the cellars of the castle, wishing that she were dead. She held a kitchen knife in her hand, which she raised slowly over her wrist… before she then started to shake and sob.

"Loure?" An old female voice said behind her. "Are you there? Come girl, I need you in the kitchen."

She dropped the knife into the darkness of the grain storage and closed her eyes shut.

"Coming." She said, with an effort.

When she opened the door, the woman's voice was heard again.

"What were you doing in the grain storage, lass?"

"N-nothing… Just taking my pain tonic," she said, trying to regain her composure. When she came arrived at the kitchen a few minutes later, the old woman looked her right in the eyes, and saw that she'd been crying. She also saw the bandages covering half her face and looked elsewhere, feeling pity for the poor thing. Most people did.

"Come my girl, peel the potatoes. Dinner won't cook itself." The old woman said while walking next to the main cook.

Loure sat on a corner stool and opened one of the many potato sacks around. She put a bowl with water on the small table next to her and began to dutifully peel the potatoes. She was lost in her thoughts when, a few minutes later, the old woman's voice was heard again.

"What do you want, son? Ahh… tell that old man he must stop eating so many cookies. They're back there boy, on a shelf next to the potatoes. Go and get them."

Loure panicked, not knowing who was about to walk in. To her surprise, it was a young boy who walked in—barely a teen… and he was also misshapen, like her. The young boy, already sporting some of the early signs of manhood on his chin and eyes, stopped upon seeing Loure in there.

"Oh… apologies, my lady." He greeted her as Radolf had taught him, as if she were a noble, instead of a common, disfigured servant.

She bent her head, not wanting to be seen by anyone, even this servant boy, and kept on peeling. Hugo, on the other hand stood there, watching her breathlessly. His eyes were wide as an owl's, as if he were witnessing a being from another world. The more he looked at her, the more uncomfortable she became.

"What do you want?" Loure finally asked, tired of the eyes on her. "Yes, I had a horrible accident… Staring won't make it go away." She told him.

"I-I'm sorry, my lady… Hideous? Why you're… you're the fairest maiden I've ever seen." He said shyly, looking at his feet.

At that moment Hugo noticed the other side of her face, hidden behind the thin curtain of her hair. He flinched for a second, but then his shock turned into happiness: a happiness which reflected on his face as a sincere smile.

"I mean it." He told her... and Loure, strangely, didn't feel absolutely terrible about herself for the first time in weeks.

"Thanks," she told him warily, not entirely sure if he was being honest or just nice. The boy just stared at her for a moment longer, then suddenly came to.

"Cookies, my lady. I'm looking for the cookies. For Radolf, you see. He likes them a lot."

Loure stared at the boy now. At his sparkling green eyes, brown, messy hair, and kind face. She found herself smiling ever so slightly, despite herself.

"There, boy," she said, showing him a shelf with the knife in her hand. Hugo nodded and silently walked to the shelf. He kept sneaking looks at her and smiling, she noticed. While he was leaving the kitchen with the cookie jar in his hands, he looked at Loure, who'd gone back to peeling potatoes, one more time.

"What's your name, my lady?" He asked her.

Loure stared at the boy, still smiling from the door, for a moment. He was looking at her like she was the most beautiful thing he'd ever seen. She knew the look well—having been sought after by many young men before coming to work in the castle. The thought that anyone could still look at her that way lit a small, but potent flame in her heart, pushing away the deep shadows. It showed on her face as a genuine smile.

"Loure."

"Loure..." The boy said. "It's a pleasure, my lady."

The boy turned to leave, nodding her goodbye, when Loure stopped him.

"What about you? What's your name?"

"Oh," he said, looking suitably sheepish. "Hugo." Then he left the room.

Loure stared at the door for a long while, feeling much better than she had moments before. Soon, she returned to her chore of peeling the potatoes, but this time, she had a very slight, but noticeable smile in her face.

"... Hugo." She repeated, under her breath.

CHAPTER 11

THE CAPTAIN OF HOUSE PENTGARD

Nighttime was fast approaching as the sun started to set beyond the faraway mountains.

Locke's party had been traveling for more than a week now and had made good time on their way to Rockpour village, but after so many days on the road nerves were strung and tensions were high. Locke himself looked weary and like he hadn't sleep well for the entire trip.

"He looks so tired," Merki said, sitting beside Axel in the modest wagon. "I hope we're still on the right track."

"Fear not. We are." Axel said, relieving her fear.

As he noticed the red leaves of the Crimson King Maple, indicating that they were close to Rockpour, Locke ordered the convoy to slow down.

"Here." He ordered, and pulled his horse's bridle, as they arrived at a wooded meadow full of apple trees, decent cover, and long grass carpeting the ground. "We'll camp here for tonight." Locke dismounted his horse.

Gerard looked around and noticed they were within shooting distance of the famous Crimson Maple Tree, the lodestar of travelers—venerated by all.

"Rockpour should be within another day's ride by horse, give or take. We should get there tomorrow by midday, if we set out early enough."

Everyone else dismounted after Locke, very grateful both for the chance to rest after the long day of riding, and the news that they would soon sleep in beds again, as well as eat properly cooked food. Merki let Rage run around the campsite as she dismounted the wagon and started to help with setting camp. Axel dismounted as well and helped Kade to a tree, tying him up as usual, though by now everyone was so used to it, most of them barely gave it a second thought.

"By Aether's mercy, at long last." Jarrie said. "I thought we'd never get out of the woods and hills."

"We're still not out yet." Leord said beside him, tying his horse to a tree.

"But we're close, yeah?" Jarrie said. "Ahh, I can't wait to take a proper bath and eat some good food."

Leord couldn't help but agree.

"Right on time, too," Ourg said. "We're almost out of food."

"Once we rest and restock at Rockpour, it'll be a straight run for the garrison, lads. That means this will be our last proper camp for a while. Be sure to make the most of it." Locke said.

Everyone nodded. Gerard approached Locke. "Permission to secure the perimeter, captain?" He asked, his voice tired and weary.

Locke nodded. "Granted. We'll set up camp in the meanwhile."

The older soldier took his horse and rode out of the meadow, hoping to scout their immediate surroundings and ensure they weren't at risk.

Now that they were so close to another major village, and closer to the heartlands of the kingdom (which meant they were farther away from the more dangerous border regions), Locke decided to risk a fire, to cook some warm food. He thought the men deserved it… even though Gerard wouldn't probably agree.

He ordered Ourg and Jarrie to help set things up, and Leord to gather water, as usual, and the three recruits went about on their way, gathering what they needed. Locke started to check their bags for provisions—then grimaced once he realized how little they had left.

"What do you need me to do?" Merki asked him.

"The boys have the camp covered. Keep watch over the perimeter while they work."

Merki nodded, then walked away to gather her things. Locke watched her go, his eyes unconsciously running down her back and settling on two... quite prominent points. He pursed his lips, then shook his head. Merki grabbed her bow and quiver, which held a couple dozen handmade arrows, and she scanned the trees around them. Finding a suitable one, she climbed its branches and sat between two, scanning the perimeter as the crimson light of twilight filled the woods with a pumpkin-orange glow.

Locke then pulled the maps of the area from his horse, using the Crimson Maple as a reference point, and started to plot the next leg of their journey to Rockpour.

Camp was set fast, and a fire—the first one they'd started since setting out from Halstead, blazed in the failing light of the day. Locke thought they could use it to cook a good stew, seeing as they still had some meat, vegetables and herbs available—along with some of the potato patties Elder Erikson had given them. They could then stamp out the flames before they went to bed.

The stew was prepared in short order, and soon everyone was scooping heapings of it onto wooden bowls. The recruits, Locke and Merki sat around the fire, gratefully enjoying the fragrant, delicious, if simple stew. It was the first hot meal they'd had in weeks. Axel had taken a bowl with a spoon to Kade, sitting over by his tree a few meters away or so, then sat back with the group to enjoy his share.

Merki didn't know if it was the bright warmth of the fire, the hot, savory stew filling their bodies with renewed energy, or the fact that they were so close to Rockpour at last—and then the garrison, but she noticed how the groups' spirits suddenly brightened. If she was being honest, in fact, hers did as well.

Even Kade, whom they kept a constant eye on, seemed to be enjoying himself—as much as the man could, given his situation.

Gerard was the only one who wasn't present in the group. He'd been leaving for longer and longer whenever he did his perimeter rounds, up to the point where he'd been spending hours out of camp. Merki had queried Locke about this, to which the captain has said: "The man likes his solitude. Just let him be. He'll always come back." And true to his word, Gerard always came back, once he'd made sure they were safe for the night... and once he'd had enough time away from them to keep himself from decapitating them the next day, Merki thought gloomily.

Well... today, he's missing a hell of a feast, she thought, sipping down some of her stew with closed, grateful eyes. She then shrugged. *Better him than me.*

"Easy there, recruits," Locke said after a while. "Make sure you leave some for Gerard too."

"No promises," Jarrie joked. "I mean, I'm almost full—which is a marvel to say after more than a week eating dried meat and fruit—but Ourg here looks like he's just getting started."

Ourg smiled like a child and poured some more of the stew. "Hmm... it's so good." He said. "Not as good as ma' used to make... but still good."

They all finished their share of stew, and put a lid over the pot, hoping to keep it at least warm for Gerard. Ourg looked at the pot, still holding food, with very longing eyes.

"So," Merki said after they'd all eaten half their bowls. "You all know I'm from Halstead... but I don't know where you're all from."

The recruits all looked at each other, then at Locke. The captain nodded to them in an easygoing way.

"I'm from a small town called Tuquan," Jarrie said. "To the east."

"Huh... Tuquan... Never heard of it." Merki said, and the rest of the group chuckled. Jarrie grinned too. Nothing ever seemed to get to him, Merki noticed. She liked that about him.

"You wouldn't have, no. It's a small farming village, really. We're quite hidden away in the valley."

"Anything remarkable about Tuquan?" Merki inquired.

"We make some damn good cheese," he said. "Lots of cows, and very good pasture too."

"Hmm… Cheese." Ourg said.

"What about you, Ourg?" Merki asked him.

"Ladervale," the big guy answered. "Near the mountains. Not big, not small. Lots of ore—but also lots of food." He said.

"I take it you were a smith's apprentice there?" Merki asked, because of the young man's telltale hammer and helmet.

"My pa' was," Ourg added. "I helped around the kitchen, mostly."

"What exactly *did* you do, Ourg?" Asked Jarrie. "You swing that hammer too good for a kitchen hand."

"I worked with the butcher. Chopped meat, tenderized it with a hammer. My da' thought a hammer would be better than a sword or spear. I was never very good with a sword or spear." He said.

A butcher's apprentice. That explains why he eats for five, Merki thought. Then she looked at the last recruit and took a deep breath. Of the three, Leord was the least social, and the least kind—the man always acted and talked like he had a stick up his ass… which he probably did. Nevertheless, he was part of the group, and Merki truly was curious.

"…and you, Leord?" She asked.

The recruit looked up from his bowl of stew, which he was drinking with extreme care and décor, then went back to it and ignored her. Everyone waited for him to speak, and the pressure of having so many eyes on him eventually caused him to give in. He sighed.

"Orvel," he said. "On the central plains."

"You're from the town of Orvel? Well, that explains a lot." Jarrie said.

"What's that supposed to mean?" Leord asked, an undignified look on his face.

Jarrie and Ourg chuckled, but Merki didn't get it. "Orvel? I'm not familiar with it." She said.

"It's one of the largest towns in the heartlands," Axel chipped in. "Not a city like Kellum, but quite well-off, if I'm not mistaken. Very fertile lands, and fields of cotton and lavender. It sees much trade, does it not?"

The young recruit nodded.

"So... you were the first of us three to join the captain here. How come only you joined? I mean, Orvel is a big town!" Jarrie said.

Leord stayed silent this time, nursing his bowl of stew, eyes down. The mood got a little uncomfortable.

"He wasn't the only recruit from Orvel," Locke said, eyes down on his own bowl. "We got around fifteen men there. Orvel is closer to another garrison, so another lieutenant from the town reserves escorted the group there."

"Why didn't you go with them, then?" Jarrie asked Leord.

The recruit sighed. He looked at Locke, who nodded encouragingly.

"Because... I didn't mean to join." Leord said, his eyes down. "My father forced me. He's a lesser lord in Orvel. My family runs a successful cotton plantation."

Locked looked away after Leord finished talking. Merki as well. To force your own son to enlist in the forward forces was equal to sending him to die. What kind of father would do that to his own son?

"I declined at first," Leord continued. "But my father insisted. Harshly."

"We were already on our way out of Orvel when Leord approached us," Locke cut in, saving the boy from saying more. "The recruit party had already left with the other lieutenant, so we decided to take him with us down on our tour of the south."

There was something else he didn't say there, which Merki knew.

Those who went to the Orvel garrison are most likely already on one of the many war camps at the frontlines. Most of them are already likely dead.

Locke had most likely shown the young boy a mercy, taking him with him instead of sending him after the other party. A noble's son, clearly unused to the rigors of battle and war... he wouldn't have lasted a day.

Merki looked at the captain with new respect. She looked hard and long at him, without realizing that she was doing so. In the firelight, she noticed that his blue eyes seemed to glimmer, like water, and found herself delving deeper and deeper into them. He suddenly looked back at her and she quickly nodded, letting him know that she understood his actions, and looked away. He cast his eyes down, smiled a little, and finished his bowl of stew.

"What about you, captain?" Axel asked him, out of nowhere. "I recognize the crest on your shoulder. House Pentgard, from the land of Freiz, is that right? The wine and merchant lords of the plains?"

That caught Locke by surprise, his eyes wide, the shock clear in his face. "How do you… yes. It is." He said.

Axel waved his hand in a dismissing manner. "Oh, I must've seen dozens of crests while working at the castle. Had to learn them all—proper etiquette and all that."

Locke looked Axel in his old, grey eyes for a long time. Then he looked away. "Yes, I am Locke Rodrick Pentgard, from the House Pentgard of Freiz. My father is Lord Franthz Pentgard."

The recruits all exchanged looks with each other. They'd known their captain was a person of influence, but the son of a high lord? That was something else entirely. Merki, for the second time in as many minutes, looked at Locke in an entirely different light.

And it was Merki, out of all of them, who asked the question in everyone's minds. "How does a high lord's son end up becoming a captain of the Kollek army?" She leaned forward.

Locke looked down and sighed. "That's a story for another day." He said. "Now, what about you, old man? You're too knowledgeable about the world for your own good. Where did *you* come from?"

Axel smiled, then squinted his eyes. "That is fair."

The other voice inside Axel's mind laughed at him—a wheezing, gut-wrenching sort of laugh. Axel waited for it to die down before continuing.

"I originally hail from a small village at the foot of the mountains to the northeast of Kellum. It was… ravaged by the Koartiz during one of their skirmishes with the border towns and left to ruin. Hollom, it used to be called—its location now lost to nature and time. I was one of the few survivors."

Merki looked at the old man and frowned—but in pity, not anger. "Axel... Is that true...?"

He nodded solemnly, the sadness in his eyes palpable. Suddenly, Merki felt guilty for having asked.

"I'm sorry... I never knew."

He nodded at her again. "It's quite alright, young Merki. Time has made that wound irrelevant. It all happened so long ago, I doubt your parents had even been born yet."

"Wow... you're really old." Ourg said in a mesmerized tone, to sudden stares from everyone in the group.

Axel just grinned from ear to ear. "I am!" He said.

"What did you do?" Jarrie asked, trying to quickly cover for simple Ourg. "You know... afterwards?"

Axel nodded several times. "I... well, I wandered. I was very young, back then. Hadn't seen my sixteenth winter yet. I eventually made it to Kellum, where I begged and survived however I could. It was ruled by Ulor's grandfather back then, king Ormir, father of Urail. Eventually, I worked my way up the slums—out of the grime and dirt, and onto the castle, working as a servant, first to the castle staff, then to the Chosen. The largest honor among lowly servants, that was—besides tending the king or queen. I learned everything a servant could learn and more in their service." He said. "Met your father too," he told Merki. "Saved his life once, after he came back to Kellum wounded after his unit was ambushed. I was the first to see his horse, galloping up towards the barracks under a heavy downpour, your father slumped on its back. That's how we became such fast friends." Axel's eyes were on Merki's, who he saw, was doing her best to hide the tears.

"Fascinating..." Jarrie said after Axel finished.

Axel saw that Locke seemed satisfied with his story—enough to let him be, and he rose from the log he and Merki were sitting on. "If you'll excuse me, I have to check on our Chosen. I'll be right back." Locke nodded, and Axel walked over to Kade.

His inner voice couldn't stop laughing like a maniac as he did.

"So many stories..." Ourg said after a moment of silence. Everyone nodded, staring at the dancing, flickering flames, drinking clean water from their mugs. As they stared at the fire, feeling sleepy and oddly soothed by the shared stories and their full bellies, an abnormal, alarming sound on the edge of their minds drove them out of their state of reverie. Rage's belly began to rumble in anticipation and the hunting dog padded over to the edge of the camp. Then, as the sound got louder, he began to bark.

"Horse hooves… Heading this way in a hurry!" Locke said. "Men, arm yourselves!"

Chaos erupted in the camp. Feet stomped over leaves and twigs as the recruits, and Merki, scrambled to get ahold of their weapons.

"Wedge formation—now!" Locke commanded, and they all stood in a semi-circle, facing the way of the incoming hooves. Merki knocked an arrow on her bow, raised it, and closed one eye.

Suddenly, Gerard burst out of the bushes in front of them, his horse heaving puffs of cold air like a creature out of hell. He reined the animal to a stop, causing it to stand on its hind legs and bellow a loud neigh.

Gerard looked down upon them like a madman, his features contorted and twisted even further by the light of the fire—which he stared at in absolute horror.

"What have you done?!" He growled at Locke from his horse. Not waiting for an answer, he jumped from the saddle and stormed his way to the pot over the small campfire. "Help me put it out—now!" He yelled.

The recruits, and even Locke, were too shocked to object. Gerard kicked the pot of leftover stew, still hot, onto the dirt, spilling its contents on the ground. He started to repeatedly stomp the fire, kicking dirt onto it, then onto the remains of the stew.

Rage continued barking madly, running circles around Merki as if trying to protect her.

Axel and Kade watched in horror a few meters away, outside the dying circle of light of the campfire.

"You… absolute… idiots!" Gerard growled. "The stew! Bury the stew!" He said, kicking dirt onto the still-warm leftovers. Merki was sure the man had lost his mind. Jarrie and Leord followed his orders without thinking it twice, while Ourg looked at the spilled, wasted stew with almost watery eyes.

Once the fire had been smothered, and the camp plunged into darkness, Locke stopped, taking huge, heaving breaths, and recollected himself.

"Gerard! What is going on? What has come over you? Are we under attack?!"

The old wolf turned on him, and what Locke saw in his eyes drove a cold knife right into his stomach and twisted it.

Fear.

Gerard was afraid. Terrified, even.

"We must pack immediately and leave this place! This is no safe haven." He said.

"What is it, Gerard? Bandits? Rebels?" Locke asked, his voice almost a plea.

Gerard shook his head. "Worse. I found tracks. Big ones. Followed them."

Rage continued to bark.

"What kind of tracks, Gerard? Where did they lead you?" Locke asked him, his blood turning to ice, dreading the answer.

"Behemoth. Here." Was all he said.

Then, almost as if on cue, Rage stopped barking and hid behind Merki's leg, whimpering. He seemed to be looking not in Gerard's direction… but eastward, into the cold dark of the woods. Merki noticed it and her blood froze in her veins.

Then, there was a rustle and a rumble in the trees. They all held their breath, listening. Merki noticed, for the first time, that the forest was silent… had been for some time now. Rage whimpered even harder, almost in a panic, looking at the woods right behind where Ourg was standing.

"Guys… I think there's some—" Ourg began to whisper, but never finished, as a dark, bulging mass of claws, muscles and teeth materialized from the darkness behind him and tore his body in half.

CHAPTER 12

THE DOVE AND THE LION

Queen Etheria played with her dinner, cutting the slice of duck on her plate into small pieces. The rice near the meat remained untouched. Her children had already eaten their food, but were waiting for their mother, who seemed utterly lost in her thoughts. Ulor wasn't with them that evening.

"Mother?" Prince Urail said.

"Yes?" She raised her head, startled, as if she'd been somewhere far away.

"What is troubling you?" Urail asked. Etheria smiled. "Nothing, nothing my son. Your brother must've tired me out, I guess… He's growing so fast."

"How do you know it'll be a boy, mother? Maybe it's another sister for Flora…"

"No." Etheria said, harsher than she meant to. "It's a boy… because your father has decreed so, my son. Therefore, that is what I'll give him." She smiled. Urail shrugged.

"I hope he likes horse riding then, so we can race together." He said.

"I'm sure he'll like whatever his family likes, my prince."

The princess looked into her mother's eyes and, just as Etheria had taught her earlier, she took mental notes of the way she spoke and how she conducted herself, hoping to learn as much as possible.

"With your permission, mother." The prince said, hoping to be excused.

"You are excused, my prince. You too, my princess." Etheria said, sending her kids away. After they left, she raised her hand, and her maid Kareen ran over to her.

"Find me the butler." She ordered.

"As you wish, my queen." Kareen knew just which butler the queen was referring to. She walked over to some of the other lesser servants and gave them instructions, sending them on their way.

Shortly afterwards, coin master Fermand entered the great dining hall and walked over to Etheria. "My queen," he said with open arms. He seemed full of joy, as always.

"Sir Fermand," she kindly said, and extended her hand for him to kiss, which he promptly did. "Please join me," she continued, and invited him to sit near her at the table. A maid hurried to pull out a chair for him, and he gladly took it.

"Apologies for my, ah, tardiness. Just came back from a meeting with the merchant lords, and you know how much they love to talk. Alas, I am at your service, my queen."

If it had been anyone else keeping someone like the queen waiting, even just for a few minutes, as was the case with Fermand now, they would've received *severe* punishment for their insolence. Etheria, however, knew how busy the small man kept himself, and how crucial his work around the city was, so he got something of a special treatment in these matters.

"That's quite alright, Fermand." Etheria said, letting it slip as always.

After the maids had served some food to the coin master, Etheria signaled them to leave. As soon as the great doors closed, and they were all alone in the chamber, she sighed.

"Fermand… I need a favor." She leaned closer to him. Her voice had a tinge of worry and rush to it, so he became all ears.

"You and I are old friends… and I've never forgotten how much you helped me back when I'd just become queen. You are my strongest ally in this castle." She looked into the depths of the coin master's tired eyes.

"Of course, my queen. And you've been so good to me in return. I am forever in debt of your generosity." He looked into her eyes with respect, then humbly bent his head. "Now tell me. What can I do for you?"

Etheria hesitated for a moment, unsure of how to proceed.

"I need you to undertake a special project for me. As coin master, you're in charge of approving every major construction done in the city, correct?"

Fermand nodded.

"You wish for an addition to your quarters? Or a new section to the royal gardens?" He asked. But Etheria simply shook her head.

"No. What I need is bigger… and riskier. I need you to authorize, and oversee, the construction of a house. A small cottage—something that won't attract much attention."

"A… cottage, my queen?"

Etheria nodded. "Then, once construction is finished, I'll need you to stock the house with emergency provisions. Everything we might need for a few months. Food, clothes, etcetera. And I need you to do so in secret. No one can learn of this—especially Ulor or Ifir."

As she spoke, she could see the small man becoming more and more anxious, no doubt as his mind tallied up the costs and difficulties in such a task.

"M-my Queen… what you're asking for… is there a threat against you, or your family? Are you in danger?" He looked over her features, his eyes searching for something she wasn't saying.

"No Fermand. This is all just… planning ahead, for the days to come."

Fermand nodded, like a ferret or a mouse, but the stress poured out of every feature in his face.

"I understand, yes, yes… but, my queen, are you sure you want to keep this from the king? I mean, if there's…"

The Dove and The Lion | 151

Etheria gave him a stern look that immediately shut him up. "It *must* remain a secret. Only you can make that happen, Fermand. Can I count on you?"

Fermand stared, wide eyed, into the queen's own eyes. Then he nodded vigorously. "Yes… yes. It won't be easy hiding it from the Songbird and her people… nearly impossible, truly…" He looked at Etheria, who frowned at him with a clear message in her eyes. "But I'll find a way. Now… where are we supposed to build this cottage?"

Etheria took a deep breath. "Under the Roaring Peaks, there is a vast system of caverns, leading under the mountains—once used for transporting ores from one side of the peaks to the other, when the lands beyond it belonged to us. They lie abandoned now, forgotten. One of the chambers holds an open gallery, with a mouth that lets in light from far above; the chamber has an underground lake, next to a shore of glittering sand. I want you to build the cottage there."

Fermand nearly fainted. He grew paler than milk, his eyes wide as an owl's.

"D-dear Queen… that is… why, it's an incredibly dangerous location! The Roaring Peaks lie on the border of Koartiz lands. Kollek don't pass through that area at all, especially since the war started!"

"That is the point, Fermand." Etheria said, sighing. "Stop worrying, and just do as I've said… and once more, make sure nobody knows anything about it. Especially the king and Ifir." She strictly warned him.

Fermand nodded.

Her body language was so calm that she didn't even move. Her eyes stared into space as if she had already made peace with her thoughts. Fermand knew she'd never ask something so ludicrous, so risky and fantastical, unless she had a very important reason for it… and maybe some pressing knowledge that *he* didn't have. He bowed respectfully.

"It shall be done as you wish, my queen."

"Thank you, Fermand. I knew you were the right man to ask." Etheria held his hand and looked into his eyes before she stood up.

"It is my pleasure, my queen." Fermand said. Etheria nodded, then walked away and out of the dining hall. As the doors closed, and the sound of her steps disappeared into the castle halls beyond, Fermand pressed a hand to his forehead, and started sweating profusely, his eyes darting all over the table… then he took the knife he'd been using to slice his meat and flung it clear across the hall.

***

Back on her chambers, Etheria found Kareen along with the butler she'd requested, called Jacobs.

"Good evening, Your Highness," the old man said, bowing.

Etheria nodded. "Evening, Jacobs. Please, take a seat." She showed him to a seating area on one corner of her private chambers.

"To what do I owe this privilege, my queen?" The old man said after sitting. Etheria sat opposite him and started to pour some tea from the pre-prepared kettle her maids had left her in the table.

"The girl from the other day… the new maid at breakfast. What happened to her? I've heard… rumors."

The butler looked down at his well-polished shoes. "I'm afraid there was an accident, Your Highness. She was badly hurt. Scarred. They think it happened in the kitchen—a misstep with one of the frying vats."

Etheria's eyes widened. "Oh… is that so? When did that happen?"

"The very same day you saw her at the dining hall. It was… quite horrifying, really."

No wonder Ulor was in such a foul mood that day. The girl must've never made it to his chambers…

"I am so sorry to hear that, Jacobs. Where is she now?"

"We put her on kitchen duty for now, Your Highness—away from the frying vats, mind you. She helps the main cook down prepare ingredients in the cellars now, her deformity making her unfit to serve in the upper rooms, as you can imagine."

Etheria gathered her thoughts for a moment, taking a sip of hot, fragrant tea. Then she nodded to herself.

"Send her to me one of these nights."

"I... I beg your pardon?" The butler asked, flabbergasted.

"I'd very much like to meet her."

Jacobs didn't understand the queen's reasoning here, but he knew better than to inquire further of the most powerful woman in Kellum... *After Ifir, of course,* he corrected himself.

"As Your Highness wishes. Just give the order, and I'll send her up."

Etheria nodded, smiling. "Excellent. That will be all."

***

On the other side of the castle, Ifir relaxed in her golden bathtub, enjoying the candlelight which softly brightened her bathroom. There were roses everywhere, and the steam of boiling water on the stove covered all the mirrors on the walls.

Mere worked around Ifir as she relaxed, setting down towels, making sure the water was the right temperature and getting her whatever she needed or wanted. The old maid, however, worked with a tight knot in her chest and down in her stomach, her thoughts going back to her niece and what she'd done to her. It'd been several days now, and she still hadn't seen Loure after she was let go from the physician's room. She only knew she had been assigned to the kitchens, on the other side of the castle, and that she slept there on a cot in a backroom.

Was she better now? Would her eye ever see again? What would Mere tell her sister?

The questions raced in her mind like wild horses. Mere filled a tankard from the pot of boiling water on the wood burning stove. The heat of the water made her feel all the sorrier for Loure.

"Mere?" Ifir called out, bringing her out of her thoughts.

"Yes, my lady?" Mere replied. Her voice trembled as much as her hands as she washed Ifir's arm with a sponge. She did her best not to look her mistress in the eyes.

"I heard a very sad news." Ifir said.

"Hopefully not related with your well-being, my lady?" Mere said, while foaming the sponge with lavender-scented soap.

"Not quite, no. It's about Loure… your niece. Was it true she accidently burnt her face few days ago?" Ifir stared at Mere to see her reaction. The old woman froze for a second and stopped her work on Ifir's arm. Just hearing her niece's name out loud drove a sharp knife into her chest. Mere nodded, sadly and heavily.

"She did, yes… It was a… terrible thing."

"Poor girl. She was so pretty too…" She put a hand on Mere's arm and looked into her eyes. "…Though I'm sure she'll find a way to bounce back up. She seemed like a very resilient young lass." Ifir nodded slightly to herself. "I took the liberty of setting aside a little gift for her, for when you see her." She pointed to a velvet red bag on a small table. "Just some change to pay the physician for her treatment. I'd hate for the poor girl to have to work for a year or more without pay just to cover the expenses."

Mere had paid for Loure's treatment as soon as she'd taken her to the castle physician, and was still paying for it with her own coin. Something told her that Ifir knew.

"Thank You, Your Grace. You do us both too much honor." Mere said.

"She was supposed to serve the king that day, didn't she?" The way Ifir asked the question sent shivers down Mere's old spine.

"Erhm… She was, yes… But she never got to." Mere said, in quick succession. "Now she's in the kitchens, working with the head cook."

"Ah, a wise, safe choice that, Mere. I'm sure she'll be safer there."

"Yes, Songbird." Mere swallowed heavily.

Ifir smiled and continued to enjoy the hot water and foams of the lavender soap. She raised her right foot out of the water and Mere moved to wash it as fast as she could.

"As I always say, only loyal families can survive during these dark times. We are all a large family here in Kellum, Mere. We all work hard for the bright future of our king."

"Long live the king, and you, my lady." Mere said, looking at Ifir's eyes.

"Well said, Mere. Well said." Ifir nodded.

She then closed her eyes and enjoyed her bath while Mere continued washing her, doing her best to ensure the Songbird of the Kollek enjoyed her soak. However, Loure's scream of pain and agony continued to ring in her ears since that day, and the pressure of the sadness in Mere's chest never let her breathe easy. Mere's desperation was like a silent hangman, hovering over her, denying her any kind of ease or respite.

As she thought of her niece, and how she'd destroyed her life in the hopes of saving it, a tear fell from her old cheek and mixed with the foamy bath water.

After half an hour of relaxing, Ifir suddenly stood up.

"Good. I am done." Ifir said.

"Sure, my lady." Mere replied and brought her towel.

While drying Ifir's shapely legs, another tear fell from Mere's old cheek. Ifir looked carefully at her, noticing it, and she extended her hand to caress Mere's hair. She stopped before her fingers reached old woman's white hair, however, took a deep breath… and started to sing a mournful melody that could send shivers down anyone who listened to it. Mere's desperation, as well as the pain in her soul, slowly went away with every note she sang. Her old eyes turned to Ifir, who continued to sing, while staring at the sky through her window. The old woman forgot the whole world for a second. Her wrinkled hands were still holding the towel but not drying Ifir anymore. She instead watched her, mesmerized… bewitched.

Ifir caressed Mere's white hair, smiled at her, then stopped singing.

"I am cold, Mere. Bring me the lilac silk dress if you will." She gently said.

Mere's eyes opened wide, as if she'd been breathless for some time. She nodded and stood up in a panic.

"Yes, immediately, Songbird!" She rushed to bring Ifir's clothes.

Her confused and sheepish attitude made Ifir smile, so she just nodded and waited.

Mere opened the engraved doors of her closet. Right in the middle of all the colorful clothes hung the illustrious lilac dress, made by the most famous Kollek tailor of all time, Sir Prageth; a gentle and gifted man who served King Fredrich, the monarch of Salut Island. The dress was sent as gift for the Songbird last year when she'd helped King Fredrich become a member of the Council of the Lords; one of the few organizations in the Kollek lands granted protection by Chosen. Being the only island protected by Chosen meant few, if any, would ever dare attack their merchant ships, and such an agreement gave King Fredrich much fame... in return, of course, for a decent down payment and a hefty increase in the taxes paid to his High King, Ulor.

As Mere helped Ifir clothe herself, she tried hard not to touch the royal woman's body with her cold hands. Ifir's eyes, however, were fixed on the lilac dress and not her, as she wondered at the beauty of its colorful embroideries. Mere's fingers nonetheless moved on Ifir's body faster and gentler than a feather in the wind. Finished putting on the elegant dress, the Songbird of the Kollek looked at herself in the mirror, while Mere buttoned up the dress' back. The embroideries on it were dense in the hemline, and gradually became less so until they reached Ifir's hips, a feature that accentuated her thin and slim waist and stomach. The plunging necklines, long, frilled arms, and wide shoulders made Ifir look like a royal swan—one that could make even a bright flame brighter with its beauty.

Mere looked at her mistress' image on the mirror with admiration. Ifir slowly walked to her dressing table and sat. With slight moves, Mere opened a specially-made hair curler—designed with small hot coals inside an iron body. She moved it on Ifir's head with practiced hands, careful not to touch her scalp, letting her glossy black hair fall on her shoulders one by one. The Songbird opened her jewelry box and gave Mere a hair pin made of gold and emeralds, to accentuate her eyes.

"The one," Ifir then ordered in the softest voice. Mere ran to pick the special necklace Ifir was referring to from her closet and soon arrived with an engraved wooden box in her hands, which had champlevé enameling on its wooden lid. The champlevé had two swans whose wings extended to the sky as they stood over an aquamarine sphere, which represented the world.

As Ifir opened the box, a necklace shone brightly from within it, as if a flower had just found life by reaching the sun's light. The extravagant piece of jewelry was made out of white gold and sapphires; a massive one at the center, with the rest of the piece adorned with smaller ones of varying sizes. If the sky could ever fit in a box, Ifir thought, it would have that necklace's blue shine… which is why she'd named it the Blue Phoenix—a symbol of renewal and rebirth, second chances… life and death.

"Every pain brings its cure along with it, Mere." Ifir said while her fingers brushed the stones on the necklace. "We just need to be open-hearted enough to see it."

Mere could still remember the night that Ulor gave Ifir the necklace as a present. It was the same night Ulor's father, Urail, had been found dead in his bed. The Songbird was a young, gorgeous woman back then, and Mere could still walk without her knees aching. Ulor was just a young prince, too.

Mere could feel the pain of that night in her heart again, as it was a day that hung heavy on the people's memories, and one the folk of Kellum preferred not to speak of, as if it'd bring some kind of bad omen.

"Only love can break all the rules… and make a soul blind enough to go astray." Ifir told Mere that distant night; something the maid would only come to understand a few years later.

The necklace meant so many things for Ifir. It was a symbol of love, betrayal… and sins. More than anything else, however, it was the symbol of her ability to write her own destiny.

"Tonight, destiny will change once more." Ifir said as she put the necklace on her thin, graceful neck. Mere silently helped her, but her eyes were afraid to meet Ifir's.

With a sharp move, the Songbird stood up and walked to the door of her chamber. As she opened the door, the maids waiting on the other side of it moved aside in a sudden panic. Like always, their mistress found ways to make them stress.

"Dismissed." She said. All the maids bowed, then walked fast back to their dorms for the night.

Ifir and Mere waited until they disappeared, then Ifir turned to Mere. "You're dismissed for the night too, dear Mere. Enjoy your evening." She said, before walking out into the corridor.

"Thank you, Songbird." Mere bent her head and waited until Ifir had disappeared. Her old eyes carefully checked the corridor, hoping nobody saw where she was going… although anyone who'd been here for long enough could risk a guess.

While walking through a corridor in the upper levels of the keep, away from the private chambers, Ifir stood in front of a door. She opened it and entered the castle library, full of bookshelves from top to bottom, lit by the gentle glow of many encased candles and a massive chandelier at its center, adorned with precious, glistening crystals. Ifir walked over to a small reading chamber at the back of the library—her private study and reading room, separated from the main room by a locked door, and approached a bookshelf to the right of the entrance. Her hand wandered on a special red book on the fifth shelf and she pulled on it. Something clicked, and the bookshelf swerved on unseen hinges, popping loose. She gently moved it open, like a door, making no sound, and walked through.

Beyond the bookshelf was a completely enclosed chamber— save for a small, covered window at the top to let some air, almost invisible from the outside. It was lavishly decorated, with plush, ornate rugs, racks of expensive wine, a long, red velvet couch and a large bed fit for a king. Her innocence, love, hopes and dreams were standing in front of her in that room—all inside one body. The king sat on a stool in a comfortable white cotton shirt, unbuttoned, and his silken sleeping pants, painting a vase full of colorful flowers on an adjacent table—something he did for her, as she collected them and then placed them around her chambers as a reminder of their nights together. He seemed so peaceful and distant from the real world in that moment—as if he were a completely different person than the one everyone else saw outside the chamber. Ifir watched him for few seconds. She knew he was aware of her presence in the room, as, aside from its builder, no one else knew about the room's existence and location other than her. And she'd taken care of the former a long time ago, so the secret was uniquely theirs.

"My king," Ifir gently bowed.

"My love," King Ulor replied, turning to see his lover with the brush still in his hand. By seeing Ifir in her lilac dress and the Blue Phoenix on her neck, the king couldn't hide his surprise.

"I hope we're celebrating something tonight." He said, looking her from head to toe.

Ifir slowly and enticingly walked to him and wandered her fingers on his naked chest.

"We will soon, my king." She smiled at him.

"Good," Ulor replied with a knowing smile, then turned back to finish painting his toile. His brush licked the canvas so fast that the colors seemed to materialize on the white vase on their own. Despite everything else that could be said about the man, Ulor was quite the artist with the brush. Part of the "refined" education his father had given him, among many other obligatory skills, Ifir knew.

She walked next to him then, interested in something other than his painting skills.

"Soon we will have the Manuscript in our hands…" She said, "and we'll know how to find and awaken the Sword of Aether." The king's eyes shone with passion and fire as he looked into her eyes.

"Then, my king, you will have all the power in the Stone. You will rule the whole world, and I will be able to give you a son."

She could see the flame of desire and hunger in his eyes. Her lips came so close to his that he could feel her breathe on them. Her eyes were on them, waiting for his next word or move.

He caressed her hair and looked into her eyes—eyes that he knew since he was a boy… eyes who belonged to the first woman he ever loved.

"The world will be ours." The king said.

Ifir nodded, then began to recite an old poem Ulor had written to her many years ago. "The world is underneath us…" She said with a smile. And the king completed it, saying: "We are but the swans in the sky. Your song hath the wings of love, which maketh this Lion fall for the Dove. We become but one, our sins amended by the sun."

Ifir smiled innocently like when she was a young, naive girl, and leaned towards Ulor's lips. He caressed and smelled her fragrant neck right before he kissed it, regarding how she had the light smell of lavender on her and the softest skin he ever felt. He took her into his arms and carried to the bed. While Ulor kissed her soft skin, Ifir opened her eyes to look through the small window slit above the bed and saw the sky, which was already dark. Her eyes immediately found Sirius, the planet of the god Odon of old, and she closed her eyes again to pray one more time before the best part of tonight's ceremony took place.

May the Lord of Fire, Odon, bless me with a baby from the king's blood.

CHAPTER 13

SCREAMS IN THE NIGHT

"TAKE ARMS!"

Locke's voice rang clear across the hollow of trees, spurring the men into action after they'd watched Ourg's torso get flung clear across camp by a ten-foot-tall shadow. The beast had then revealed itself from the darkness of the trees—massive and hulking. It closely resembled a bear, but three times as big, and completely black. The hair on its back stuck out like needles, and its arms were covered in thick plates that looked like rock. Its face was something out of nightmares or storybooks—a huge, gaping ursine maw full of fangs, and two massive tusks like a boar.

The beast began to gorge on Ourg's remains, which gave the soldiers time to pick up their weapons. Thankfully, they were all wearing their armor already—not that it'd done much for poor Ourg.

"What in the world is that?!" Jarrie asked, eyes wild as he picked up his spear.

"A Behemoth!" Gerard roared.

"Gerard, how do we kill it?" Locke shouted.

"Kill it? Shouldn't we *run*?!" Leord asked, fumbling to put an arrow on his crossbow.

The old soldier rounded up towards the captain, eyes wide. "We can't run, Locke. Not from this! It will follow, and it will kill every last one of us! Our only chance is the soft skin on its underside—it's the only way to hurt it!"

"I can hit it!" Merki said, already kitted with her bow and arrows.

Locke nodded. "Aim for the neck, chest and stomach soldiers—and be brave! We haven't come this far to die just yet! You too, huntress!"

Leord, Jarrie and Merki nodded. The huntress then snapped her fingers and gave her hound a quick command to stand back and away, hoping to keep him out of harm's way.

"Captain!" Axel yelled. "What about the Chosen?"

Goddammit! Locke thought. "Cut him free from the tree and get out of here!"

Gerard was about to say something, then the massive beast finished goring over Ourg's remains and rounded on them, blowing huge clouds of steam from its bear-like snout. The rumble on its stomach made the very earth and trees shake… then it roared—a booming, moaning, barreling sound that sent shivers of pure terror down all it struck, and pierced their ears with shrill agony.

"Here it comes!"

The Behemoth pawed the dirt, getting ready to break into a charge, when an arrow hit it square in one of its terrible eyes. It squealed a wail of pain, moving back a couple of paces, then rushed the soldiers. They all rolled out of the way, and the beast slammed into a nearby tree, shaking it to its roots. A crossbow bolt glanced off its thick hide. Another of Merki's arrows flew past it, scratching its cheek. The beast doubled over to them and charged again—this time focusing on Merki. The huntress shrank at the sight of the monster heading her way, then rolled out of the way of its charge—but before she'd even managed to get back on its feet, the Behemoth was upon her, swiping its massive paws full of dagger-like claws. She stumbled backwards, scrambling on all fours, trying to avoid the deadly limbs at all costs, but the cluttered state of the campsite and thick darkness around them made it difficult to maneuver. She dodged, rolled and spun, scrambled and then jumped again just out of reach each time…

until her foot tripped on an exposed root and she fell on her back, dropping her bow, while the wounded beast continued making progress towards her. She scrambled on all fours, trying to crawl away from it, but she knew it was too late—the thing's gleaming claws were within reach. Realizing its triumph over its prey, the Behemoth lifted a paw, coiling its entire massive body into the pounce—when Jarrie's spear got it square in the chest.

It roared in agony once more.

"Get away from her!" Jarrie said, eyes wide, spittle flying everywhere. He tried to push the beast away, but his frame, and the spear's poor shaft, couldn't budge it. The thing flung its arm towards Jarrie, lifting him in the air and sending him sprawling over the camp, while splitting his spear in half. It roared that terrible, ear-splitting roar again and raised both of its thick, plated arms up in defiance—just like a bear.

Then, out of nowhere, a crossbow bolt slammed right into its chest, pushing it, making it roll over on its back. Leord quickly knelt, trying to reload his crossbow. The beast got back up and growled, intent on charging the newcomer, but before it could, Gerard jumped on it, sword in hand, and pressed his advantage. The man tackled the beast with the force of a bear himself, pushing it to its back once more, then slashed with his blade, slicing a clear gash across the monster's chest before it had time to react. He then ducked out of an incoming swipe which would've decapitated him, then rolled back and out of another, which would've also proved fatal. He came out of his roll in an experienced crouch, sword held to his side, eyes locked on his enemy. The Behemoth pounced at him, but he rolled back to the side, stabbing with his blade and catching it under the arm—but before he could push the sword all the way to its heart, the beast leaned into the blade and snapped it, then slammed its plated arm against Gerard, sending him sprawling across the campsite.

Immediately, another arrow struck its chest, and a bolt slammed into its side, and yet, the thing kept coming, this time rushing towards Gerard who was still gasping on the ground, the wind knocked out of his lungs.

Screams in the Night | 165

The beast reached him in a matter of seconds and reared its neck back, intent on impaling its massive tusks right through him. The old wolf's eyes went wide. He tried to move out of the way but couldn't, his lungs compressed and his entire body searing with pain. Then, out of nowhere, Locke's voice rang clear over him.

"Aaargh!"

The young captain jumped over his lieutenant with his sword and shield at the ready, somehow deflecting the killing blow from the animal, parrying its tusks to the right with his shield. The thing slammed its tusks on the dirt, and Locke took the opportunity to draw his blade clean through its throat—but the Behemoth shrugged, and the blade caught it on its shoulder instead, sliding off with a hiss. The beast then dug its tusks out of the earth… and right into Locke's leg, punching through a gap in his greaves. It bit the captain's leg and dragged him through the dirt like a toy, mauling him, before flinging him clear across the campsite and against a tree.

The Behemoth roared at Locke… forgetting the old soldier at its feet for a moment.

And Gerard saw his opportunity. Taking a deep breath, he drew one of his daggers, pushed himself forward with very ounce of his strength, and slit the thing's throat right where it stood. A splash of blood sprayed right onto Gerard's face, making him choke and sputter, while the beast slowly shuffled its weight from leg to leg, wavering, not fully understanding what had just happened. Then, without warning, its legs gave out and it fell clear over Gerard, who howled in pain as his legs got pinned under its immense weight.

The Behemoth twitched a time or two… then laid completely still.

Silence consumed the campsite. Leord, Jarrie and Merki stared, wide-eyed, at the black, bristling body of the massive creature. They all waited, bow and crossbow at the ready, for any sign of movement… when Gerard's voice croaked from under the thing.

"Can anyone… get this fucking thing… off of me?!"

The soldiers snapped out of their shock and moved towards the massive corpse, very cautiously at first. Upon seeing its glazed eyes and large tongue spilling over the side of its mouth—as well as the pool of blood under it, they grabbed Gerard by his arms and pulled him out from under the massive carcass. The old man was almost completely covered in blood—something that probably saved him, as it made it easier for them to pull him out in time.

"Are you alright? Can you walk?" Leord asked him after a moment, still holding onto his arm.

Gerard grunted with a grimace, then nodded. "I'm fine," he said. "Go check on the captain. He took a worse hit than me." He pointed over to a nearby tree—and to everyone's horror, there was Locke, his body sprawled over some roots like a discarded marionette. Jarrie and Merki made their way to him, while Leord helped Gerard to a nearby log.

"Captain…" Jarrie whispered. Locke, like Gerard, was dirtied and bloodied beyond recognition—his face caked with mudded, bloody dirt. His chest, however, was rising and falling, so he was alive.

"Locke," Merki said. "Can you hear me? Can you speak?"

The captain slowly opened his eyes and groaned. Then, he shuffled forward, trying to stand up, and immediately whimpered desperately, his face a mask of utter pain and agony.

Merki and Jarrie both saw it at the same time. His leg was a mangled mess… and part of his tibia was poking out of his greaves.

"God above…" Jarrie said.

Merki just watched with wide eyes, the horror plain in her face. Locke stared at her past all the blood, barely able to speak, clearly in physical and mental shock. He groaned, trying to ask her what was wrong, as he couldn't even move his neck to look, but the words wouldn't come out.

"Will he live?" Jarrie asked her.

She shook her head. "I don't know."

Gerard stalked over to them, leaning his weight on Leord. "How bad is it?" He asked.

Then he saw Locke, and Locke saw him. Gerard saw the wound, then looked away.

"Fuck," he whispered.

"Fuck, fuck, FUCK!" He roared.

Axel walked over to them then and saw Locke's wound. "By the graces of Aether…" He spoke.

"You!" Gerard immediately rounded on him, grabbing him by the scruff of his shirt and twisting it. "This is all *your* fault. You and that damn whore!" Axel just looked, meeting his eyes as bravely as he could. "Where's the Chosen? What did you do with him?"

Axel looked towards the camp. Kade was there, released from the tree, but still bound hand and foot. He looked at the scene from afar with caution, and more than a little shock and dread. Rage, was by his side, growling defensively.

"He could've run away, soldier." Axel croaked, the knot in his shirt choking him. "He's still there."

Gerard looked between him and Kade.

"Let him go, Gerard, you're hurting him!" Merki yelled.

"Shut up, harlot!"

"I can help him," Axel said again, his voice hoarse. "The captain."

Jarrie and Leord didn't know what to do. They looked at each other, then the captain, Merki and Axel. Gerard grunted, then let the old man go.

"Do what you can… and hurry." He started to limp away towards the campsite. "For fuck's sake! Why do these things keep happening to me?" He walked over to the discarded pot, which had been full of warm, savory stew a few minutes ago, now speckled with blood and bits of Ourg… and kicked it as hard as he could, howling as he did.

***

Axel had Merki make a familiar antiseptic poultice out of their stock of medicine back at camp, then applied the salve over the captain's severe leg wounds, and around the bone. He gave Locke an infusion that slowed his heart rate, then, with the soldiers' help, he moved him back to camp, placing him on a clean bedroll. That had been the easy part.

Having stemmed the blood flow to the wound, he now had to reset the bone back to its place, then bandage the leg properly along with a splint. He gave Locke a stick to bite into. "I need someone to hold him down when I reset the bone… or he's definitely going to hurt himself." He said.

Jarrie volunteered. Merki watched from the side, ready to help. Axel grabbed Locke's leg, then stared at his face. "This is going to hurt, lad…"

Locke, barely awake, grunted weakly, and nodded. "Alright… here it goes."

Gerard watched from afar as he finished bandaging his own wounds.

SNAP.

"*Ghhh…Aaahhh!!!*"

The captain howled, his torso arching back, the veins in his neck popping out like roots on soil… then passed out.

Axel then signaled for Merki to bring the rest of the cloth they were using for bandaging. He stitched up the wound as best as he could, wrapped Locke's leg along with a sturdy piece of wood Leord had brought him and set it against the splint. Axel then sat back after all the work, wiping thick beads of sweat from his brow.

Gerard eventually made his way to them.

"Will he walk again?" He asked, his temper somewhat cooled now, arms still crossed.

Axel took a deep breath. "In a few weeks' time, with the herbs I'll be giving him… yes."

"Shit… Will he ride?"

Axel hesitated. "No. Not until his wound fully heals. He'll have to ride on the wagon… with Kade."

Gerard pinched the bridge of his nose and let out a long sigh.

"This is just great." He finally said, then shook his head.

Everyone in the group looked at each other, not knowing what to say. Gerard walked over to his horse and drew a flask of very strong alcohol. He downed a couple of gulps in one go, then sighed.

"What are we going to do now?" Jarrie asked Axel.

Axel was the one to sigh now. "Your captain will be out of action for some time. Lieutenant Gerard is the next highest-ranking soldier

Screams in the Night | 169

in this group, so he'll be your commanding officer until the captain is at least able to speak again."

"Aether…" Leord said from a few meters away, standing beside a tree. He was looking down at the remains of Ourg's upper half. "Poor Ourg… He didn't even see it coming." He said.

"What will be do about him?" He asked Axel.

"If your acting captain allows it, we'll give him a proper burial tomorrow before we set out. I can say a prayer for him and send his spirit back to his loved ones. It's… all we can do for him now."

"Damn…" Jarrie said, visibly upset. "How could this happen? How did we not know we were walking right into a Behemoth's territory, of all things?"

Axel took a deep breath. "Behemoths are creatures from before the time of the Kollek. From when magic was abundant in the world, and it permeated nature in mysterious and powerful ways… Before the creation of the Stone, which sucked the world dry of it."

"We're quoting old legends now, old man?" Leord asked.

Axel shrugged. "Legend or not—this creature is a relic of another time, very rare, and it usually keeps to itself high up in the old places, rarely thread by men. The fact we ran into one was, to put it simply…"

"The worst of luck?" Merki added.

Axel nodded. Gerard walked over to them then and stared at Locke. He looked deep into his face, breathing heavily, for much longer than was comfortable, and Axel feared the thoughts he might be having.

"Who was hurt the least in the battle?" He asked.

Leord stood up. "Me, sir."

"You've got first watch. Make sure nothing else creeps up on us… and keep an eye out on the Chosen while you're at it."

"Aye, sir." Leord said, hefting his crossbow in his hands.

"Tomorrow we set out at first light. We ride for Rockpour as fast as we can and leave all this… madness behind. Maybe we can get him a proper healer there." He said, nodding towards Locke. Then, he looked at Axel and Merki with nothing but pure hatred in his eyes. Axel looked away, but Merki held the big man's gaze. If he was trying to say something with his eyes, Merki wanted to make sure she did as well.

"I'm going to sleep," Gerard finally said. "Jarrie will have second watch, then wake me up for last." The soldiers nodded, and Gerard limped back to his bedroll. He spared a look towards Ourg's mangled upper half, then shook his head. Then he looked at Kade, who'd been tied back to a tree, and was intently and silently watching everything that happened.

You better be worth it, you big, damned bastard, Gerard thought. Then he lied down to sleep; his daggers clearly visible at his side.

CHAPTER 14

A Moment's Rest

Right after dawn, they buried Ourg's body—or what was left of him, on a shallow grave, and held a short funeral for him. They placed his hammer on it, and Axel said a few words—an old prayer to guide Ourg's soul back home first, then to Aether.

Shortly after, they were all on the road. Axel gave Locke the same sleeping tonic he'd been giving Kade, sending him into a deep slumber. He'd used the last of it on Locke, so their Chosen captive was up and awake today. Seeing as Locke had been placed in the back of the small wagon, Kade had been given Ourg's horse to ride, but his hands had been tied behind his back instead of his front so he couldn't take off with the animal if he wanted to. His horse had also been tethered to Gerard's, so it could only follow his lead, and then both Leord and Jarrie had been assigned to ride on either side of him, keeping constant watch. Merki and Axel, along with Rage, rode on the wagon at the back, keeping a much slower pace than usual as to not shake Locke so much.

The tension in the group was palpable. They'd lost one of their men last night, and now their captain was badly hurt and unconscious. Axel was the only one who wasn't tense. He held the reigns of the wagon horse easily, and even seemed to be enjoying the autumn sunshine on his face; taking in the beauty of the colorful trees and little red squirrels that scampered away from the horses as they passed.

Kade suddenly looked back from his horse and stared at the old man over his shoulder. "Are we far from the capital?" He asked.

The unexpected question interrupted Axel's moment of reverie, bringing him back to the present.

"Yes… I believe we are." He looked into Kade's eyes and saw something akin to concern there.

Kade nodded thoughtfully. "Can we really make it there?" He boldly asked.

Jarrie, who was all ears, didn't say anything as he wanted to see where the conversation went. Kade's question, however, stabbed him like a knife, as he'd also been thinking the same thing.

"We most certainly will," Axel said. "We're close to Waterval. Once there, many more soldiers will join our escort. Your passage to the capital is all but assured." Axel said.

Kade nodded. "Alright. As long as we make it." He said.

Jarrie watched him closely, not saying anything. *Does he know what's going to happen to him once he gets there? Aether… he must have one hell of a case of amnesia… or he's one hell of an actor.*

Kade's busy mind was interrupted by Gerard's voice.

"Rockpour is within sight." He announced.

All the horses stopped over a ridge. They could see the village below them, through the trees, a few dozen meters away. A field of grass surrounded the town, keeping the forest away like in most of the villages around these parts of the Kollek kingdom. With Gerard's signal the group started the slow ride down the ridge towards the picturesque mountain village.

After a couple of minutes, the main road took them into the outskirts of Rockpour, and soon after, their convoy was rolling down the main street of the village, drawing the gazes of every villager on its way.

Gerard led the group towards the biggest building in town, and a short, round man with a braided beard and bald head came out to greet them.

"Soldiers of the king!" He said. "Welcome to the humble, loyal village of Rockpour. I am the village ealdorman, Harlon Karst. How can this servant of the king assist you?"

The man's eyes shifted between Gerard, the prisoner he was clearly escorting at the center of the convoy, and the wagon at the back, which seemed to carry a badly wounded man.

Gerard nodded back to the captive.

"We're soldiers of the king's scouting forces on an important mission. We have a captive here with us who needs a room to stay in—preferably one with a sturdy lock and some bars. Do you have a jail here?"

The ealdorman shook his head respectfully. "I'm afraid not, captain. Being so close to the Waterval Pass garrison, we hadn't a need for it. You could secure your prisoner in our lumber shed, out near the sawmill. We have the strongest locks and doors there, and a few of my men can prepare the place for you."

Gerard looked around the small village and located the roof of the sawmill in the distance. He nodded. "That will do. We need it ready for our prisoner as soon as possible."

The man nodded. He called a few of the townsmen, out of the many that had gathered around the novel cavalcade, and sent them to prepare the shed for Gerard."

"There. It should be ready in less than an hour. How else can we serve?"

Gerard looked back towards the wagon. "We… suffered an attack last night during camp. One of our soldiers, the captain of this unit, suffered harsh injuries. Do you have a healer in town?"

The man bowed. "Just the one, but he's very skilled. He often travels to the garrison to help the soldiers there."

"Is he in town right now?"

"He is. I will call upon him immediately. In the meanwhile, why don't you and your group head into the common house? We'll serve you cold drinks and warm food if you haven't eaten."

"That would be excellent. Thank you, master Karst."

"Harlon is fine, my lord."

A Moment's Rest

Gerard smirked at the sound of that. He like the ring of it. He simply nodded.

A few minutes later, a group of Harlon's men had taken the soldier's horses to the only stables in town and secured the wagon to the side of the common house – what passed for an inn around such a small village.

They helped bring Locke inside, to one of the many rooms available for travelers, and set about helping the other soldiers and their escort find suitable accommodations. Gerard took Kade inside the common house, making sure his amethyst binds were tightly on his wrists, and locked him inside a room, using the house's master key to lock him in until the shed was ready for him. Just to be safe, he ordered the windows be boarded up—even if the Chosen would only inhabit the room for an hour.

A few minutes later, one of the village men arrived with the healer, a man by the name of Oolar—old, balding and wearing loose-fitting robes. The healer examined Locke in the small room he'd been placed in, sitting on a stool before his bed. Axel explained what he'd done for him, and the healer then moved to examined Locke's leg, running his fingers gingerly down its length. He also placed a hand on his forehead, another on his neck, very cautiously, and one on his exposed hand and wrist. Gerard and all the other members of the group stood around the man as he worked, watching carefully. Eventually, the healer turned back to them—though mostly Axel, and spoke.

"Your treatment helped stabilize his injury, but he's running a fever. He's very weak. I surmise he must've also broken a few ribs during the incident you mentioned. He'll need rest, fluids, and careful application of one of my special healing salves—which should help the fever. Otherwise... he's very lucky. He'll live."

Most of the crew released pent up breaths of relief.

"How long will he be in bed?" Gerard asked, arms crossed, the perpetual frown on his forehead.

"At least a week. Maybe two. Ideally, though, he'll rest for about a month."

The old soldier pinched his nose and shut his eyes tightly as he sighed. "We don't have that long. Isn't there anything else you can do?"

The healer stared at him from over his small, square spectacles for a moment. "I'm afraid not. As I said, he's lucky to be alive. One of his ribs seems to have lacerated a lung, to say nothing of all his bruises, and his broken leg." He turned towards the rest of the group for a moment. "You said a bear did all this?"

They all looked at each other and then nodded at the man.

"My… I mean… I've never seen injuries like these from a bear before."

"It… was a big bear." Jarrie said, looking down.

"I can only imagine." The healer said. "Your captain will need rest and silence now. Please give him some room. I'll be back to check on him in the evening, and again tomorrow morning."

Gerard sighed, then nodded. "Thank you, healer. You have your king's gratitude."

The old man nodded. "And that's all I require. Especially in these dangerous times. Aether's blessings upon you."

"And you," everyone replied in near unison.

***

A few hours later, the group had all eaten a warm meal, as promised, along with some cold ale (though not too much, as they were all still aware of the possibility of a rebel attack, and Gerard made sure they didn't overdo it). They now sat at one of the tables of the common house's main room, while the village men finished preparing their rooms for the night—or realistically, the few days they'd have to stay until Locke was well enough to travel again.

Jarrie and Leord seemed much more relaxed now after having eaten, and their spirits, dim and fallen since losing Ourg last night, seemed to have picked up ever so slightly. Merki seemed less on edge as well. Axel was just being Axel, occasionally whispering to himself, but otherwise as placid as could be. There weren't any smiles at the table, but neither was there the deathly heaviness that had followed them throughout the whole day.

Gerard, however, felt that something wasn't quite right—even though he couldn't put his finger on it. He ate and drank, mostly in silence, but his eyes kept a constant vigil of the room—and the door to the common house, while also checking on the door to Kade's makeshift prison every once in a while.

Eventually, Merki stood up, intent on taking some food over to Kade. Jarrie accompanied her, wearing a club one of the villagers had given him after losing his spear last night.

Jarrie opened the door to Kade's room with the master key, which Gerard had lent him, club in hand. Kade was inside, looking out a slight gap in the window, which had been thoroughly boarded from the outside, his hands and feet still shackled together.

"Lunch," Merki said to him. The tall man turned to face her, and he nodded.

"Thank you."

She put the plate on a small table in the room and turned to leave, while Jarrie watched from outside the door.

"Hey... Um... Merki?" Kade said. She turned around.

"Yes?"

"You were very brave last night," He continued. "I've never seen anyone fight like you did. Like any of you, really."

She stared at the big man, eyeing him for a moment.

"How could you not? You're a Chosen. Fighting is all a Chosen ever sees, from the moment they're old enough to hold a weapon—whether at Kellum or... in the woods."

Kade sighed, then slid down the wall, ending up with his legs stretched out on the floor in front of him.

"Do you really believe I'm one of those... rebels, they keep mentioning?"

Merki stared at him right in the eyes and held his stare for quite some time. He met her gaze, unflinching.

"I..." She said, momentarily looking away. "I'm not sure what you are." She took a deep breath. "Other than dangerous. I saw you kill those men out there. You were feral."

"I've never done anything like that before." He said. "I swear, I only want to find my brother and take him back home. I... Our mother. She needs us. Needs *him*."

"Your… mother?" Merki asked, and she took an involuntary step into the room. Jarrie, listening from outside half-covered by the door, perked up his ears.

"Yes. I've had glimpses of her during our journey. I know I'm supposed to bring my brother back to her. That much is clear to me."

Merki took a deep breath and assessed the man further. She had no way of knowing if he was telling the truth, and yet… his body language seemed genuine. That could all be part of his rebel training, of course. Wouldn't be the first time a man had lied to her—convinced her he was something he absolutely wasn't.

"What's your mother's name, Kade?" She pried, testing him. Chosen were taken as babies and never told of their families. If Kade responded with a name, he was either lying… or truly not from Kellum at all.

"Lilian." He whispered.

Merki hid her shock and surprise, then asked: "And your brother?"

"My mother didn't get to name him, but… if she had… it would've been Ellyad."

"Ellyad…" Merki mouthed.

Kade perked up. "Do you… know him? Is the name familiar?"

The young woman shook her head. "I'm afraid not."

Kade settled back, looking suitably crestfallen.

"I have to go now." Merki said after a moment.

Kade nodded. "Of course. Thanks for the food."

She nodded, and closed the door. Jarrie locked it tight, then watched her leave the common house. He looked at Gerard, who was already looking at him. The lieutenant nodded towards Merki, and the rookie nodded in acknowledgement. He dropped Gerard the master key and followed after her.

He found her outside near the wagon, washing her face in a washbasin and pouring some of the water to Rage, who she'd ordered to stay outside to keep watch on their things. The dog pranced around her, tail wagging, eager for a drink and some of the food he could smell from inside.

"Soon, boy, soon. I'll get you something to eat soon. I'm so glad you're ok… after everything that's happened." She said, kneeling down to rub his back. "I don't know what I'd do if I lost you." The dog turned on its back in the grass and started wiggling around, begging Merki to rub its pink belly… which she, of course, did.

Jarrie spied her from the corner of the common house, trying his best to stay hidden. He smirked, enjoying the scene.

"That old wolf send you to watch me?" She said, surprising Jarrie, her back to him. "Make sure I don't run into the woods and tell them all the orders the Chosen just revealed to me?"

The rookie soldier chuckled soundlessly to himself and walked closer. He knew what Kade had told her, having heard it too, and unless they were speaking in some kind of code, he knew she was in the clear.

"Just doing my job." He said, hands up in a mock acceptance of defeat.

Merki smirked at him, standing up and leaving Rage to his water bowl. "I know. You're quite the nice one, you know? You should look for something else to do other than the army."

"Too late for that," he said, shrugging.

Merki scoffed. "Yeah… I guess it is."

Jarrie had stopped a few feet away, and now he just looked on as Merki continued to wash her hands and arms, the water glistening off her pale skin. He leaned against the side of the building, arms crossed, and raised an eyebrow.

"What?" She asked.

"You believe him, don't you?" He said.

"Who?"

"The Chosen… Kade."

Merki kept washing, then stood upright and shook her hands over the basin.

"What makes you so sure?" She asked after a moment.

"The way you look at him."

"Hmmm," Merki said, turning to him, crossing her own arms. "You wish I looked at you the same way? That it?"

Jarrie did his best to hide a smirk, and failed. "Nah… I just… I think he's pretty convincing too, is all. I mean… He hasn't given us any trouble since we set out… and he could've run yesterday, but he didn't."

Merki watched the young man with curious eyes. "Don't let Gerard catch you saying that. He'll threaten to behead you, then send your head back home to your family or something horrible like that."

That made Jarrie chuckle. "The lieutenant is… grizzled, sure." He said. "But he's just lived a lot, you know? He killed that thing yesterday. That was *him*. We owe him our lives."

Merki nodded, sighing. "I guess he did. Though… he would've been an asshole kebab if it weren't for Locke."

"That's true," Jarrie added, with another grin.

"You did good too. I… would've been a kebab as well, if you hadn't charged that monster with your spear. Thank you."

Jarrie lowered his eyes. "No need. Just a soldier-to-be doing his duty, ma'am."

That made Merki smile. Actually smile—something Jarrie hadn't seen once in the weeks they'd already spent on the road together. It was a beautiful smile, he saw—the kind that reached the eyes. He was happy to get to see it.

"Well, I appreciate your service, soldier. And… to answer your question… yes. I want to."

That caught Jarrie by surprise. "Uh… what?"

"I want to believe him. Kade."

The young man nodded several times.

"He might be lying to all of us, waiting for a chance to slit our throats and go back running into the woods… and a lot about his story doesn't add up, like how he apparently knows his mother's name, despite being a Chosen… But I don't know. I don't see him being that kind of person."

"Then… what do you think he is?" Jarrie asked.

"One way or the other? Rebel or not?" She said, biting her lower lip.

Jarrie watched her expectantly.

"I think he's really lost."

A Moment's Rest | 181

CHAPTER 15

REBELS

Merki sat at the table in the common house, making new arrows to replace the ones she'd lost the other night.

Jarrie hovered around her, clearly hoping for more conversation, while Leord sat at Gerard's table, maintaining his crossbow and checking his equipment. Gerard sat hunched forward, watching the recruit work and giving him tips, while Axel sat on a corner chair, hidden by shadows. He seemed to have dozed off, but Merki could see him opening his eyes every once in a while, and scanning the room.

"Ahh… here we go," Jarrie said, placing a fresh mug of Ale in front of Merki. "One for the lady, on the house."

Merki looked up at the young man and raised an eyebrow. "I've already had one, thanks."

"You can't handle more than one?" Jarrie asked, an expression of mock surprise on his face.

Merki smirked. "I can handle many more—but your lieutenant over there might not agree." She kept her voice low, but Gerard still heard her and threw her another one of his warm looks.

"Nothing I can do to convince you, then? I already paid for it, you know."

"You mean you put it on the poor villagers' "soldier" tab?" She smirked.

Jarrie shrugged. "Perks of enlistment." He said.

"Thanks… but I really don't want any more. I need a clear mind to fletch these arrows. Otherwise, they won't fly well."

Jarrie nodded, resigned to his fate, then shrugged. "Ah well. More for me, I guess." He sat opposite Merki and took a swig of his ale. "So… the capital, eh?" He said, looking at her very seriously.

Merki pursed her lips and nodded, focused more on her work than on Jarrie.

"Why there? Plenty of other towns and cities in the Kollek lands, if you just wanted to get out of… what was its name? Ah, Halstead."

Merki seemed to ignore him for a moment, putting the finishing touches on an arrow, then moving it to her "ready" pile. She sighed.

"Because it's the farthest away from home I can think of. Most opportunities are there too."

"To do what?"

"To hunt."

"So… you're thinking of joining the guild once you're there?"

Merki got started whittling another arrow from a piece of wood.

"Bigger." She said.

Jarrie thought long and hard for a moment, taking another swig of his ale. "What's bigger than the Hunter's Guild of Kellum?"

Merki spared him a quick sidelong look, then her eyes went back to her knifework on the wood. "The Ranger Corps."

Jarrie's eyes opened wide. "You mean… the royal hunters of the king? You're an ambitious one, aren't you?"

Merki nodded, then smirked. "I'm always more interested in bigger prey." She returned to her whittling.

Jarrie let out a whistle of exclamation. "Big indeed—the Rangers of the king are almost legendary in their feats—best archers in the kingdom hands-down. They say even the Songbird uses them from time to time to scout out enemy territory… and more."

"So I hear." Merki said, her focus still on her current arrow.

"Wow… so… you must be a very good shot, then. I mean… of course you are. You got that thing right in the eye yesterday." He looked at his mug of ale and then back at Merki, then smiled, his cheeks rosy. "The ale must be getting to me."

Merki raised an eyebrow, then allowed herself another slight smirk. "That's… what? Only your second now?"

Jarrie looked suitably embarrassed. "I… yes, but… What's that supposed to mean?"

Merki smiled lightly. "Take it easy, soldier. You'll draw your acting captain's ire if you get hammered."

Jarrie mulled over the words with a very pensative look on his face, lips pursed, head nodding. "Maybe I will… but only because Gerard's watching us. On any other time, I'd easily down five mugs without as much as a hiccup." He said, took another swig as if to confirm his point, then continued. "Anyways, why go to Kellum now, with us? Why not travel there sooner?"

Merki stopped whittling, then put her tools down on the table. Jarrie sat back, noticing the shift in tone.

"I tried. Several times before." She said, her tone definitely heavier than before. "I had to turn back."

Jarrie hesitated for a moment, and considered dropping the topic there and then… the alcohol, however, had already loosened his tongue a bit too much. "What happened?"

"The first time? Bandits. They ambushed me on the road, not two days away from Halstead," she said, her eyes suddenly getting lost in the distance. "There were six men. I killed three, but the others grabbed me, disarmed me, then pinned me down. They beat the pulp out of me… Then they started undressing me."

Jarrie had stopped drinking now. Leord had also stopped maintaining his crossbow, and was staring her way as well. In fact, many of the villagers and patrons in the common room were now attentively listening to her story, she noticed. Despite that, she continued.

"They took off my top… then my trousers… then stopped, as soon as they saw the knife I kept strapped to my leg. I took the

Rebels | 185

opening, pulled my arm free, grabbed the knife and slit the throat of the man pinning me down."

Silence, all across the room. Merki pursed her lips and cast her eyes down in a frown, mulling over the memory.

"What about the other two?" Jarrie asked, eventually.

"They hesitated, seeing their leader grab his throat, the blood spilling through his fingers. So, I took the chance and I pounced on them too. Sunk the knife into the other's chest, all the way down until it *crunched*. Then the last one slammed his club against my back and knocked me down. He was going to finish the job too, but I pulled the dead man's dagger from his belt and stuck it on the last one's leg. Then his throat."

More silence.

"The Kollek lands aren't what they used to be in our fathers' days," she said, picking up her arrow and knife once more. Jarrie watched with slightly parted lips—as did most of the other men in the common room. Gerard even grunted in what Merki thought was his version of a sign of approval. "I barely made it back alive, my horse dead, badly beaten up. Had to walk for two days. Luckily, Axel found me outside of town, passed out, and brought me back. I don't think I would've made it if he hadn't nursed me back to health."

Jarrie looked at the old man, still apparently asleep in his chair at the other end of the large room.

"Wait..." he said. "You said 'the first time' before... You tried to leave again after that?"

Merki smirked. "A year later, yeah."

"W... what happened then?" Jarrie asked, after taking a moment to consider if asking her was a wise thing to do.

Merki simply smiled this time. "The horse I borrowed stumbled on a ditch and buckled me over. I broke a leg."

Jarrie almost sighed with relief. "Oh... I'm... sorry to hear that."

Merki shrugged. "I took that as a sign. I needed to wait for a caravan, or convoy, or any other group large enough to guarantee at least some degree of safety. Halstead being in the middle of nowhere as it was, though, no one came. Until you."

Jarrie nodded, eyes wide, completely overtaken by Merki's story. He held up a finger. "I'll be right back," he said. "I need to take a leak." Then, he got up, the look of shock still in face, and left the room, to several chuckles across the table. Merki smiled to herself and continued whittling wood for her new arrows.

Karst's men entered the common hall then, walked towards Gerard and told him that the lumber shed was ready for Kade. The old soldier stood up and nodded, then made ready to go get the Chosen in his room.

Then, not ten seconds later, Jarrie rushed back inside, his face pale, slamming the door behind him.

Merki jumped in her seat.

"Aether, Jarrie... what's wrong?" Leord asked. "Did the woman's story really haunt you so much you couldn't even piss right?"

He looked at him, then at Gerard. "R-rebels!" He muttered.

The old man looked between him and Leord, who stared back in terror.

"Outside! Coming up the road! R-rebels!"

Gerard stopped in front of Kade's door, and his hand flew towards his new sword, which Harlon had given him after he'd requested new weapons. He crossed the way to the door in a few strides, then opened it just a crack, peering outside. He slammed the door shut, and leaned his head against it.

"God—DAMMIT!"

He looked at Merki, then stared at the door to the room Kade was being held in. The few villagers in the common room all stood up, and started massing up against the back door of the building—near the kitchens.

The ealdorman, Karst, stared at Gerard with utter terror in his face. The old soldier beckoned him over.

"Get outside," he whispered, "and keep them busy. Do *NOT* let them in here, no matter what you do." He growled. "All of you—stay inside. Do *not* leave the building." He told the villagers. "I can't guarantee your protection if you do."

Leord had armed himself and promptly joined Gerard at the door. "How many, sir?"

Rebels | 187

"At least ten of the bastards. Go, go, go!" He told Karst, who nodded almost neurotically, then headed outside.

"A-ah, dear travelers... how can this servant help you this evening?" He heard Karst say outside the door, addressing the group of armed men getting closer to the building by the second.

"They're here for the rebel," Gerard said, looking at Merki. She shook her head frantically, eyes wide. "She must've led them to us. Or the old man. Kill them both before they have a chance to turn on us or announce our presence," he whispered. "Now!"

Merki dashed across the room towards Axel and shook him awake. "Axel! Axel!" She said, looking at the soldiers, who exchange troubled glances, hesitating by the door. The old man woke up and read the scene, instantly realizing something was wrong. Merki had already drawn one of her daggers and was holding it towards the soldiers, standing between them and Axel. Jarrie had already started loading his crossbow.

"We didn't do anything!" She whispered fiercely to them.

"Do it, now! They're almost here!" Gerard whispered to the soldiers. Jarrie shook in place, his knuckles white over the handle of his borrowed club. Leord brought up his crossbow.

Merki looked around frantically, hoping to find something to cover herself and Axel with, trying to think of a way out from the impossible situation. She could see Leord's hesitation--the strain on his face, the beads of sweat coming down his brow, the shaking of the crossbow. He didn't want to do it—but she knew he would do it all the same.

But then, a man's voice rang out from outside.

"Harlon, my friend. We're just passing by on our way to the northern camp. We though to quench our thirst first, and perhaps receive some supplies for the road... if you'd be so kind."

Gerard's eyes widened as large as they could. He looked at the villagers—and their expressions told him everything he needed to know. He realized now why Karst had been so nice and accommodating to them all along—why everyone had been acting so overly lenient... they were working with rebels.

He aimed a sword at them. "Any of you move—any of you shout, or try anything, and you're dead! You hear me?"

"We're not working with them!" One of the men said. "We have no choice but to do as they say!"

Gerard wasn't sure he believed the man.

"What are we going to do?" Jarrie whispered. "It's just three of us, plus the girl. The old man can't fight!"

Gerard frowned heavily, his eyes darting all over, thinking of a plan.

"The element of surprise!" Merki hissed. "They don't know we're here yet. We can gain the jump of them—they aren't expecting a fight!"

Gerard breathed heavily, still frowning. He stared at Merki, at his men. Then at the dozen or so villagers in the corner of the room, who seemed genuinely terrified.

Then he nodded, fiercely.

***

"Ahh, Makon, yes, of course. Ahh… do you mind if I bring the ale out to you?" Harlon Karst said to the man. "You see, we just had an accident inside—a terrible fight. One of the men, ah… vomited all over. The other… defecated all over the floor. It's horrible, just horrible. My men are…"

The leader of the rebel cell never learned what Karst's men were, as the door suddenly exploded behind the fat man and a roaring beast of a man materialized from it, wielding a longsword at the ready. Blinded by the sudden brightness of the light that burst onto the street, he had but a second to react—and he didn't take it. He immediately found himself suspended in the air, his face a mask of surprise and horror, as the old wolf's sword cleaved clean through his gut, then spilled them all over the road.

The other nine men looked at the scene in shock for but a second, then branded their large swords, axes and maces. Immediately, an arrow slammed into one of them, right between the eyes. Then a crossbow bolt hit another in the gut, toppling him to the ground. A blood-curling roar blasted from inside the alehouse then, and five men, counting Jarrie, spilled out onto the street, holding swords, clubs and even hot pokers from the fireplace.

"The people have turned on us!" One of the rebels said before a man pushed a hot fire poker through his throat. Hearing the man's words, and recovering from the surprise attack, the rebels rallied and retaliated, first with another roar of their own, then with swinging steel and iron.

Chaos ensued.

Heads rolled across the streets of Rockpour, both villagers and rebels, and swords clashed in the night as the tired men of the woods suddenly found themselves besieged by their expected allies, and soldiers of the king, no less.

Gerard cut down man after man, the bloodlust overtaking him, while Merki rained down arrow after arrow from atop the building, having climbed a ladder on the back. Jarrie quickly traded his club for one of the rebel swords and swung as well as his father had shown him—which wasn't very well, but still well enough to kill a rebel and hurt another before taking a bad cut to the ribs. He pulled back, holding his wound, as Leord moved in with his sword now, covering his flank and parrying a blow to the side, then thrusting his blade through the man's heart.

"Never knew you could fight like that!" Jarrie said in the brief moment of respite, out of breath.

Leord spoke without looking away from his next foe. "Mandatory noble fencing classes!" He said, then locked swords with another rebel.

"Keep going men, they're almost all dead!" Yelled Gerard, bolstering the soldiers and the few villagers left standing. Eventually, the last of the rebels dropped down, his throat cut wide open by a savage slash from Geralt's blade.

"We did it! They're all dead!" Jarrie yelled.

But then, a blood curdling war cry reverberated through the night—something that sounded like a mix between a man and a monster.

Gerard looked down the road and, to his horror, another group of men was running up towards them, larger than the first... and some rode on horses.

"We're not done yet!" He yelled. "Pikemen up front! Defend Rockpour from the heathens!" A single man wielding a spear stood forward, then another, holding a long fire poker. Then, to Gerard's surprise, Harlon appeared from the other side of the street, rallying a group of about a dozen other men, all wielding proper weapons—though mostly lumber axes.

"For the glory of the High King!" The ealdorman yelled, and the villagers rushed forward, supplementing Gerard's meager forces. The two groups met in front of the common house, and the clashing of steel and wood began once again, fiercer than before.

Merki tried picking out riders from their horses, while the pikemen impaled them on their spears or felled the horses themselves. The rebels were onto them this time, however, having heard the previous skirmish before getting there, and were now fully prepared for the attack. Their terrifying savagery and superior fighting skill started to show through, as they slaughtered villager after villager, cleaving them apart, dancing around them, slicing off their heads. It was utter pandemonium—hell on earth.

Gerard, the soldiers and the villagers of Rockpour all fought for dear life. Then, to make matters worse, a massive man—the size of Kade himself, and wielding a two-handed sword the size of Jarrie, appeared. Where every other rebel was clothed in animal furs, leaves and leather—this man was actually robed in the furs of a Behemoth—the beast's terrible fangs hanging from his neck as a trophy. Gerard took a sharp breath as he beheld the monster heading their way.

"Incoming!!!" He yelled. Then, the giant man spurred his equally massive horse into the fight, dismounted with a leap, and fell upon a villager with his two-handed blade, slicing him clean in half from head to groin. Another swing of the weapon and another village's torso toppled over to the side, cut diagonally in two. The massive man stared down at Gerard and growled—literally growled. Then his eyes flickered upwards, he leaned back, and somehow, with amazing superhuman speed, dodged one of Merki's arrows. He grabbed one of his men's torches then and flung it at Merki, setting the common house's thatch roof on fire.

Gerard heard the young woman yelp, but he couldn't look back to check on her; the beast of a man was heading his way, sword in hand, ready to cleave him in two. The old wolf gripped his longsword tightly with both hands. He knew blocking a hit from the monster's two-hander was impossible—his hand-me-down replacement longsword would break like a twig. No, he'd need to be agile and to strike fast and true—then get the hell out of his way.

While the hellish battle raged all around him, Gerard took a deep breath, yelled his most blood-curdling war cry, then rushed the big man, taunting him into a swing. The man did as he predicted, swinging horizontally, but Gerard was as fast as a jester, and he slid on his knees under the swipe, came up, slashed the giant across his exposed leg—which was as thick as a tree trunk, then bounced back to his feet behind the man, leaping away just in time to avoid another massive diagonal swing from the rebel.

He dodged another, then another, then sliced the man's waist, drawing a thin curtain of blood—not deep enough to truly hurt him, he knew. The man, on his side, was surprisingly fast and agile, swinging his weapon faster than any man had any right to. As he fought him closer, Gerard noticed, too late, that the man was… of course, a Chosen. One of the so-called Musal—if he was correct, which explained how he could swing the massive blade around like it was made of feathers.

So… this is how I die, he thought, realizing he didn't stand a chance against a Chosen.

Still, if he died, he would go down fighting. And fight he did, dodging, slicing, dodging, cutting, weaving in and out of range, and doing his best to keep up with the giant in front of him, while the villagers and soldiers fought off the other men. The rebels were superior fighters without a doubt… but they were only a dozen against several dozen villagers. The men of Rockpour were winning the fight by sheer numbers alone—but Gerard knew, unless they somehow managed to kill this Chosen, the whole village was done for—there was simply no way any number of untrained villagers could face off against a battle-trained Chosen--especially a Musal, which were rumored to be able take down a house with their bare hands alone. No, the Chosen had to die for there to be any hope for the people of Rockpour. However, his superior reflexes, speed and strength made that more and more unlikely with each passing heartbeat.

Suddenly, Gerard realized, with a pang of anger and shame, that his only hope resided in a room inside the burning common house—shackled in amethyst cuffs.

Amethyst.

"We need amethyst!" Gerard yelled to the people around him, while making some distance from the Chosen giant. "We need amethyst *now!*"

"No amethyst, sir!" Said one of the townsfolk, fighting near him. "Not in town! Aghck!" He got cut down by a rebel axe and crumpled down on the ground with a bloody, wet grunt.

Dammit!

Gerard continued to dance with the Chosen beast, but his stamina was quickly running out, while his foe's only seemed to grow. He knew he was running out of time and considered, just for a moment, running back inside and slicing the cuffs off of Kade—that is, if the poor bastard hadn't burnt to a crisp already. Then he checked himself—he must be mad to consider such a thing. Under no circumstance could that rebel scum be let loose—not even to save his life from the flames. He was just as much a threat as the thing before him right now, if not worse—if what the girl had told of his abilities was to be believed.

No, Gerard would need to find a way to fend off this impossible threat on his own, or die trying.

He was still entertaining that though when the massive hulk of a man knocked his sword away with a surprise flat-sided bash of his blade, then grabbed him by the throat, lifting him up in the air. The lieutenant kicked and struggled, feeling the pressure crushing him more and more, making his eyes and veins pop out. He drew two of his blades and started to jab the Chosen's thick arms with it, again and again, but the man didn't falter. He stared at Gerard with hatred and disdain—not just towards him, but for everything he represented, as a man of the king. Soon, the pressure around Gerard's throat was so great, his head began to pound like a hammer, his eyes rolled to the back of his head, and his hands dropped the knives. He went limp, convulsing, choking, about to break, as the world went black…

…when out of nowhere, another force slammed into the Chosen and sent him flying clean across the street, and onto an adjacent house. The house exploded in a cloud of dust and wood upon impact, instantly collapsing upon itself.

Gerard fell limp to the ground, numb and nearly dead. He could hear his own rasping coughs as the blood slowly returned to his brain and his vision focused. When it did, the sight he saw both terrified and relieved him. Kade, the Chosen scum himself, was standing over him, his body swollen almost as much as the other Chosen, his eyes white with rage.

He wasn't wearing the amethyst cuffs anymore. Gerard drew enough energy to whisper a weak "fuck," then passed out.

***

Kade saw only red.

A few minutes ago he'd been in his room, locked up, confused by the commotion outside, when suddenly, it began to get very hot. He soon saw the flames licking the ceiling, the wooden beams starting to groan and splinter, and he knew he was dead unless he did something.

He got up and threw himself against the door as best as he could, which wasn't very hard, as his feet were still bound at the ankles.

I can't die here! He said to himself. *I need to find him! I need to bring him back home—for her!*

He threw himself against the door again, making it rumble. It didn't open. The lock was sturdier than it seemed—or he was just too weak to break it. He yelled at the top of his lungs.

"Axel! Merki! Heeeelp!"

No answer. He tried again, bashing his shoulder against the door, but no dice. A ceiling beam fell from the roof and landed on top of his bed, setting it on fire. He yelped, then tried the window. Grabbing a nearby chair, he slammed it against the window and broke it—but try as he did, he couldn't break through the wooden barricade beyond them. He panicked.

"HELP!" He yelled once more, then got on his knees, as the small room began to fill with smoke.

"I can't die here... I can't die!" he told himself, over and over. "I see the sun... I see the sun, and its light guides me!" He prayed, eyes closed, now on his stomach, trying to escape the deadly gas that slowly filled the room.

He started coughing, trying to keep himself alive and breathing, when the door's lock suddenly clicked open and it swung away from him, revealing Merki and Axel on the other side.

"Kade!" Axel said. They dragged him out of the burning room just in time, as another ceiling beam fell across the room, landing where his legs had just been.

"We need you Kade—there's another Chosen out there, and he's going to kill us all!" Merki said.

Kade looked at her and Axel like they were mad. Axel nodded. "It's true, my boy. You need to fight now—give yourself to your gift, or we're all dead."

"But I can't control it!" Kade said. "I don't know what *it* even is—this "gift" you keep mentioning!"

Axel and Merki exchanged worried glances. "The Curse, Kade." Axel finally said. "You need to give in to the Curse."

"Wha... but I thought you said..."

"I know what I said," Axel interrupted him. "But you need to do what I say *now*, or we're all going to die—you as well. If that happens, you'll never find your brother—never go back home. Is that what you want?"

Kade looked between them desperately, his eyes pleading. "No, I... No! But I can't just... I can't! Not the Curse!"

"It is not a Curse, Kade. It was your gift, manifesting in you for the first time. Let it in now. You must."

"I... I don't know if I can!"

"For all of us, Kade." Merki said, putting a hand on his shoulder. "Do it for us. Please."

He looked her right in the eyes. "I… Ok, I'll try."

Axel nodded, then said: "One more thing—whatever you do, do *not* touch your forehead to the other Chosen's. Do you understand?"

Kade was about to say something, but before he could, Axel took out a dagger and sliced his cuffs clean off his wrists.

"Good, now go!" The old man said, then both he and Merki got out of the way.

Immediately, Kade felt the same rush he'd felt in the forest—all the sensations. His world turned upside down, the building exploded in all directions, and suddenly, he could hear everything around him—everything outside, in the woods around Rockpour, in the mountains beyond. His ears opened, and he struggled to contain the power surging through him. Suddenly, he focused his senses to the battle outside, and heard each sword blow, each clang of steel against steel, each rip of flesh, squirt of blood and crunch of bone—he heard Gerard choking, dying.

The cacophony of death was too much for him, and his powers burst loose. The bindings on his feet snapped like strings, his body swelled, stretching his clothes… then, with a sudden move, Kade sunk his foot into the floorboards and shot out of the common room like a bolt of lightning—straight for the worst sound of all, the heart of the whole conflict—that of the other Chosen's dark, sadistic laughing.

He hit the man with the force of a hundred speeding boars—sending him crashing through the next house over with a loud bang and crunch.

He ran over to the Chosen and saw him among the rubble of the house. Now, it was him who was choking, gurgling blood. Dying. He was impaled on a large, broken beam of timber—the shaft coming clear through his abdomen, red with his blood. He stared at Kade with shock and surprise—and more than a measure of betrayal in his eyes. They said: *"How could do this to one of your own?"*

Kade held his head in his hands, looking at the fruit of his actions, then screamed—a roar just like the one the Chosen had bellowed before—a monster, and not a man. He was about to lose himself to his powers again, go fully feral, just like he had back at the woods near Halstead... when a cooling sensation washed all over him, clearing his senses, bringing the world back into focus, and drowning out the sounds of death all around him.

Axel was standing behind him, pressing two amethysts against his back with his palms. Kade's muscles went back to their usual size, and the man knelt on the ground, soothed, calm, sleepy. Axel placed both of the amethysts next to his neck—his arteries, and the power of the stones touched his very essence, seeped into his blood... and knocked him clean out.

With Kade pacified, Axel looked around. The rebels were all dead, lying in pools of blood along the main street of Rockpour. The villagers had won.

The battle for Rockpour was over.

CHAPTER 16

IMPERATION DAY

Gerard opened his eyes slowly.

He was in a clean room, lying on a bed, and he noticed his wounds had been bandaged. Stiffly, he tried to get up, and noticed a sharp ache in his neck. He groaned, but sat up all the same. How had he survived? The last thing he remembered was that massive Chosen rebel, crushing him, standing over him and…

… Oh no.

Gerard jumped out of the bed and limped as best as he could outside the room. He noticed many other beds and cots set out across the floor of the house—a temporary infirmary, full of injured villagers wrapped in bloody bandages.

Gerard looked around the place. He didn't see any of his men—or the Chosen Kade. His heart hammered in his chest. He walked outside into the broad daylight, shielding his eyes from the sudden brightness, and soon saw Axel, the old man, walking around town, collecting grasses and plants.

"Old man!" Gerard yelled, walking towards him. Axel perked up at the sound, looked his way.

"Lieutenant! You're up and well, I see! The herbs must've worked faster than…"

Gerard grabbed him by the cuff of his shirt and pulled him up real close. "Where the hell is the Chosen? Was it you who let him loose?"

Axel looked to his left, down the village's main road, and nodded. Gerard followed his eyes… and in the horror of what he saw, he fully released the old man's shirt.

"By the gods."

Kade was walking along with some villagers, holding a pile of broken wood and debris on his shoulder—helping with the cleanup of yesterday's attack. Instead of cuffs, the Chosen was wearing a quickly-fashioned necklace holding two big amethysts around his neck—and he was smiling as he talked with some children.

Gerard almost fainted.

"How did… how can you…" Gerard was at a loss for words.

"With all due respect, lieutenant…" Axel began. "The young Chosen saved your life yesterday… And most of the villagers' as well. He's been working all morning to help them put out fires, bring injured to the sick house and remove debris from the ruins of the common house. The people have taken quite a liking to him."

Gerard stammered, putting a hand to his forehead. "I… But he's…"

"If he'd been a rebel, he would've joined the group that attacked us yesterday, lieutenant. He's had plenty of chances to escape by now. He's chosen to stay and help—as well as wait for you and the others. He seems dead set on travelling to Kellum with you."

"I… I can't… This is madness. Where are the others?" Gerard asked him. "Where's Locke? Did anything happen to him?"

"The captain is fine. Merki and I got him out of the burning common house, with the help of some villagers, and secured him in a house not far from here. He slept through the attack—but I heard he woke up this morning. His fever seems to have died down. Why don't you go see him?"

"Where is he?"

Axel pointed the way.

"And the rest of the men?"

"Alive. Jarrie suffered a bad wound, but is recovering in the sick house. Leord only suffered minor injuries, and should be somewhere in town, helping the injured."

Gerard took a deep breath and nodded. "That's good. That's good. Keep an eye on him, old man," he added, pointing towards Kade. "Do *not* let him out of your sight." Axel nodded, then Gerard headed towards the house he'd pointed out, leaving the old man behind, staring after him.

"You should've waited a bit longer to help the Chosen," said Axel's inner voice. *"Just a few seconds longer, and the other Chosen would've crushed that sourpuss' neck like a twig. Saved us all a lot of trouble."*

That is not our way, Axel said to himself. *Now shut up and help me look for more yarrow for the villagers.*

***

Gerard entered the house—which turned out to be ealdorman Karst's home, and found Locke sitting in a couch in the living room, the hunter girl at his side.

"Gerard!" Locke said, from beneath his many bandages. "You're alive!"

The old wolf nodded, then looked around the room. The ealdorman was there giving orders to some of his men and, as soon as he saw him, he walked over to him and bowed.

"Good soldier. Thank merciful Aether you're alright."

Gerard nodded. "Karst," he said.

"Merki told me what happened yesterday, Gerard. Aether… we must have the worst luck out of any unit in the whole Kollek kingdom. First the Beh…" He saw the warning in Gerard's eyes, then hesitated. "The *bear* attack," Locke corrected. "And now rebels!"

Harlon Karst lowered his eyes to the wood panels of his home.

"I'm afraid I owe you all an explanation… and an apology," he said.

"You're damn right you do. You were harboring rebels here all this time? Helping them? What in the seven hells were you thinking?!" Gerard said, then regretted raising his tone as a sharp jolt of pain ran up his stiff, swollen neck. He flinched and rubbed a hand over it.

"We didn't have a choice, my lord," Karst said. "The… bear, or rather, the *Behemoth* you faced," he said, and all eyes perked up towards him. "It appeared in these mountains a few months ago. We requested

Imperation Day | 201

help from the Waterval garrison, but the soldiers there…" He looked at Gerard, then shook his head. "They weren't as brave as you. They told us they couldn't deal with something like a Behemoth, that they didn't have troops to spare for such a risky hunt."

The cowards… Thought Gerard.

"That… thing, that beast, posed a danger to our very existence, to our very way of life. Left unchecked, it would've wiped us out—completely destroyed our village. So, when that group of rebels first passed by, and we saw they were mostly Braves—warriors of their highest caliber, we begged them for help. You see, there wasn't just *one* Behemoth here at first, but two. A pair. Left to their devices, they would've reproduced, and this whole region, this whole area, would've become uninhabitable. We offered them sanctuary and supplies, in exchange for their service in dealing with the beasts… Especially after we saw they had a Chosen among them—one of those strong ones."

Gerard grimaced, then unconsciously rubbed his sore throat. Karsts hesitated for a moment, then continued.

"And they helped us. They killed one of the beasts and pushed the other one back, further away into the mountains. They promised they would come back for it at a later time… but then, due to having lost many men in their first hunt, they began to lean into our favors. Ask more and more of us… Never too much, but obviously, they felt we owed them, and took their time exacting payment for their services. Because of the surviving Behemoth, the soldiers from Waterval seldom came down here anymore or patrolled the area either, so the rebels decided to… take their time dealing with it. We were at their mercy."

Gerard took a deep breath, then looked around the room. The villagers there all cast down their eyes. Locke met Gerard's gaze and nodded.

"They made the right choice when it counted the most," Locke said.

Gerard sighed. "I suppose you did," he said, looking back at Karst. "How many men did you lose yesterday?"

Karst lowered his eyes again. "Too many. More than half the men in the village."

Gerard nodded. "Then you've paid enough for your mistake. We will not report this transgression against your king and country to the authorities... and will instead ask for aid when we get to the garrison. You will be remembered as heroes who fought against the rebels and struck a decisive blow against their ranks."

Karst bowed, as did the other villagers. "Thank you, my lord. You do us too much honor. We shall keep you and your men in our prayers during the incoming Imperation Day ceremonies."

Gerard frowned—something the ealdorman wasn't expecting. Then, a look of horror overcame his features and he looked at Locke, only to find the same look in his face.

"By Aether's grace... Imperation Day is this year." Locke whispered. "How long have we been out here in the mountains, Gerard?"

"About three months... Give or take." The old man mouthed; his eyes lost in thought.

"How far away is the holy day?" Locke asked the ealdorman.

"About a fortnight, at the full moon, I believe."

"Goddammit..." Said Gerard.

Merki looked between the two men, a look of confusion on her dirtied and tired face.

"Imperation Day? Is that the holy celebration where the king speaks to Aether? What's the issue?"

"You don't observe Imperation Day back in Halstead?" Locke asked her, almost shocked.

Merki frowned, then shrugged. "I'm sure they do... but I've never been very devout. The villagers observe so many traditions and holidays, it's hard to keep track of them."

"Once, every ten years," Locke began, "The kings of all the Kollek lands gather in the holy city of Kellum. The High King himself enters the Great Aetheliour—the grand temple of Aether, and prays inside for a week, communing with our god, receiving guidance and wisdom for the next decade. It's the most holy, important event in Kollek culture... you should know of it." He told Merki.

Again, she shrugged. "I know of it, but I'm not sure I get why you're so worried. What's the problem? It's just another holiday, isn't it?"

"Just another holiday..." Gerard began, then stopped, as Locke held up a hand.

"The holiday lasts a whole week," Locke explained. "During that time, every city, every town, every garrison, closes their gates. The people hide inside in an act of devotion mirroring the king's actions and pray for him, for the Kollek, and the world. Soldiers stay inside the towns and garrisons—all patrols are called back. The roads..."

"... Become much more dangerous." Merki finished for him. "My god... We have less than a month to get to Kellum, then." She said.

"Indeed."

"But wait..." She added, frowning. "Can't we just make it to Waterval, then wait the festivities out there? What's the problem? I mean—half of us are hurt anyways... it wouldn't hurt to spend some time to recover."

Gerard scoffed, then shook his head. "You're a real backwater yodel, aren't you? I'm almost ashamed I thought you smart enough to be one of the Sons."

Merki frowned at the big man, and Locke held up another hand.

"It's not that simple. You see, after the Imperation Day ceremonies are observed comes the month of fasting and prayer—where the people purify themselves to receive Aether's guidance, as spoken to our king."

Merki still didn't get it. "So?"

"They purify themselves with amethysts." Gerard said. "Which means that every garrison sends most of their stock to the capital—keeping only what they need for binds and weapons. Waterval isn't that big a garrison. They'll likely only have a handful of the stones left... if any at all."

Understanding was starting to dawn on Merki's eyes. "There'll be an amethyst shortage. And Kade needs amethysts."

"Correct," said Locke. "Our big friend has some on him now... but they'll run out of power way before we can replenish our stock. Even if we make it to Waterval, it's unlikely they'll have enough to keep him under control for a whole month."

Merki bit her lower lip, thinking.

"So... what? We're better off rushing towards the capital instead of getting Kade to Waterval now?"

"More likely to another garrison, a bigger, more central one." Locke said.

"And where is the closest one?"

"The city of Alladon. About two weeks' ride away—if we're fast."

Merki looked between Gerard and Locke. "But Locke... your leg. You'll have to stay behind."

The young captain shook his head. "It's alright. I can ride."

Gerard let out a long sigh. The tension in the room became palpable.

"No... You can't, captain. Not fast enough," Gerard said. "We'll have to go ahead and escort the Chosen without you."

Locke held Gerard's gaze for a long time. "That's not going to happen, Gerard. If you present Kade without me, I'll... I won't..."

Merki saw his troubled expression. *I won't get the recognition for it*, it said. *The catch, and all the honor tied to it, will go to you.*

If Gerard was thinking the same thing, he didn't show it. "Well, we can't leave him here—and Waterval might be a pointless detour. What other choice do we have?"

"I'll go with you. We'll ride a little slower... but we'll make it."

Gerard sighed, then pinched his nose as he habitually did. "But we won't!" He exploded. "We'll be late for the festivities, then get locked out! You know what happens to soldiers who get locked out, Locke. We'll get *butchered* out there!"

Karst had been following the discussion closely, looking between one man and the other, but now, seeing which way the wind was blowing, he politely excused himself and left the house, taking the other villagers with him.

The captain looked at his older, wiser lieutenant... and to Merki's horror, she saw the look in his eyes. He knew Gerard was speaking the truth.

And yet, he didn't relent. "I can't stay back, Gerard. That Chosen—Kade—he's the key to regaining my father's respect. My family honor. I can't let that happen."

"And you'd risk all our lives in the process? You'd have us risk dying out there on the road?"

"We won't die. I'll ride on the wagon… and we'll prop my leg up with straw or something. It'll be fine. We'll make it."

"No, captain… We'll get stranded in the middle of the road and get butchered by the scores of bandits, rebels and other filth that come out, looking for *exactly* this kind of opportunity." Gerard said, frowning, seething with barely contained anger.

"We'll *make* it." Said Locke, looking away from him, then back.

The two men looked at each other for a long time.

"You'll get us all killed… and you don't even care." Gerard finally said, shaking his head in disbelief. Then: "Fine. Have it your way. We'll set out at midday today."

He turned on his heels and left the house, slamming the door behind him.

Locke stared after him and sighed. "We'll make it." He said. "We will. We have to."

However, Merki could tell, plain as day… he didn't believe the words any more than Gerard did.

CHAPTER 17

THE LORD OF THE SLUMS

Efilia slowly awoke in Odmund's bed, enjoying being naked under the soft blankets in the morning breeze.

The first light of the sun lit the perfectly engraved cupboard in Odmund's chamber. Aside from the main door, there was another room in his chamber which opened to his bathroom. That was one of the perks of being the Kollek champion: he had a little of everything to call his own.

However, for a man with so many privileges, Odmund was a very plain person at heart, just like his room. The room given to him was spacious, but not as big as Ifir's, for example, or the coin master's chambers. Efilia had seen Fermand's chamber once and she could still remember the golden statues, which gleamed like the sun when the light hit them right. In Odmund's room, the only fancy things were the championship medals that King Ulor had given him. Efilia loved Odmund's room anyway, as it was bigger than hers, and allowed so much sunlight in. She smiled and turned to give a kiss to Odmund in bed as he slept, but immediately realized something was wrong with him; his face was wet and clammy with sweat and his legs were twitching and moving, as if he were fighting some unseen force in his dreams. His palms were closed, but Efilia could see small flames escaping from between his fingers. Suddenly, the flames leapt to the bedsheets and the whole bed caught on fire.

"Aaaah!" Efilia screamed and jumped out of bed.

Her scream woke Odmund up and he threw himself out of the burning bed as well.

"What the hell?" He said, and they both went to work, trying to put the fire out with the pillows.

Somehow, they managed it, then sat near the end of the bed, still naked, with burnt pillows in their hands. They silently watched the rising sun through the window in front of them. Efilia's hand grabbed Odmund's and held it tight, then she looked at him.

"What's wrong Od? That must've been some horrible nightmare you were having."

He didn't look at her, so she insisted.

"Is it about the boy?"

"No," he finally said. "Not this time."

"Then?"

"What I saw back in Outer Silence before."

"The slavers?" Efilia's eyes popped up.

"Yeah… I have to find them, Lia. We can't allow anyone to go around selling Kollek people as slaves anymore. Not as long as us Chosen live and breathe." The anger in his voice stoked the fires in Lia's heart too.

"I'm sure you'll find those responsible. Our people might've been slaves to the other races long ago, in the times of the Cursed King and his reign, but not anymore—not since Aether gifted us Chosen to the Kollek." Efilia held his hand tighter.

"I will solve this if it's the last thing I do. We can't go back to those times, Lia. Our people have come too far."

"And I'll help." She said, then put her head on his shoulder. He then hugged her, not caring about the burnt bed behind them.

***

Two floors up from Odmund's chamber, Ifir took a sip from her herbal tea and let her thoughts take her to the festival of colors on display in the sky. The sun was about to rise; the most beautiful period of the day that could be seen from her room.

Mere's sleepy eyes resisted the lure of unconsciousness, of the deep sleep she desperately needed at that moment. Her deep desire to sleep without nightmares grew in her like a torn in the spring. However, life hadn't been so kind to her for a while now. If Ifir wasn't the one giving her bad dreams, then her niece's scarred face hunted her down in her sleep. Although she hadn't seen her for a week now, her ghost was still there in her room. Because of this, she was happier to be here, working, than back there, with the nightmares.

Ifir, on the other hand, enjoyed her warm drink as she watched the autumn sunrise. She didn't care what situation Mere was in, as always. As was their way, Ifir did as she pleased, while Mere took up the burden. That was the ultimate duty of being a maid: Forgetting yourself and putting your master before everything you knew, wanted or felt.

The sudden knock on the door made Ifir almost jump on her seat. She instinctively held her stomach. Mere's sleepy eyes suddenly flew wide open.

"Come in." Ifir said and Mere ran to open the door.

In entered Josiah, the coordinator of the castle: the man above all the butlers and maids. His once-dark hair had brightened into a mane of silvery white, as he'd turned sixty last year. His light-brown eyes were brighter than a cloudless day, and his hands contained two opposite phenomena not found in this world of servants: they were both clean and strong. He was the only man Mere knew who didn't need to get his hands dirty to stay strong.

Mere's eyes shone when she saw him. His smell was fresher and sharper than that of the royal rose gardens, but entertaining fantasies around him was as dangerous as being in the Direhalls beneath the castle, she knew. That was what he meant to Mere: an unreachable peak. An untouchable core that cauterized her heart.

She greeted him with a bow.

"Good morning, Meredith." Josiah greeted Mere in a low voice, careful and respectful as to not disturb Ifir.

His silky voice comforted Mere's soul.

"Good morning, my lady, Songbird." He saluted Ifir.

"Inform me." She ordered.

Josiah laced his fingers under his abdomen.

"We are almost ready for the Imperation Day ceremonies, Songbird. The rooms of the kings and queens are cleaned and prepared. Queen Karmen's flowers are ready to be cut as soon as she arrives. Six hundred sheep and two hundred-fifty goats are ready in the slaughterhouse. And, as you ordered, King Hourak's chamber will be next to his ex-wife Queen Karmen."

"Good." Ifir smiled. "Don't forget Karmen likes blue silk bed covers and pink flowers." Ifir added.

"They are all prepared as per your orders, Songbird." Josiah confirmed.

"What about King Derkel?"

"I have arranged ten blonde girls, ages between sixteen to twenty. We also bought thirty gallons of pink rose wine from Karte island just for him along with sour green grapes."

"Perfect, Josiah, perfect." Ifir signaled him to come closer with her index finger. The man came next to her and bent to hear her better.

"What about the clerk holes?" She asked in low voice.

"They are all ready, Songbird. Even our men can't tell where they are."

"Excellent," Ifir announced with joy. She then stood up so suddenly, Josiah stumbled back a step, as to not to bump into her.

Mere instinctively moved to hold him as he did, but before she stepped out, he managed to stand straight. Ifir walked out to her balcony with a dubious smile on her face.

"You can leave." She ordered. Josiah bent his head and walked back to the door. While passing by Mere, he smiled and nodded at her. His white teeth and well-shaped lips took Mere under their spell, so she smiled back.

After he left, Ifir took few more breaths of fresh air into her lungs and enjoyed the morning light for a little while longer, then headed back inside.

"Love is nothing but a liability, Mere." She said. Then ordered: "The cloak." The maid froze for a second, as she processed Ifir's words. "The cloak." Ifir repeated, louder this time. Mere ran over and grabbed Ifir's black cloak—one with a hood, which ensured nobody could recognize Ifir when she wore it, and put it on her. The coat, Mere knew, meant Ifir had some dirty business to take care of.

Mere didn't follow her, but stared into the emptiness instead. Watching her broken dreams dance with the life she once hoped she could have.

Ifir left the room, then stopped at the middle of the corridor going to the stairs. She made sure nobody was in sight, then pulled a stone to open a secret door to an old staircase, which was full of spiderwebs. She lit up a torch and descended the stone staircase for about twenty minutes.

When she arrived at the bottom of the stairs, she was greeted by a plain, straight tunnel. She kept on walking for another five minutes until she reached an intersection in the tunnel, then immediately turned left and kept walking in the dark, lit only by the flickering torch. The rats ran around her, hoping to escape the light of her flame. She didn't care if she stepped on them or not, as the leather boots she wore were high and thick enough to protect her from any bites or scratches.

Before she reached the end of the tunnel, she took a right turn on another intersection, then another left, and walked straight for another few more minutes. Eventually, she reached a stone wall. She pulled a little stone there to open a hole, which let her see outside. She was just under the city center. The narrow street before her, she saw, was empty, so she pulled the stone gate to open it and climbed up, then closed it back again. She was right behind Gorin's Temple: a small building within a very small community, in the poorest street this side of the city. The temple would've already been turned into a whorehouse, or been completely abandoned, had Ifir not personally funded it for many years just to keep her secret tunnel safe.

She walked through the street outside and when she came to the corner she found herself in a completely empty street. The heavy smell of blood covered the alleyways and cobblestones here. Ifir stepped over a bloodstain, then headed towards the exit of the dark alleyway. A moment later, she came out into a flood of people. She was in the middle of one of the largest markets in the city; the booths full of fresh vegetables and spices everywhere. There were so many men and women shopping, fighting over prices, and poor children crying due to the crowds and noise. Ifir hated that place with all her heart; hated how it smelled like nothing but sweat and dirt. She elbowed her way across the folks and reached Fran Square, located at the west end of the city. After two more streets, she found herself walking along the city walls, in the Outer Silence district, right before the place she sought. Here, a few people were laying in the shadows of the trees, hiding from the sun which hurt their bodies. She could sense the sickness growing in them, the death that was about to take their soul from their bodies, which were nothing but skin and bones by now. The sound of their breathing faded in her ears.

Children and women sat on the sidewalks in front of the old, wrecked houses. Seeing Ifir approaching, a boy ran up to her, without recognizing her.

"Please help us, my lady. Would you honor us with a coin? We're so hungry… Please, my lady." His voice slowed Ifir down—but it wasn't enough to stop her. She hid herself more, bent her head not to be seen, and started walking faster. The skinny, malnourished boy followed her for few more steps, but eventually, his weak legs couldn't do more.

After passing few more houses, she eventually reached a house with two floors. It was the only house which seemed like a normal home, rather than a decrepit ruin. It belonged, she knew, to the most respected man of the area: Derum Shine. He was a man who kept to himself, and who was known only by the poor of the city… and smugglers.

Ifir knocked the door and a half-naked young girl opened it. She seemed like she'd just gotten out of bed.

"Yes?" She asked with half opened eyes. Ifir pushed her away and made her own way inside. The door opened to a yard full of flowers and weeds. The inside of the house looked as if a wild party had taken place here just a few hours ago. There were empty glasses, discarded undergarments and food everywhere. A few small boys and girls were eating the leftovers. They ran to hide upon seeing the intimidating stranger robed in black arrive. Ifir knew that they were still watching her from their hiding places as she walked past them.

"Derum!" Ifir shouted.

A minute later, a man who was trying to pull his trousers up ran out of a room from the second floor, to the laughter of some of the girls from downstairs. He looked down from the indoor balcony circling the first room, and noticing the black cloak, ran down the stairs as fast as he could. He had a well-built body, dark-brown hair and dark eyes that seemed sharper than any sword. His tanned skin was smooth, and his six-pack adorned with ornate tattoos.

He stopped in front of Ifir and looked at her long enough to recognize her green eyes, then suddenly shouted as loud as he could.

"Everybody out!"

All of his "guest" ran into the rooms both downstairs and upstairs, to leave the master and his guest alone.

As soon as they were alone, Ifir removed her hood. Her face shone under the little sunlight that got in through the roof of the yard.

"Welcome, my queen!" He opened his arms to Ifir.

"Hello again, my old friend." Ifir hugged him.

"It's been while. I almost missed you, my beauty." He said. Ifir laughed at him.

"I don't think you ever find the time to miss anyone, Derum." She said, looking at all the lady clothes on the floor around them.

"Ah… but you are not just anyone, my queen. You are like a winter rose for men like me. We can only imagine your beauty; never smell it, never fully partake of its riches." Derum said with a smile.

The Lord of the Slums | 213

"Oh, enough Derum… Cut it short." Ifir playfully said, looking like a flirty eighteen-year-old. Derum could see how much she liked the words he spoke, however.

"As you wish, my queen." He obeyed.

"I've known you since I was a child, Derum, and you haven't changed a bit. Always sweet… but oh so dangerous." Ifir said, touching his cheek. As her fingers slipped on his face, Derum closed his eyes and took a deep breath.

Before he woke up from her enchanting touch, she said: "The number of children around your house has increased, I see?" Her fingers reached his shoulder and caressed him. Was she really looking for a straight answer? Now? Derum searched her eyes, but couldn't find any answers, so he just pursed his lips.

"Let's go upstairs then, shall we?" Ifir said. "We have things to do." Her voice was softer than her touch, her words hotter than a summer day, so Derum followed her upstairs.

As they reached the roof, Derum opened the door for her. The roof of the house had three parts: the right corner had a small room, like an office, while the left side was full of bird cages. The rest of the roof was open to the sky and full of water and feed for the birds that walked or slept on it. Derum was the only bird trainer in Kellum, aside from the ones in the castle, and only served a few elite people in the city. He trained his birds to fly different routes, as they were the fastest communication agents in the world. The hardest routes to fly were the islands, however. Every time Derum sailed to them, he tied sticks with sharp needles on his birds, urging them to fly along with the ship all the way back and forth. Every time he traveled, only a few of the birds learned the route, as most of them died on the first day. He had so many birds for so many different routes, and yet, nobody would've ever guessed that his roof was full of birds from the outside, as they never flew over the house. That was the first lesson they got: to never reveal the home of their master.

"I really admire what you do here, Derum." Ifir said. "And you know me—I admire so few things in life."

Derum smiled enough to show his white teeth.

"Thank you, my queen. I am flattered." He said and opened the door of the small room on the roof.

Ifir walked in. The room had a big library, full of books and rolled maps. On the other side of the room was a desk.

"You keep on writing poems." Ifir said to Derum, touching the leather notebooks on the desk.

"I do. I am a true romantic." He said by coming close to her.

"Indeed you are." Ifir smiled. Her fingers moved around his body as she walked into the room. "And I need you to send a romantic message on my behalf." She said with an impish smirk. Derum laughed at her.

"Romantic massage? From my queen?" Derum rolled his eyes with a naughty smirk of his own. "Dirty, dirty games of yours. You never get tired, do you?" Derum asked.

"I learned from the best. And as you told me, only two types of people never give up: those who always win, and those who have nothing to lose. I am both." Ifir said, by touching his chest with her finger. She came so close to him that her breath swept him off his feet. Derum held her hand as she touched him, then pulled her to himself. He whispered to her ear.

"And you know I'm always right." As she was about to step back, he pulled her back.

"But the day you tire of all these games of yours… know that I'll be there to receive you in my arms." His lips were about to touch Ifir's fleshy red lips.

Ifir smiled, trying to suppress the strong desire in her. Her swelled chest touched his naked skin. She held her breath and nodded. However, the moment their eyes met, and their lips were about to feel each other, Derum stepped back. He then he opened a locked drawer from his desk and took out an inkwell and a small, sealed cylinder with a piece of papyrus in it, then passed a pen to Ifir.

"Write, my queen. The room is yours." He said, then walked outside the office as fast as he could, as if the room were on fire.

Ifir took the papyrus out and opened the inkwell. She wrote her words as small as she could.

When the fruits of love complete their ripening period,
The desires will be set free,
Our beloved must see the day effortlessly.

Then she rolled the papyrus and put it in the cylinder.

"Okay. I'm done." She said, and Derum walked next to her to seal the box with melted candle.

"Excellent. Then where shall the bird fly to, my queen?"

"To Ma'Tael."

Derum nodded and they walked out to the roof. He walked to a cage to their left.

"Do you have a special choice?" He asked.

"The fastest."

Derum laughed at her, "Of course, my queen." He extended his hand to the cage and a black bird that looked like a raven settled on his hand.

"This gentleman is the one then." He said, then tied the small cylinder on its leg. He caressed its head then shook his hand to let it fly. Ifir's eyes shone at the sight and Derum was charmed by her beauty one more time.

As the bird flew away, Ifir walked back to the door. At the stairs, she suddenly stopped and extended a bag of coins to Derum.

"You know I never charge you, my lady." He said with a sharp voice, pushing her hand back.

"Not for you. For them." Ifir extended her hand again and looked at a child's shoe on the floor.

Derum nodded this time and took the bag.

"Your heart is brighter than your eyes, my queen." He said. Ifir smiled at him before she left.

"Make sure they are comfortable." She said before she left.

"Only first-class." He said behind her.

As the door closed, Derum clapped his hands. His butler and a score of other servants came out from the rooms they were in. "Let's enjoy ourselves!" Derum said with joy and gave a few coins to the butler. Everyone was smiling happily, and soon, a group of women started to play music with tambourines, flutes and sitars.

Derum's house brightened once more, as everyone returned to their dancing, singing and drinking, completely transforming the mood of the place… and masking any sounds coming from the small agents in the roof as they flapped away on their journeys.

CHAPTER 18

SHADES OF RED

Hugo checked his new, fancy look in the mirror one more time, right before he left his bunk. His hunched back was still there, but somehow, he felt himself as good as if it had never been there. He fixed his hair and made sure it was well-separated from the middle. His well-ironed cotton clothes encouraged him, so he raised his head and left the room like a proud soldier returning from a glorious victory.

Out in the corridor there were so many male servants and cleaners, all walking around. Although nobody really noticed Hugo, he examined them all without missing any of the faces passing him by. Before he arrived at the at the stairs to the upper levels of the castle, he heard a sound like the clicking of a shoe's fine heel. *Click, clock, click, clock ...* He slowed down and waited to see who was passing by.

"Girls, girls, girls…" Hilek, the master jester of the kingdom, shouted to be heard from the hall, right before he entered the gathering room full of maids. There was a chaotic atmosphere in there and Hugo could hear the voices of so many women talking at the same time.

He curiously walked towards the door of the gathering room, adjacent to the stairs, and peeped over the room from the half-open door. There were more or less forty-five girls: the most beautiful village girls of the Kollek kingdom, and they were all talking and laughing. They were so much more beautiful than the usual whores Hugo would see at his previous place of work. Their cheeks were pink, like fresh peaches, and they had very well-shaped bodies, as if engraved by the royal sculptor. For him, however, it was impossible for any woman to feel more real than Loure. He remembered the love in his mother's big eyes when she told to him:

"Perfection isn't for humans, or any other living thing, Hugo. We all have our faults, so the good parts in us can grow more and enlighten our souls. Never forget, son, that if someone seems faultless from the outside, he or she may carry the biggest faults inside—and that kind of fault is the only thing that can stand between us and Aether: the one who loves us the most. You are beautiful and loved as you are, son. Don't look for any other evidence of it, other than in the knowledge that you're a creation of Aether."

The warm hug came right after her words as a true believer. For a second, Hugo wished his faith was as strong as hers.

The girls in the room were all so excited. Hugo could hear two girls talking to each other although he couldn't see their faces.

"Are you a virgin?" One girl asked another.

"Of course I am." Hugo could sense the sarcasm in her voice.

"Me too. I'm so excited… Chosen are so handsome, aren't they? I hope one of them picks me as his mistress."

"That's the dream of all of us, honey." The other one said and walked away from the other girls. Hugo saw her red hair and marble-white skin flash in front of him.

"In line, please!" Hilek shouted again. He was standing in front of Hugo. The boy couldn't clearly see his face, but he noticed how his body was very thin. He also saw he wore a dark-green jacket, colorful trousers and a cotton shirt, along with a hat that seemed like a hunting cap, with a feather and all. No matter how hard he tried, without his uniform or soldiers around him, he couldn't draw the respect of the girls he worked with, especially those who had no idea about his position in the castle. His hands turned red as he tried to clap harder and harder, hoping to be heard among the din and noise in the room.

Seeing no benefit from his current attempts, Hilek walked into the crowd and started to get the girls in line manually.

"In line, in line, in line…" He repeated as he softly pushed them.

"Alright, alright!" A blonde girl with green eyes said, pulling her blue dress and her arm away brusquely. Seeing her disrespect, Hilek suddenly had enough. He lost his calm and let the monster in him show up.

"Enough!" The man yelled. The anger in his voice made Hugo tremble along with the girls. He threw his hat on the floor and his voice changed into that of a roaring lion. All the girls shut up and immediately got in line. Hilek clenched his fists as if he were ready to beat someone to a pulp, and the veins in his thin arms could be seen from the other side of the room. His anger swallowed and blew out the excitement in the room, replacing it with a fear strong enough to make the girls shiver.

"I am Hilek, Master of Jesters, and I am your master from now on. If I say go, you go. If I tell you to fuck, you fuck. If I order you to die… then you die! Do you want to survive here? Then *obey* me!" The fire in his eyes fanned the flames of fear in the girls.

He then turned his back to them, staring at the floor, and walked to the center of the room with his hands tied behind his back. He took a deep breath and raised his head, looking to the ceiling, which was filled with paintings of Aether and the king. He took his green jacket off and threw it at a maid waiting near the door. Seeing him turning, Hugo was panicked and moved aside, hoping to not be noticed. Hilek clapped his hands then turned to the girls. All of a sudden, he was smiling. But it wasn't a normal smile, but the most unnerving, psychotic grin the girls had ever seen.

"Welcome to the castle, girls." He said, grinning from ear to ear. His voice was as thin as a woman's now, and his hand gestures as flowery as a lady's.

"I will be your guiding star in the complicated structure of life in the castle. I can assure you that, as long as you follow my instructions, you will have a wonderful life here as mistresses of the Chosen."

Hilek cleared his throat before he continued, then walked in front of the girls, keeping his beady eyes on them.

"We have strict rules to obey, for your own safety and well-being. Rule number one: Never forget or skip taking the herbs given to you by the herbalist. Those will keep you safe and strong. As you all know, getting pregnant with a Chosen baby will kill you in just a few months, due to the blood poisoning. Never forget that a mother can only give birth to a Chosen if she is picked by Aether; not just because she happened to fuck one." Hilek made an exaggerated face, rolling his eyes to heaven, as if the topic had come up more times than he cared to count in the past.

"Chosen are sacred Kolleks, who are gifted to us by Aether for our king's service… and you are one of the few special girls who are considered worthy enough to serve them. Never forget that they are sacred people, and that you must serve them wholly in soul and flesh."

"Rule number two: never, ever talk in the castle unless you are asked to do so."

"Rule number three: Never *ever* sleep with someone else other than who you are appointed to by me. No girl has the right to pick a Chosen or sleep with two different Chosen, unless I say so."

"Rule number four: Never get fat or ugly. Eww. Finally, any other characteristics you must have will be taught to you in next few days. Hopefully, if you follow these instructions to the letter, you will be ready to serve by the Imperation Day celebrations."

He stopped in the middle of his walk with a disturbing grin on his face, looked at girls, and ordered: "Now be ready for the healer's examination."

The girls looked at him with empty eyes, as they had no idea what to do, so he clapped his hands: "Be naked girls, be naked." He shouted. As the girls took off their clothes, a few middle-aged men walked next to them to examine them from the corner.

As he walked out, Hilek paused next to a healer who had a red and white pointed hat, denoting him as the chief healer of the group. He came closer to him and said: "That blonde with the green eyes… the one next to the blue dress. She will visit Captain Urk tonight."

The healer's eyes became bigger. "But he…"

"A welcome lesson for them all." Hilek interrupted him, and walked to the door without caring for the befuddled looks of the healer. The maid was waiting for him at the door, holding his jacket. As she put it on him, he pinched her old cheek and smiled.

"Thank you, my love, thank you." His voice was all feminine again. Hugo ran as fast as he could and hid on a corner, out of sight. Once Hilek was out of sight, the young boy rushed back to the servant dormitories, in fear of what he'd just seen.

***

Out in the training fields, Efilia was teaching younger Chosen how to fight.

"Hold it up, Fredric." She said as she raised a wooden sword in Fredric's hand, who was training with another Chosen girl. They were both sixteen years old—the new graduates Odmund had addressed recently at the ceremony.

"Good. Now fight." Efilia ordered, and the kids started to fight with their practice weapons, following the forms they'd been taught. Fredric jumped so high that his feet rose almost a meter off the ground and Efilia pursed her lips out of surprise and admiration. She nodded, pacing among them.

Odmund was on the other side of the garden, training another group of young soldiers. His eyes searched for Efilia for a second. Seeing her so devoted to her duty comforted him.

Soon, the ring of the big bell echoed through the yard. All the soldiers stopped their training and got in line.

"Soldiers." Odmund said. "You're all dismissed."

All of the young soldiers said, "Sir, yes, sir," then retired for the night.

Odmund walked to Efilia as fast as he could.

"Champion?" She said in a very coquette tone.

"Lieutenant." Odmund smiled and kissed her on her cheek. All the sixteen-year-olds around them smiled. The girls among them, especially, were big fans of their love story—the best one told in the Chosen army.

"Let's go get some dinner," he said, and Efilia nodded. As they walked among the roses in the garden, the young lieutenant didn't speak at all, but Odmund didn't mind. He was just content being there with her, walking close to her. He kept on planting little kisses on her golden hair along the way.

When they reached the stairs to the castle, they saw a score of very young, very attractive girls leaning out the windows of the second floor.

"Looks like Hilek brought more girls," Efilia said in a sour tone. She frowned as the group of scantily clad girls giggled and waved at Odmund from the windows.

"Yeah, for the Imperation Day celebrations. Ifir wants only the best..." He said, in a tone that implied, *"you know how she is..."*

"Will she make it better by supplying literal whores to the soldiers, though?" Her anger showed through her voice. Although it could be dangerous for anyone else, Odmund found it cute.

"You know... When you get angry like that, your green eyes look like a forest on fire. They get dangerous... and I like it. Very much." He flirted, then kissed her on the forehead. That destroyed any hopes the new girls could have, and they turned their looks away to find another Chosen to flirt with.

The Chosen pair was kissing and playing with each other on the empty corridors as they passed by the sleeping quarters of the other Chosen captains on their way to dinner. Captain Urk, however, Efilia's friend, could hear them behind the closed doors of his room. Being an Acris, he had ears that could hear the sound of a leaf falling from a mile away. Because of that, he couldn't really miss hearing Efilia's voice or laughter—even when she was far from him. Laying on his bed, he listened to Odmund and Efilia's laughter; to their kissing and flirting with each other. Unwillingly, he gripped his pillow and squeezed it hard among his fingers.

Shit, shit, shit…!

The more Efilia giggled, the angrier Urk got. He got up and drank some wine. Tried to tune out the sound of her voice as she walked down the hall, but he just couldn't. Out of all people, out of all sounds, hers was the one he couldn't free himself from. Most days he could tune her out, if she was far away enough, but today… it just seemed impossible. Finally, he threw the glass of wine hard against the wall, shattering it. He walked towards the door, hoping to leave the room and get some fresh air—put as much distance between himself and Efilia as he could. When he opened it, however, he saw a blonde girl looking at him with large, green eyes. For a second, he thought it was Efilia—which was impossible… but then she spoke in a very different voice.

"Greetings, Chosen. I was told…" Urk cut her off and pulled her in without waiting for her to finish. He kissed her as if she was the love of his life. The girl was very impressed, and immediately smiled, letting herself get swept away by the tall Chosen man. He was more handsome than she could ever imagine; and so concupiscent and wild. He ripped her dress with one pull and threw her naked body on the bed. She smiled at him and beckoned him closer with her index finger. He kissed her and tried his best to turn his focus on her; to tune out Efilia's voice.

The moon lit the room in a pale, ghostly light. A cold wind blew past the curtains. Time was passing fast, and Urk got right in the mood. While making love to the newcomer, he suddenly stopped and asked her in low voice:

"Do you love me?"

"Yes," she said, just as she'd been ordered to by the man who brought her here.

"How much?"

"More than anything." She said, while enjoying his touches.

For a second, Urk lost his concentration and heard Efilia's voice, giggling at something Odmund had said, all the way down in the dining hall. He looked at the girl under him. She wasn't even smiling. He looked at her and asked again:

"Do you *love* me?"

And the girl, who had no idea what was happening, answered fearfully.

"Y-yes…"

Suddenly, Urk lost his temper and slapped her hard across the face, making her yelp.

"Liar!" He shouted, and slapped her again. The girl screamed in fear, but she had neither the power to escape, nor anyone to help her. She was all alone in the room with Urk, who had no limits when it came to using power—who would do anything to keep his broken heart beating, despite the pain it felt.

Less than an hour later, Urk was standing in front of his window, looking up at the stars. The wine in his glass was as red as the blood on the sheets. He drunk his wine in a sip, then looked at the girl lying dead on his bed. With no sign of mercy or regret, he walked towards the door and knocked on it.

"Clean the room!" He ordered his personal servant, who'd been standing outside the door. "Tomorrow I go on my holy mission, as given to me by Ifir herself. I need to rest." He then walked into his personal bathroom to wash himself. The old servant came in, looked at the dead girl on the bed, her body broken, and acted as calmly as Urk, showing absolutely no remorse nor emotions. He simply pulled her by her arms like a big bag of meat, then threw her off the bed to change the sheets.

On the other side of the corridor, Efilia and Odmund had finished having dinner, and Od had accompanied her to her room, which was on the same hallway as Urk's. She was now enjoying some fruit on her desk for dessert. They'd both bathed together and gotten comfortable for the night, choosing to spend it together on Lia's room for a change. Odmund held the sheet covering Efilia's body and pulled her towards him. She sat on his lap and he kissed her shoulder. They both looked at the stars shining on the dark sky and lighting the streets.

"What if I'm not wrong? What if she meant what she said?"

"I don't know who'd ever dare to sell our people as slaves, Od, but we can't leave it to chance." Lia supported the doubt in him.

"I should go and check." Od looked into her eyes. She nodded.

"Tonight?" She asked.

Odmund nodded. "I can't sleep thinking about this, Lia. There must be something I can find—anything."

"Alright… then if you think you're going alone to the worst part of Kellum, at night, without your guards, then you have another thing coming. I'll go with you." She smiled at him.

"It will be dangerous," he said.

"I know. That's the point." She replied, blinking. Odmund smiled back at her and kissed her, showing her how much he cherished her support. "You may be the Champion of the Kollek and the only Odon we've seen in ages… but you're still flesh and blood. You could use someone to watch your back."

Odmund nodded.

"Then get suited up. We're going hunting."

***

In less than half an hour, they were both on their horses, riding in the night. The streets of the city became less and less crowded as they passed through Edgetown. They both stopped at the gate before they entered into the Outer Silence and Odmund took the lead. The streets were almost dark as the torches in this part of the city were poorly maintained, and half of them weren't even lit, as was the way in the side streets of the Silence. Odmund burnt a flame on his palm and slowly rode his horse through the street where he'd seen the dying woman before.

When they came closer, he put the flame out and dismounted from his horse. Lia followed him. They silently walked through the narrow streets, ready to defend themselves at any moment.

Suddenly, a child screamed in pain in the darkness.

"There," Odmund said, and they ran towards the voice, avoiding all the debris and junk littering the sidewalks and alleyways. Although they looked everywhere, they couldn't find the owner of the voice in time. The streets were eerily empty—with not a soul in sight. It was almost as if the boy, if it had been a boy, had vanished into thin air.

Odmund was just about to give up hope when Efilia pointed at something in the darkness.

"There!" She said, aiming a finger at two shadows moving in the dark. The lieutenant and her champion ran after the men, following them through several alleyways, turns and twists. Od ordered them to stop, but they, of course, only ran faster. Soon, they'd disappeared, just like the boy, as if swallowed by the very ground.

"Shit..." Odmund said, balling his hand into a fist.

"We almost had them." Efilia said. "I wish Urk were here. He could hear where they went and point us in the right direction..." She added without thinking. Her words made Odmund pause for a second, and his eyes became as dark as a starless sky. Noticing the effect her words had had on him, Efilia added: "I mean, his power would be useful. Not that I'd rather be with him. Ugh, I'm sorry, Od... I am so useless. I didn't mean it that way."

Odmund realized she was only trying to be helpful, and shook his head, dismissing the topic.

"Nonsense. You mean the world for me." He ran his hand up and down her back. However, his touch was cold.

"Come on. Let's just keep searching. Acris or not, we're bound to find something, eventually. No one expects two Chosen to be on the prowl here at night. They'd have measures in place for common guards, but not us." Efilia agreed, and they continued to stalk through the dark, empty streets of the Silence, hoping to pick up the trail—or find a new one.

Eventually, as they walked among the dark houses, Efilia heard a voice. She held Odmund's arm to stop him. They walked silently to a corner, and saw two men talking near a wrecked house, close to Harborside. One of them had a torch in his hand, which lit up their faces. Lia listened carefully to him.

"The ship will be here in a few days. We need more girls. You bring only boys. Nobody wants boys. They want *girls*. The more use these kids have, the more money we get. I've told you this a thousand times, idiot." The first man slapped the other one's head. "Bring me *girls*." He hissed angrily at him. The man tried to hide his head behind his weak shoulder, afraid to be beaten by the other man.

"Yes, sire... sorry sire. It's just... boys are so abundant, ye know?" He said. "Plus, they can carry more weight too! Work for longer... that's valuable too, ain't it?"

"Are you questioning my orders...?" The other man said, raising a hand.

"No! No... girls it'll be, aye."

Odmund looked at Efilia and signaled her to go around the house. When she started to move, however, a sharp whistle pierced the night. The Chosen looked around to see who'd done it, but in a second, many other whistles and screams joined the first, as if they'd suddenly been surrounded by an army. Efilia and Odmund came closer to each other for protection. Odmund burned a new flame in his palms and waited to see his attackers. Efilia opened her mouth and screamed in the direction of the nearest din. The sound waves that came out from her mouth shook the stones and walls of the wrecked houses, but her warning wasn't enough to stop the racket. Both of them were on high alert now, and utterly ready to fight. Unlike Odmund, Efilia had never actually been in such a dangerous situation in real life before. She could feel the excitement rising up in her. Her heart was beating like it'd burst out of her chest.

The sound got louder as if they were getting closer, but then suddenly hushed. Odmund looked around, then turned to the wrecked house to look at the men. There was only the torch on the ground, now, and both had disappeared.

"Dammit!" He shouted. "They tricked us."

Efilia was silent. She sighed with the relief, seeing the men had left.

"We must find them before the ship they spoke of sets sail." Odmund said. Before Efilia turned her back, she noticed something whistling past her, splitting the air, and heard Od's voice.

"Ah!" He screamed in pain, as he threw himself against the wall for protection.

Without realizing what had happened, Efilia did the same. Next to her, Odmund was holding his shoulder, and in the faint light of the torch, she saw blood dripping from it. An arrow had flown past his arm, cutting his uniform and flesh, but thankfully missing him otherwise. Another one whistled over them, making them flinch. Seeing his beloved's blood was enough to make Efilia lose control. She suddenly stood up, took a deep breath, and shouted with such a strong voice, that all the walls in front of her came rumbling down, and the glasses of lamps and windows shattered. The sound waves coming from her throat hit everything in front of them, in the direction the arrows had come, with the force of a hurricane. In the middle of that storm, two men holding bows fell from the roofs on which they hid, tumbling down into the dirty streets. Thick blood flowed from their ears.

Odmund was shocked at Efilia's incredible display of power. His eyes grew bigger when he saw how much damage she'd caused to the surrounding buildings, and he was grateful for having been behind, rather than in front of her.

"My love," she said, looking back at Odmund. She held his arm to see if he was okay. However, Odmund's eyes were wide open, looking at her. Her hands were ice cold, and her skin had turned a deadly pale.

"Lia... That power... That was almost like... Like Ifir herself. Are you alright?" He asked, looking her up and down.

"I am... Don't worry." She said, though she didn't look like it. Odmund pulled her into his arms and hugged her as tight as he could, then kissed her on the head. She hugged him back and, secretly, tears fell down from her eyes and onto his chest.

"I'm alright." She repeated. "Oh Od... For a second there, I thought... I can't lose you. I don't know how to live without you." She said with tears in her eyes.

"You won't, Lia." Odmund said, and held her close.

"You won't."

Chapter 19

Crossroads of Fate

The group of soldiers had left Rockpour a few hours ago.

Merki had watched them as she put her things on the wagon; watched as Gerard had taken Leord and Jarrie apart, away from anyone else, and given them what appeared to be some kind of orders. Jarrie had been acting strange ever since, barely speaking a word, while Leord seemed almost… relieved?

Gerard had taken the lead, like before, while Jarrie and Leord rode behind on either side of Kade, who was once again bound, wearing a new amethyst necklace Axel had fashioned for him after he'd cut away his cuffs the previous night.

Axel and Merki manned the front of the rickety wagon while Locke laid in the back with their belongings, his leg sprawled over a stack of hay. He seemed to be in considerable pain, despite the padding.

"Is this really necessary, lieutenant?" Axel asked Gerard, despite his better judgment. He nodded at Kade. "The Chosen did save us all yesterday, and he's proven that he truly wants to go to Kellum. We can at least unbind his hands."

Gerard looked at Axel over his shoulder.

"Not a chance. The Chosen stays bound until we reached the next garrison—or Kellum itself. I'm not taking any chances."

"But…"

"Drop it, old man. He might've saved us… But that doesn't mean that his story adds up. He could still have some ulterior motive. I'm not risking it. Now shut up and ride… we've got long enough to go as it is, and precious little time to waste." He looked back at Locke, who was sitting in the wagon looking away from him, then back onto the road.

"And… what happens if we can't make it in time?" Axel asked Gerard.

The old man didn't look at him when he replied. "We die." He simply said.

They all knew it was because of Locke's insistence to go with them. They understood the reason behind it too—if he stayed behind at Rockpour, then the spoils and merit of delivering Kade would go to Gerard. He'd miss out on all of it. They were surprised, however, that he was willing to put them all at risk for his own glory and gain like that. It just wasn't right… nor like Locke, from what little they knew of him.

Still, he *was* their captain, and the one who'd fought for the opportunity the most, where Gerard just wanted to kill Kade and get it done with. He definitely understood where the captain was coming from, even if he didn't agree with his decision to come along. Put in his position, he wondered if he would've chosen any differently himself.

Leord wasn't so convinced, however. He kept looking at Gerard, then back at Locke. After the stress and trauma they'd all experienced in the last few days, the young recruit, who was definitely not used to any of this, seemed to be near his breaking point. Now, without barely any rest, he was being forced to escort a wounded man across bandit-infested country, in the hopes they might make it to the next big city in time… or else die a very painful death at the hands of the worst the kingdom had to offer.

As the sun was starting to set, Gerard looked upon the horizon. They were still crossing mountain country, but he could see the faraway plains between the distant peaks—a sign that they were about to finally leave the mountains behind, and finally descend to smoother terrain.

"We'll camp here for the night." He said, stopping his horse.

"Wait… why are we stopping? Gerard, keep it going! We can still ride for an hour more or two!" Locke said.

The old soldier hung his head and scoffed. "And stop to make camp in the darkness, captain? Are you sure that's wise at all?" He looked at Leord, who was looking straight at him.

"No. We stop here. Then pick right back up in the morning." Gerard finished.

Locke did his best to turn his torso to face Gerard, straining with pain as he did so. "No… No! We need to make as much time as we can. We need to keep moving!"

Gerard took a deep breath, facing the setting sun in the distance, beyond the plains, then let it go.

"Captain, I'm afraid your judgement is flawed due to your injury. You're not thinking straight. We will stop, and rest. You need it as much as we all do." He said, his voice even and calm.

"I *order* you to keep moving, Gerard. All of you!" He said, in clear frustration.

Merki and Axel exchanged looks, then looked at the lieutenant and the other soldiers. Kade didn't look at anyone, but kept his eyes down. Even he knew this wasn't such a great idea. He feared, most of all, what they'd do to him once the amethysts ran out of power… or worse, what he'd do to *them*. He knew he couldn't control himself yet without the stones—not for long, anyways.

Gerard didn't listen to Locke, and instead led the convoy into a glade of trees, a few dozen meters away from the main road. He dismounted and the recruits did the same, all the while Locke howled in anger, repeating his orders, threatening to have him court martialed for insubordination, cursing helplessly in the back of the wagon.

The old wolf ordered camp to be set as if nothing was happening. He ordered Kade tied to a tree, as before, and then Locke to be left in the wagon, until he calmed down.

Then, he called the two recruits over and began to speak to them again, apart from the rest, in the distance. Merki saw him from afar as she filled Rage's water bowl, stroking his warm, fuzzy fur and kissing his furry head. She spoke to him as she prepared her sleeping area for the night. "Keep an eye out tonight, huh boy? And stay close to me." She gave the hound the commands to do just that, then patted him one last time on his head before looking back towards the soldiers.

Gerard remained calm as ever as he talked. Leord nodded profusely, a look of grim determination in his face. Jarrie looked crestfallen, like the weight of the last few weeks had finally caught up to him. Merki gave Axel, setting up his own bed besides her, a sidelong look.

"I don't like this," she said.

Axel nodded. "Neither do I. Stay on your guard."

Merki nodded right back.

The group set camp, ate some of the food they were given in Rockpour for their trip, then went to bed for the night in silence, the tension hovering over them like an evil, sentient thing.

It was Rage who felt it first.

Merki's faithful dog and lifelong companion started to rumble a warning. She didn't pay it any mind at first, being deep in sleep… but then, his sharp, agonizing yelp brought her right up out of unconsciousness. She jerked wide awake, pushing herself into a sitting position, and right into the point of Jarrie's sword, aimed squarely at her throat. Her hand was halfway towards a dagger she'd hidden under her bedroll.

"I'm sorry…" The young recruit said, literally weeping. "I'm so sorry."

"Jarrie… please don't—" Before she could finish speaking, the young man slammed her on the side of her head with the pommel of the sword, and Merki's world went black.

***

Merki opened her eyes slowly, feeling a dull, pulsing ache in her temples.

She was tied to a tree… and the first thing she saw was Rage, lying dead at her feet in a pool of blood. He had a crossbow bolt coming out of his neck.

"No… NOOO!!! RAGE!!!" She yelled, and tears immediately started to form in her eyes. She looked up and saw Gerard standing by the fire, his dark frame silhouetted by the flames, arms crossed. Jarrie and Leord stood beside him on either side. They were facing Merki… and Axel, who was also tied to a tree next to her. He was still unconscious, a small sliver of blood trickling down his forehead.

"Axel… AXEL!" Merki screamed.

The old man slowly blinked himself awake, looking weak, frail and tired.

"M-merki…? What in the blazes… Oh. Oh no." He said, as he realized their situation.

Merki stared at Kade, who'd been bound hand and foot, a few meters away from them. The amethysts in his neck glowed brightly, working overtime to keep his powers suppressed. He groaned and grunted, trying to break free of his bonds, but the knots and rope were too strong for him while the gemstones weakened his body.

Locke, Merki noticed with horror, had been pulled out of the wagon, and currently lied on the ground before Gerard, his mouth muffled as well, his hands tied behind his back.

"You BASTARD!" Merki spat at Gerard, and the old man turned to face her, his face obscured by the shadows. "You killed my Rage! My only family!" She screamed.

"W-why would you do this, lieutenant?! After all we've been through?" Asked Axel.

Gerard drew a long breath… then let it go. "Isn't it obvious?" He asked. "Our captain here… in his *feverish* delusion… has not left me any other choice."

Locke grunted and squirmed in the dirt, right in front of the fire. His eyes squinted with pain.

"I'll kill you for this, you old piece of shit!" Merki yelled.

"Merki!" Axel hissed. "That won't help us… please."

Crossroads of Fate | 235

"I don't care!" Merki said, struggling madly against her bonds. "That bastard killed my dog—my poor Rage…"

"I know Merki, I know," Axel said, sadly.

She stared at the animal's dead body at her feet and her eyes began to stream with tears. "Rage… was all I had left of him… All I…" She started to sob… then, after taking a ragged breath, her eyes suddenly got lost in the distance, as if something suddenly snapped inside of her. A sudden cold overcame them—a lifelessness. She fixed those very cold, very dead eyes at Gerard.

Axel looked away from her. "Weren't you supposed to protect the captain, lieutenant?"

Gerard nodded, several times. Axel noticed he'd been holding one of his daggers—the very same one he'd used to kill the Behemoth just a few nights ago, in fact. He stared at it now, and in the light of the flames, she actually saw the conflicted look on his face. The man grimaced with an expression she'd never seen before—he almost looked like he hated himself.

"I was," he finally said. "And I tried my best to hold onto that promise. That command from my superior, Commander Siegen."

Merki's eyes twitched at the mention of the name—just for a second—then turned dead and cold once more.

"He's a downright bastard of a man, you know," Gerard continued. "Threatened to send me to the mines if I didn't take this job. Just because I messed up one of his cruel, inhumane military operations and tried to save my men from an impossible situation."

Merki, Kade and Axel just watched the man as he spoke. Leord and Jarrie stood armed on either side of him; though the former looked poised, confident and fully on board with this whole madness, and the later as if he'd cut his own throat at any moment, his eyes downcast, full of horror… and almost a glint of madness.

"Now, after all these years, fate has placed me at the very same crossroads, it seems." Gerard said. "Honor… versus duty. And old man, I choose honor. For my men."

"There is *no* honor in this!" Axel said, casting a quick look at Merki's dead companion in front of him, then at the young huntress and the dead, wild look in her eyes. Her chest rose and fell like that of a wild beast waiting to pounce on its prey. "You don't have to kill us! You can just take the Chosen with you if you want him so badly and leave us here. Leave *him* here." He said, nodding at Locke. "We'll just go back to Rockpour and…" He realized the flaw in his logic as he said it.

Gerard nodded. "And rat us all out. Turn us into fugitives. Deserters of the army—just for doing what we had to in order to survive. You do realize he was going to get us all killed, right? That there was no way we'd be getting to Alladon, let alone Kellum, before the celebrations? Not with his leg dragging us down."

Axel looked at Merki, at Kade, at Locke, lying on the ground, looking for a way out of this, a way to plea their case… But he knew there wasn't one. Not this time.

"This is it, old man." His inner voice whispered. *"We tried and failed. It was good while it lasted."*

"It's ironic, isn't it?" Gerard told them. "All this time, I thought you were rebels. 'Sons of Forest.' I wanted to kill you for it… but you really were just a couple of yodels and a lost Chosen—*however* he came to be down there in your neck of the woods. And yet, here I am. About to kill you lot all the same, in spite of it."

"Gerard… you don't have to do this. I beg of you." Axel said.

"Listen to her soldier… You're better than this." Kade added, speaking for the first time.

But Gerard was shaking his head fiercely now. "No, no, NO! You're not listening! There is no way, no scenario, in which you live and we survive. You knew the risks of coming on this little trip of ours—these boys did not. They don't deserve…" He stopped, then looked around wildly. "*I* don't deserve to walk into my death on the *petty* whims of a rich, spoiled daddy's boy, who wants to make his *daddy* proud, and fuck everyone else! I've lived too long… sacrificed too much already." He stopped fiddling with the dagger, then stared at Merki, his eyes filled with dark intent.

"I'm tired."

He then started to walk towards Merki, very slowly, his dagger glistening red in the firelight in his hand. The young huntress

Crossroads of Fate | 237

continued to hold his stare, her breath almost even now, her eyes growing wild and full of barely contained hatred.

"So, here's what will happen. I'll kill you two—quick and painless. Then I'll kill our captain there—not that he'll last long with that wound out here, but we can't take any chances, see? Then, me and the boys take the Chosen to Alladon, cash in on whatever they give us there, and each go our separate ways, splitting the money... Twenty-five, twenty-five, fifty." He looked back at the recruits. "That's fair, right?"

He stopped in front of Merki, who stood still as the tree she was tied to, staring the much taller man down with those cold, baleful eyes.

"Merki... no! Don't do it, Gerard!" Axel blurted out. "Kill me! Just let her go, out in the wilds if you must—the girl won't say anything! She'll start a new life somewhere and forget all about this! Tell him, Merki!" Axel said.

Merki didn't say anything. She couldn't.

Axel shook his head. "Soldier! Spare her life! Don't do this!" Said Kade.

But Gerard didn't listen to him. He stood in front of Merki, tall as a mountain, as she stared up at him with those cold, dead eyes, seething with deep-black hatred.

"Please... Lieutenant." Axel said. "Don't do this..."

Suddenly, Gerard heard movement behind him and Leord yelped in both pain and surprise. The old man turned towards the campfire... and saw Jarrie, his eyes wild, his sword struck clean through Leord's chest.

"I... I can't let you do this! I can't!" The youth whimpered.

Leord looked at him in surprise, and more than a little confusion... then the light left his eyes and he fell on his knees, then sideways onto the campfire.... and began burning.

Jarrie stared at Gerard, shaking, every bit of his body trembling, and held up the rusty sword at him, its tip swaying wildly from side to side.

"Jarrie... Don't! Just run!" Axel yelled at him.

"I... I c... I can't. This isn't... this isn't right! Ahh!!!"

He rushed towards Gerard screaming, blade held high, and Axel closed his eyes. Merki only saw the old wolf's tall silhouette; as he easily parried the sword to the side with his dagger, then plunged it right into the young man's heart, embracing him like a father saying goodbye.

"*You damn fool...*" Gerard whispered as he let him slide down, his eyes wide and shocked, looking up at him. He stared right into his eyes until they glazed over, then lay there, motionless, the look of horror and shock frozen on his dead face.

Locke screamed as hard as he could with his mouth gag, his face turning as red as the flames. Merki began to hyperventilate, her chest rising and falling, her eyes filled with a darkness that filled Kade with horror as he watched. Axel kept his eyes shut as tightly as he could.

"Dear Aether..." The old man prayed. "Receive your children into your bosom. Forgive them of their sins, for they know not what they do, and grant them peace everlasting." He continued repeating the same sentence over and over and over.

Gerard turned over to Merki, his eyes wide. He looked down at the two dead bodies of the soldiers, to his hands, then to her. For a second, she thought she saw remorse in those old, grey eyes. That Jarrie's sacrifice would spare them after all. Then, with a crazed look in his eyes, Gerard said:

"I guess it's a hundred percent of the bounty for me now."

And he strode towards her, lifted her by her hair, and put the dagger to her throat. However, before he could swipe the bloody blade across her flesh, the old wolf heard a popping sound, then he flinched and grunted.

"Ugh..."

He shook, then a sliver of blood slipped from the corner of his mouth. He looked down with wide eyes, and instead of the scared, broken young woman he thought he was about to kill, he saw something else looking up at him. He couldn't tell what it was, but he immediately knew it wasn't the huntress he'd gotten to know in the past several weeks.

Merki held a long, thin stiletto knife stuck most of the way into his gut. She twisted it, her eyes wide and wild, and Gerard stumbled back. He dropped his dagger—the very one that'd tasted both Jarrie and the Behemoth's blood by now. Merki caught it in the air, pushing away completely free of the ropes, and plunged it into the old man's gut—again and again. Then, once more into a lung, twisting it all the while she looked into the Gerard's eyes. The man shook and convulsed, eyes wild, as she held him, her grip much stronger than he would've ever expected. Blood spilled in bursts from his mouth, soaking his beard and Merki's chest. He started to choke on it, spasming uncontrollably, as the brown-haired huntress looked down at him with those dead, cold eyes... holding him. Waiting until the realization fully sank into him.

Then, once he'd agonized enough, Merki drew the blade from the collapsed lung and plunged it into his heart, twisting it with a sickly crunch, grimacing as she did.

She watched the life go out of the big man's eyes almost instantly... then let him slip down to the bloody earth with a thud.

**

Next morning came by in a daze.

Merki, Axel, Locke and Kade all sat around a second fire, away from the first. Gerard and Leord's bodies had been piled on top of it, and they were now little more than charred husks of the people they'd been yesterday. Just silhouettes: no hair, no features... nothing.

Jarrie and Rage had been buried next to each other, some distance away from camp, little wooden effigies marking their resting place. Axel had, once again, said a few words for them, commending their souls to Aether.

They'd taken their clothes, weapons and armor off, and packed them neatly in the wagon. Merki had kept Gerard's knives.

Locke had asked Merki about what happened last night. She'd answered by saying:

"I always carry an extra knife or two on me. Ever since that day," she said, going over the story of the time when bandits had almost raped her. "I've had that stiletto strapped to my lower back since we set out from Halstead… just for such a situation. I'd started cutting from the moment I woke up, and realized I was bound. Thankfully, Gerard had used most of the rope we had left on Kade," she said, nodding at him, "and only had a few coils to spare on me, or else I wouldn't have been able to cut through them in time. I still had to dislocate my hand to pull free though." She stared at her bandaged right hand, which she'd reset since then.

"How *did* you cut through them in time… and without Gerard noticing?" Locke asked.

Merki looked down at the flames. "Jarrie."

The young captain nodded, a look of deep sadness in his eyes.

"I… I still can't fucking believe it." He said. "I… I thought I knew Gerard. I knew he had a strong will and temper, but… to turn traitor like that?"

Silence.

"And… It's all my fault." Locke finally said, barely more than a whisper. "I drove him into it. All of them… just because I wanted to join in the glory of the King's Bounty."

More silence.

"You didn't put that dagger in his hand, captain." Axel said, breaking the silence. "He made his choice. They all did."

The captain frowned deeper. "But only because I didn't leave them an option. I… I knew my plan was flawed. That it wouldn't work. And…"

Axel took a deep breath. "And that's something you'll have to live with for the rest of your life, young Locke. Let it teach you… instead of break you. It's all you can do to honor their memory now." He said.

Kade and Merki nodded. Locke swallowed the words like a man holding onto a log for dear life.

"I guess it is." He nodded. "I'll make it up to them. I have to. Even Gerard. They deserved better than this. I was stupid, and selfish, and I…"

"Let it go," Axel said, gently, and all eyes turned to him again. "Just let it go. What's done is done. They are at peace now, free from war, sickness and pain. Take solace in that… and let it go."

Locke sighed deeply, and stared at the fire for a long time. Everyone respected his silence. Then nodded, almost imperceptibly. "Ok."

Silence overtook the campsite again for a very long time. The group had a meager breakfast out of duty, as none of them had appetites of any kind. Eventually, it was Kade who broke the silence.

"What are we going to do now?" He asked.

Locke shrugged. "What can we do? Other than going back to Rockpour. We won't make it to Alladon in time, not with my leg as it is, and without Gerard, or me, none of you can just waltz in and deliver Kade to the army—not unless you find another officer who can verify your claim… and doesn't just skewer you on sight, like Gerard wanted to do."

"Alladon is to the west… through God's Plains, and then beyond. It's almost the same distance from where we are as Kellum." Axel said.

"No… it's not." Locke said. "To get to Kellum, we'd had to go through the Orkail Mountains after the plains, then take the river roads up north. That kind of terrain easily doubles the time."

Axel nodded several times. "Yes… But there is another way."

All eyes perked up to look at him. "What other way? There's no other way to the capital." Locke said.

"Not for a young Kollek soldier such as yourself… But for an old man like me, who's been around for so much longer… There are still old paths that most don't remember. That most dread to cross, and have even stopped mentioning altogether."

Seeing as how all eyes were utterly glued to him now, Axel continued.

"North of here, a short day's travel or two up the plains, there's a pass that few remember, and fewer still dare mention. It is known as the Dreamer's Oasis—a valley that runs through arid land, desert as dry as you've ever seen, and bypasses the plains, the detour west, and the snaking riverways to Kellum. It is almost a straight path to the capital."

"The Dreamer's Oasis?" Merki asked. Axel nodded.

"How come I've never heard of it, if it's so close to Kellum?" Locke asked.

"You have," Axel smiled, sadly. "Your people call it the Valley of the Dead."

Locke took a sharp intake of breath and leaned back. "You don't mean... the cursed lands to the east? That's... That's Koartiz territory! Past the borders of Kollek lands!"

But Axel was already shaking his head before he finished. "No... That is only what you're told. While the Oasis *is* technically outside of Kollek lands, yes—it is not Koartiz land either."

"Why not?" Asked Kade.

"Because the Koartiz also avoid it, just as the Kollek. It exists as a natural buffer in the east, between the two nations. No one force dares cross it."

Merki shook her head. "But we're supposed to?"

"If we want to get to Kellum in time, yes. It is literally our only chance."

"Why are they so scared of it?" Merki asked. Locke answered her this time.

"Because the Valley of the Dead claims any Kollek who venture into it. It is a cursed place—where the undying forces of the Cursed King Luden met their demise thousands of years ago. They say their ghosts, and those of the Koartiz that died there, still haunt the empty wastes. That the darkness of Luden's army seeped into the land, corrupting it. It's why no life grows there. It's a vile, fell place."

Merki frowned, then looked at Axel. "Again... and we're supposed to cross that how?"

Axel smirked. "By not believing every rumor or legend we hear," he smiled at Locke as he said it. "You see, the land is an enigma, yes. A desert valley, in the middle of such lush lands. But life does grow there. And there is water to be found. Otherwise, why would it be called an Oasis?"

"Who calls it that, anyways?" Locke asked. "As far as I know, it's always been the Valley of the Dead."

"People from long ago—from before you were born. Like me. We can safely pass through the valley, as long as we prepare accordingly

Crossroads of Fate | 243

before heading into it. Thankfully, there is a city on its outskirts that we can use to replenish our goods."

Locke thought long and hard. "Orkail?"

Axel nodded. "The same."

"And what about amethysts…?" Merki asked Axel, sneaking a look at Kade, who looked away.

"Ahh… well… I have some thoughts on that. We'll be able to replenish our stock in Orkail as well."

"How?" Locke interrupted. "The sale of amethysts is illegal. You'd have to either steal them from a garrison or from another captain, like me."

Axel stared at the captain, wondering whether to proceed or not… then realized they'd already come this far together, so he might as well go all the way.

"I have a… friend, who can acquire the stones for us. No stealing. Just… outsourcing."

"You mean, the black market?" Locke frowned at the old man.

"You want to get to Kellum in time? You'll have to make some concessions. The black market is, and will always be there, young captain. We might as well avail ourselves of it. It's not like you can… ahem, excuse my bluntness, *walk* into a garrison and request more stones. And even if you did, not that they'd let you leave, with your leg as it is—it'd cast suspicion on your motives. No, this is our only option."

Locke didn't like the idea, but he eventually nodded all the same, after realizing that they didn't really have much of a choice. "… Only if we must."

Axel nodded. "On that same note, if we are to get to Kellum in time, we must avoid all other guards and soldiers on the road—for the same reasons. We can't afford to have them stopping us to check on you, and Kade here, and risk them trying to appropriate the Bounty for themselves, or even try to assist with it."

Locke let out a long sigh. He didn't like this either, wandering around like fugitives, but he saw the sound counsel behind it.

"Now, about Kade here… I have an idea. A proposition, if you will, that will allow us to use our current amethysts for longer, and also lessen the absolute necessity of finding more."

Everyone edged forward in the fire, especially Kade. Axel waited, giving them time to prepare... as he knew the gravity of what he was about to propose.

"In my years at Castle Kellum, I trained several Chosen in their abilities. In how to control their powers."

"Oh, no..." Locke said, leaning back. "Oh no, no, no... You must *really* be mad to be suggesting what I think you're suggesting..."

Axel smiled. "And yet, I am. I can show you how to control your powers, your gift, young Kade. It is clear that you do not come from any rebel group, nor Kellum, and have thus not received proper training. I can show you how to control yourself—how to channel your abilities."

"Axel... I have to agree with Locke, here. That's mad." Merki finally said.

"I... also have to agree." Kade added, to the surprise of all. He looked up, at each one of them. "I don't know how to control my powers. The moment you take this off," he pointed at the necklace, "I don't know what I'll do."

"Were you always feral before we pacified you, Kade?" Axel asked.

"No... but."

"You've gone feral twice, correct? Once when Merki found you, and dangerous-looking men were trying to rob you, then again when we unleashed you to save us all from the other Chosen."

"What's your point?" Kade asked.

"On both occasions, you were under extreme duress. That is a common trigger for feral behavior in Chosen—which is why self-control, breathing and discipline of the body and mind are some of the first things your kind is taught over at the Nest, in Kellum. We can practice those same things without removing the amethysts... then take them off, little by little. Only for as long as you feel comfortable. You'll find you'll be able to control your abilities more and more each time before you feel them... overtaking you."

"This still sounds dangerous." Locke said.

"It will be." Axel added. "But think of the rewards. Young Kade here will learn to control his powers, and push the feral state further and further away. He'll not only become more of an asset to us, but at the same time, he'll become less of a threat. Don't you want that?" He asked the last of Kade himself.

The young man nodded. "I do."

"Then if everyone else agrees, we can start your first session as soon as tonight." Axel looked at Merki and Locke. Merki shrugged, then nodded. Locke shook his head and scoffed.

"This still sounds like madness to me… But what the hell. Every single thing we're about to do is pure madness." He looked at Kade up and down, and raised his eyebrows and hands in a philosophical gesture of defeat.

"Fuck it. Let's do it."

CHAPTER 20

THE IMMACULATE TEAWARE

"Be careful, you idiots!"

A lavishly clothed merchant by the name of Bermand shouted loud enough to be heard over at the city walls, while his carriers tried to lift a huge wooden chest with engravings. To control his nervousness, the man kept on turning and fiddling with the gold rings in his fingers, which were decorated with rubies and emeralds.

As each of his men managed to lift a chest on their shoulders, their thin, malnourished legs could barely move them over the unsteady planks of the river boat. With one eye on his carriers, Bermand stopped next to the port captain, standing at the side of the gangway, watching and counting the goods and passengers that left the merchant's lustrous river boat, the *Goldswift*.

"I hope you had a pleasant journey?" The captain asked him, eyeing him curiously.

"We did, captain, thank you. The God's River was as calm and bountiful as ever." Bermand winked at him while passing a small coin bag.

"Good to have you back in Kellum, master merchant." The captain shook his hand vigorously after feeling the weight of the bag.

Bermand grinned his yellow teeth with pride and crossed the gangway. His poor carriers were waiting for him on solid land, beyond the grand lake port.

Lake Kellam was the largest man-made lake in Kollek history—acting as a gateway to the city due to its large port. The lake connected the north and south tributaries of the God's River, which snaked for miles, and provided a large-enough body of water for the dozens and at times even hundreds of vessels traversing the rivers to dock and unload their goods. It was instrumental to Kellum's economy, and the main gateway to the Kollek capital, as the God's River connected both the north and the south of the kingdom, allowing for rather safe, easy, (if incredibly monitored and taxed) access to the capital.

The lake gleamed beautifully in the early morning sun, its surface shinning as if made out of gold. Its banks and shores had been carefully manicured with trees, stone walkways, gazebos and gardens filled with flowers of every kind, letting travelers know they had indeed arrived at the most powerful and wealthy city in the Kollek world.

"Walk, idiots!" Bermand shouted again. "My carriage is over there!" He gestured at two black carriages waiting close by—one in the front, with red velvet curtains and golden details, and another one behind, for storage. As the merchant's aides carried his chests to the storage carriage, one of the port's customs inspectors approached him.

"Bermand!" He said from behind, and the merchant cursed under his breath. "Welcome back, dear friend." The man said with a smile. With a forced smile, Bermand turned around and greeted him.

"Kair... hello. So good to see you on duty once again." Even as he spoke them, his words tasted like sour milk on his tongue. He and the man had both grown up together in the slums of Kellum, and Kair had always had a flair for making his life difficult. The man seemed to live for it, actually.

"What did you bring to our beautiful lands from Karte this time? Wine? Pearls?" The inspector smirked. "Perhaps... a Poly-sister?" He winked at him with a raunchy smile, showing him his foul set of teeth. The merchant forced another smile, hating himself and his luck.

Bermand had arrived from the island kingdom of Karte a few weeks back, but touched down at another port down south to trade some goods along the way, before making it up to the capital. He'd then taken the river north, hauling his wares with him on his boat (and making some more money ferrying people), as it was the safest and fastest way to move goods once inland. God's River was one of the most patrolled and guarded routes in all of the kingdom, after all.

"No, no… just goods to sell before the ceremony."

"So business is that bad, eh?" Kair looked at the chests suspiciously, but Bermand simply nodded.

"Not as good as last year, I admit." He forced out.

"Why don't you open this one and let me see what you brought this year?"

"Actually, I already got my goods inspected over at the wharf by another officer. Already paid the tax for them too. Here's the inspection slip." Bermand handed Kair the piece of parchment with a record of all the goods he carried, and the weight tax associated with them. It was already stamped by another inspector.

"Ah, I see," Kair said. "But you see… *I* haven't seen them yet, old friend. And I know how you like to sneak things in that you shouldn't, as you did back in the Silence when we were kids…" He smiled easily, showing his putrid teeth to Bermand again, making his stomach squirm. "So, you see… I need to look. You can't leave until I do. So, if you will…" He gestured with his hands.

Bermand started at the man for a moment, then finally sighed and nodded. "Of course, Kair. Of course. I have nothing to hide."

He ordered his aides to bring the chests full of goods back and placed them in a row before the inspector, wasting valuable time that Bermand absolutely did not want to be wasting right now.

The aides opened them, and the lanky inspector walked in front of them, looking at all the exotic trade goods inside, confirming everything that'd been written on the slip. There were many bottles of Kartean wine, little jars of spices, some dried fruit and scores of glistening, traditional jewelry and trinkets from the island kingdom. He took his sweet time going through each chest, looking back at the slip, then finally, once he felt he'd wasted enough of Bermand's time, he walked back over to him.

"Everything looks to be in order," he said in a chipper tone, then handed the slip back to Bermand. But just before the stocky merchant had a chance to grab it, the other man pulled it away from him. "Except… what's this? Says here you're being charged two Kolls for every pound… that's not right." Kair took out a pen and some ink, then amended the tax to three Kolls (silver coins) instead of two.

"Ahh… there we are." He signed his name under the other inspector's, so that the tax money would pass through his desk, stamped it with his own signet over the previous one, then handed it back to Bermand, an easy smile on his face.

Bermand grew red in the cheeks and ears. He thought of the times Kair had humiliated him before, beaten him up, cheated him when they were kids. How he'd made his life miserable. He wanted nothing more than to tie the skinny, miserable, rat-looking man to a stone and shove him over the pier. However, knowing his place and the way of things, Bermand simply nodded, and forced a very fake, wide grin.

"Welcome to the capital, Ber. It's *so* good to see you again." Kair said, then left to see to another traveler—and possibly rob them as well. As soon as he left, Kair's assistant moved forward with a bag, and the merchant paid the extra Koll per pound his "friend" had amended on his receipt. The man then nodded, turned away, and left Bermand to his silent, seething rage.

The merchant's aides closed his chests, placed them on the carriage and mounted on its sides, while Bermand simply stared out over the port, wondering how he could get back at Kair someday—make him rue the day he decided to make a fool out of him. He then got on the front carriage, knocked twice, and the driver ushered the horses forward, climbing the paved stone road up to the city and leaving the dreaded port behind.

A few minutes later, they'd arrived at the eastern gates to the city, and the rider stopped. Another customs officer opened Bermand's door.

"Welcome to the capital, sir. Your paper please."

Bermand passed the receipt he'd gotten from Kair and the previous inspector, along with two more coins. The officer looked the Kolls over carefully, ensuring that they were real. Then, seeing the minted image of Ulor on one side and the symbol of Aether on the other, the man nodded. He quickly looked over the storage carriage, then came back.

"Thank you." He bowed and closed his door.

As Bermand heard the carriage rider whipping the horses into action once more, he took a deep breath… and a smirk appeared on his dry lips. Soon, he'd arrived at his store in the Merchant's Row district; a building with many beautiful flowers rolling down its walls, ornate wooden carvings and exquisitely polished stone. A huge sign outside the main entrance read: "*Golden Delights.*" Elegant noble women strolled in and out from under it, fanning their faces and giggling among one another.

Bermand looked through the glass windows, while still inside his carriage, and saw his son tending the front desk. He wasn't the smartest boy, but at least he kept the store going in his absence. Thanks to Aether, Bermand had also been smart enough to hire his two business-savvy nephews to aid his son in running the store—otherwise, he feared the dull boy would run his business into ruin.

Seeing the store running properly, he knocked the carriage's wall again and signaled for the rider to move on, the storage carriage full of goods having been left safely in the alleyway behind the store—which Bermand had made sure was always guarded by armed hired hands. As soon as the wheels rolled gain, the merchant pulled a small box from a secret pocket in his ornate robe—one that had not been inspected—or taxed, but hidden away in his person. He carefully opened it and looked at his face on the mirror inside. He took out a comb made from Ardfant bone; a huge, three-meter-long animal with four long tusks, a huge snout and a long tail covered with soft, colorful fur. Then, he simply fixed his hair. Finished, he dropped some perfume on his wrists and neck, to hide the musk he'd built up traveling along the hot river all day, and smelled the air to ensure the new scent was strong enough. He checked how he looked, smiled at himself a few different ways in the mirror, considering which of his smiles was more impressive. Then, after a few tries, decided on his modest smile, which didn't show his yellowing teeth, and closed his "grooming box," putting it back on the secret pockets of his coat.

***

At the castle, Ifir and Fermand were interviewing bureaucrats who represented the Kollek lands. She was sitting at her desk, pretending to enjoy listening to the men discuss taxes and regional issues, like the drought that some of the kingdom had faced this year.

"We'd... uh... we'd like to ask for the mercy of our king—to make an exception on behalf of the taxes of his affected vassals this year." Offered bureaucrat Shurk, doing his best to avoid Ifir's penetrating looks. Fermand grimaced as if he saw a ghost. Seeing his reaction, Sir Shurk moved fast to explain himself better.

"Lord Franthz Pentgard, for example, said he had almost no harvest this year to feed his subjects and citizens. That the droughts have left him and his subjects on the brink of famine."

"His subjects?" Fermand said. "We are all subjects of our king. Besides, when have we done exemptions in taxes? Have we ever done that?" He looked at Ifir as if she had the answer.

"Never." She answered, looking at her nails.

Then she stared at all the bureaucrats in turn, one after the other. They all looked at the floor like grounded children. Even Shurk seemed to already be regretting bringing forth the notion—even though it was on everyone's minds.

"Any other propositions?" Fermand asked, keeping his eyes firmly on them.

No one said anything.

"Jerome?" Fermand asked one of the bureaucrats—the one in charge of representing the lords of the southern lands.

"I...I th-think it's too soon to ask for such a large demand of our king.... Especially in times like these." He spoke so fast, the other barely understood what he said.

"Right." Fermand said and stood up. "I think that's enough for today. Jerome has made it very clear on your behalf that there's no need to demand such an unnecessary thing from our king right now… at least not until we have more solid evidence, like reports of people actually starving. As long as we're getting by, even if just barely, we need to keep in mind that every other resource we have must go to the war effort. After all, our king is the voice of Aether, and he has decreed so… we wouldn't want to incite the ire of Aether, would we?"

"No, no, never." The men in the room chorused.

As Ifir's stood up, the men in the room followed suit as well. Their trouble expressions seemed at ease now that the meeting was over.

"Thank you, respected servants of our God's Hand." Ifir emphasized the last part of her words with a stern look, then she respectfully bid them farewell.

As soon as the bureaucrats left the room, she walked over to the window to gaze upon the city—see some of the life outside the walls that surrounded her, rubbing her hands on the silk fabric of her dress as she did.

"We can't keep them silenced for long." Fermand said, looking at Ifir in his usual sweaty, fidgety way.

"We don't need to." Ifir said.

"They won't have a big enough harvest this year. They didn't last year either." Fermand said, pouring a glass of wine to himself and drinking it.

"Don't worry, Fermand. You and I will solve it like always, my old friend. Like always." She walked over to him and caressed his shoulder.

Fermand nodded. "I know, Songbird." He said and put his hand on hers.

"I have to go make some payments now in the lower city—for Imperation Day services." He smiled. "If you'll excuse me." Ifir smiled back at him and nodded.

As soon as the coin master left the room, Mere ran in to see if she needed anything, and as she expected, Ifir was in a foul mood.

"Wine." She ordered as soon as Mere walked in. As the servant poured a glass, someone knocked at the door.

"What?!" Ifir shouted. A soldier faintheartedly informed her: "The merchant Bermand is here to offer you gifts from his trip, Songbird."

Ifir sighed, then rolled her eyes. "Tell him to leave. I'm busy right now…" But she suddenly stopped, and looked sidelong at the soldier. "Wait. Where is he returning from?" She asked.

"Karte Island, Songbird." He answered without raising his head, missing the smile that appeared on Ifir's lips.

"Oh… Well in that case, tell him to come in."

The soldier nodded and let Bermand in. The merchant bowed deeply before Ifir then walked inside, two of his men following him with a heavy chest between them.

"It's an honor to see you, Songbird." Bermand said. Suddenly, Ifir's eyes got bigger, and a smile appeared on her face. Mere looked secretly at the merchant. She could easily see he wasn't from a rich family, from the way he overcompensated in his exaggerated clothes and jewelry. The way he held himself, however, revealed much of how he'd become rich on his own merit—especially though his particular gift of gib.

"Welcome, Bermand. It's been a while." Ifir said. "Wine?" She asked him kindly.

"If you deemed your humble servant worthy, my lady." He answered and signaled his men to leave the room. The men walked backwards, without turning their backs to their boss and Ifir. As soon as they were out, Ifir raised her hand to signal Mere to pour wine for her guest.

Bermand had a well-practiced smile on his face. Mere served them both their wine and stood at the corner.

"I hope your trip was fruitful?" Ifir asked Bermand.

"More than I expected, Songbird." The man smiled and rubbed his hands. "I brought you something very special." He said, after taking a sip from the tasteful wine. He opened the chest for Ifir and she walked closer, appreciating the nicely painted handmade teaware set inside.

"A piece of priceless art without equal." He informed her.

"Good" Ifir said, looking into the depths of his eyes, and asked: "Is anyone else aware of the existence of such a great teaware?"

"Oh no, my lady, no eyes have seen it. Even its creator died right after finishing this great work. A very unfortunate accident." He said.

"Even better." Ifir said. "Mere, give Bermand a box." She ordered. The old maid walked to the cabinet behind Ifir's desk, opened it, and took out a small box.

"The other one." Ifir warned her. Her dried hands reached to a bigger one, then she walked in front of Bermand and extended the box to him.

"A small gift from me to you, Bermand. Accept it as compensation for your kindness." Ifir said.

The merchant bowed respectfully and took the box from Mere's hand. "There are none as generous as you, Songbird. Our race is uplifted because of your presence." He said, trying to sound composed, but pushing back the happiness and giddiness building up inside him.

"Always a pleasure to see you," Ifir said, and waved him farewell. Even with some wine left over in his cup, Bermand immediately walked out the door with the box in his hands. His face was full of excitement; he couldn't wait to open it, as he noticed how heavy it was. His mind tried to make calculations as to the worth of the treasure inside, but failed. As soon as he left the office and walked away from the guards, he slightly opened it to see his gifts' worth. The sunlight reflected off of countless small emeralds and amethysts, among a great score of glistening golden coins.

"She is a real queen." Bermand giggled and happily walked out of the castle.

***

Back in Ifir's office, Mere awaited another order, and Ifir walked around nervously. She rubbed her hands together.

"Clear out the chest." She ordered Mere. The old maid was confused, but she obeyed as always. She gingerly picked up each of the pieces of teaware and put them on Ifir's desk for displaying. Bermand wasn't wrong: the teaware's handmade design and material

The Immaculate Teaware

was incredibly special. Mere loved touching the pieces, despite being afraid to drop them. On the other hand, Ifir showed no interest on the teaware whatsoever. As the last piece of it was removed from the chest, Ifir looked into the empty space inside.

"Leave!" She shouted at Mere. The old woman had no idea why Ifir was so tense, but she had no intention to do anything else but leave—and as soon as she could. So she did.

After she was left alone, Ifir grabbed her letter knife and bent over the chest. She stabbed the knife on one side of the bottom of the chest to remove the base. She heard a *click*, then the thin wooden bottom came out. There, staring at her from a secret compartment, was the true treasure Ifir had paid so much for: a leather-bound journal. She carefully took it out and sat on a nearby chair.

She opened the first page and began reading:

Poly-souled Sister Mathie,

who left her soul that was from the fifth daughter of

the Lord of the House Gallion.

Ifir turned the pages carefully. In her hands, she held the diary of a poly-sister from a Karte temple, in which young girls of respected families were trained to serve men in the ways of bodily pleasures. It was another tradition that King Ulor's great-great grandfather had come up with in order to collect more money from men, and reduce the incidents of rapes across the kingdom—which were rampant at his time. He'd also instilled this new concept as a way to lead people to respect Aether more… and him as well, being the god's hand and voice—as the institution of the poly-sisters had been decreed as an order from Aether Himself, and as a new way to venerate him. Even Ifir felt bad for those stupid girls and for the ignorance of their rich families.

As she passed through the pages, her hands and eyes hesitated for a second. Such writings usually carried so much pain. While turning the pages, she remembered what Bermand had told her: *"Even its creator had died right after finishing this great work."* She jumped to the next page right away. There, she found the last day of sister Mathie's life. Ifir took a deep breath, sipped her wine, and filled herself with courage before she started reading.

> *Day 2392*
>
> *Dear Lord Aether, owner of this world and the worlds above and below,*
>
> *I, Mathie, who left her soul that was from the fifth daughter of the Lord of the House Gallion, to be honored with the soul of Poly-souled sister, swear that I live this life you gave me to serve you and cherish your presence in every breath I take, as your loyal servant and subject.*
>
> *For the peace of the communities and your subjects, today I served my holy duty and satisfied two of your subjects, a grain merchant and a teacher from Kellum, Asthian. I also taught a young man who is about to become a warrior, from the island of Jortel, how to make love.*
>
> *During my duties, I tried my best to serve you as always. I taught the young man how gentle he should be to a woman, even if he is warrior. I served to help the gentle soul and body of the teacher.*
>
> *However, forgive me, creator of us all, for not being successful in my all duties today. Although I did my best to fulfill the wild desires of your subject, the grain merchant, I couldn't be enough for him, and prevented him from sinning by killing one of your servants, dear Poly-souled Sister Laine, who left her human soul as the second girl*

of the house Firk, to serve you. Through his wild desires and behaviors, the merchant took two of my teeth and bloodied my back. But that wasn't enough for him. Saving my sister was my duty, but I wasn't strong enough to stop him as he strangled her. This helpless and desperate subject of yours is begging you, Lord Aether, to please have mercy on me and my soul. Please let it reach your world when it leaves this one.

As a Poly-souled sister, it is my duty to report the sinful soul who murdered one of your servants, and thus bless her memory. The name of the grain merchant is Franthz Pentgard, from House Pentgard. A traitor who lost himself in the emptiness, and whose desires were the darkest…

The indescribable physical and emotional pain I have been suffering may only be the stones you pitched on my path to your high garden. So, please, forgive my soul if my confessions ever sound like complaints.

I am ending my day by consecrating my soul to you, Lord Aether, God of this world and the others.

Your faithful servant,
Poly-souled sister Mathie

Ifir's eyes got bigger. Mathie was an experienced poly-sister who'd worked for 2392 days on the service of men. Ifir wondered how she died for a second. Her mouth curved with pity.

"Franthz Pentgard, you sly bastard, you… Now we'll see if you say another word on the topic of taxes, or dare steal amethysts from me ever again…" Ifir said after a while; a wild light in her eyes.

CHAPTER 21

THE DREAMER'S OASIS

The Dreamer's Oasis. The hidden darkness of history, the unspoken secret of the ancients… The last great connection between the past and the future.

They were nearly there, they knew, when Locke suddenly spoke from the back of the wagon.

"I don't think I can make it." He said, his dried lips barely moving as he spoke.

"Here. Drink mine." Axel opened and extended his water skin to the captain. However, his body was barely sitting upright on the wagon by this point. His weak fingers grabbed the waterskin; his dry lips wanting nothing more than to feel the cooling sensation of water. The skin, however, had only a few precious drops left in it. Locke swayed in place, looking like he'd pass out at any moment. Kade put a hand on his shoulder.

"He's on fire," he said.

"We're almost at Orkail." Merki said, riding her horse next to the wagon. She was the only one riding a horse now, with Axel and Kade sitting on the wagon and Locke resting in the back. They'd brought two more horses with them, tying an extra one to the front of the wagon for speed and another at the back, in case they needed him, then set the others free back at camp. Kade checked his water skin as well, but it had nothing to offer. His desperate eyes met with Axel's. Looking around them, the old man couldn't find anything. They had crossed into desert land already, long before reaching Orkail, and resources had been incredibly scarce.

"We have to get to the other side of this hill. Can you go ahead and scout for us?" Axel told Merki. She nodded.

"Hiya!" She rode her horse as fast as it could go through the low side of the hill they were crossing. They followed Merki as fast as they could—which wasn't very fast, as even with two horses, the wagon was still a clumsy, stocky thing.

Locke finally passed out as they reached the top of the hill. Kade looked back at him.

"Will he be alright?" He asked Axel.

The old man nodded. "As long as we can make it to Orkail before the day's up and get him some water."

Just then, as if on cue, Merki's voice rang out. "We're here!" She said, slowing her horse. As they crested the top of the hill, the large town of Orkail appeared before them down below, surrounded by sandy stone walls. A small river snaked around the wall just outside, between them and Orkail.

"Alright," began Axel. "As we rehearsed, we will make camp outside town—on our side of the river. You will all stay there—help keep Kade out of sight of the town guards and any passing villagers... I'll go into Orkail and bring some food and clothes—as well as amethysts, from my... contact." The old man said. Kade's stomach rumbled when he heard the word food, as they hadn't eaten a proper meal for the last few days. There had been very little game to hunt on the way, and they'd quickly eaten through their remaining provisions from Rockpour, while most of them had gone bad from the drastic change in temperature.

Merki agreed with Axel and he passed the reigns over to Kade while he checked Locke's pockets. He found an almost empty coin bag, made a slightly disappointed face, then pocketed the purse.

They eventually reached a suitable spot on their side of the river, out of sight and covered by a few palm trees and bushes, and Axel stopped the rickety wagon. He and Merki exchanged places, with her taking Kade's side in preparing the camp, and Axel mounting her horse.

"I'll be back soon. Be sure to give him water—but a little at a time. He's too parched to swallow too much and will choke otherwise." Axel said.

Merki and Kade nodded, and the old man rode his horse into town as fast as he could—though he did stop for a quick drink once he reached the river. He also washed his face and arms, not wanting to enter town looking like a dirty rat fresh from a dirt hole.

Wateerrr! His inner voice screamed with joy. He washed himself with as much water as he needed, then mounted his horse and rode to town in a much more pleasant mood.

Orkail had high stone walls surrounding it and there were just few isolated homes and farms around it, all made out of a combination of wood and stone. As Axel rode through the farms, more of the well-built stone and wood houses and barns appeared. The main road to the town was crowded with carriages and horse riders, entering and leaving its gates.

Axel got in line to enter and waited for the soldier at the gate to usher him forward.

"What if they suspect us, you old bag? What if they catch us and throw us in one of their sandy prisons?" Axel's inner voice asked, in a panic.

They won't, Axel told him. *They have nothing to suspect... Unless we make ourselves look and sound suspicious, which we won't. We're just a traveler passing through town on our way to Kellum for the celebrations, as everyone else.*

After around ten men and two carriages had been allowed through, Axel was finally face-to-face with a well-dressed soldier wearing much more airy and comfortable-looking clothing than those in other parts of the kingdom. Even his pointed shoes were shiny, he noticed.

The soldier looked at Axel and studied his features—his face, clothes and belongings.

The Dreamer's Oasis | 261

"Welcome to Orkail, stranger," he said, warily. "What's your name?" He asked, rather unpleasantly.

"Derek Dareil, sir." Axel smiled.

The soldier looked suspiciously at Axel's old, worn clothes and horse.

"And from where do you hail, Derek?" He asked.

"Halstead—down in the southern wildlands." He answered, truthfully.

"And how long do you plan to stay in Orkail?"

"Not long, good soldier. I'm on my way to Kellum to see our High King during the Imperation Day festivities one more time before I die. I'll just buy some food and clothes, then hit the road again." Axel answered once more… mostly truthfully.

"Can you afford the riches of Orkail? The village of Bern is just a few miles west of here." The soldier said, looking at him suspiciously. Seeing as the Imperation Day celebrations were coming, and the town would be closing its gates, anyone entering might get locked inside for the duration of the festivities. That meant guards such as this one needed to be extra cautious not to let any criminals or troublesome elements in town before the festivities began. Axel understood that, and showed him Locke's velvet money bag, then shook it for him, making the coins inside clink nosily.

The guard looked at the coin bag suspiciously.

"And that is yours?" He asked.

Axel nodded. "I've been traveling the wastes for almost a week now, good soldier. Lost my escort to hungry jackals. I'm looking for a change of clothes and food once I'm in the safety of the walls."

The guard squinted at him for a while longer, then suddenly bowed.

"Apologies, sire." He said. "One cannot be too careful during these times. You're free to enter. Obey our laws while in Orkail, and we won't have a problem."

Axel nodded, then entered the city.

"That was too close," his inner voice said. *"You almost got us thrown in a sandy prison cell, you old fool."*

We're still free, aren't we? Axel retorted. *Now shut up and go back to sleep. I've got work to do.*

Orkail was very well-organized and structured, with a large main street full of vendors, stalls and shops, and more than a fair number of rich people. There were many traders and soldiers here right now, Axel saw. He also took note of how most of the town was covered with autumn flowers and citrus trees. The inside of Orkail offered a very different life than that of the desert lands outside—it was like Aether's Garden, surrounded with his flame.

Axel watched the people crossing him in the street. Most of them wore silk clothes decorated with laceworks, and preferred to ignore him, seeing as he looked the very picture of a dirty beggar after spending days traversing the badlands leading to town. The carriages, passing him by, he saw, were covered with velvet and handmade cotton flags, with fancy looking drivers.

"Ulor is smart enough to have the rich people live in towns closest to the capital," Axel's inner voice said. *"Oohh! Rich people really love being alive, don't they?"* Axel's other self looked though his eyes at the rich ladies looking at the window of luxury shops. He could hear one of the salesmen say to one of them: "This jewelry is fit for the queen herself, madame! You would shine during Imperation Days like a light from Aether." The women giggled and examined the piece.

Axel shook his head and silently rode his horse to the side streets. He was in a hurry, but he couldn't ride his horse too fast and risk drawing too much attention. Eventually, after riding around the side streets for some twenty minutes or so, Axel found the store he was looking for. Outside the store, he saw a small pot made from clay with a lotus painted on it. It stood right next to the door, which was itself painted with a nicely decorated garden full of trees and flowers. The entire store was made of wood, which was uncommon in Orkail, as most buildings were made out of stone and clay.

"Here she is." Axel said to himself and dismounted his horse. It was a fabric shop, full of silk, leathers and laceworks. Axel stopped and looked at the lotus flower, making sure it was the right one, before he slowly and carefully walked in. He smelled the air of the shop picking up the scents of a freshly bloomed rose garden.

"Is anyone here?" He gently called out. An old lady in a nicely sewed dress walked out behind the coils of fabric and lace. Her eyes examined Axel.

"How can I help the stranger?" She asked. She was almost his age and was cross-eyed—with one eye looking left and the other looking right. Her wrinkled skin was almost fully covered with silks, revealing only her face. Her hair was covered with a white silk scarf and pinned under her chin as well, and she wore colorful leather shoes that made almost no sound as she glided through the stone floors and walked closer to Axel.

"I'm looking for some special items, Lady." Axel said, bowing slightly to her.

Her hands moved over the silks she hung at the counter, to present to her customers. "Then you are at the right spot, stranger." She replied. It became evident she was also a hunchback as she came closer.

"Do you require silk or laceworks?" She became more specific. Axel shook his head.

"No, I need more... *special* things." He walked closer to her and looked into her eyes. "Things that can only be supplied by faith during war times." He said in low voice. Her little nose moved up and down, smelling Axel, before saying another word.

"Says the man who smells as dead as a Dreamer." The old woman replied.

"Life is for the ignorant." Axel told her. The old woman smiled.

"Welcome to my humble shop, my lord." The old woman locked the door of the shop and walked through a room behind it.

They entered a room like a kitchen. She pulled a chair and sat at the table. So did Axel.

"How may I serve you?" she asked.

"I need amethysts, food and nice clothes that can fit a Chosen and two others—a young man and a woman."

"Foods and clothes are easy... but amethysts?" She said in confusion.

"I'll pay you well." Axel informed her.

"Oh, my lord, I am not worried about coins. They are very rare these days and the war..."

"I know, my lady. You'll have enough of the stones back to protect yourself as soon as I reach Kellum. Think of it as more of a… temporary investment."

"Thank you so much. That is very generous of you." She said, and pulled a counter. Then, she moved a piece of wood from the wall, took out a velvet bag and extended it to Axel. He opened it to see how many amethysts it had. There were enough stones in the bag to suck all the power out of Kade ten times over.

"Come with me." She said, after pushing the counter back and putting all the dried meat and bread she had in a bag. They walked back to the shop again. She gave the food to Axel and took out some pants, cloaks and shirts she'd already prepared for such a request—as Axel wasn't the only traveler that came by, looking for similar items. While the old man picked among the clothes for all his friends, and himself, she extended him a pair of large leather boots.

"The trousers will be short for a Chosen. Use these tall boots and a good, strong belt." She advised.

Axel had no words to say concerning her taste, as everything she gave him was of the highest quality. She wrapped up his needs in a bundle, and Axel beamed at her with the biggest smile he'd had in years.

"May Aether bless you, sister." He said to her while extending her the coin bag. She pushed it back to him.

"No money needed, my lord: favors in hard times should always come from the heart." She smiled at him and Axel slightly nodded. He held her hand from her wrist.

"You are thus marked then, sister. From my hand to Aether," Axel raised his right hand: "When the darkness rises, you will be protected." Axel swore to her. The old lady paused for a second without knowing what to say. Her eyes shone with happiness.

"Send word: the Destiny is at the doors of the capital." Axel said, then left the shop with his goods.

The old lady walked behind him and watched him leaving with a smile on her face and hope in her heart.

***

While Axel was busy in Orkail, Kade was keeping a low profile back at camp, watching as Merki washed Locke with a piece of cloth from water gathered in the river.

They'd already set a small camp and filled their water skins to the brim—after drinking their fill. Merki had given Locke some water, a trickle at a time, until his breathing had smoothed out and stopped rasping.

Now, she pulled him next to her and washed his face, neck, arms and torso with a piece of cloth, careful not to move his injured leg too much. She'd removed his shirt, and her hands moved deftly over his body, cooling him down. The more she touched his face, the softer her touches became. She eventually put his head on her lap, and ran her fingers through his hair, waiting for him to wake up. Despite herself, she could feel her heartbeat rising higher and higher. She found herself worrying that the young man wouldn't wake up at all, as his fever had been quite bad before. Then, suddenly, Locke's lips moved in weak, wordless speech.

"Locke? Locke… Wake up." She said. "Drink this… C'mon, drink."

She grabbed the flask next to her and gave him another trickle of water, which he greedily gulped. His temperature seemed to be stabilizing, she noticed with a sigh of relief. She allowed herself a small smile. She didn't know why—she had never felt like this before about anyone… but here, she realized, she cared about this man. About all the people she was traveling with. The thought surprised her and gave her pause for a moment. Then, she realized it felt good to care for others that way again. It'd been so long since she'd done so, only focused on her own goals of wanting to get out of Halstead, she'd nearly forgotten…

Locke's paled skin slowly found life again. He turned his head to Merki with a pleasant murmuring sound. He wasn't fully awake yet, but he seemed stronger, and awfully happy, laying on Merki's legs as he was.

"Locke…" She whispered. "You with us again?"

"Yeah…" He croaked, his throat still dry. Merki gave him more water and continued ministering to him, until, eventually, the young man managed to prop himself up on his own.

"Thank you." He said.

"Of course. Take it easy—you're still weak."

Locke nodded, then looked at Kade. "You're still with us, huh?"

Kade looked up from what he was doing. "Are you surprised? With all the chances I've had to run away by now?" He smiled. "I told you already—I'm heading to the capital to find my brother, and you're all my best shot at doing that in one piece."

He still doesn't remember what happens to Chosen who are found guilty of treason... Locke thought, feeling a sudden pang of guilt.

"Plus..." Kade continued, then hesitated.

"Plus?" Locke asked.

Kade smirked. "I'm not going to leave you to fend for yourselves—not as you are right now." He nodded towards Locke's leg.

Locke smiled, despite himself. "I... appreciate that, Chosen."

"It's Kade... You know that." He said. "Anyways, I'm glad to see you're up. We thought we'd lost you there for a moment." Kade continued.

Locke offered him a painful smile. "Oh, you're not getting rid of me yet either—not that easily. I have my reasons to make it back too—and they're just as strong as yours... Kade."

Kade smiled, but it was a sad smile. He looked down at his feet. "I'm... not so sure about that." He said.

Merki and Locke perked up. "What do you mean?" Locke asked him. "Do you finally remember?"

Kade nodded.

"How much?"

Kade looked up, sighing. "All of it."

CHAPTER 22

THE SCENT OF ROSES

The stars and the moon shining brightly above Kellum complimented the dying light of the candles and fireplace in Ifir's room, through the windows. Already asleep in her bed, Ifir suddenly opened her eyes as she heard a weak knocking sound coming from her wall.

Slowly, without making a sound, she grabbed the dagger under her pillow and slid noiselessly out of her bed, padding towards the source of the sound in the wall. Her hand reached the keystone that opened the secret door in her chambers—which she thought, until know, that only she knew about. As the hidden stone door slid open to the side, Ifir's eyes met with near total darkness—but her senses warned her to the man standing there, shrouded by the shadows. She grabbed the man by the wrist in a flash and then, using her superior strength as a Chosen, threw him out of the shadows and onto her carpet, landing on him in a heartbeat, her dagger at his throat.

"Finally." He said, feeling the cold edge of the dagger on his neck. "I'd rather be killed by your dagger than die in a rat hole." He said with a smile, his breath smelling of wine.

His half-buttoned cotton shirt, leather belts and tight trousers were familiar to Ifir; as simple as an ordinary man's, but as high-quality as those in a king's own wardrobe. Despite the faded light of the candles, the moon and stars revealed the man's face. His hand slowly reached out to Ifir's like a feather floating in the air. She loosened her fingers, feeling his soft touch, and her rush of adrenaline suddenly receded at the calm feel of his skin. His long fingers covered her hand, holding the dagger, then pushed it away from his neck as he moved forward to kiss her hand like a gentleman, not caring for the sharp edge of the dagger, inches away.

"My queen." His voice was to Ifir as a cool breeze on a hot summer day.

"Derum." Ifir asked, the question clear in her eyes. "What are you doing here?" Her face got lost between surprise and confusion, while her hand showed him to the chairs near the dying fire.

Her voice wasn't very welcoming, but still respectful. Derum shrugged, understanding her surprise, and sat on the chair she'd offered him. He silently watched Ifir's beauty, lit by the fading, flickering light of the fireplace. Even with her bed hair and tired, confused eyes, she seemed as radiant to Derum as always.

"You never change…" He said, his eyes wandering all over her, his mind remembering every inch of her body—especially the tips of her breasts, clearly visible through the silk of her gown in the cold night. Ifir watched him closely, wondering how to begin. He finally stopped ogling at her and added: "… my queen."

"Derum… I could've killed you. What are you doing here?" She asked.

He took out a small cylinder from his shirt pocket. "Urgent message for you, my love. Sent via Peregrine falcon." He said. Ifir nodded, looking at the cylinder held between his fingers… but a part of her felt oddly disappointed by the news.

"… I see. And you couldn't send the message via bird? You know they know their way here." She said, with more than a little hint of playfulness in her voice.

"And miss seeing you in all of your… bedridden glory?" He asked with a mock frown. "Never." He smirked at her, then extended the cylinder to her, still held between his fingers.

Ifir reached out to grab it, then he pulled it back, leaning forward. "Ah, ah, ah… don't I get a pre-payment for delivering this personally?" He winked.

Ifir gave him a knowing, playful smirk, then snatched the message out of his hand. "We'll see." She said. She broke the seal and unrolled the paper. Her eyes glowed as she read the message:

Love and loyalty cover my heart like bramble roses. No matter how many thorns prick my heart, my commitment is sealed with my blood to this love, and the roses are mature enough to envelop the world.

Ifir took a deep breath and burnt the coded message in the nearest candle. While the paper turned to ash, the strong smell of roses covered the room. Derum knowingly smelled the air and his eyes searched for a clue on Ifir's face. Was it a love message? A hidden business deal? A… conspiracy of some kind? No… the rose scent said otherwise. So… a lover then, he thought grimly. Ifir, however, didn't give him any hints, just another smile like she usually did.

As the message curled up into smoke, Ifir looked into his eyes and her lips slowly moved. "Thank you, old friend." Then she moved back, away from him.

"Always a pleasure, my queen." Derum slightly bowed his head, looking suitably deflated. It didn't look like he'd be getting what he'd come all this way for, after all. Ifir looked at the night sky, already starting to glow with the hues of the sunrise as a thin line in the horizon, over the sea.

"Beautiful, isn't it?" She said, beholding the display of colors in the distance like a painting, slowly revealing itself over a dark-blue canvas However, Derum's eyes were on her rather than the sky. "Not as much as you, my queen."

Ifir stood up and smirked knowingly at the man. "You are so kind Derum, as always. And… while I'd love to enjoy your company a bit more while you're here…"

Derum stood up and bowed. "It is time to get lost in the darkness from whence I came…" He said.

Ifir looked honestly regretful. "I'm afraid so."

"And yet…" Derum said, moving closer to her… "A good man knows when to take things slow… and when to move fast. We could still have our way, my queen… And be done before the day beckons you elsewhere." He ran his fingers up Ifir's bare arm, sending shivers up her spine. She felt the familiar rush pulse through her, her heart skipping a beat, and her pupils dilated.

"I…" She began.

"Shh…" Derum said, putting a finger to her lips, looking right down at them with the hunger of a wolf that hadn't seen meat for a whole week.

She was about to let herself get lost in her desires, their lips awfully close to each other, when the sound of carriages down below suddenly reached all the way up to her chambers. There were many of them, she realized—and they were being escorted by soldiers. All of a sudden, the magic swelling inside Ifir was snuffed out, her mind flying in every direction, assessing the new situation. An escorted set of carriages meant royalty. Was Ulor or Etheria out on some clandestine task that she didn't know about? Where they about to set out on one? She knew all of their moves, their schedules, and knew they weren't supposed to go anywhere today… Derum saw it in her eyes—how his chance was gone now for good, and stepped back to leave. Before he did, however, he cleared his throat. Ifir looked at him again, as if realizing he was standing there for the first time.

"Do let me know if I can be of any other service in the future, my queen." He said, and disappeared through the hidden passage once more. Ifir just nodded, without bothering to say another word. As soon as the man's footsteps disappeared down the winding staircase beyond the wall, Ifir pushed the keystone again, and the hidden door slid back in place, the system of pulleys behind the stones going to work.

Ifir then ran to her balcony to assess the situation below. The king's carriages were in front of the castle, a troop of elite Chosen ready to move all around them.

"Dammit Ulor… Dammit!" Ifir exhaled, then rushed to get clothed and ready without waiting for Mere.

***

Etheria and Ulor stopped in front of the carriage, seeing Prince Urail and Commander Siegen already inside. Etheria gently placed a kiss on her husband's cheek.

"Enjoy the hunt, my king. I'm looking forward to your return already." Her fleshy red lips smiled brightly as she bent her head. Ulor held her chin and put a kiss on her lips. His hand hovered over the queen's belly, saying a quick farewell to his future son in there. Etheria put her hand over his and smiled, then he got into the carriage. Prince Urail waved at Etheria from the soft, plush, red-velvet seats inside.

"Mother."

"Good luck, my prince. May Aether be with you." She waved back to her beloved son.

Siegen saluted the queen as appropriate, adding "my queen," and the carriage left the castle. After waving her hand long enough, until the carriage and its escort had all but disappeared, the smile on Etheria's face left on the wind. Etheria then entered the keep and climbed the stairs to the second floor—and to her surprise, she saw Ifir and Princess Flora walking together in the corridor, the princess' maids following them close behind. Mere, Ifir's personal maid, was also tagging along closely. Etheria stopped in her tracks upon seeing them. She saw how Flora had a huge smile on her face, laughing at the things Ifir told her. Etheria could see the admiration in her daughter's eyes for the Songbird of Kellum… and it made her squirm all over.

"Mother." Flora said in greeting.

"My queen," echoed Ifir, bowing her head slightly.

"Flora. Ifir," Etheria smiled, as kindly as she knew how. "Where are you two going?"

"I have archery lessons today, mother… remember?"

Etheria nodded. "Ah yes… of course. I just thought she'd be taking her first lessons from the master of the Ranger Corps." She turned to Ifir, directing the unspoken question at her.

"And she is, my queen," Ifir said, bowing again. "I just ran into her on my way down and decided to accompany her."

"Ifir is so kind—look at the gift she gave me, mother!" Princess Flora extended her hand to the maid behind her and the maid

The Scent of Roses | 273

passed her a small wooden horse, posed in the middle of its gallop. She passed it to the queen and she looked it over, turning it in her hand.

"A masterpiece. Incredibly well-sculpted." She said. The horse was indeed a work of art—carved to such a level of detail that even its muscles and bristling hair could be seen and felt along its body.

"Thank you for such a thoughtful gift, Songbird." Etheria said, nodding slightly.

"My pleasure. Only the best of everything for my princess," She said, smiling widely. "Now that you're here, my queen, if you'll excuse me…" She said, urging Flora to join her mother. With a nod from the queen, Ifir left the second floor and walked down the stairs to the castle's entrance. Etheria, on the other hand, kept looking the horse as if she expected to find some sort of secret purpose in it. Flora could see the distrust in her eyes.

While Ifir walked furiously out of the castle, heading for its main doors, a male voice suddenly called out from behind her.

"Songbird?"

It was none other than Odmund, she realized. She stopped at her spot and took a deep breath. Mere saw it and felt a shiver rise up her spine. Fearing what could happen, she stood away and to the side, head down. Ifir clenched her teeth, put a fake smile on her face, then turned back to face Odmund with wide-open arms.

"My dear Champion." She said. "How are you today?"

"Fine," he answered, rather coldly. "I'd like to have a word with you, if I may?" He looked all business today, and Ifir had a suspicion she knew why.

"Sure." She answered kindly, looking the very picture of an innocent lamb.

"Can we… go somewhere more private?" He asked, looking around at all the people walking back and forth in the castle foyer.

Ifir nodded, then led him to an elegant side room where castle guests were usually made to wait before audiences with the king. The room was lined with comfortable couches and chairs, and held an impressive table at its center, which would be topped with food and refreshments on particularly busy days. Today, the room was nearly empty, save for a few servants.

"Everyone out," Ifir commanded upon entering, and everyone scuttled away. She locked the doors behind them, then turned towards Odmund.

"Now... what did you want to speak about, my dear?" She asked Odmund, her voice as soft as silk.

"You didn't allow Efilia to participate in the Chosen Tourney." He said.

"No." Ifir replied, as if nothing was wrong.

"Why?" He asked. "What did she do wrong? She got the top scores in the preliminaries to the tourney—best Veruter in her class. Why keep her from participating? From the opportunity to rise in the ranks faster, as she should?"

Ifir listened closely and nodded as he spoke, arms crossed. Then, she walked closer to him, almost gliding, like a snake, and stood before him. She looked deeply into his eyes, and held out a hand to his cheek.

"Why, my dear... Because you love her." She said, causing Od to flinch in place, eyes wide. "And she loves you... But you'll mostly likely become the Sword of Aether, my champion—you'll have powers that the rest of us can only dream of. You are the destiny of all the races; the destiny of the world, even. Efilia... she needs to be so much more than she already is. She has to become better for you, for herself, and for our race. If she is to..." Ifir looked for the word carefully, almost as if she were savoring it in her mouth with her tongue. "If she is to *survive,* yes... then she needs to be up to par. You will, after all, face dangers such as the Judges, and their foul creators. You will stand against all our enemies. In truth... I am doing both of you a favor here... even if she can't see it yet." She stepped away and looked at the young man—at the effect her words had had on him.

Odmund considered her words for a moment, then shook his head. "But... even so... how does denying her the opportunity to gain glory and fame, to rise up faster, help her in any way? She's worked hard for it—she deserves it!"

"Efilia is very skilled, that much is true." Ifir said, nodding. "She even stands a good chance of winning the tourney. But what she has in natural potential, she lacks in restraint and self-discipline. Have you not noticed, dear Odmund? How prone she is to fits of emotion and outbursts?"

Odmund looked away from Ifir's penetrating emerald eyes.

"She's much too reckless. She needs to learn to temper that, ah, *temper* of hers, to control her emotions and power—if she's to survive the times that await her. Having her compete in the tourney and win would be doing her a disservice. She needs the experience that comes with climbing the ranks normally, as any other Chosen does."

Odmund took a deep breath. Ifir's words made sense, and… she really did seem to have Efilia's best interests in mind. But how could he explain something like that to Efilia? Tell her that it was all for her own good—because she was too gifted, to reckless?

Especially after what he'd seen her do the other night.

Odmund stayed silent for a moment longer, and another thought hit him—something else Ifir had brought up. The idea and reality of awakening as the Sword of Aether pierced him like a cold blade, running him right through the chest. Did he really have that power? Could he really defeat something like a Night Judge with his bare hands, as the legends and myths foretold? And… was it right of him to force Efilia to share in that destiny—and all the dangers involved with it?

Eventually, after letting out a very long sigh, he looked back into Ifir's eyes.

"I'm… I'm sorry, Songbird." He said. "I just thought… I mean, she was so sad and upset. I just want her to be happy."

Ifir put a hand on his shoulder. "I know, Champion. Now… is there anything else? I do have the world's largest intelligence network to run, dear." She said, a smirk on her lips.

Odmund shook his head. "That was all, Songbird." He nodded.

Ifir nodded back, then turned to leave, ordering Mere to open the doors, when Odmund spoke.

"And Songbird…"

"Yes?" She looked at him over her shoulder.

"Thank you. For looking out for her."

Ifir smiled. "Of course."

Then she turned and left the room, but her smile stayed there, with Odmund, replaced by a visage as cold and calculating as stone.

Ifir then summoned her horse outside the main keep's gates and mounted it. She covered her head with her silken hood, leaving Mere behind to see to her tasks, and rode out into the city—alone, as she tended to do.

***

Back at the castle, Hugo trained in how to help a Chosen dress in full armor, using a wooden model. He first put a cotton shirt on it, then he tried placing the back portion of a steel cuirass on the mannequin's back, but dropped it at his feet with a loud clang.

Radolf, watching him from the side of the room, took a deep breath.

"Maybe it would be the best if we train you for bath duty...? Those pieces of armor look far too heavy for you to carry." He said.

Hugo lowered his head. "I'm sorry, sir."

"That's quite alright. We'll find a proper task for you yet. Come on." Radolf beckoned him to follow and they exited the room, heading down the maze-like corridors under the castle. Eventually, they arrived at an area Hugo didn't even know existed—somewhere under the Nest. It was so humid and hot, but smelled incredibly nice. Hugo could barely breathe, however, due to the heavy smell of roses in the air.

In the room, there were so many women washing sheets and clothes with bars of rose-scented soap and pouring rose essence in their cleaning water. Some other of them ironed the pieces by putting hot coals in the iron pressings. A stairwell then led to a garden behind the Nest—the Chosen training building, full of clotheslines, holding a sea of washed clothes and linen from all around the castle grounds. Among the fluttering sheets, Hugo thought he saw a familiar face. He

The Scent of Roses

walked away from Radolf, weaving under bedsheets and soggy pants, and soon got a good look at the girl. He stared at her, eyes glowing, beaming. It was the girl he'd met in the kitchen… Loure. The young woman saw him staring in the distance, beyond the fluttering clothes, and slightly smiled, holding up a hand. The young man grinned even wider and held up a hand as well.

"Are you done ogling the grotesque, then, boy?" Radolf said, standing beside him.

"The grotesque… she's beautiful!" He said in her defense.

The old butler rolled his eyes in an expression that said: *"I'm too old for this."*

"If you say so. Now come, I need to introduce you to the bathhouse mistress."

"Wait, wait! Just a second. What happened to her?" Hugo asked, nodding towards Loure in the distance.

"Nobody knows," Radolf said. "They say it was an accident. She was apparently working on the frying vats by the kitchen, and got some of the burning oil on her face somehow. Others say she was cleaning the head physician's office and accidentally splashed a glass of acid on her face—the kind used to treat certain poisons. However, that theory sounds like rubbish to me." He curled his lips then turned his back. "Either way, there's a lesson to learn here, young Hugo. It's best to keep to your own business around these parts. Just do your job well and keep your head down. You'll live longer and easier that way, believe you me." Radolf shrugged his shoulders and walked away. "Now come. We've got work to do."

Hugo turned his back to see Loure one more time, but she was already lost among the white, dancing sheets. Radolf then led Hugo down an adjacent entrance to another basement in the yard. This one wasn't a washroom, but the Chosen baths and steam cellars. Radolf introduced Hugo to the bathhouse mistress, the head maid in charge of the area, and she showed him over to one of the baths; one where a bath servant was currently washing a Chosen.

"You have to be gentle," the bath mistress showed Hugo. "All of your moves should be circular, like she's doing. Slow, gentle, circular…."

She showed Hugo all the tricks to bathing a Chosen the right way—providing the ultimate relaxing and invigorating experience. Eventually, they got Hugo in washing clothes and set him next to a newly arrived Chosen—another young man in his late teens, who happily sat in the hot water of his copper bathtub. Hugo then proceeded to wash him, under the instruction of the bath mistress, then another, and another, until his hands were all pruney and his clothes all wet.

"I think we finally found what you're good at, young man." Radolf proudly said. "You may start your new job soon."

Hugo's eyes grew big, and he was speechless. His eyes shone with the pride of finally finding something he could excel at in the castle—something he could be recognized for.

"Excellent work, Hugo, I'm sure Master Odmund will be thrilled to hear of your progress. Now go change into your regular clothes, son. You don't want to get sick in that soggy uniform." Radolf reached out a hand and ruffled his wet hair like a son, which Hugo did not object to in the least. Humble work as it was, he couldn't believe he'd found a place where he could fit in, and where his work would be valued and appreciated.

"Yes, sir." Hugo said, and watched as Radolf and the bath mistress walked away, talking amongst each other, no doubt discussing his services and future work details. When he was left alone to go change, he heard a soft voice behind him.

"Congratulations… You'll soon be serving the Chosen themselves." Hugo's heart beat so fast, he actually felt dizzy for a second. The voice behind him was no other than Loure's.

"You! Uh, I mean… hello! Loure, right?" Hugo said, wiping a hand dry on his apron and extending it to her. The young girl shook it, and Hugo enjoyed the soft feel of her hand against his for the little time it lasted.

"You remembered. That's very kind of you." She said, smiling. "You were… Hugo, right?"

The young man nodded vigorously. "Um… yeah. Yeah. You remembered too!" He said, feeling like he was about to throw up and pass out all at once.

The Scent of Roses | 279

"Well… you were very nice to me, back on the day we met."

Hugo nodded, then stared, not sure what to say. "So…" He began. "You work here in the baths too?"

But Loure shook her head, a little sadly. "No… Across the yard. In the washing cellars."

"Ahh," said Hugo. "I'll be working here from now on. We'll be close!"

Loure smiled and nodded. "Looks like we will. How did you get to bathe Chosen right from the start, though? Usually, it takes a servant years to get close to the Chosen… Do you… know people here at the castle, Hugo?" Loure asked, giving him a curious look.

"Who, me? I, uh…" He considered whether he should tell her or not… then decided that yes, he would tell her, of course. It was Loure, after all. "I do. I'm uh… friends with the champion, Odmund. He's the one who brought me here to the castle. Do you know him?"

Loure blinked several times. "You… are friends with the Champion of the Kollek?" She asked.

Hugo nodded vigorously. "Yeah. He, uh… he brought me here and gave me a job. He was friends with my… um, family, before, when I was little." He was ready to tell her about Odmund, and hopefully impress her… but not about his brother. Not yet.

Loure looked at him with different eyes. She couldn't tell whether to laugh or to sigh. This kid? A poor hunchback, friends with the Champion of Kellum? Yeah, and she was the queen's head masseur… She stared at Hugo for a long time, wondering what she should say, or do. The young boy stared back, eyes wide, not looking bothered in the least.

"Well… good for you!" She finally said. Liar or not, the kid had to be well-connected, given the circumstances, so she'd be smart to stay in his good graces… at least for now.

"Thank you!" Hugo said, beaming at her.

"Maybe I'll come by here and there and watch you wash some of the Chosen?" Loure asked him, smiling.

Hugo felt like his heart would jump out of his mouth. "T-that'd be great, yes!"

Loure grinned, then got close to him and whispered on his ear. "And maybe one day you can wash me too… Yeah?" Then, before waiting for an answer, she turned around and left, giving him a sly, slightly mischievous smile.

Hugo just watched, eyes wide as a barn, mouth slightly open. He tried to say something, but the words just wouldn't come. Then, after a few minutes of him standing there, staring at the entrance of the bathhouse like a slobbering pup, he realized he was sodding wet, and ran back to the nearby servant room to change back to his regular clothes.

Maybe one day you can wash me too… yeah?

Hugo repeated Loure's word over and over in his head long throughout the day, and if there was any doubt in his heart before, now he knew it for a fact: he really was the luckiest boy in all of Kellum.

Chapter 23

Disassociation Sickness

The group huddled all around Kade in the campsite, outside the town of Orkail.

Upon his insistence, they'd all waited for Axel to come back. Now that he had, they huddled around their fire in silence, waiting for Kade to begin.

"So… you've finally remembered everything?" Axel asked him.

The large man nodded.

"Well? What are you waiting for, then?" Locke said. "Out with it!"

"I…" Kade said, looking down at his feet.

"It's ok. You can do it." Axel said. "You can tell us, Kade."

"I'm Kade, son of Lilian—the hardest-working person I ever met. About my father… I knew him very little. He left home in search of my brother when I was young and never returned. Taken by the Curse, the people always said. I left home to seek my brother after him… because he's the only one that can save Agnes… my sister. She suffers from a rare blood condition that can only be cured by an infusion from a sibling."

"A blood sickness? That can only be cured by the blood of a sibling?" Locke asked. "I've never heard of such a thing."

Kade shrugged. "It must be native to our people, then. It's very real to us."

"And you say only a sibling can cure it? Did you try some of your own blood?" Merki asked him.

Kade nodded. "We all did… Nothing worked. It has to be Ellyad's blood."

"How can you be so sure?" Merki asked.

"Because of a friend. A priest from our temple. He assured me that Ellyad was, indeed, alive—and that his blood is the only cure for Agnes' illness."

"Do you trust him that much?" Merki asked. "I mean… this just seems like such a big quest to undertake on a single man's word…"

"He's a very respected healer among my people… and a good friend. He wouldn't lie to me about such a thing."

"And… who are your people exactly, Kade?" Locke asked, his eyes firmly on him.

"I come from the ancient temple-city of Norzou," Kade said, to the shock of everyone present. "Beyond the Mountains of Antler."

Merki's face went pale at the mention of the place, as did Locke's and Axel's.

"But… that's impossible, Kade." Merki said.

"How so?" Kade asked.

"If you're really from the Antler mountains…" Locke began. "Then that would make you… a Nor."

Kade nodded, seeing no problem with the statement. "I am a Nor." He said.

But Locke shook his head aggressively. "But you *can't* be. The Nor all perished after they followed the Cursed King into war, Kade, thousands of years ago. Those who survived became little more than animals—mindless monsters that are hunted and used for sport at the royal coliseum in Kellum; kept by the king as prized pets in the Direhalls. You're a Chosen—a special Kollek, born to us by a miraculous birth, blessed by Aether to protect his chosen people. Can you really not remember that?" He asked, very passionately, as if Kade's lack of religious awareness offended him.

The big man shook his head, then looked away. "I don't know anything about Aether, or being born 'special' like you said… All I know is growing up in Norzou, among others like me. All of us Nor."

Locke and Merki stared at Kade, and each other, with confused expressions. Axel, on the other hand, stared fiercely at the young man, a deep frown in his forehead, revealing a multitude of creases.

"But… That can't be, Kade. If what you say is true—if you truly are a Nor from Norzou, then the implications are…"

"Immense." Said Merki.

Locke nodded. "I don't even want to think about it, honestly. I mean… did any of the other… *Nor* in your village show any powers or abilities? Like those we see in the Kollek Chosen?"

Kade shook his head. "We're all just common people back home. Like you, or Merki… Uh, no disrespect." He shrugged. "I was just a farmer before I left, myself. Nothing special."

"But they all look like you?" Locke said. Kade nodded. "And you say you first experienced your abilities… the *Curse*, as you call it, after you left… Norzou?"

Kade nodded again. "It's why we're forbidden to leave." He said. "I… broke taboo. I had to, for the sake of my family."

Locke and Merki seemed to reflect deeply upon Kade's words, while the young man just watched them. He stared at Axel several times, but the old man just looked him in the eyes, searching, clearly deep in thought, his expression unreadable.

"What do you think about all this, Axel?" Merki asked him, eventually breaking the silence. "You're awfully quiet."

"I've… been thinking back to my time at Kellum," he began, "working with the Chosen there. There was an… affliction, yes, which was mentioned here and there. It was very rare—something that only affected Chosen who'd been separated from their units after a battle, or left behind after being thought dead, and gone feral in the wilds. The very few of them that were rescued, and subsequently restored, spoke of… things that weren't, as if they were."

Kade actually frowned at Axel's comment. "Are you… are you saying I'm lying? That I'm making all of this up?" He looked suitably upset.

Disassociation Sickness

Axel shook his head slowly, but very deliberately, keeping his stern eyes on Kade's.

"No… not consciously, anyways."

"What are you talking about, Axel?" Locke asked him.

"Disassociation Illness," the old man finally said.

Locke exchanged looks with Merki. She shrugged.

"I've never heard of it," Locke said.

"You wouldn't have. It's something that's happened only very few times throughout Kollek history. Less so nowadays, since Ulor restricted Chosen exposure to going feral so much, and established such strict rules and training to keep them safe. It's very rare for a Chosen to go feral nowadays, especially one from Kellum, and thus, for one to suffer from Disassociation Illness."

"But what is it, old man?" Locke asked. "Is he telling the truth about his sister and brother?"

Axel nodded. "When a Chosen go feral, their abilities, the power in their bodies, turns on them, taking over their minds. Their physical vessels cannot contain it properly, and it runs rampant. In this state, some Chosen create false memories based on what they'd heard before. The longer a Chosen remains feral—that is, controlled by their God-given powers, the stronger this effect becomes."

"So… you really are saying that I'm lying?" Kade asked him, looking outright angry for the first time since they'd brought him with them on the trip.

"Not lying, no. Your sister and her illness are, in all likelihood, real. So is your mother, and your brother. Such strong ties are not easily made up, nor forgotten. However, being a Nor, from Norzou—that, in all likelihood, is a fantasy created by your mind to help you cope with the trauma of going feral for so long. In all likelihood…"

"In all likelihood *what*?" Kade asked, his voice taut and strained, his brow clearly furled.

"… You were on a mission that went horribly wrong… and saw your other Chosen comrades die a horrible death. Maybe by rebels, or even a Night Judge attack."

"We heard of such an attack during our travels south… a Judge attack near Carmeuse Lagoon, which wiped a whole platoon of Chosen." Locke said.

"That's just a few weeks ride northeast of Halstead…" Merki added.

Axel nodded, then turned back to Kade. "The shock of going through such an experience must've pushed you towards the feral state, young Kade."

"That still doesn't explain how he remembers Norzou in such detail, though." Merki said.

"Well, all Chosen learn the history of the Cursed King during their training—it's part of their conditioning as soldiers and protectors of the Kollek race. Maybe young Kade here had an affinity—a special interest in the history of the Nor people, prior to his… ordeal. Thus, when he faced whatever crisis befell him and went feral, his mind grabbed onto his preconceived notions of Nor history as a way of keeping itself whole—a lifeboat amidst a sinking ship, if you will."

Kade's eyes trembled as he listened to Axel's words. He threw the water cup he was drinking to the side and rose suddenly, angrily, causing Merki and Locke to flinch. The amethysts at his neck glowed brightly.

"I know who I am, old man. I know where I came from. Norzou, the temple, the fields, the people—I remember them all clearer than I see you all now before me. They are more real to me than this world of madness; of war, Chosen, kings and Night Judges. Do *not* tell me what is real and what is not."

"Kade… calm yourself." Axel ordered him, seeming unfazed by his sudden outburst, where the other two had turned pale. "I am not against you here. I'm just stating the… difficult, yes, and painful truth. But the truth all the same."

"But it's not!" Kade said.

Axel sighed, but kept his oddly cold, even menacing eyes on Kade. A moment of heavy silence passed between them, and the Chosen man, despite his anger, pain, and clearly superior strength, felt a sudden chill run up his spine.

"Norzou is no more, Kade… A legend, lost to time. Neither are the Nor—not as you remember them." Axel said, in a tone that brooked no further argument.

"I…" Kade began. "I don't understand."

"No one expects you to."

"It all feels so real to me." He finally said, sitting down. The other two visibly relaxed a bit more after he did.

"It would… And I imagine it still will, for some time. It'll get better with time, though." Axel said, looking down at their cooking pot.

"Will… will I remember the truth then?"

Axel nodded. "We'll find you help once we get to Kellum. Your brother is still, in all likelihood, still there as well—or we'll find someone who can help you track him. He should still be a Chosen, like you—not that hard to find. Either way… all will be well, young Kade."

Kade let out a long sigh, then nodded, looking very tired.

"Well… alright." He shrugged, then stood up and walked over to his bedroll. "I… need some time alone. To think, if that's alright."

Axel nodded, and the Chosen lay down, turning his back to the group.

"Axel… will he…" Merki began.

"He'll be alright," Axel said. "Just give him time. It's not an easy thing to hear; that your entire past, your memories and identity, aren't fully what you thought they were."

The other two nodded in silence, then Merki and Axel moved to cook the group some dinner with the goods Axel had brought back from Orkail. They sat and ate in silence after that, glancing at Kade occasionally, who seemed to be asleep in his bedroll, his back to them, staring out into the desert. Merki had offered him something to eat but he'd refused, saying he wasn't hungry. After they'd all eaten in companionable silence, they all headed right to sleep, seeing as they would head out into the Dreamer's Oasis properly tomorrow, and as Axel warned them, they'd need all of their strength for the crossing—even if it'd only take a few days. As the rest of the group drifted swiftly into sleep, Axel tossed and turned in his own bedroll.

He scratched his face, grimaced, and mumbled to himself, unable to find the release of sleep…

… not only because of the kind of pain he knew he'd inflicted on Kade—making him question his own identity, but because of the incessant din of maniacal, wheezing laughter grating against his ears from deep inside of him, from the moment he had.

CHAPTER 24

THE RHYME OF AETHER

In such a hot day, even the few dried grasses on the ground were too lazy to move. There was no breeze to suppress the heat nor shadow to soothe the dried bodies of the travelers, who'd been traversing the unforgiving plains for the better part of three days now.

Their horses trotted slowly through the valley, pulling the little wagon. The dry weather of the Dreamer's Oasis, less than two weeks away from the capital, was a perfect barrier against invasion to Kellum's southeastern flanks, as no large force could survive the trek through the arid, punishing and disorienting land—if they even dared brave it, given the stories. As the group crossed the Oasis, they saw the skulls and bones left of those who had attempted the crossing before them, and dark thoughts clouded their minds.

The Dreamer's Oasis was a wide valley surrounded by sharp mountains that no horse could ever cross. Beyond the western mountains, one would find the lush lands of the southern tributaries of God's River—though that route would be a horrible option for them even if they could access it now, due to Kade being with them. Beyond the eastern mountains was a massive marsh, as wide as the eye could see, known as the Gates of Darkness. The marsh, with its yellowing grasses, was a deadly trap to those who had no idea of the kind of world that laid under the surface of its mirror-like pools of rotting water.

Locke would've preferred following God's River and easily reaching Kellum with a boat, but he knew it just wasn't an option—not with the Chosen in tow.

Kade reached out to his water skin to refresh his dried body, and yet, as soon as it touched his chapped lips, he grimaced in pain and put it back.

"When will we come to the end of this cursed land? I thought it was only supposed to be a few days, Axel, but I only see more desert ahead of us." Merki asked, rather desperately. She shielded her eyes from the burning sun, trying to catch a glimpse of some trees in the horizon, to no avail.

"We should still have around two more days of desert before we reach the green lands beyond…" Axel replied, his voice echoing across the plains and bouncing from the nearest mountains.

"I don't think our water will last us for two days," Merki said, looking at her half-empty flask with worry.

"You did say it'd only be a *few* days, old man." Locke said, from behind them in the wagon. "So, we only prepared for a *few* days. If we don't find water soon, we'll surely die here."

"No worries, no worries," Axel said, his voice raspy and dry. "We will find another source of water soon, of that, have no doubt. Remember the name—there are a number of Oases in the area, remember? Or… was it just the one?" He said the last part to himself, under his breath.

His inner voice started cackling again. *"You old fart, you can't even remember something as vital as this! You've killed them! They're all going to die because of you, hahaha!"*

Kade sighed. "I hope we can find them… or *it*, soon, then." Then, all of a sudden, the young Chosen frowned. He perked his ears up, looking from left to right, and even lifted himself a little in his seat. Merki noticed his strange behavior and rode closer to the wagon.

"What is it, Kade?"

"Can you hear that?" He asked, looking visibly concerned.

"Hear what?" Merki asked.

"There's a sound out here… like drums." Kade said in low voice, unsure of what he was really hearing. "Who could be playing drums out here?" His hand instinctively reached to the amethysts on his neckband, and gripped them tightly.

Merki frowned, then slowed her horse's pace slightly to see if she could pick out the sound too. Suddenly, her eyes bugged out, and she rode back towards the wagon.

"I hear it! By Aether… what is that? Could it be…?"

"What?" Kade asked.

"You know… the ghosts that are supposed to haunt this place? The undead army, marching out there somewhere in the desert?"

Kade's eyes grew big and he looked at Axel, who was looking forward, smiling as he led the horses.

"The Rhyme of Aether." He said.

"The… temple musicians?" Merki asked. "But there's no temple here!"

"Not here, no..." Axel smiled more. "A holy procession of temple musicians from all over the kingdom are walking to Kellum before Imperation Day, and on the way, they always play the Rhyme of the Aether— as a way to remind people that the day is soon to come. Then there'll be silence for a week, while the High King is in the temple, receiving the commands of Aether for the next decade."

"Oh… ok." Merki said, and rode her horse a little farther away again.

"So… no ghosts?" Kade asked.

"No ghosts. Just music." Axel said.

"But how come we can hear it all the way here?" He asked.

"Because of the valley's shape—and the many dotted caves on the western mountains, which eventually open up to the other side. The Dreamer's Caves. They amplify the sound from the river basin, so we can hear its echo all the way here, miles and miles away."

Kade nodded, visibly relieved, then asked: "The Dreamer Caves?"

"Yes. An old name, nothing more." Axel said. "In the ancient days, sorcerers lived in those dark caves alone for days, hoping to

The Rhyme of Aether | 293

find enlightenment in the divine light of Aether. They were known as the Dreamers."

Merki looked at a skull on the ground, next to an old dark piece of cloth which could've been part of a Koartiz flag, and said: "Looks like it didn't work out too well for them, though."

Axel smiled. "No, it didn't. They lost all of their lands here to the Cursed King."

Kade suddenly felt a shiver run up his spine. Locke looked back at Axel, twisting from behind him.

"Don't mention the name of that heathen. Especially not in a place like this." He said.

"… I agree." Kade added.

"Very well. My apologies." Axel said.

The rhythm of the Rhyme was so powerful and ominous that Kade started to get goosebumps. At the start of it, there were only a few beats of drums. But then, the rhythm had gotten louder and grown to include more drums between the first, creating a beat that felt like two armies clashing in the middle of a blood-soaked valley—like the herald of holy judgment, or the coming of a god. The strong beat shook Kade to his very core.

"It's different now, isn't it? Powerful, glorious and terrible: all at the same time." Axel smiled at the big guy and Kade nodded. "This part of the Rhyme describes how Aether created the worlds." He explained. Three short drum solos were followed by other instruments, like pipe and strings that Kade wasn't familiar with. Suddenly, the Rhyme became more jovial and uplifting, like a song of celebration and victory. "Now we are created," Axel said. "All the races."

Locke looked at Axel and saw how much he seemed to be enjoying the Rhyme with eyes of approval. "You seem so well-versed in terms of religion, Axel. When did you become such a devout follower of Aether?"

"Oh, long ago… serving at the castle in Kellum taught me many things, young Locke. I was so furious at first, having lost my family to the raids and spent so much time alone. I hated Aether and everything he stood for. But then, serving the Chosen at the castle, wondering at all they could do, all that they *were*—I understood that Aether has a purpose for everything. That we're all part of a greater tapestry woven by the Master of Fate Himself. We all fit into it and complete it, no matter how small or insignificant the person—the tapestry cannot be complete without each and every one of us."

"Wise words…" Locke said, nodding. "Of course, for a man who got us lost in a desert without water, and didn't count the days properly," he smirked.

Axel smiled. "Who says I didn't? Maybe I planned for us to get a little lost—teach you lot a thing about faith or two."

Locked shrugged. "As long as we don't die out here."

"We won't. Axel said. "And how about you, young master? How did you come to be so devout towards Aether? I've seen the way you act whenever he's brought up during our journey; your prayers and gestures. You're a man of faith."

"The teachings of Aether were… a friend to me, growing up. When I didn't have any. I found I could always find comfort in them—in Aether's promises. Then, as I got older, I just stuck with it, I guess."

"But you do believe?"

"Of course. Any proud Kollek citizen does. We all know Aether's word is the truth—and his Right Hand, our King Ulor, his envoy in this world."

"Of course." Said Axel.

"What about you, Merki?" Locke asked.

"What?"

"Are you a devout follower as well?"

The young huntress shrugged imperceptibly from her horse. "I've never given it much thought."

Locked gazed at her as she trotted besides the wagon.

"If he's real or not—it doesn't make much of a difference to me. I make my prayers here and there, just in case… but I've never gone out of my way to seek his favor or anything, if that's what you're asking."

"Maybe that's why you couldn't make it to Kellum until now." Locke said, before he could stop himself.

The Rhyme of Aether | 295

Merki gave him a long look, which he avoided, hanging his head in regret of having spoken so carelessly.

"I... uh... didn't mean it like that. I'm sorry."

If Merki received his apology, or cared for it, she didn't show it.

"Maybe it was," she eventually said, then seeing Locke's confusion, added: "The reason why I had such back luck getting out of Halstead."

He nodded.

"Or maybe the world's just rotten," she said, and rode away from the wagon.

They then rode silently, listening to the Rhyme fade away as the musician's path took them farther and farther away from the mountains, until the sun started to set.

"Alright, let's stop here." Axel said, and they drew the wagon to a halt. "It'll get dark in a few more minutes. We should get a fire going now."

Merki nodded, then rode towards the back of the wagon where they'd stored bundles of kindling they'd gathered to use for their nightly campsites.

"Remind me why we're riding during the day and not at night, when it's cooler?" Locke asked Axel as the old man dismounted the wagon and stretched his old, wiry limbs.

"Oasis jackals, young Locke. They sleep during the day out here and hunt during the night. We don't want to be out here when they're out there in droves. Our campfire will keep us safe."

"So you've said... but we could easily carry torches at night." Locke said. "They'd help push off the biting cold too."

Axel nodded thoughtfully. "Alright. Have it your way. There's something else other than the jackals and the unnatural cold of this place."

"Let's hear it." Locke said, as Kade and Merki helped him off the wagon.

Axel hesitated for a moment, then shrugged and spoke, smiling. "Just call me a suspicious man... but I wouldn't be caught dead roaming these fell wastes after sundown."

"Why not?" Merki asked, smirking. "Is the wise Axel really afraid of ghosts?" She winked at Locke, who smiled.

Axel chuckled.

"Maybe he is." Locke said, smirking as well.

Then, Kade, walking past them with a bundle of kindling, added. "Or maybe he knows about something that we don't—something worse than ghosts."

Merki and Locke exchanged glances, then looked at Axel, who was now pretending to be busy with something else, the smile all but gone from his lips.

"Fire, fire!" He said. "Let's get that fire going, everyone."

The group got the fire going and tied their horses to some of the nearby cacti. As Merki patted her brown spotted mare down and set a bit of water for her, looking into its eye, a tear fell down her cheek. This surprised her, and she looked down, only to realize that she was holding Rage's water bowl, filling it with what little water she had as usual. She'd done that a few times since… well, since he'd died protecting her—but with all that had happened to them until then, she realized she hadn't had a moment to fully process it—or rather, that she hadn't let herself do so. Now, in the darkness outside the campfire, after hearing the Rhyme of Aether, she thought of her faithful companion. She closed her eyes and let the tears flow, saying farewell to her lifelong friend.

Suddenly she felt a presence near her—a large one. She turned to look and saw Kade, standing her next to her, outlined by the campfire behind him. She couldn't see his features, but when he spoke, his voice was kind and tender.

"Are you alright?" He asked.

Merki quickly wiped away her tears and nodded. "Yeah, yeah… It's just… I was thinking of my dog. Rage."

Kade nodded then looked at the water bowl, from which the horse was now drinking. "He was a fine animal. Seemed to have taken a liking to me back when we set out."

Merki smiled, her eyes lost in thought. "Hah… yeah. Rage could always sense people's intentions. He was a better judge of character than I ever was. He… he was a gift from my father." She said.

"Your father?" Kade asked.

She nodded. "He was my best friend. My father, I mean."

"Was he... I mean, did you... leave him back in Halstead?"

Merki nodded, her eyes distant. "In a way, yes. He died many years ago, back when I was barely more than a child."

"I'm sorry." Kade said. Then added: "What happened to him?"

Merki looked away. "It was an... accident. In the forest."

"Ah... I see. I apologize, I didn't mean to..."

"No... It's alright." Merki said, shaking her head.

"I can see why you'd want to leave your village behind." The big man said. Merki nodded. Then, he put a hand on her shoulder, which greatly surprised her. "I hope you find what you're looking for in the capital." Then, with that, he left, heading back to camp. Merki watched after him, eyes wide, for a long moment. Then, she composed herself, finished tending to the horses, and headed back herself.

I'm sure I will.

Back at camp, Axel was checking on Locke's leg, removing some of the bandages and replacing the healing salve he'd been using to treat the wounds. Between his work and the Rockpour healer's, Locke's leg had been saved, and was now looking well on its way to a full recovery.

"How does it feel?" Axel asked him. "It doesn't look terrible anymore."

Locke smirked. "It sure feels terrible."

"That bad?" Axel asked.

Locke shook his head. "Well... not really. It *is* getting better with each week."

Axel nodded. "Well... you shouldn't put weight on it yet—at least for a few more weeks. But if it doesn't hurt as much, you can try to start standing up with your good leg. I'll be sure to fashion a walking stick for you once we reach the other side—that way you'll at least have a way to move by yourself."

Locke nodded, then grabbed Axel's arm before he left. "I appreciate it." He said. The old man nodded.

Kade appeared next to them then and helped Axel prepare their meal for the night—mostly dried meat, some dry fruit Axel had procured in Orkail and a bit of water. They were rationing what they ate as to not need too much water to process the food. After their meager, but satisfying meal, Axel took Kade to the side, as he'd been doing every night to work on his breathing and focus exercises.

"So, Kade... You've been doing exceptionally well for the past couple of nights."

Kade nodded.

"I... think you're ready to try something different." He said, and Kade frowned, unsure of what the old man meant.

"What do you mean?"

"I think it's a good time to teach you full control." Then, seeing Kade's look of confusion, he added: "The necklace, Kade. I think it's time to finally take it off." Kade's eyes grew wide—and so did Merki's and Locke from across the fire.

"Axel... Are you sure now is the right time to do this? We're in the middle of a desert. What if he goes berserk and..." Locke asked.

"That's precisely why now's the best time to do this, captain." Axel replied. "There's no one around to disturb us, and no one to put at risk."

"Except ourselves."

"Well... I have faith in our friend here that he won't hurt us. Furthermore, I believe he's ready to control his power now... and that he won't go feral."

"But if he does?" Merki asked.

Axel nodded. "You'll hold onto the necklace, Merki. Kneel behind him while he meditates." He turned to Kade now. "As for you, you will continue to breathe, Kade—only focus on your breathing. You'll feel things, hear things... but you will not let them distract you. You will only focus on your breathing, you hear?"

Kade nodded.

"If I see you losing control, I'll signal Merki here." He turned back to Merki. "You'll press the necklace to his skin and the stones will do the rest. Though... I have faith we won't need to."

"How long will I take the necklace off for?" Kade asked.

"Let's shoot for a minute, seeing as it's your first time."

Kade thought about it for a moment, then nodded. "Alright."

Axel looked around. "Everyone ok with this?" Merki and Locke exchanged looks, then nodded as well.

"Here's hoping we don't all die a horrible death tonight…" Said Locke, then sat as comfortably as he could to watch. Merki took position behind Kade and knelt on the ground behind him. Axel sat in front of him, legs crossed. Kade, for his part, took off his shirt first, then sat like Axel.

"We'll begin with breathing exercises first, as we have before. You'll just focus on your breathing." Kade nodded, closed his eyes, then did as told. He began to breathe as deep as he could, then exhale. The cool wind, the warmth of the fire, the sounds and sensations of the desert—they all started to recede to the back of his mind. Soon, Kade's world became his breath, in and out. He only felt his breath, only heard his breath.

Axel nodded to Merki and she slowly lifted the necklace from Kade's neck, over his long hair, and completely away from him.

Everyone watched the Chosen closely.

"In and out." Axel calmly told him, watching him with the eyes of an eagle, looking for any signs in his muscles, veins or neck. The Chosen continued to breathe, his muscles rippling with each rise of his large chest, relaxing with each fall.

Kade was focusing wholly on his breathing—on the sensation of the air flowing into his lungs, when he suddenly felt it.

The Curse—as he'd known it.

However, this time, it didn't seem to come from outside, as he'd previously thought, but from within him. It was like a flame, growing larger and larger inside of him, first in his stomach, then spreading over his body, through his veins and to the very tips of his fingers and toes. He twitched and grimaced and Axel saw it. Kade almost panicked and broke his meditative trance then—but Axel's words, louder this time, guided him back to that centered place.

"In and out, Kade… You've got this… In and out. You are its master… not the other way around."

Kade's breathing stuttered here and there, as if he were sobbing, but he always came back to a steady rhythm. He felt the fire inside him fill his entire body, his mind, his whole self. Then, he realized that it wasn't burning him like before. As he continued to breathe, he noticed that the fire in him swayed, back and forth, along with the rhythm of his breathing. It was alive, like him. It was truly a part of him.

Almost as if reading his thoughts, Axel said: "It's not just a part of you, Kade… It *is* you. Acknowledge it. Accept it. Become it."

Kade continued to breathe, and the fire turned into a pleasant warmth that covered his entire being. The large man suddenly smiled, and so did Axel, upon seeing him.

"There you go… You're doing it. You're doing it, Kade!"

The Chosen nodded and continued to breathe, beholding this new state of being—the purest euphoria coursing through his veins as his body recognized and welcomed his power. He was just about to open his eyes and take it a step further, feeling the flames completely under control, when the entire campsite became surrounded by the bone-chilling sound of agonizing howling and barking. Locke and Merki looked around, and way off in the dark, they saw the shapes of many, many jackals, running around the fire like a swarm of darkness.

"Jackals!" Merki said.

"Don't worry. They won't get too close." Axel told her, then to Kade. "Focus, Kade. Focus on your breathing. In and out…"

"But… the horses!" Locke said.

Axel heard the animals whining and neighing, some pulling against their bridles in an attempt to run away.

The din of sounds overcame Kade's senses, just like they had back at Rockpour. His ears suddenly flung open, and he realized he could not only hear every individual jackal running around them, but also their breathing, the rustling of their fur, and even their heartbeats. The feeling hit him like a crashing wave, knocking him off his centered place, and the gentle flame within him fanned into a roaring fire. He frowned, grimaced and began to sweat.

"Focus, Kade, focus!" Axel said.

"I… I can't…!" The man replied, straining. His muscles began to bulge and his veins popped out all over his skin, running up to his neck. The Chosen groaned, gritting his teeth, trying to control himself.

Axel looked at Merki and, immediately, she pressed the stones against his back. The cooling sensation started to fill Kade's mind, refresh his body, and quench the fire… then the stones burst, their power utterly spent.

Kade's body continued to swell and grow and Merki stumbled back, pushing herself away from the emerging titan before her.

Axel looked up at the Chosen with wide eyes, and Locke, sitting a few meters away, tried to stand up, then fell back down with a yelp, grimacing in pain.

Kade stood up, holding his face with his hands, fearing what was about to happen—what he was about to do, when he suddenly heard Axel's voice through all the others.

"You own your power, Kade—it doesn't own you! BREATHE!"

Amidst the storm of noises, growls, bellowing animals and shuffle of feet and claws, Kade breathed. He took the deepest breath— held it, then let it out. The roaring flames reacted. Another inhale and another exhale. Suddenly, the noises began to focus—instead of coming at him all at once. He realized he could choose what he wanted to hear; Axel and Merki's heartbeats, Locke uttering a prayer of confession and rescue to Aether under his breath, the animals running around them, scaring the horses…

Kade took another deep breath, arched his back, looked to the skies… and unleashed a monstrous roar that shook the very soil beneath their feet.

The jackals all stopped dead in their tracks, whimpered, then scampered away for their lives. The horses neighed and pulled madly against their bridles, threatening to hurt themselves against the cacti, or worse, run away and leave them stranded in the middle of the desert.

Kade looked back to Merki and, with effort, said: "The horses… Go!"

Merki stared at him with wide eyes, trembling, her skin pale.

"Go…" Kade whispered, trying to control his voice, and managed a nod. Merki nodded back, looking into his eyes and seeing him there. She clambered up to her feet then ran towards the horses, shushing them, calming them down, averting the potential catastrophe. Kade looked down to Axel and held out a massive hand. "The stones…" He said.

The old man took out the bag he'd received from his contact in Orkail and produced several amethysts. He walked towards the towering Chosen and, looking him in the eyes, he placed them in his hand, keeping his own firmly over it.

Kade gripped the stones and Axel's hand in his own, closed his eyes, then breathed.

He took one deep breath after the other, feeling the sensation of the fresh stones in his palm; as they cooled the fires within him, tempered them. His muscles returned to normal, his veins disappeared under his skin… and the Chosen continued to breathe.

He opened his eyes, then nodded at Axel.

The old man stared, his eyes full of surprise.

"By Aether, Kade…" He whispered. "You did it. How did you… How did you overcome the power, the feral state, so easily?" He asked, his mouth half-open.

"The Rhyme of Aether," Kade said, smiling. "I heard it in my mind. Mirrored the steady beats with my own breathing."

Then… it worked. Axel told himself. *It really worked. He's finally ready to meet him.*

CHAPTER 25

THE GREAT CITY OF GREENCREST

Urk and his men rode their horses out of Kellum like the wind. The sun was at its zenith, bathing the land with its rays whenever they found a way through the gray, overcast cloud cover, as the soldiers ran their horses north, then west, along the coast, at a consistent gallop.

Maybe this was Urk's golden opportunity, or maybe it was punishment for his antics around Kellum—but Ifir and the king had seen fit to choose Urk, out of all the other Chosen officers in the city, on one of the most important missions a Kollek could ever receive… a Holy Expedition to secure one of the fabled, legendary Manuscripts, left behind by the previous Sword of Aether, which, when put together, would reveal the identity of the new Sword. This would turn the balance of power of the world in favor of whomever claimed them all first, he knew, so it was one of the greatest of privileges a Chosen could receive.

Such a search was also of course incredibly dangerous, as the Koartiz guarded their Manuscript pieces with their lives—and quite often also with the only beings capable of killing Chosen without fail: the Pentaghast's Night Judges.

Now, under the cover of the Imperation Day celebrations, and the confusion and movement involved in the holiday, Urk had been sent to slip into foreign enemy lands and bring back a lost piece of the holy relic—hopefully before the lockdowns began.

After riding for half the day, they were just about to arrive at the sizable walled city of Greencrest, the last bastion of rest before the massive Elderwood. Cresting a small, rolling hill Urk and his men saw the city in the distance, rising tall and grey just before the massive sea of green, yellow and orange treetops that spread behind it. A melody from afar reached his ears then—a song, coming from a shepherd girl, singing a common regional lullaby to her sheep… The melody, together with the peaceful voice of the girl, tugged at his memory in a way he hadn't felt in a long time, reminding him of the nights he spent with Efilia and the other Chosen in the Nest, whenever Ifir would come down and sing for them. The Chosen of his generation cherished those nights—and grew to look up to Ifir as a sort of mother figure because of them, seeing as none of them were ever allowed to know their real mothers. Ifir was, to his generation of Chosen, the mother of all the Chosen… at least until she suddenly changed one day and stopped treating them as such; stopped coming to the Nest, or singing to them, or even treating them as family, as she once had.

Because of Od, no doubt, Urk thought, thinking back to how it all coincided with his childhood rival's ascension to champion—after his Odon powers revealed themselves in full.

Urk remembered Ifir's voice now, as the young girl sung the mournful lullaby.

>*"Hush, hush, little sheep….*
>
>*Don't wake the wolves in sleep.*
>
>*The sun shines upon us.*
>
>*Enjoy the meadows which endlessly lie…*
>
>*Your shepherd's here to guard you.*
>
>*Hush, hush, little sheep…*
>
>*Don't wake wolves in sleep."*

Urk found himself unexpectedly enjoying the melody and slowed down his horse, not to scare the herd.

"Captain?" Hukail called out. His voice distracted Urk and he was broken out of the reverie of the girl's song. A sudden feeling of rage suddenly overtook him—the rage of living his childhood as a Chosen, of never knowing who he really was, where he came from... of losing both Efilia and Ifir, her true love and surrogate mother, to Od.

"What?!" He shouted at Hukail.

The other Chosen soldiers looked at each other. Urk looked angrily at Hukail, waiting for an answer. The soldier tried not to look into his eyes as he spoke:

"Are we stopping at Greencrest for supplies before we head further out?" He asked in a low voice. "I notice we didn't bring much with us... as none of us know where we're heading but you."

Seeing his soldiers' confused and concerned faces, Urk pulled himself together.

"Yes... yes, we are. Even better: we'll sleep in town today before setting out towards our objective. You deserve comfortable beds before the long ride ahead."

His soldiers looked at each other. Hukail spoke again.

"Are we leaving the Kollek lands, sire?"

Urk sighed and looked away towards the town... and the endless forest beyond it.

"Our objective is to be revealed once we're close to it... by order of Ifir. Now, let's go. We're burning daylight, men." He said, then urged his horse to a canter down the grassy hill.

As soon as Urk turned his back, the other Chosen looked at each other again with questions in their eyes. However, they all knew the rules—when Ifir gave orders, they followed them; even to the grave, if need be.

Soon after, they were nearly at the gates of Greencrest, looking up at its huge stone walls. It was one of the most important of Kollek cities, as it was the closest civic center to Koartiz lands in the northwest. Because of this, Greencrest had one of the largest military forces of any other Kollek town or city—but no Chosen, as they'd all been recalled back to Kellum to serve as protectors during the holy ceremonies.

Hukail saw the gate guards send runners inside, telling them: "Chosens are coming! Alert the mayor!"

Urk stopped his horse outside the gates, and the gate guards saluted him and his men, beckoning them forward among the other citizens waiting in line to enter the large town.

"Hail the king's Chosen—Soldiers of Aether!"

"At ease, men." Urk said. "We're here to rest and restock before setting out on an important mission. Send for your mayor or ealdorman, for we need to speak with him."

"Sir, yes sir! He's already on his way, sir!"

Urk nodded. "Good."

A few minutes later, a lavishly clothed man came to greet them at the gates, followed by a group of servants in horses. The man quickly dismounted his own steed and knelt before the Chosen on one knee, bowing his head deeply.

"My lords—I am Bancroft, and this is Captain Audrey, of Northmont." He waved an arm towards a man in full armor and kit, wearing a band of Kollek colors over his chest plate and an elaborate red cape, like Urk. "We weren't expecting Chosen so close to the celebrations. How can we serve the king's own today? We are *honored* to have you here." Bancroft continued, bowing again.

The man was clearly a very well-to-do noble, Urk saw. His big belly hung over his trousers, which were of the finest make, as were his laced silk shirt and lavish red overcoat. His entirely bald head was perch to a circlet of pure gold, a single ruby adorning its crest. The mayor's round face had no signs of any wrinkles, he saw, and his hands were as smooth as a young maiden's. Urk tried to guess which of the noble family he was from… then decided he didn't really care.

"Hail, Bancroft, servant of the king." Urk said, his voice monotone and even. "We are Chosen Knights from the Great City of Kellum, on a mission of the utmost importance. We're here to rest and restock before setting out properly."

"Of course, of course." Bancroft said. "And Greencrest will happily provide. Have you all had lunch yet? What am I saying—of course you haven't, you've been riding all day, yes? Come with me, come with me." The round man said, beckoning them, and barking some quick orders to one of his servants, who galloped away ahead of them on his horse. "I have just ordered my servants to set the table, and I always have extra food prepared in case of guests such as yourself."

Urk looked around the town's entrance square—at the crowd of commoners staring in awe at the cavalcade of Chosen knights entering their city in their glorious, glistening red armors and golden capes. He saw all the poor, starving folk too, and thought upon Bancroft's words with mild disdain.

Him and his men were hungry, however, and they hadn't eaten yet, so he simply nodded at the man. "That would be best. Lead on, Bancroft."

"Excellent!" The stocky man said, promptly mounting his horse with the help of the captain and setting it on a trot towards the city. "Follow me, Chosen!"

As the Greencrest's Captain Audrey mounted his own horse behind Bancroft, Urk silently noted the man's peculiar, yet incredibly well-crafted sword, hanging at his side in a golden, intricate scabbard, and his eyes widened in a flash of sudden shock. He immediately checked himself, hiding his reaction, but filed away the detail for later.

As they rode through the ample streets of Greencrest, Od's sensitive sense of hearing hovered around the citizens like a ghost, selectively picking out their words right out of their mouths and carrying it over to Urk's ears.

"They look so different from our Chosen…" One person said. "Larger… stronger."

"That one looks so scary…" A little boy said on another street.

"Are they here on their way to the Koartiz lands?" A middle-aged woman whispered to her husband.

"An Expedition, this close to the holy celebrations?" Another said.

"Them royals over in Kellum must be mad, sending Chosen away so close to Imperation Day deadline…" A gruff man said.

"Yeah… unless they sent them to die." Another replied to him.

Urk took a deep breath, then continued to follow after Bancroft, disregarding the din of words flowing around him like an invisible hurricane. He decided to keep them there, around him, in case he needed them, but away from him, focusing only on the sounds of his horse and the immediate area.

After passing the square and riding through more narrower streets, they finally arrived at a lavish mansion on the rich part of town. Greencrest wasn't that different to Kellum in that the richer folk lived in the higher districts, while the buildings and houses got poorer the lower the land dipped, all the way to the city gates. However, as with Kellum as well, the main street reflected only the best the city had to offer, with the side and back streets quickly turning uglier the deeper one delved into them. All in all, Urk though, Greencrest wasn't a bad-looking place… especially considering how close it was to the Koartiz border. Most houses were two-story and made of wood in the poorer parts, or stone in the more upscale ones. The major attraction of town, however, was its massive keep—a castle by all means, built right into the northeastern section of the city wall—surrounded itself by a double wall. This was Greencrest Keep, or Anvil's End, as it was commonly known, and it was one of the largest garrisons in all the Kollek lands. That whole part of town, Urk knew, was filled with military barracks, training yards and workshops, housing hundreds if not thousands of soldiers at any one time.

Urk's attention was drawn back to the moment when his ears picked up the many footsteps of servants, running out of the mansion to help Bancroft and the Chosen dismount. Urk refused the servants' help and dismounted himself, however, as did his men. As the servants held the bridles of their horses, about to lead them to the mansion's stables, Urk held the arm of the servant who was leading his horse in a firm grip.

"Never touch them." His words were so sharp and certain that the servant's face grew pale. He just nodded in fear and carefully lead the horse away, looking back at Urk and his men as if they were the Pentaghast themselves.

Bancroft waited for his guests at the door, rubbing his chubby hands, with Audrey at his side. Once the horses were taken care of, he graciously led Urk and his men inside his manor, through the posh and ornate foyer full of columns, priceless vases, paintings from the best in the Kollek lands, and a plush red rug—then left to the dining area. The dining table, made of exquisite, lacquered wood, was already topped to the brim with plates and bowls of hot, steaming food, silver pitches smelling of at least three different kinds of wine at their side. The smile on Bancroft's face showed how proud he was of himself for offering his distinguished guests such a feast in such short notice. He walked towards the table and pulled chairs for each of the Chosen; first for Urk, then the others.

The Chosen captain gazed around the dining room, looking at the many paintings lining its walls, which described the line of Kollek kings as Aether's right hands. One special painting took his attention: one where a young Ulor was held by his father through the clouds, so he touched the sun. In another painting, the moon was standing in King Ulor's palm and stars were falling from his hair.

After they'd all seated, with Urk taking Bancroft's usual position at the head of the massive table, the round man sat next to one of the other Chosen and addressed the captain.

"Please, enjoy yourselves. You're now honored guests of Greencrest, and I hope I don't disappoint."

Captain Audrey stood by the door to the dining room like a ghost, eyes on the room, but not on any particular person.

"Alright. Eat, men. Let us partake of Greencrest's hospitality, then." Having said that, Urk took a piece of meat from the baked turkey in front of him and bit into it, the Chosen soldiers followed suit. They all ate heartily from the feast laid out for them, drinking exotic juices and fragrant wine while Bancroft watched closely. After they'd finished, the round man stood and bowed towards Urk.

"I hope our esteemed Chosen guest is happy with his servant's hospitality?" He asked.

"He is." Urk said, sitting back, noticing the tense atmosphere in the room. He stared at the lavish man and Bancroft froze in his chair. His round face faded like a rose in autumn.

"We are not here for you, Bancroft." Urk explained. "As I said, we are *just* passing by. That said… I'll make sure to mention your kindness in my report when we're back at Kellum. I'm sure our king will be glad to hear of his… ah, *servant's*, hospitality." Urk said, enjoying the moment.

Hearing the last part of the speech, Bancroft fumbled with his fork, dropping it on his plate by accident. He bowed again.

"Thank you, captain. You exalt me with your kindness." Urk nodded and drank the rest of his wine. As soon as he noticed that his men's plates were empty, he stood up.

"The meal was more than delicious, Lord Bancroft. Now we must set off. I thank you for your hospitality." He nodded at the man and left the room, his men doing similarly. Bancroft, surprised by the quick farewell and exit of his guests, didn't know what to say except: "My… pleasure." He stared after Urk and his men as they exited his manor, then, after they'd left, he slumped back onto his seat, grateful to see they weren't here to collect his head.

Urk and his men rode their horses back through the streets of Greencrest, passing the upscale neighborhoods around Bancroft's manor and reaching the town center, where Greencrest's biggest market was currently bustling with vendors selling goods for the upcoming celebrations and trying to draw the passersby's attention.

"We'll come here tomorrow morning to stock up on provisions," he told his men. "Make note of all you'll need. The journey may take us several weeks." His men nodded in response. Urk then dismounted his horse in front of a large smithy.

A huge man with muscles as big as Urk's head was forging a sword, while his two helpers were busy sharping knives. Urk noticed swords of all kinds hanging at the entrance to the shop, carefully crafted out of steel and perfectly engraved. Another older man working at a desk at the end of the shop drew Urk's attention, as he carefully engraved a steel piece. The captain entered the shop and walked towards him after greeting the large smith at the back with a nod, who'd stopped working upon seeing the Chosen enter the shop.

"I hope you're having a good day, master smith." Urk respectfully said to the old man.

The old man kept on engraving, yet answered, his back to Urk. "You too, young man. Let Arron in the back know if there's something you need." He carefully engraved a snake and a falcon on a steel pommel. The others in the shop were all silent, tending to their work. Noticing how his master had no idea who it was who'd just greeted him, the large smith at the back kindly called out to him.

"Master?"

The old man took a deep breath and raised his head. Seeing Urk standing next to him, his eyes got big at first, but then the old man simply smiled at the captain.

"Ahh... welcome, sacred soldiers." He said. Urk looked into his eyes and saw respect and wisdom, instead of fear. He nodded in appreciation of it.

"It is our honor. We are passing by on an important mission and I noticed your works... which look very similar to the ones from the times of the Red Clash."

Hearing mention of the Red Clash made the old man uncomfortable, and his face suddenly got more serious. "You are very kind..." The old man looked at the medals on Urk's right chest. "Captain." He completed his sentence before he turned back to his work.

"Is there any chance you may know the works of Weisor?" Urk asked him.

All the other soldiers got excited after hearing that name. The great master Weisor was the most famous sword master and smith of Kollek history. Despite that, he'd been hung after the last great, full-scale battle between the Koartiz and Kollek armies, known as the Red Clash, fifty years ago. His swords were still kept on display in Kellum, in King Ulor's private collection; as sharp as Aether's nail and lighter than a feather. The blades got famous after King Ulor's father sliced a notorious and publicly loathed Koartiz commander in half with one of them in the great battle—which some historians believe caused the Kollek to win the most important battle in recent Kollek history and prevent the Koartiz from launching another all-out force against them since then. The glory of Weisor's work spread through the kingdom so fast, and people added so many embellishments to the tale as they passed it forward, that Weisor's work had become mythical by the time the war was over. At the end, it was said that Weisor's swords were so sharp they could even cut a Night Judge, despite being creatures of pure magic. That upon seeing their gleaming blades, the vile creatures ran away like scattered, frightened mice. However, after the war, Ulor's father had executed Weisor with the excuse that his ancestors were from Koartiz lands—that the man was a half-breed between both races. Moreover, he accused him of being a sorcerer, and of forging his blades using forbidden magical techniques, and so he hung him one unexpected dawn. Because of this, the myths of the swordmaster had turned into stories of horror.

Presently, the master didn't answer Urk's question. Urk extended his hand to take a sword from the shelf. "May I?" He asked the big smith at the back, who nodded.

Urk hefted the sword in his hand, feeling its perfect weight and balance by holding it by the flat of the blade. He curled his lips as the sword was neither light nor the best he'd ever seen. And yet, he could tell the old man could do so much better. He walked next to the old master, and whispered, very close to his ear.

"We'll be leaving tomorrow morning. Make me a sword that only Weisor's son can make before we do. A blade that can make a Night Judge bleed." Urk stared at the old man, who seemed frozen in place, then stepped back without turning his gaze from him. The old man looked into his eyes and nodded with no sign of any emotion; he just slowly blinked his eyes. Urk nodded and left the shop with his men without saying another word.

Urk walked out into the streets with a knowing smirk in his lips, his men wondering what that whole exchange had been about.

He then looked at some of the other shops in the busy market, selling clothes, herbs, meat and many woodcrafts. After browsing many of them, the Chosen arrived at some stalls selling dairy products and farm goods. Urk took a red apple from an old woman's stall, and bit it. The old woman was surprised, but didn't dare say a word to the massive Chosen soldier in the red cloak before her. Urk looked into her eyes and said: "Hmm, tasty." Then he threw her a silver Koll, which was ten times what an apple was usually worth. Seeing the shine of the coin, woman gasped and looked back at the Chosen. The man on the next stall over looked at the silver Koll with wide eyes.

"I have fresh fruit, TASTY FRUIT!" He announced as loud as he could after Urk, yet the Chosen didn't pay him any attention and walked towards the end of the market.

Eventually, Urk and his Chosen entered the Loon district of Greencrest—a long, wide street lined with Inns, taverns and several bordellos. Seeing as Greencrest held the Kollek's largest garrison, and soldiers needed company, this was easily one of the most lavish red-light district for adults, Urk had ever seen. Drunk men everywhere tried to walk in the arms of whores, laughing and swearing. A woman was trying to take her husband back from a whore's arms, but the strumpet was complaining about not being paid. Urk and his men looked at the lesser whorehouses in disgust, but they eventually found the premier establishment of the street—a tall, ornate, three-story building that did not look like it belonged with all the others, and walked in. A golden sign above the posh entrance read: "The King's Hall." Hukail walked ahead to open the door for Urk and the others. As he did, his special eyes scanned the whole building in just a few seconds, witnessing all the dirty things the men inside were doing, but assessing that the place was safe to enter. With a nod of his head, the Chosen walked in. All of a sudden, the music being played by the high-class bards on the raised, red stage inside stopped. The men and women at the tables stopped eating. Only Urk and his men's footsteps could be heard. A few young, scantily clad girls sitting in the laps of Kollek soldiers stood up. Urk looked around to find an empty table big enough for them, noticed a big table on a dark corner, and walked over to it. Seeing them pick their own table, the girls ran to clean it.

"Bring us wine." Urk ordered to one of the serving girls, and she nodded. "The best one," Urk added before he left.

Looking around, one of the Chosen noticed some other Kollek soldiers sitting few tables away from them. None of them were speaking, and were trying not to come eye to eye with Chosen, wondering what they were doing there at that specific time, so close to the celebrations. Like everyone else outside, they all feared the Chosen were there to exact the king's justice on someone who'd crossed a line—to make a public statement. Their fears were put to rest when Urk next spoke:

"At ease, soldiers. Tonight, we have fun before we hit the road again." Urk said, smiling. He then raised a hand to signal the bards to continue their show. As the music resumed, the jovial atmosphere returned to the high-end establishment. His men nodded with a smile.

The girl brought a wine bottle and several glasses, then poured the wine to the Chosen. Urk held her arm quite strongly before she could pull away. "You drink first." He said in a sharp voice, then he added without letting her arm go. "Please."

The girl couldn't move out of fear. Her eyes looked at the owner of the place, standing behind the counter. With his nod, she brought the glass to her red lips with shaking hands. As the wine went down from her throat, Urk waited for few seconds, then said: "Great." With one flick of his wrist, he sent her away.

"Captain?" Frain, one of the Chosen asked. "The smith… Do his swords really look like Weisor's?" He asked. Seeing the kingdom's heirlooms, such as Weisor's blades, was an award given only to Chosen lieutenants and above. Urk was one of them, and the only one at the table who'd had the honor of seeing some of the king's heirlooms.

Urk pursed his lips thoughtfully. "We'll soon see." He answered.

The Chosen soldiers drank a few bottles of wine then talked and laughed together for few hours, as if they were back in Kellum. Once they were finished listening to the bards and watching the girls dance in the raised stage, Urk left three gold Kolls on the table, then walked over to the master of the house, behind the counter.

The man bowed. "How can I serve the king's Chosen tonight?" He said.

Urk placed a velvet bag full of coins on the counter.

"Give us your cleanest quarters for tonight… and send the most beautiful girls you have up to them." He said. The man nodded. "Your wish is my command, Chosen." With that, Urk walked outside, leaving his men to enjoy the night as thoroughly as they could.

He knew, after all, it might very well be the last time they ever did.

CHAPTER 26

FIRE IN THE NIGHT

The voices rising from the dining hall echoed throughout the castle.

The king and his men had recently arrived from their hunt with many deer, boar and rabbits, and the members of Kellum's high society were enjoying a feast traditionally set before the Imperation Day ceremonies known as the Advent Feast, along with the royal family. The great dining hall was decorated with pinecones and pine tree branches, which symbolized the incoming festivities, set in ornate displays. Red silk curtains complimented all the green and many fireplaces kept the people warm during the gathering, as the weather was starting to get truly chilly. Maids ran around the hall, setting the tables and properly allocating all the food the chefs had prepared for the dozens and dozens of guests. The royals were at their table, while the rest of the folk ate at long tables lining the hall, seated according to their ranks; the lower the noble's rank, the closer they were to the hall's great doors, near the exit.

Prince Urail stood up after receiving his father's blessing. With his clap, the royal crier clapped his hands noisily to hush everyone, calling for their attention. All of a sudden, everyone in the room stopped talking, and Urail stepped forward. Flora watched her big brother from with admiration, seated beside him at the table, the look of pride in her eyes no different than that of her mother's. Seeing such a moment of unity in the royal family, Ifir looked away from the royal table for a moment. She then bit her lip and turned her eyes back to the prince, not to depart from the proper etiquette that was expected of her at such a public gathering.

"Subjects of our High King Ulor. As your prince, I am honored to present the spoils of our latest hunt, in which my father and I recently took part." Suddenly, many animal heads were brought to the hall in large plates by maids, which they then presented to the people.

"All of our spoils will be distributed to the citizens of Edgetown and the Silence, before the festivities, as a sign of the great generosity of our king." Those assembled clapped politely at the announcement. Urail raised his hand again.

"Behold, the spoils of our hunt!" The young man said, and a small army of servants walked into the room with trays upon trays of deer, rabbits and boar—enough to feed half the people in both the Silence and Edgetown for a day. The people clapped as the dead carcasses passed them by, more out of etiquette than anything else. This was the young prince's moment, and they all saw it simply for what it was.

"To the prince who would be the hand of Aether one day." Said the crier, holding up a glass of wine.

"Long live the prince," the people in the dining room echoed in one voice. Urail beamed at the recognition and praise his subjects bestowed upon him, too young to see that they were really doing so out of respect to his parents and self-interest.

Sitting at the long table right in front of the royal's, Ifir clapped for Urail as loud as she could. Then, once the prince had sat back down and the festivities resumed, Ifir stood up, and respectfully left the gathering, excusing herself before the king and queen.

She left the dining hall with Mere behind her, among some curious looks from the nobles. Then, when she had gotten far away from the music, laughter and nauseating smell of food, she stopped and leaned against a wall and held her stomach… then heaved as if she would vomit. Mere was standing next to her, ready to hold her if she fell.

"I am fine." Ifir said, raising her hand with the other one still on her belly. "That whole display of dead animal heads disgusted me, is all." She added, with a wave of her hand. Mere nodded, but couldn't help her disbelief. If there was a person in this castle who'd felt disgust from a dead carcass, it definitely wasn't Ifir. Mere remembered how, not too long ago, she'd murdered innocent babies in front of her like it was nothing, smiling all the while with that cruel grin of hers.

Speaking of: on the way back to her room, Ifir had a suspicious smile on her face just like back then, which greatly disturbed Mere. The old maid watched her mistress carefully, hoping to glean some information as to what was going on, but Ifir's smile never left her lips.

When they arrived at her room, Mere removed Ifir's clothes and helped her change into her nightshirt. Ifir then sat down on her bed, but before she laid down, she held her belly like a mother protecting her baby. It was there that Mere understood what was happening... Her face turned pale and her old heart nearly gave away. She could feel her hands sweating. She stood by Ifir's bed, waiting for a command, almost holding her breath. "You may leave." Ifir finally said, setting her free for the rest of the night.

Mere slowly left the room, then, once she was some distance away from Ifir's door, she leaned against a wall in fear.

"May Aether help us." She told herself. Her breathing was shallow and panicking, her heart gripped by a cold hand. Suddenly, the old maid felt like she would pass away. After a few seconds of collecting her thoughts and wits, she gathered her strength and walked back to her room at the bottom of the castle. Her steps were fast and unstable, as if she were on the border of a panic attack. While she was climbing down the winding staircase to the basement, an arm suddenly grabbed her and caused her to lose what little balance she had.

"Is she okay?" A male voice asked her. She was taken aback in fear as his face appeared in the dim light of the basement torches. However, Mere then realized it was just Fermand, and allowed herself to relax a little.

"She is. She's just… tired."

"Good, good." He seemed like he was talking more to himself. Mere could see the worry and anxiety in his face. "Make sure she's well tomorrow. She's got a long day ahead of her and she absolutely can't afford to miss it." He warned her. Mere nodded, and he climbed back the stairway, leaving her to make her way back to her room. Her legs had been tired and cold, and now they were also weak and trembling; there was just so much going on at once.… So much. She pulled out a little candle from her pocket and burnt it with the torch on the wall. The light of her candle had barely lit the latch to her room, when suddenly, as she moved to open the door, she noticed a light coming from under it. There was someone walking in the room with a candle in their hand. Mere froze at her spot and swallowed all her hopes for a restful night's sleep. She took a deep breath and checked the small dagger she carried in her belt, which had been given to her to protect Ifir, but might now save her own life instead… and slowly pulled the door open, to peek inside. A woman hidden mostly by shadows was sitting on what used to be Loure's bed.

"Who's there? Who are you?" Mere asked from outside the door.

The woman turned her face, and with a start that almost gave her a heart attack, Mere realized it was Loure. There was no sign of Mere's previous sins on the side of Loure's face she showed to her aunt. However, soon after, Loure turned all the way towards her, showing her the fullness of what she'd done—the grotesque result of her hasty actions. A half-melted face stared back at her, the one eye white and blind—like a creature risen from a grave to punish Mere for her recent sins. Loure, despite her one blind eye, could see the fear and shock in Mere's old face. She couldn't believe the consequences of what she'd done.

"Lou-Loure!" She stuttered. Loure smiled at her with half of her lips, as the other half was burnt so badly it could hardly move. She opened her arms to her aunt as if she hadn't been the one who'd done this to her. "Come, aunt," she said.

Although she wanted to, Mere just couldn't move for a whole moment. She wanted to run to her niece, hug her, throw herself at her feet and beg for mercy, but she just couldn't move. Loure could see her pain from the tears gathering on the old maid's eyes.

"It's ok," she said. "Don't be afraid." Mere's old, trembling legs eventually started to move, and she shambled toward her disfigured niece. She could barely breathe, feeling the heavy burden and pain swelling on her chest. She hadn't seen Loure in nearly a month, and now here she was—and the sight of her pierced Mere to her very core. Loure walked over to her the rest of the way and hugged her old aunt tightly.

"I'm sorry, Mere… Please forgive my ignorance. I was so stupid. So *very* stupid." She pulled back from Mere, still holding her shoulders. "I would've caused the destruction of our entire family with my actions—I see that now." Loure said to her as tears fell from the old woman's eyes. Seeing Loure made Mere understand how she herself had become the kind of monster she'd once warned people about; how she'd become exactly what she'd never wanted to be. Loure's face was the perfect reflection to Mere of who she'd become after serving under Ifir for so long.

The old maid's mind was so confused, it struggled to feel something other than pain. She opened her mouth to say something, but she couldn't produce a single sound. Eventually, however, she managed to say something.

"What did I do to you, dear Loure?" She whispered, between sobs.

Loure stared at her for a long time, then said: "What you needed to. I didn't realize what I was doing… how life works here. I should have been wiser. Now… I've paid with my beauty." Loure nodded as she spoke. She had no sign of anger or hate in her, and sounded like she meant what she said.

"Can you really forgive me?" Mere asked, tears running down her old, creased cheeks. Loure thought about it for a moment, fixing her one good eye on Mere.

"I do," she finally said. "You only did what you had to so you could save my life… and our entire family name. I've learned how things work around here in my time at the kitchen and the bathhouse… How ruthless Ifir can be… and how jealous. Had I slept with Ulor that night, she would've erased us and everyone we know from Kellum." Her hand reached Mere's arm. "And so I talked with Majordomo, and asked for his permission to stay with you here again. To be honest... this room is far better than staying at the Bosom. Least it's just us, and not a dozen other girls" She smiled as she said the words. Mere didn't know how to react. "If that's ok with you." Loure finished. Something seemed off about the way she spoke—the way it all seemed rehearsed, and the even tone of her voice as she said it.

Still, Mere dismissed the thought and hugged her again. "Of course, dear niece... of course."

"I'm happy to hear you say so." Loure said, then started preparing her bed. "Now neither of us has to be alone again, aunt. We'll look after each other... and I promise I'll keep my nose clean this time around." She looked at Mere with the half smile on her face. The old woman nodded, but then something hit her—a feeling that sent a chill running up her spine, making her shiver. She realized what about Loure's tone of voice, her words, seemed so troubling; what that something that'd been nagging at Mere from the moment she'd started speaking was, exactly. It'd been a certain familiarity that she couldn't quite place... but now, it hit her like a ram to the chest.

Loure sounded just like Ifir.

The decades Mere had spent serving the Songbird of the Kollek had burnt the woman's ways into the very core of her mind like a hot iron. She knew when she was plotting something, when she was lying through her teeth and when she intended to cause harm or engage in violence. It was almost like a finely tuned sixth sense for Mere at this point.

And now, here, she sensed the same energy from her niece's voice—and it chilled her to the bone.

"O-of course... we will look after each other," Mere said, her voice breaking at parts. "I am always here for you Loure... and I will never hurt you like that, or in any other way, ever again." Mere spoke the words truly, but in her mind, she nurtured a sudden, deep fear.

Loure nodded. "I know, aunt. I'm glad we were able to talk tonight. I'll see you tomorrow, then. Sleep well." She said and laid down in her bed, then turned her back to Mere, making sure her scar didn't touch her pillow. Mere went into the tiny adjacent chamber—a cramped bathing room, and took a quick bath in cold water before settling down to sleep. Once in her bed, she felt a fear the likes of which she hadn't ever felt before. She laid down staring at the ceiling, looking sideways at Loure... and hoping against hope that death wouldn't visit her that night.

***

Mere wasn't the only one facing her fears that evening, however.

Back at the Outer Silence, Efilia assessed Odmund's wound after he'd just been shot by an archer. Holding the light close, she saw the archer had scored a glancing strike just off of Odmund's shoulder and tore at the skin—but it wasn't anything major. Still, seeing her lover's blood trickling down his arm made her insides jump in circles and her blood turn to icy slush.

"Od... will you be alright?" She asked.

The big man grunted, looking at the wound, feeling the burning cut in his flesh. "Yeah... I should be. It's just a flesh wound." He said. "Help me out here." He then added, nodding towards the sleeve of his shirt. Efilia understood what he meant and cut a long strip of cloth from his shirt's long sleeve with her dagger, using it to bandage the wound. It quickly started to soak up his blood, turning red.

"You'll need to get that checked back at the castle," she said. "It might need disinfecting... and a stitch or two."

Odmund nodded. Efilia looked around them at the darkness of the night, made even more blinding by the torchlight next to them.

"We should go back, Od." She whispered to him. "You're hurt, and we're sitting ducks out here. If there are more archers in the buildings..."

But Odmund stood up, shaking his head. "No... we can't. We need to press our advantage and see if we can find one of those archers alive."

Efilia realized that there'd be no convincing him otherwise, she eventually, she just nodded. "Alright. But you're going straight to the infirmary when we get back, you hear?"

Odmund smirked and nodded. "Not going to argue with you there."

They left their horses in the shadows and pulled their black cloaks up to disappear in the night. Efilia, however, couldn't stop thinking of the danger that could be looming, waiting for them at every corner. They made their way to the ruin of the house Efilia had just blasted into rubble and found one of the archers—or at least his stiff limbs, sticking out of the mess. He was clearly dead. Crushed under the stones and bricks. Realizing they wouldn't get anything out of him, they decided to follow after the second archer, who was nowhere to be seen. He couldn't have gotten far though, not after the fall and tumble he took.

Slowly, carefully, the pair stalked into the night, losing themselves among the twisting streets of the Silence, hoping against hope to pick up the trail once more… and eventually, their persistence paid off.

While they were turning a corner into a nearby street a few blocks away, a man with a torch stepped out of a house. The pair crouched low and waited, watching from the shadows.

The man was wearing old pants and a ragged shirt, with no shoes on his feet. He looked around to be sure nobody was following him, then walked through a narrow street. After a few meters he thought he heard something, so he stopped and looked around. Seeing no one, he shrugged and kept on walking.

"Didn't he hear the literal building crashing a few blocks away?" Efilia said to Odmund in hushes tones. "Or my scream? You'd think half the neighborhood would've woken up after that."

"We were near the harbor. Maybe the sound of the waves masked the noise? Or maybe they're used to hearing women screaming in the night and things crashing down around here…" Odmund said, shrugging.

"I mean, he's just walking around like nothing happened."

"Either way, let's just follow him—he might just lead us to whatever's going on around here."

And so, they did. They followed the man around the ring of the city, always staying in the Outer Silence, for nearly half an hour. The man took detours, walked around back the way he came and entered dead ends, waiting for a while and then coming out, until eventually, he met with another man at a corner. The man gave him a coin bag, and said: "For the Edgetown boys."

"They took children from other zones too?" Efilia asked in a low voice. They were far enough away that the men wouldn't hear them.

"Seems that way." Odmund whispered back, barely audible. The man who'd just gotten paid looked around towards their hiding spot, and they thought that, for a moment, they'd been spotted. They crouched low, holding their breath, until the man shrugged and quickly walked away from the other man, who quickly disappeared inside the building next to them.

Odmund and Efilia continued to follow the first man. He whistled a song as he walked, looking like he was enjoying the bag in his hands. He shook it few times next to his ear, listening to the clicking sounds of coins.

Suddenly, Efilia saw a woman closing the wooden shutters of her home in fear. She held Odmund's arm. "Something's wrong," she warned him right before the man looked around in the direction of the sound, then broke into a sprint.

"Dammit!" Odmund said, and they both ran after him. Odmund burnt a ball of fire in his palm to stop him, but Efilia shook her head.

"I'll catch him!" She said, then inhaled and shouted so strongly, it was as if hurricane-force winds had suddenly barreled through the street. Everything on the path of her voice trembled, and the man rose into the air, then fell down, holding his head between his hands as he rolled to a stop. The leather coin pouch he had fell down and all the coins spilled out of it. Screams of fear and noises of fleeing feet were heard from some of the nearby houses too, as the common folk were suddenly woken up by what seemed to be a storm outside their homes.

"Great job," Odmund said, and ran to capture the man. Efilia ran behind him with pride, having used her abilities twice tonight with great results and proving her power both to her lover and herself. She just wished Ifir had been there to see just what she could do when she tried. As she entertained those thoughts, Od grabbed the man by his shirt and pushed him up against the wall of a nearby home.

"Who do you work for?!" The Chosen asked. The man stared at him with wide eyes. "Tell me!" Odmund insisted, while Efilia looked around, making sure nobody tried to take a shot at them again.

Odmund burnt a fire in his hand and brought it next to the man's face. He could see that the man was afraid of him… but seemed to be more afraid of something else, his eyes looking past Od into the darkness.

"No one!" The man said. "I work for no one! I don't even have a job! Please, just let me go… I don't know what you want!"

"Speak…" Efilia's spoke, standing next to Od. Her voice was so soft and hypnotic that the man suddenly looked as if he'd fallen into a trance. "Who do you work for?" She asked.

"I… I don't work…" The man said, half asleep.

Odmund could see his effort not to speak, but he couldn't resist the power of Efilia's voice.

"I serve…"

"Who do you serve?" Efilia asked him.

"I serve…" He said, right before an arrow entered one side of his skull and exited through the other.

"No!" Efilia shouted, her scream hurting even Odmund's ears. He let go of the man and bent his head to cover himself. Efilia knelt next to him, and they hid behind a small nearby wall for protection.

"No man can make such a shot in the dark… unless he's a Chosen.'" Efilia said, her eyes growing wide.

"Rebels!" Odmund said, with no amount of uncertainty, and Efilia nodded.

"If so, this whole thing is bigger than we thought." Efilia said.

Odmund tried to raise his head to see the shooter, but just as he did, another arrow with fire on its tip whistled over him. "Damn it!" He said. "He can see us in the dark!"

The arrow fell near them and offered some light in the dark, which made Efilia notice the coins on the ground. She picked one, realizing it wasn't a regular Koll, and hid it in her chest pocket.

"Alright, I'm going in, Lia. Bastards aren't going to score a hit on me this time. Cover me!"

"Od, wait!" Efilia said, but it was too late—Odmund was already on his feet, two bright fireballs swirling atop his palms.

He used the balls of fire to deflect two arrows flying towards him, turning them to cinders, then threw the fireballs the way the arrows had come—at a spot between two buildings. Efilia stood up and focused her voice, launching it in bursts that also deflected arrows aimed at them. One of her blasts slammed hard against a building, and Odmund saw a man fall from the roof while another jumped out of a window, both of them landing on the street as if it were nothing.

They were indeed Chosen, Od confirmed, and they ran so fast, they disappeared in the darkness in only a few seconds. Odmund tried to give chase, but the men moved like the wind, and he realized that, even in horseback, he wouldn't be able to keep up with them.

"Did we get them?" Efilia asked him.

"They got away," Od said, shaking his head. "They were definitely Chosen rebels, though... They've been right under our noses this whole time. Just what are they doing here in the city?"

Efilia shook her head. "We should probably leave before they come back with friends. Regular folk we can handle, but a whole group of Chosen..."

Odmund sighed deeply, then nodded. "I agree... Let's get back to the castle for now. I'll bring this to Ifir and the king as soon as I get a chance. These rebels won't stay in Kellum for long..."

Before they left, Odmund held out his hand towards the buildings he'd set on fire, and the flames all flew into his palm, as if being sucked right into his body, sparing those inside the buildings from a fiery death.

"Let's go." Odmund said, then they jogged back to the place they'd left their horses at, and rode them into the safer, brighter districts of the city. Passing through each one, they rode back to the castle in silence, the sound of the horse's hooves and breathing their only companion. About half an hour later, they'd reached the castle up on its hill, and Odmund handed his horses' reigns to the servants waiting outside, who led them over to the royal stables.

"Dammit," he finally said after the long silence, as he walked back to the keep with Efilia. "All that effort, all that risk… and we still got nothing."

Efilia took something out of her shirt pocket and extended her hand to Odmund. "Maybe not." She said. It was the coin she'd picked up from the first man's money bag. Odmund held it between his fingers and then close to a nearby torch, turning it in the light. The coin was silver, and there was a man's engraving on it with a snake on his head, and olive branches on both sides. On the flip side of it there was a sun figure with six stars around it. Little stars were placed like a protecting circle, one above the sun, another one below it, and the other four on the sides.

"This coin…" Odmund began. "It's not a Koll."

"Then what is it?" She asked, hoping Odmund had the answer. "Where would that man spend a coin like this?"

Odmund shook his head.

"I… don't know. But this isn't a good sign. Them being paid with another kind of currency implies something much bigger than we initially thought… a whole new network of smugglers—a new black market, right here in the city. This operation could go deeper than we think." He said in low voice, his eyes still on the coin.

Efilia stared at him in silence, wondering what kind of thoughts could be coursing through his mind—what connections he could be making right now… and which people were first among his lists of suspects. Something this big couldn't possibly go unnoticed by at least some of the powers that be in Kellum. Someone must've been either allowing it, or even outright encouraging it… but who would do that? Who would benefit from such a horrible thing as Kollek slavery? Not knowing what to think of it beyond it left Efilia speechless and frustrated.

The two Chosen exchanged a worried look, confirming each other's thoughts.

"Do not speak of this to anyone," Odmund told her. "We don't know who could be behind something like this… and how far they'll go to keep it hidden."

Efilia nodded, then gulped, despite herself. This night had left them stranded in a dark ocean of unknowns, and Efilia couldn't shake the feeling of dread that crept over her, squeezing her chest... like they'd just stumbled onto something they wouldn't be able to get out off.

CHAPTER 27

DARKNESS RIPPER

As the night turned into another day, the streets of Greencrest were all in silence.

Urk was laying down in his bed, wearing only his sleeping pants, a chestnut-haired whore sleeping soundly beside him. His eyes were wide open; his mind estranged from peaceful sleep. He watched the sunrise from his room's window, watched the trees dancing in the cool morning breeze, enjoying the mid-season weather. The whole scene filled Urk with a meaningless hope. He remembered Ifir's words the day she made him a captain.

"There are no coincidences in this world, Chosen. You pave the stones for your life's path with your own choices. Always be on the lookout for opportunities... always be ready to seize them when you see them."

She'd been so brutal and serious when she'd said the words, emphasizing them one by one, as if making sure that Urk understood her well. And maybe he hadn't that day... but today, he could definitely feel their meaning as clear as the sunrise before him... as he stepped into the day where he would likely die. Would his choices save his life? He took the cold air into his lungs and stood up. He got suited in his full kit of armor, somehow without waking the woman in his bed, and walked out of the lavish room.

The door creaked noisily as Urk pushed it open. He walked to the door next to his and knocked on it. The door opened a crack and Frain, one of his Chosen, peeked through the gap. Upon seeing it was his captain, he opened the door fully, and stood at attention in just his breeches.

"Captain." He said.

"At ease. Wake the others up. We meet downstairs in fifteen minutes."

"Aye, aye, sir." He said, then went back into the room. Before he did, however, Urk caught a glimpse of all the other beautiful prostitutes he'd paid for the previous night, all still soundly asleep in the Chosen's beds in various stages of undress." He smiled to himself then closed the door, leaving his men to prepare.

Urk made his way to the establishment's dining area and ordered breakfast for him and his men. While he waited for the food, his men all marched down from the stairs, fully uniformed and ready to move, with the wenches right behind them waving them goodbye. They all sat down around the table, and Urk stared at them, smirking.

"Did you all sleep well?" He asked.

His men all nodded at different intervals. Urk smiled.

"Good. Eat as much as you can without getting sluggish—you'll need the energy for the ride ahead. After we're done here, we'll head down to the markets and buy our provisions for the trip… Then we head out—ideally before the eighth bell tolls."

His men all nodded, and soon after, their breakfast was served—eggs, boiled ham, lard-fried bacon and roasted potatoes dressed in goat butter and fragrant spices—along with freshly baked rolls of bread. The men wolfed down the breakfast with gusto, then left the upscale establishment. Balto, one of the Chosen, looked back longingly at the place.

As they walked down the red-light district and towards the central market, they witnessed as the city slowly woke up, its peoples heading out in every direction towards their day's work. Greencrest, due to being the largest military city in the Kollek lands after Kellum, enjoyed a substantial amount of wealth in its more upscale districts. However, the very source of that wealth, the heavy military presence, caused a stark divide between the upper and lower classes. Because of this, the poor districts of Greencrest were *immensely* poor—with the people living in rags, staying in little more than shambling huts and tents.

Urk scowled as they rode through such streets, remembering how some of the rich people, like Bancroft, literally wasted food without reason while half the city starved and begged in their dirty corners. He'd even seen how, if a beggar as much as made their way to one of the better-off parts of town to beg, they were quickly kicked back into their holes by the guardsmen—likely under orders from the mayor himself.

When they arrived at the market, Urk ordered his men to procure their provisions while he took care of some business at the master smith's workshop. The store was just opening but wasn't yet receiving customers, he saw. All the same, he walked inside and leaned against the counter.

"Weisor's son." He called in a firm voice. "I've come for my weapon."

The old master smith appeared at the counter, the dark bags under his eyes signaling he hadn't slept a single hour last night. He ushered Urk past the counter and into the smithing workshop behind it.

The man led him to a long worktable, lit by a nearby window in natural sunlight, and stood aside. On top of the table laid a weapon the likes of which Urk had never seen. The blade of the sword was inlaid in gold, runes in the old tongue written across its center. The crosspiece and handle were also cast in gold, and the sword's pommel glittered in the morning light like a jewel. The edges of the blade seemed to have been coated or rubbed in a special substance, as it also reflected the sunlight in a way that seemed as if it were almost absorbing it. Other parts of the blade had been polished to such an extent, they reflected Urk's face like a mirror. The engravings on it were written in an ancient language, and its ornate hilt had been engraved with a sun and snake motif. Urk held the longsword and hefted its balance in his hand. It was perfect.

"Erain sheina odto sorko de dourkain kaisek." Urk read the text in ancient language which meant: "The Sun's justice shines upon the Darkness Ripper."

"Is the Chosen satisfied?" The old man asked weakly, tiredly.

Urk slowly, but surely, nodded. "He is. This is… incredible work. Far beyond what I expected of even you, the son of Weisor himself."

The old man sighed, and the look in his eyes told Urk everything his words did not. *Please stop saying that. You're going to get me killed.*

Urk smirked, then nodded.

"How did you manage to do this in a day?" Urk asked the man. "A regular sword takes weeks to put together, so that means…"

"That this one was nearly already done, yes. It was a commission from Lord Bancroft. I'd been working on it for months. Just needed to add the last few… ah… special touches."

Urk nodded. "I see." He grinned a very wide grin. "Well, you tell Lord Bancroft I said thanks for the sword, master smith." The fact that the sword had been meant for Bancroft made the whole thing all the sweeter for Urk. He doubted the fat bureaucrat even had the first notion of how to draw the weapon, let alone wield it. Urk's hand reach to his coat's inner pocket and he pulled out a heavy coin bag—containing the rest of the money he'd been given for provisions before his mission. He extended the bag to the smith as payment… but the old man didn't take it.

"I see," Urk said. "So you want the payment in the old ways. Alright." He remembered Ifir's words one more time: there was no coincidence here. Urk was sure that his ancestors were showing him the way now. He walked in front of the old man and bent with the sword in his hand. Meanwhile, his men had stopped by the entrance of the shop and were now watching him in amazement—staring wide-eyed at the gleaming sword in his hands. The old master knelt before Urk as well and placed his right hand on the sword. He closed his eyes and prayed.

"The steel that birthed this sword is forged to be your blood. It will shine to protect you, soldier of Aether. Its sparkling power will be your sun until the last day you live."

When the old master rose, Urk swore:

"The master forged the steel, as I forged my vanity. The sword is my blood, and this blood will spill no innocent blood. The sun's justice shine upon the Darkness Ripper."

"Then arise, soldier, and shine like justice upon all the races." The old master said, and extended the scabbard he made for the sword. Urk rose and sheathed the blade in its scabbard—just as intricate and special as the sword itself. The Chosen soldiers outside watched the ceremony conclude in amazement. They'd never seen something like that before in their lives, as the old ways were mostly forgotten in Kellum—but they'd certainly studied them during their time at the Nest. Three of the Chosen gazed in amazement, but one of them, Balto, frowned instead.

"What's wrong, Bal?" Asked Hukail, noticing his companion's expression.

"That man," Balto said, gesturing towards the smith. "There's something wrong with him. I... can't read his mind." He whispered to Hukail, hoping that Urk could hear him. Hukail frowned, then said. "But that means..." Balto cut him off with a hand gesture, then nodded towards Urk. Hukail made an "O" with his mouth, then nodded, shutting up. Urk got the message and he looked back at his men, nodding. But he didn't care about its implications. He placed the sword in its scabbard, then left the coin bag on a desk. Before leaving, he said:

"Thank you, master." And the old man just nodded.

As they walked away from the shop, Balto came closer to Urk, but the Chosen captain just held up a hand: "I know, Balto." Urk said. "It's alright."

Hukail, on the other hand couldn't let the matter go so swiftly. He turned back to see what the old master was doing after they left, casting his superior Chosen sight into the shop as if he were there, standing next to him. He saw the old master in a hurry, wearing his cloak and collecting some of his tools in a large knapsack, as if he were about to leave the city. Hukail's vision was stopped by Urk's touch, who knew what the soldier was doing.

"There are no coincidences, Hukail. Let him leave." Urk said and smirked. "We have to leave Greencrest now... and I doubt we'll ever see him again."

***

They reached Lossen's Forest a few hours after leaving Greencrest, just before noon. The forest was near the ocean; partly a mangrove forest in which trees' roots grew in the water and partly a regular forest, spread throughout marshlands and swamps. They rode north as fast as they could, hoping to make as much progress today as possible. At around midday, Urk and his men stopped to rest and eat under the cover of some of the tall, blossoming trees by the side of the road. He pulled the map from his horse's saddlebags and looked at it while his men drank water and tended to the horses, which were visibly sweating and panting. According to the map, and given the towering mountain in the distance serving as a landmark, they were almost at the border of the Kollek lands. The border line between the kingdoms should've been less than half an hour of riding ahead of the—decorated with animal skulls.

Nodding to himself, Urk folded the map and stowed it away.

"Men?" He said, turning to his soldiers, and they all turned to face him, stopping whatever they were doing. "It's time I told you where we're going... and what we're doing. You're all bright men and probably have an idea already, based on our heading. There's only one possible destination to be reached by taking this road, after all." Urk said, then looked at them in turn, waiting to see if any of them gave him an answer.

"We're heading into the Koartiz lands... aren't we?" Frain finally said, his voice showing how he was resigned to his fate. Not many people, not even Chosen, came back from the Koartiz lands.

"That is correct," Urk said, nodding. "But we're not just on *any* kind of mission here. This isn't a sabotage or scouting operation."

The men's eyes widened, and they exchanged looks with one another.

"Ifir's spies have confirmed the location of a Sacred Manuscript—perhaps the most important piece yet. We are going to find it and bring it back home, where it belongs."

"We're on a… Holy Expedition?" Hukail asked. Urk nodded.

"But… if we succeed in bringing back the piece of the Manuscript… then we'll become Saints!"

The men got visibly excited at the news, as most Chosen usually did upon hearing they'd been chosen for an Expedition.

Urk nodded, but he did not share in their enthusiasm. "Indeed…" He said, his voice grave. "However… there's something else you should know."

His men stopped their excited celebrating and turned to face him once more, the joy slowly draining from their faces due to the gravity in Urk's voice.

"This piece of the Manuscript is kept in one of the Kollek's holiest sites—the temple where they entombed the last Sword of Aether. Resistance will be fierce… and there's a high likelihood we'll run into Night Judges."

That did it for them. Urk saw as the color drained from his men's faces.

"We are all bound to this task now. There is no turning back… but I thought it wise, and fair, to let you all know what we're about to walk into."

His men all looked at each other, then back at their leader, and Urk could see the struggle in their eyes. Before, they'd been celebrating what they thought could be the greatest highlight of their lives… Now, they were clearly dreading what would most likely be their end.

"That said," Urk continued, and his men rose their eyes to meet him. "We are proud Chosen soldiers, hand-picked by the Songbird herself for just this very mission. We will not fail… for Aether *Himself* is with us." He said, growling the last part as he drew his special sword from its scabbard, its blade gleaming in a rainbow of colors under the midday sun. "We will march into the heathens' lands, take what is rightfully ours, and come back home to Kellum as Chosen Saints—bearers of a Holy Manuscript!"

His words stirred the hearts of his men, and seeing the brightly glowing blade and his leader's confidence, the group of Chosen nodded.

"For Kellum and the Kollek, men. For Aether and his right-hand, King Ulor. For Sainthood!" Urk shouted. "Are you with me?!"

His words rippled inside his men's hearts and they all drew their weapons, raising them towards the heavens along with him. "For Kellum and the Kollek!" They echoed. "For Aether and his chosen king, Ulor! For Sainthood!" They shouted, bolstered by Urk's words, then broke into cheering and whooping.

Urk looked at them, slowly lowering his blade, and smiled.

Deep inside, however, he desperately hoped he believed his words nearly as much as his men did.

CHAPTER 28

THE LEGEND OF THE CURSED KING

It'd been four days since Kade's display of power and control at the Oasis.

Today, as the sun rose on the horizon, the young Chosen sat on the cold desert ground, wearing only his breeches, his legs crossed in front of him. He breathed in the cold morning air deeply, eyes closed, and felt his inner fire react to his command—felt as the energy entered through his nose and coursed throughout his entire body, fully under his control.

Axel sat opposite him (fully clothed and more than a little cold), in the same sitting position. His eyes were open, however, as he assessed Kade's efforts to remain in control. They'd continued to train the Chosen every morning and every night, teaching him more and more control.

"Good, Kade… good. How does it feel?" Axel asked him.

"It feels… right." He said.

"As it should. You've made tremendous progress in the last few days. More than I would've expected from any Chosen, in fact."

"I take it that's a good thing?"

"Very good." Axel said. "For someone who's never had proper training until now, your display of control is nothing short of miraculous. You're definitely cut from a different cloth, young one. It's almost like…"

"Like what?" Kade asked, seeing Axel hesitating. The old man just shook his head and smiled.

"Nothing, nothing."

"Axel…" Kade insisted.

The old man sighed. "Fine… but keep it between us. The others are already wary enough of you as it is."

"Alright," Kade said in a hushed tone, looking back at the camp, ensuring that everyone was asleep. "Tell me."

"Have you noticed how many abilities you display, Kade?"

The large Chosen considered it for a moment. "I'm not sure I follow."

"Most Chosen only ever develop one ability, and are thus assigned a category to tell them apart. Scal. Musal. Cauda. Etcetera. However, you, Kade… you show several. You have the strength of a Musal… the hearing of an Acris… and occasionally, you move with the speed of a Fetear. This is uncommon, and might be part of the reason why you've felt your powers overtake you so strongly in the past."

The young man frowned for a moment, thinking. "So… what does it mean?"

Axel pondered the question for a long time, then chose his words very carefully. "I'm not sure. It's too soon to say. However, you'd do well to keep this a secret—as much as you can… and pay special heed to your training, so you can learn to control your abilities."

Kade nodded. "Ok."

Axel nodded. "Good. Now, back to your training. Breathe deeply…"

"One more thing before we continue, Axel…"

The old man raised an eyebrow. "Yes?"

"Why did you warn me against touching that rebel Chosen's forehead back then? You were… so insistent."

Axel held Kade's sight for a moment, then sighed. "Alright then… I guess I owe you an explanation there, don't I? Chosen like you have a… ah… special connection to one another, you see. When two Chosen touch their foreheads to each other, sometimes, rarely, a literal exchange of thoughts might happen… which incapacitates both Chosen in the process. It's a process known as a Mind Link."

"A… Mind Link?" Kade asked.

Axel nodded. "Your thoughts and the other Chosen's intertwine, and you get to see parts of their life; their memories, for one, while they get to see part of yours. But the process is supposed to be very taxing on the body and mind, and causes both Chosen to pass out—something we needed to avoid at all costs in that battle."

Kade mulled over the information for a moment, then nodded. "Alright. I'll keep that in mind."

Axel nodded. "As you should. Now, are you ready to continue?" The large Chosen nodded, and so Axel resumed his breathing instructions. As he continued to lead Kade in his control exercises, Merki woke up. Realizing how heavy the chill in the air was that morning, she moved to stoke the dying embers in their fire.

"Good morning." Axel said in greeting, hearing her shuffling around the campsite.

"Good morning." Merki said. "You're both up early today."

"None of us could sleep very well last night." He explained. "I think the fact we're so close to Kellum now has us both on edge."

Merki nodded. She could feel her stomach twisting into knots as well. "We're really that close now, then?" She asked.

Axel nodded. "We should be out of the Oasis by tomorrow. Then it's just a few more days until we reach the gates."

"Ahh… at long last. I've seen enough desert to last me a lifetime!" She said.

Locke stirred in his bed then as well. He slowly started to get up, pushing himself upright, then squinted in their direction. "What are you lot doing up so early?" He asked.

"Training," Axel told him. "Did you sleep well?"

Locke didn't reply right away, rubbing his eyes one at a time. "I guess so. So… I hear we're close to leaving this place?" He asked, and Axel nodded. "Oh, by the sweet mercies of Aether! At long last!" He exclaimed.

"At long last," Kade repeated, smiling slightly, eyes still closed.

"You focus on your breathing! No talking." Axel said.

Kade grimaced. "Sorry."

"But yes, we're almost out of here now." Axel continued. "Merki, if you'd be a dear, can you get a breakfast going?"

Merki shrugged. "Sure." She got up to get the materials and more kindling for their fires, then asked. "What's the deal with this place, anyways? I mean… I know part of the story… the battle against the Cursed King and his immortal army, and how nothing will grow here since… but what about before that?"

"Before that… as legends tell, this was a green, lush valley—like those over the west ridge near God's River." The old man said.

"Hard to believe this place used to be anything but a desert." Merki added.

"Indeed. But that's the way it was. A lush green field like any other, with a great river coursing through its middle by the name of Vrbain—which time and dust storms have long since erased. You can still see the remains of the Vrbain even now though, in the form of the oases that cropped up here and there."

"Yeah…" Locke said. "Good thing we stumbled into one of those the other night too, or else we'd all be bones by now."

"Stumble?" Axel chuckled. "I'd like to think my sense of direction had something to do with that."

"I'd like to think not." Locke said, then shrugged. "But we've got enough water to get out of here now—so that's all that matters."

Merki began to ration out some of the dried meat and fruit they'd bought back at Orkail, which was running dangerously low. She passed some of it to Axel and some to Locke, as Kade usually waited until after he'd finished his exercises to eat anything.

"Did you know that this valley was called the 'Dreamer's Oasis' among the Koartiz before it became an actual desert?"

"How so?" Merki asked, biting into her portion of dried fruit and meat.

"Because of what this place represented," Axel said. "For the Koartiz, this valley was an oasis—a place of retreat, in the midst of a cruel world."

"A cruel world?" Locke asked, after swallowing a piece of meat with some water. "Didn't the Koartiz have all the power back then? If there was ever a race the world wasn't cruel to back then, it was the Koartiz—and the Nor. They ruled over these lands with powers we could only imagine—treated the Kolleks as nothing but slaves to build their great cities and monuments."

Axel nodded grimly... almost sadly. "You know your history, captain." He said. "You're right... in a way. But also wrong. You see, the Koartiz had unlocked the secrets of magic ages before even the Cursed King made his first appearance in these lands, tainting them with his darkness. How the Koartiz came to do so is a secret only they know... but in discovering the way to tap into magic, into the essence of creation itself, their minds expanded to understand the universe. It... is said that their minds operated on levels far beyond that or regular mortals—Kollek or Nor. However, after touching the very fibers of creation, and witnessing the realms of the immaterial firsthand, it is said that the Koartiz found it a struggle to live in carnal bodies anymore—to be bound to the world by their flesh, with its rules, laws and limitations.

Their more skilled users of magic, the sorcerer castes, thus traveled here, to this valley, which was supposedly a place of great power in the magical realms—a wellspring of magic itself. They came here to commune with Aether himself, it is told, and rejected all of the material in exchange for staying in dark caves with no water or food—sustained by the love and power of Aether only—the God of Magic and Creation Himself. Those were the Dreamers. Those among them who completed this mission were then called the Awakened— and from these were members of the... *Pentaghast*, chosen to lead the rest of the Koartiz people. From among the Awakened, came the Five Head Sorcerers of the Koartiz—each a leader in an aspect of government pertaining to their culture and society. They were the Sorcerer of Magic, of War, of Culture, of Spirituality and Religion, and finally, of Progress. And so, the world was like a desert to them, and here, at the Oasis, was the one place they could rest and relax."

Merki, Axel and now even Kade, who'd stopped his breathing exercises to focus on the story, looked intently at Axel. The old man realized Kade had stopped his training and poked his leg with a stick. The Chosen closed his eyes with a deep sigh, then continued breathing deeply.

Locke frowned. "The historians back in Kellum say that the Koartiz used those caves to ambush Luden's troops during the war—not as places of prayer and meditation. They'd come out of the caves, strike, then retreat back inside."

"You heard right," Axel replied. "They did. These group of warriors were called the Matured—those who'd attained a great level of affinity in the use of magic. They could strike and disappear into the caves, never to be found by the enemy."

"Why didn't Luden's soldiers just follow them inside?"

"Because the caves were, of course, magical in nature. They could only be traversed safely by sorcerers. Anyone else who tried to pass through them became inevitably lost, and was never heard from again…" Axel replied.

"If the Koartiz were the only people who learned to wield magic… then how did Luden's army become immortal?" Kade asked with his eyes still closed. "I mean—even my people know about Luden and his immortal army—he is the ultimate enemy and shame of the Nor."

Axel took a deep breath. "You mean, even the Nor *knew* about Luden, Kade. Back then… when they were still alive." He said, very softly.

Kade looked away. "Yeah… that."

"Well," Axel continued. "It's not really known. As the war between the Nor and the Koartiz raged on, and it seemed as if the Koartiz would prevail over the physically superior Nor troops with their magic… One day, the Nor just started to get back up after being struck down. The Koartiz had just defeated one of the largest Nor forces in the war, as history goes—killed every Nor down to the last man, then marched out of the blood-soaked grounds…

the next day, the Nor army appeared on their doorstep—the same men they'd slaughtered just a day before, and killed most of them. Some people said Luden tapped into a dark power—darker than any known to man or Koartiz before, to obtain this foul gift, but its name and nature were lost to time and history. The very power that almost gave him the world turned against him and his people, devouring them after the creation of the Stone of Eternity—as the records go."

"You keep mentioning these 'records' and 'histories' Axel…" Said Locke. "But not in my father's library nor at the Great Library of Kellum have I ever read of such things. Where did you get all of this information?"

The old man looked at the three pairs of eyes around him, fully fixated on him now. He nodded, then smirked. "Why, from the Koartiz themselves, of course." He said.

That drew a gasp or two from the those sitting around him.

"You mean, you… You've visited the lands of the Koartiz?" Merki asked.

"The only way to visit the Koartiz as a Kollek… is by becoming a Koartiz." Locke said, frowning. "What are you saying, Axel?"

The old man began to chuckle. "Yes, I got it from the Koartiz… and yes, I traveled to their lands to do so, young Locke… however, it's not what you think at all. The Koartiz, you see, used to live *here* in the Oasis, did they not? Before they were pushed away from their land, that is."

Understanding began to dawn on Locke and Merki's eyes.

"Just as so, there are many other places in the Kollek kingdom that used to belong to the Koartiz once. One such place held the ruins of a library full of tomes and records of the sorcerers' history. During my time as a traveler, I stumbled into it and spent weeks poring over its tomes, learning them by heart. You see, after my time caring for Chosen at the castle, I… moved around a bit. I traveled the land for some years, working as a storyteller and a merryman whenever I went, capturing pieces of stories from people all over the kingdom… and searching for places just like that library."

The Legend of the Cursed King | 347

"How come the king's scouts never found such a place? One would think they would've added these tomes to the Great Library's collection." Merki asked.

"Oh, they did," Axel said, sadly. "But I'm afraid our fair king wasn't very interested in preserving history from the *Koartiz's* point of view… so he ordered the library and all of its contents burned to the ground."

"Ah…" Locke said. "That… makes sense. I *have* heard of ancient Koartiz sites being burned to the ground after new acquisitions of land."

"Indeed," Axel said, and his inner voice started to cackle with long, wheezing laughter. "We should probably get ready to leave now, however. We don't want to spend more time here than we absolutely have to, after all."

Locke and Merki nodded, then Axel began to get up as well, stretching his stiff lower back. Merki started to tear down the camp and get things ready, while Locke tried his best to get up on his one good leg and hop over to the back of the tiny wagon, as usual.

Suddenly, as Axel was picking through his things, he heard a voice behind him.

"Can I stop breathing deeply now?" Kade asked.

"Oh… dear Kade, of course, of course. Your training is over for today. Please have something to eat before we set out and help Merki pack our things."

The large Chosen stood up and, same as Axel, stretched his back.

"That was quite a story, old man." He said.

Axel nodded somberly. "Stories are all I have anymore, I'm afraid." He looked deep into Kade's eyes for a moment, enough for it to become uncomfortable, then he turned his back to the Chosen, fixing his attention on gathering his things.

Something about those words, and the way he said them, stayed with Kade long after they left that place, hovering over his mind like dark clouds.

Was that just an old man's regrets coming to the surface…? He pondered as they rode further and further away from the dead campsite where the tales had been shared.

Or a warning of some sort?

CHAPTER 29

THE CHAMPION'S LAMENT

Hugo poured more hot water in the silver bathtub, which gleamed like a polished mirror, reflecting the hundred candles burning in the bath chamber.

He stared at his own reflection on the sides of the tub he'd recently and perfectly polished. Next to the tub Hugo was preparing was another, that one golden, set before he'd arrived at the chamber. Another woman he'd seen around the baths but whom he didn't know was preparing it, while Hugo was doing his best to lather up the water on his silver one.

"Do you need help, boy?" The woman asked. Her voice was firm, but well-intentioned.

"No ma'am, I'm alright. Thank you."

The woman shrugged and returned to her own business. Before Hugo could say anything else, the door to the private bath chamber opened and a servant walked in.

Both Hugo and the woman placed folded towels on their arms and stood at attention... then Odmund and Efilia walked in. A woman and a male servant appeared from behind them as they walked to a screened-off area and began to remove their armor and clothes. While they worked, Odmund looked at Hugo, whose eyes were shinning with pride and excitement to finally serve his friend and rescuer.

"Hugo!" Odmund said, his head above the screen. So, you've already started your duties I see!" He smiled.

"Yes, sir!" The boy answered.

"How have you been liking life at the castle?"

"It's amazing, sir. Everything I could've ever dreamed."

"And your mother?"

"I see her at the end of every week, sir. She's very grateful for your mercy. I'll soon be able to move her out of the Silence, if all goes well."

"I'm very glad to hear that." Odmund said. "Looks like it's my lucky day today then, eh?"

Hugo didn't know how to respond to that, his cheeks growing red, and he just bowed. "It's my pleasure to serve you, Lord Odmund."

"I told you before at Jack's, Hugo—it's just Od for you. Always."

The boy just bowed deeper. "Yes sir, Lord Od!"

Odmund sighed in resignation.

Efilia, on her part, immediately knew who the boy was just from the joy in Odmund's face. She fixed her eyes on him with a concerned look on her face until her maid had taken off all of her clothes. Odmund looked back at her with a raised eyebrow and just shrugged, until her bath maid held her by the hand and helped her into her bathtub. While it was customary for women to be helped into their tubs, men were expected to get in on their own, regardless of status, so Hugo didn't have to strain himself to help Od enter his own. He did cast his eyes down at the brick floor of the chambers until the naked Chosen had walked past him and settled into his own tub, however.

As soon as Od laid down into the hot water with a sigh, Hugo grabbed a large piece of cloth and dipped it in a hot water bowl placed on a small table next to the tub—mixed with special oils and fragrances meant specifically for Chosen. He then climbed onto a small wooden step he'd been given, and began to slowly rub Odmund's shoulders and arms, as he'd been taught. The boy really had a knack for the ministering arts, and soon enough, his slow movements had Odmund completely relaxed. He closed his eyes and enjoyed the notes of a harp being played by a girl behind another of the room's curtains. Hugo could see her long, slender fingers sliding on the strings of the huge instrument. As he looked at the silhouette of the girl playing the harp, his eyes briefly hovered over Efilia over in her bathtub. While he couldn't see anything below her shoulders and face, the young man still turned red as a beet and looked quickly back at Odmund. He was, after all, fourteen, and was starting to experience an oddly overwhelming attraction for the opposite sex. After he was done with rubbing his arms, Hugo moved onto giving Odmund a strong neck and shoulder massage, just as the Bath Mistress had taught him.

His long fingers worked wonders on Odmund's stressed, stiffed muscles, and the man just enjoyed it, his eyes closed. Hugo noticed a recent scar on Odmund's right shoulder, and did his best to avoid the area, despite it looking like it was well on its way to healing.

"You're really good at this, Hugo. They definitely gave you the right job." Odmund said. Hugo grinned to himself, suddenly feeling like he was at least ten times taller and stronger than he really was.

"Thank you, sir. There was a lot of trial and error, but eventually Radolf seemed to think this was where I belonged as well." Hugo happily answered. "Do you… do you mind me asking what happened?" Hugo asked, very hesitantly. The other maid threw him a long look. Servants weren't supposed to talk to their patrons unless talked to first, or unless it pertained to their bathing service, like "is the water hot enough," or "do you want me to sing to you as well?" Hugo ignored her.

"What do you mean?" Odmund replied, clearly not caring for the usual rules.

"Your wound," Hugo said. "You were recently hurt, weren't you?"

Odmund looked at his shoulder. "Oh, that there? It's nothing. It'll probably be gone in a few more days."

"When did you get it?" Hugo asked.

"Boy!" The other bath maid said.

Odmund smiled to himself. "It's alright," he said to the maid. "He can ask me all the questions he wants." Then to Hugo, "I got it a few days back while patrolling the Silence. Ran into some… erh…" He threw Efilia a questioning look, almost as if asking for her permission. His lover was staring at him already from her bathtub, frowning. She slowly shook her head.

"I ran into some undesirable types down that way."

Hugo nodded. "You mean rebels." He said.

Od stared at the young man, then at Efilia. She was now looking between him and Hugo with wide eyes. Od pushed himself up in the bath a little.

"Hugo… what do you know?" Odmund asked the young man.

The hunchback boy smirked, feeling very useful all of a sudden. "Back at Jack's, Lord Od. The day you came to get me… there were rebels there, plotting something. I was just serving their table when you walked in."

Odmund raised half his body out of the bathtub now. "Rebels? Hugo, are you sure? What were they saying? Did you hear? Wait, you two," he said to the bath maid and the harp girl. "Out of the room. Now." The other bath maid looked between him and Efilia, and the Chosen lieutenant nodded towards the door.

"You heard the Champion. We'll call you back in when we're done."

The bath maid bowed deeply and left, along with the harp player. Once they were alone, Hugo stood beside Odmund's tub, then nodded. "I heard some of it, yes. They mentioned a "load" of some kind… leaving out Savior's Gate, I believe."

Odmund looked at Efilia, who was leaning from the edge of her tub now, both arms under her chin.

"Did they say when?" Odmund asked Hugo with urgency.

The young boy shook his head.

"Dammit!" Said Odmund, and Hugo recoiled, his eyes wide. Odmund extended a wet, soapy hand. "I'm sorry Hugo, I didn't mean to yell. You're doing great. Did you hear anything else?"

"I… it was very noisy, and I was really scared." He said.

"There must've been something else, Hugo. Think. You can do it." Odmund said, putting a hand on the young boy's shoulder.

"I think… I think they mentioned a lady? And an old man. Yes, that's it—they said the 'load' was leaving with 'the old man.'" The boy said, frowning in concentration.

Odmund clapped his hands. "That's it," he said, looking at Efilia. "We just have to watch Savior's Gate—look for either a suspicious-looking lady or an old man, Lia. We've got a solid lead." He grinned at her, and she nodded, smiling as well.

"Sounds like it." She said.

Odmund turned back to Hugo and smiled a big, genuine smile at him. "You incredible boy, you. Excellent work, Hugo. Excellent work." The young man bowed deeply, unable to contain the ecstatic grin in his face.

"I'm happy to serve, L… Od. If there's anything else I can do for you, just let me know."

The Champion of the Kollek patted Hugo on his shoulder, then Efilia spoke.

"What about the coin, Od?" She said. "It's still in my pocket."

Odmund told Hugo to get the coin from Efilia's clothes—which again, made him blush like a ripe tomato. The boy walked back towards them, frowning at the odd-looking coin in his fingers.

"Have you ever seen this type of coin before? Or either of those insignias?"

Hugo looked deeply at the coin, his bright-green eyes shining with intensity as he tried to remember.

"I'm sorry," he said. "I haven't. Though… one of the rebels was about to pass a coin bag to the other one. Maybe they were the same kind?"

Odmund nodded. "They could. That's another lead there—we can look for more of these coins among the suspects. Thank you, Hugo. You've given us more here than you can imagine."

Hugo bowed. "It's my pleasure sir."

Odmund then told Hugo to return the coin to Lia's pocket and speak of their conversation to no one, which the boy promptly agreed to. Then, he had him call the servants back into the bathroom and reached out an arm towards Efilia, grabbing her shoulder. She did the same. Before the servants walked back in, he said, softly.

"This might be it, Lia. If we find another man—or woman, with a bag full of these coins, we might unravel this whole smuggling problem."

Efilia nodded, glad to see Odmund so uplifted… but worried about what would happen if they really did. What if the people behind the smuggling operation had enough power to hurt them… or worse, outright silence them? Silence *him*.

She was still holding onto those thoughts when her maid walked back into the room and resumed washing her legs.

***

The next morning, the king's breakfast table had been prepared prior to his arrival in his special chamber, full of enough fruit, bread, cheeses and select cuts of high-quality meats for several families. Ulor's private dining room was large and bright, well-decorated with flowers and statues. The table was also massive and the chairs also tall, their backrests towering. Everything here was designed to make people fell small before the king, and the walls were decorated with swords and shields with different emblems on them, symbolizing the many lords under Ulor's command, reminding them of his influence and power. As the doors to the chamber opened, both Ulor and Odmund walked in. The maids stood at their places, then waited for them to sit while other servants pulled their chairs for them.

"So, tell me, my Champion…" Ulor began. "What kind of show are you planning for the ceremony?" He put his hand on Odmund's shoulder as he spoke.

"I am to light the path you'll walk ahead of you, my king." He said.

"The whole path?" Ulor asked, surprised.

"Yes, my king." Odmund said, while Ulor sat on his chair.

"To use your powers for such an extended period of time… You must be really making progress towards becoming the Sword of Aether, my child." Ulor leaned back in his chair with pride.

Odmund bowed, then sat on his own chair after Ulor.

"What about that lieutenant?" The king asked him.

"Which one, my king?" Odmund asked.

"The blonde one, with the green eyes. How is she doing?"

"She is doing excellently, my king. Becoming a better soldier every day."

"Good, good… as long as she makes you happy." After saying that, Ulor began to eat, slicing up his eggs and putting them on top of his steak. Odmund, on the other hand, hadn't touched his food yet.

"My lord… I have some vital news to share with you, today." Odmund said, unsure of how to begin.

"Of course. Go ahead. That's why you requested this audience, is it not?" Ulor said before putting everything he could in his mouth. Odmund nodded.

"During my patrols of Edgetown and the Silence, I notice some… strange happenings." Upon hearing the name of the two notorious districts, Ulor stopped eating and waited for Odmund to continue.

"Go on."

"I have strong proof pointing to a smuggling operation in and around those districts. They seem to be taking young children—boys and girls, and selling them into slavery." Odmund said it all at once. The maids looked at each other without raising their heads.

"Is that so?" The king said, then resumed eating. Contrary to Odmund's expectations, Ulor seemed surprisingly calm and relaxed. The monarch's attention was mainly on the pies on the table. "Did you find who's behind it?" He finally said.

"I followed up on some leads and gained new ones—promising ones… But I haven't had the opportunity to follow up on them yet. I thought it best to come to you with the news first." As Odmund's spoke, Ulor seemed more and more intrigued by his breakfast than anything else—especially the meat pies.

"These pies…" He said as he chewed the piece on his fork with joy. "These are the best pies I've ever had. Would you like some?"

The young Chosen smiled politely and held up a hand. "I'm quite alright, my king, thank you."

Ulor shrugged. "Suit yourself. All the more for me."

Odmund didn't know how to react, so he just smiled and nodded. He was surprised that pie seemed to be more important to Ulor than the news of children being kidnapped on the street. As he watched Ulor gorge himself on his breakfast, Odmund cleared his throat and continued.

"We found that some of those responsible for the disappearances leave through Savior's Gate. We're planning to hold a stakeout in the area and see if we can identify two of the people we heard about during our patrols—an old man and a woman."

Ulor nodded several times, then continued eating.

Odmund blinked, staring blankly at his lord and king. He thought the gravity of the situation hadn't yet landed home for the monarch, so he pressed a little further. "My lord—the Kollek, our proud people, haven't been slaves since the times of Luden, the Cursed One. We can't allow such a thing to start anew, much less in our holy city, to spread to—" But Ulor raised a hand, stopping him as he spoke.

"Odmund..." The king said, looked into his eyes. "I love you like a son. You are a very special symbol of Aether's trust to our nation... blessed by Him, and by *me*. Because of this, I don't want you to focus on anything but preparing for the Imperation Day ceremonies. Our priority for the following weeks is making sure that the city looks its very best in front of our guests—not waste time chasing stories and lost children. Besides, folk disappear all the time in the Silence. The matter can wait."

Odmund blinked again. "M-my Lord... if we don't act now, these people might slip past our fingers. All I'm asking is for a force large enough for an operation, so we may catch these villains before they..."

Ulor held another hand.

"The price for the freedom of our race entails a heavy burden for all of us, Champion. While we pay it as best as we can, there will always be a few... leaks. We can't save them all. Focus on the ceremonies first, then we'll see what we can do about that matter. It's a time for celebration, Odmund! Not any of this dreary stuff." Ulor smiled and raised his glass to Odmund. The champion had to raise his too, but he couldn't manage to smile as Ulor did.

"To our nation," Ulor said.

"To our nation," Odmund repeated. Ulor drank all the wine in one gulp, then continued, his tongue a little bit looser.

"You know what truly bothers me though, Odmund?"

"Tell me, my king." Odmund said.

"All those kings and queens coming here to ask for favors and all… It's all so tiring. They all believe themselves so smart and wise just because they sit on tiny thrones, in their tiny corners of the kingdom… but they have no idea what it takes to rule the world of men."

Ulor looked really troubled for a second, then he added: "Only I do." The king looked deep into the champion's eyes and his face became more serious.

"Here's some advice for you Odmund—stay away from any unnecessary risks or dangers. You are a more than just your own man. You are a symbol to the Kollek; poor or rich, noble or peasant. You can't afford to run around putting yourself in danger like you did the other night." He nodded towards Odmund's shoulder, where he'd taken the glancing hit from the arrow. Odmund's eyes widened. He hadn't told Ulor about that, and his current clothes didn't show the wound at all.

"Thought I wouldn't hear about it? That you and your friend went for a little ride in the night and played investigators on the lower districts, bringing down houses and flinging fire in the middle of the night? And… don't get me wrong—I couldn't care *less* if you burn down the entire Silence just for the fun of it, Od—in truth, you'd be doing me a favor. But you *need* to prioritize your safety and welfare. You're not immortal. And if something happens to you, son… I, we, the Kollek as a race, lose so much more than just a man."

Odmund watched Ulor carefully as he took another sip of wine, almost holding his breath.

"Because of this, I will authorize this operation of yours later, yes, *after* the festivities are done and things get back to normal…" He said, swishing the wine in his cup… then he raised his eyes to meet Odmund. "But I forbid you from this point onwards from having *anything* else to do with this. No more nighttime escapades, not even future patrols in the lower districts, until after the ceremonies. Do you understand?"

Odmund felt his stomach tie into heavy knots, his heart fill with lead and his veins freeze over. He stared at Ulor, eyes wide, face growing paler by the second.

"Yes, Sire." He softly whispered.

"Good," Ulor said, then drank the rest of the wine. "Now, if that is all, I do have a kingdom to run here. Go back to your duties, Champion, and prepare yourself for the celebrations. Be ready to show the people just how blessed by Aether we truly are."

Odmund stood up and bowed. "So it shall be, Sire." He then walked out the door, leaving his breakfast fully untouched on its plate.

As he made his way down and out of the royal chambers, he met with Efilia, who was waiting for him on the second floor of the castle keep.

"What did he say?" She asked, accompanying him as he keep walking. Eventually, he stopped, then leaned outside a window overlooking the back gardens.

"He only cares about the ceremonies right now. He… forbid me from continuing the investigation. Said he'll take care of it after the festivities are done."

Efilia frowned. "But… that's more than a month away! The culprits may be long gone by then!"

"I know."

Lia put a hand on Od's arm. "What are you going to do?"

Odmund looked at her, the pain visible in his eyes and the lines of his face.

"I'll find a way to save our people before it's too late… with or without his blessing."

CHAPTER 30

DIVERGING PATHS

The tall mountain was covered with pine trees.

It was one of the six hills surrounding Kellum, and the air near its peak was refreshing and bewilderingly relaxing. From the spot Kade and the group were camped at, the stars seemed closer than ever, and Merki felt like she could catch one if she just reached out as far as she could. The night was cold and windy, but the campfire warmed up the chilled bodies of the travelers as they extended their hands towards it, hoping to push back the cold winds of the turning season. The members of the group, having recently (and finally) exited the dreary expanse of the Dreamer's Oasis, had entered lush, forested land once more and covered most of the remaining distance to Kellum. They were all in silence tonight—their first night making camp outside the desert in more than a week… but it wasn't just the fact that they'd made it out—that they were finally outside the desert, which took their breath away and left them speechless. No, it was the grand view of the capital city of Kellum, Jewel of the Kollek, spreading far and wide in the distance with all its glistening and glittering lights that did it. Neither Merki nor Kade had ever seen anything like it, and upon reaching their camping spot near the top of the hill, they'd just stared in wonder and awe for nearly half an hour, taking in all the details of the majestic sight into the very depths of their being.

As they ate some stew from a couple of rabbits Merki had bagged on the way here, along with their last pieces of dried fruit and meat from Orkail, Kade was the first to break the silence.

"How can any man of flesh and bone build such a grand thing?" He asked the group. "I mean—it's easily ten times larger than…" He looked at Axel. "Than any other city I've ever seen."

"It is the Jewel of the Kollek for a reason," Locke said, lying against a log, his leg propped over his bedroll.

Axel, for the first time in weeks, had nothing to say. He sat in silence, staring through the trunks of the trees at the impossibly large city beyond the hill, surrounded by an equally massive forest. Despite Kellum still being several kilometers away, the city took up most of the landscape before them, rising tall and monstrous over its central hill and completely dominating the lush valley—a massive lake to its right, and the dark, glittering, open ocean to its left.

"So… I imagine my brother has a good life there, then?" Kade continued, almost in a whisper.

"If he's truly a Chosen like you, then certainly," Locke said, looking at the glittering lights in the distance, smelling the salt and brine of the ocean. "He'll most likely live at the castle," he stretched out a hand, pointing. "Over there, at the very top of the hill."

"Wow…" Kade said. "To think that my brother lives in a castle. My mother would never believe it if I told her." He took a scoop of hot stew and sipped it gratefully. Then, he asked. "So… what will you all do once you get to Kellum? You'll first take me to castle, right?"

Locke cast his eyes down. "That's the plan."

"And what then?"

"Then…" Locke began. "Well… I'm mostly convinced you're not one of the Sons myself, but…"

Kade frowned, a look of confusion on his face.

"A rebel," Locke clarified. "But it's not up to me to make that judgment. Once we take you to the castle, you'll most likely meet Ifir—the Songbird of the Kollek."

"Songbird?"

"The commander of the Chosen forces, and Spymaster to the king. She's the one who oversees all the Chosen in Kellum—or at least, those who manage them. She'll decide your fate, then."

"My... fate?" Kade asked, frowning.

Locke shrugged. "Don't worry. As long as you're not really a rebel, you have nothing to fear. They'll probably take you to a healer who can help you regain your memories... and then to the Chosen compound at the castle. If your brother's there—that's where you'll find him."

Kade nodded several times. "And... if I *am* a rebel?"

Locke raised an eyebrow. "What do you mean?"

Kade cast his eyes to the fire and sighed, very deeply. "As you all said... I've lost my memories. I'm sick... due to all the time I spent feral in the wilds. So..." He raised his eyes, then looked at Locke and Merki, who stared back in return. "What if I really am a rebel, and I just don't remember it?"

Silence overtook the campsite.

Merki and Locke exchanged looks. Axel stayed fully silent, looking only at the dancing flames.

"You're not a rebel, Kade." Merki said.

"How can you be sure? How can anyone?"

"Because..." Merki began. "You're nothing like them. The Sons of Forest—the rebels, are wild, violent people, Kade. Folks who've decided to stand against Ulor and even Aether, and tear down everything they stand for—everything the Kollek stand for. If you were that kind of person... it would've shown by now."

Kade pondered over the words for a moment, then nodded, sighing. "I hope you're right."

"It'll be fine. You'll get help first, then they'll help you find your brother—wherever he is." Locke added.

Kade nodded. "Then I can take him back home and save my sister."

Locke and Merki exchanged glances once more. They both knew it wouldn't be that simple.

"One step at a time, Kade," Merki said. "First we need to get to Kellum before they close the gates, and get you to the castle."

The Chosen nodded. "So, Axel's detour really helped us make it in time after all." He said, looking at Axel, hoping to get something out of him, but the man still wasn't speaking.

"It looks like it did," Locke said, smirking. "Can't believe it myself either. Old loon gets us lost in a godforsaken desert, and we still come out with nearly three whole days to spare before the celebrations."

Kade and Merki smirked as well, but Axel just smiled, nodding, his eyes wide as they stared into the flames.

"Axel..." Merki said. The old man didn't respond. "Axel!" She repeated, louder.

"Hmm?" He looked up from the flames as if he'd been lost in a trance. "Yes, dear?"

"Are you alright? You seem... not like your usual self tonight. You haven't even touched your stew."

The old man shook his head several times, smiling. "Yes, yes, I'm quite alright." He spoke, but the tone in his voice said otherwise. He sounded very weak, tired and frail all of a sudden. "I'm just so tired." He smiled.

"Makes sense," Locke said. "I mean, someone as old as you crossing a desert? That's a miracle unto itself."

Axel smiled, but said nothing.

"You should at least eat something," Merki said, truly concerned for the old man—the friend, she'd grown to appreciate after the month or so of traveling together.

"I... I'm just not hungry tonight, my dear, thank you." He kindly said, his voice very weary and slow. "When you get to be my age, you can do with much less than other folk. Better if you all enjoy it tonight."

Merki stared at him for a moment, then shrugged. "Alright. But you're eating extra for breakfast tomorrow. I'll make sure of it."

Axel smiled wearily. "If you say so, then so I shall."

Kade cleared his throat, realizing that, whatever the old man was dealing with, he probably wanted to be left alone. "So... you didn't answer my question." Kade said to both Merki and Locke.

"We didn't? I think we answered it quite thoroughly." Locke said, gulping down his bowl of stew with gusto, mouth half full.

Kade shook his head. "You told me what will happen to me... but not what you'd do once you get to Kellum. I imagine once you turn me to this 'Songbird' woman... it'll be goodbye, yes?"

Merki cast her eyes down at her feet, and so did Locke. A whole moment of silence passed between them.

"I guess so," Merki finally said, barely more than a whisper. Suddenly, she looked and sounded just like Axel had all evening—tired, weary... lost in her own head.

Kade gave them a sad, knowing smile, and nodded. "It's ok," he said. "This was always a temporary union. Our paths were always meant to diverge at some point. So... what will you both do after you get your bounty for "catching a Chosen,'" he said, smirking, not realizing the many implications hidden in that statement.

Locke was the first to speak. "I'll first book a night at the "*Commodore*," Kellum's finest Inn, up in the Noble's Row district. Then I'll lie in their comfiest bed, eat their best food, and sleep like a king—if just for one night."

"That sounds great," Kade said, still smirking.

"It will be," Locke said. "Then I'll go report to the royal garrison, where a proper physician will see to my wounds and get me back up on my feet in no time—ah, not that I'm not incredibly grateful for your help, Axel." He said the last while nodding towards the old man, who nodded back.

"Especially these crutches you made for me," he nodded to a pair of wooden sticks lying next to him. One of the first things Axel had done after they'd left the desert that morning was to procure a set of small, sturdy trees with Kade's help, then sit on the back of the wagon with Locke, whittling the day away until he'd carved him two simple wooden crutches, as he'd promised. These had finally enabled him to walk on his own after weeks of depending on others for even the most basic things. They were still very uncomfortable, it should be said—but at least he could move around on his own now.

Diverging Paths | 363

"That sounds wise," Kade said, then turned to Merki. "What about you?" Merki looked up from the fire as if she'd been a thousand miles away.

"What *about* me?"

"What will you do? You know, after you drop me off at the castle and get your gold?"

Merki sighed deeply, looking back into the flames. "I… I guess I'll use the money to secure some lodgings during the festivities… and make the best use of the opportunity as I can." She shrugged.

Kade raised an eyebrow and frowned, not fully understanding the meaning behind how she'd phrased her statement. "You mean, you just want to enjoy the festivities?" He asked.

Merki nodded, silently. "Sure."

"And then?"

She shrugged. "I… don't know. I guess I'll figure it out."

Locke frowned. "Didn't you say you wanted to join the Royal Rangers Corp?"

Merki smiled ever so slightly. "… I guess I did, yeah."

"So? Is that what you're going to do?" Kade asked.

"I guess so." She then seemed to come out of whatever waking dream she was having, her eyes coming alive once more. She smiled, and said: "Sorry… it's a big moment. Got lost in thought there for a second. I mean, I've dreamt of making it here most of my life… and now it's there." She looked over her shoulder, and the sparkling lights in the distance. "It's *right* there." She shook her head. "Where does one even start?"

Locke chuckled. "That's what most people experience on their first visit to Kellum. Don't worry—I'll help you find your way around town. Then, after the festivities are over, I can put in a good word for you over at the garrison—maybe help you get a hunter license, so you can start somewhere."

Merki smirked. "I'd appreciate that."

Locke nodded, staring into her eyes, the fire glistening off of them. "It's the least I could do. You saved our lives many times during our journey—fought as bravely and hard as any of my men…" His eyes suddenly got heavy as he remembered Jarrie, Leord and Ourg… and even Gerard. "And you saved us from *him*, too." He looked up at her, his demeanor changed. "You deserve a chance at whatever you want to do in Kellum, and I'll make sure you get it."

Merki took a deep breath… then nodded. "Thank you, Locke." She said. "You're a good man." Then she hesitated for a moment, and added: "During the celebrations, there's a parade, right?"

The question caught Locke a bit off guard, but he nodded. "Uh… yeah. Why?"

"And during that parade, all the major officials of the kingdom march down the main street to the temple, right?"

Locke nodded. "That's the way it was ten years ago."

"Do you know which major figures will join the procession? I'd really love to see the king and queen—and all the other members of the court, at least once."

Locke nodded. "I believe you will, then. Ulor and all the royals will be there, of course… then there's Ifir, the Songbird," he looked at Kade as he said it, "then the rest of the royal court—the coin master, the commander of the Kollek forces, the high lords of Kellum, and of course, the Kollek champion."

Merki nodded, satisfied, then her eyes fell upon the fire once more.

"The Champion of the Kollek? Who's that?" Kade asked.

"He's the strongest Chosen in the corps. Probably in the whole world, too. Some say he's the Sword of Aether as well, waiting for the Manuscripts' revelations to awaken to his true form."

Before Kade could say or ask anything else, Axel cut him off.

"We should probably all turn in early tonight," the old man said, surprising everyone in the group. "We'll need a full night of sleep for tomorrow—when we finally enter Kellum properly. There'll be time for questions and answers then."

They all agreed, as they too were all incredibly tired, so they finished the savory stew, said their goodbyes for the night and laid down in their bedrolls. Despite their minds being full of thoughts—of worries, hopes and dreams for the following day, they all managed to fall asleep surprisingly fast, leaving the crackling of the fire and rustling of the trees as the only remaining sounds.

***

When the moon appeared among the clouds, the old man suddenly opened his eyes.

Right on time... You must hurry. His inner voice warned him.

He checked the moon on the sky, then quickly got to his feet and gathered his things, which very few. He then tiptoed silently over to Kade, who was sleeping like a rock next to him, and shook him gently. The young Chosen woke up, startled, but Axel quickly put an index finger to his own lips. Seeing the sign, Kade nodded.

"What are you doing?" He asked in a whisper. "What's going on?"

"Gather your things," he told Kade. "We must leave. Now." Then, he padded over to the horses and started preparing two of them.

"Leave? To where?" Kade walked behind him a few moments later, his bag of things—also precious few, slung over his shoulder.

"To Kellum." The old man replied, while tightening the horse's saddles. "Come, help me with your horse." Kade began to do as told, readying his horse, his mind still partly asleep. He was struggling heavily to understand what was happening.

"What about them?" He asked, nodding towards Merki and Axel.

"They have served their purpose, Kade. It is time to leave them behind and fulfill both of our goals—to take you to your brother." The old man said as he looked deeply into the Chosen's eyes.

"You... you know Ellyad?" Kade asked, eyes wide.

Axel nodded gravely. "I do. And it is my mission to take you to him, unharmed."

The young man couldn't move for a second. Axel leaned towards him with a serious, intense look in his eyes, in a way that Kade had never seen before.

"Listen... they do not know this, but once you're delivered to the king... the Songbird, Ifir... She will kill you, Kade. She won't even interrogate you or try to heal you—she will take you to a backroom somewhere in the castle and plunge a blade straight through your heart."

"What? Why? How could you know this?"

"Because of who you are, Kade. Because of who your brother is. She'll know it the moment she sees you... and she'll make you disappear. Your very presence in Kellum upsets the balance of power... *Her* balance of power. But I have another way of helping you reach Ellyad. One that doesn't end up with you dead. You have to trust me."

Kade searched the old man's eyes. He seemed to be telling the truth, despite the insane circumstances they found themselves in. Kade looked back towards the sleeping forms of Merki and Locke.

"They will be fine, Kade. They will make it to the city in time."

"I... I don't..." Kade began, but then they heard voices coming from the campsite. "H-hey... wwwhere are you goinnng?" Locke said, pushing himself up from his bedroll. "Are you... are you *lllleeeeaving*?" His voice was horribly slurred. The captain clearly didn't seem to be doing very well.

"What's wrong with him?" Kade asked Axel.

"Strong dose of sleeping herbs... I put it on the stew while I was helping Merki prepare it. They shouldn't be able to walk properly for hours."

Kade frowned, then fiercely whispered. "Hey—I ate from that stew!"

"I measured the dose. Your Chosen metabolism already processed the drugs. Theirs are just starting to. Come, Kade, we must leave! Now!" He whispered fiercely back.

"Axzzzel, answer me!" Locke said, blinking fiercely, trying to get up, but stumbling on his back like a baby.

"We're just going on a quick ride, captain." Axel said. "We'll be back before sunrise."

"Jussst going for a quick ride...?" Locke said, looking very, very drugged. "But... wait... why ar you taking all your thhhhings with you? Yyyyou're not going for a ride...! Yyyou're leaving!" He then turned to Merki. "Morrrki... wwwake up!" He grabbed one of his

Diverging Paths | 367

walking sticks and prodded her on the leg, missing half the jabs. "Wwwwake up!" He yelled, his voice still drawling something terrible.

"Aether, Axel... How much of the herbs did you put in that stew?" Kade asked the old man.

"Plenty..." He said, grimacing. "I might've put in some mushrooms I found on the desert too." Then, upon seeing Kade's horrified look, he added: "Completely harmless to you, of course, but to *them*..."

The big Chosen frowned, clearly distressed. He looked between Axel and the others, his heart breaking.

"Axel..." He began. "We... we can't just leave them here like this... we can't."

Locke's stick finally managed to poke Merki the right way and she woke up, turning on her bedroll, groaning loudly. "W-whatdoyouwon, Axel?" She asked, her voice just as slurred as Locke's.

"Iz nnnot Axel... Iz me... Lok!"

Merki tried to prop herself up in her bedroll and, just like Locke, her whole world began to spin wildly around her and she fell back on her bum. She blinked hard for a few seconds, staring at Locke. The captain waved his arms wildly towards Kade and Axel.

Merki looked at them, blinking fiercely, then her eyes shot as wide open as they could, which was still not much, given how heavily drugged she was.

"Hey... wwwhere ar you guyzzz goin?" She said, her eyes drooping. She tried to get up again, but her legs wobbled under her and she fell back down on her backside, almost limp.

"The hell?" She said, looking down at her legs and feet, as if she were discovering them for the very first time.

"Come on Kade, we must leave. Now!" Axel shouted. Although Kade had very strong reservations about this, he though upon Axel's words, and his conversation with Merki and Locke the night before.

The Songbird will decide your fate then.

He could tell neither of them knew exactly what would await him once they reached Kellum... but Axel did. And nothing—not even the friends he'd made throughout this journey, could come between him and finding his brother. With a pang of great guilt in his chest, the Chosen climbed up on his horse, and grabbed its bridle tight.

"I'm sorry!" He told the other two, then urged his horse forward and down the path they'd come. Axel gave his two companions one last, guilty look. He walked over to the other two horses, holding his by his bridle, and slapped them hard in their bums, sending them galloping away from the camp.

"Axxzel…" Merki said, trying but failing to stand up again, landing on her knees on the damp dirt. "Yyyyou can't do diz… Pleaze… don't take him…" She said, reaching out with a quivering hand.

"I'm sorry, dear Merki… Take good care of yourself… and him." He whispered to her, looking at Locke, who was worming his way onto the dirt trying to catch up to him. Axel suddenly realized that the man was sobbing. His mind was fully realizing what was happening—and just how helpless he was to do anything about it: that his prize, the Chosen for which he'd almost died—and for whom he'd lost his men, was escaping… leaving him with nothing at all to show for all his pain and loss. Realizing this, Locke wailed, long and hard, like a wounded animal.

Without looking back, Axel mounted his horse and left both of them alone in the camp… fully expecting to never see either of them again.

CHAPTER 31

THE SONGCALL

Ifir was silently watching the preparations for the Imperation Day celebrations from the hill near the Street of Kings. Countless servants were running back and forth, moving chairs around and cleaned the streets. She watched the head servants leading groups of many lesser ones, all of them running around according to the orders in their supervisors' hands.

"Did you really order thousands of Moonlight Lotuses from the Crescent Islands?" Fermand asked, walking next to Ifir while trying to control his anger and desperation.

She slightly turned her head. "Good day to you too, Fermand." She smiled without turning her gaze from the street far below her.

"How can it be a good day when you make such an expensive purchase without running it by me first?" He asked, almost in a squeal.

Ifir smirked. "I couldn't wait for you to punch out the numbers, dear Fermand, or else the lotuses would've never made it here in time. You know how rare they are—being that they grow exclusively on the islands nowadays." She calmly answered.

"Precisely why they are so expensive! What do you need them for, anyways?"

"Why, to make a statement, of course. When the kings and queens of the isles sail into our harbors, only to behold the bay covered in Moonlight Lotuses, they'll remember who holds the power in this world... and they'll know to behave themselves while in our fair city. Besides the cost my flowers is not a big issue... especially when compared to the wishes of our beloved queen." She said and raised her head to look at Temple of Aether.

Fermand launched his hands up in the air in frustration. "What's the point of having a coin master if you'll just do whatever you want anyways?" The irony in Fermand's voice didn't even disturb Ifir.

"Just make the payment, dear Fermand." Ifir smiled and then simply turned to leave. Fermand took a deep breath and checked his anger, remembering who it was he was speaking to.

"Let's go and welcome our beloved lords before our king receives them, shall we?" Ifir said, waiting for Fermand. The small man nodded, letting out a long sigh, and the two of them walked back to the castle, heading towards the royal audience chambers at the back of the keep's first floor, just past the foyer with the stairwells.

When the gates to the audience chamber opened for Fermand and Ifir, the twelve High Lords of the Kollek were already there waiting for them. The inside of the chamber was so noisy as everyone was up, arguing about something.

"Welcome, lords." Ifir said as she and Fermand walked to their chairs below the king and queen's. The High Lords of the Kollek sat in their places before the meeting started, and Ifir's eyes wandered through the crowd, specifically seeking High Lord Franthz Pentgard—Locke's father. She came eye-to-eye with him, then smiled a very knowing smile. Lord Franthz unwillingly smiled back at her.

A few seconds later Siegen walked in too, and sat near Ifir and Fermand. The room had a podium with raised seats at its end, with twelve chairs at the floor level. The highest chairs in the audience podium belonged to the royal family, the king and queen, while those below them were for Ifir, Siegen and Fermand. The lowest chairs—the twelve on the floor, belonged to the lords. In the corner of the room was a desk with many pots of ink and stacks of parchment. A king's steward stood next to the door, waiting for everyone to take their seats.

With Siegen's signal, the king's steward shouted: "Rise for the High King of the World, and Right Hand of our Lord Aether—His Royal Majesty, King Ulor!"

Everybody stood up. The doors to the chamber suddenly opened once more, and Ulor came in with Etheria in his arm. All the lords, as well as the three members of the high court, knelt as they passed by their seats, heads down, and a fist on their chest.

"Rise, my lords and ladies!" Ulor shouted as he sat on his throne, and all the lords, Ifir, Siegen and Fermand rose.

"Welcome, my lords." Ulor said.

"Long live the High King!" The lords said in unison as loud as they could. Then, with Ulor's signal, Fermand proceeded to start the meeting. The king's steward hit his weighted rod on the ground three times, signaling for silence and for everyone to pay attention.

"Dear Lords of the Kollek kingdom, in the presence of our High King Ulor and our god Aether, the annual Meeting of the Lords has begun." Fermand said, and with his hand signal, the court writer turned his focus on the parchment in front of him and began writing every word he heard.

"Today marks the seventy-second annual Meeting of the Lords of Siran, our fair continent and seat of Kollek power. The twelve High Lords of the Kollek, those of you who pledged their loyalty to our High King Ulor, are all gathered here today to speak your problems, wishes and needs before our king, so he might deliver them to Aether during the holy festivities." As Fermand announced, the court writer recorded. All of the High Lords waited silently for their turns to speak.

"Let's start our agenda with the topic of security, then." Fermand announced, and a hand rose from the second row. High Lord of Drakendon—the feudal district that contained all the lands from the Golden River to the Stepping Rock Mountains, (between which Halstead was located), stood up with all the pomp that his position allowed him and spoke directly to the council. His name was Frederick Montresor, and he was almost as tall as a Chosen; a well-built warrior with red cheeks and flaming red hair, slicked back with oil. He wore an elegant coat of fine fur and pelt, as people of his district usually did during the colder months, marking him as a wilder lord among the others. He cleared his throat before he spoke.

"My High King, my Queen, Esteemed Council of Lords… in the lands of Drakendon, rebel numbers have increased considerably during the last month. My scouts suspect that they're nested somewhere near the Arten Forest, as they occasionally rob people along the forest paths, as well as my trading convoys. My scouts searched for any sign of them, combing through the entire woods, but couldn't find their base of operations. We've suffered massive economic damage because of this, and lost many good men trying to weed them out, to no avail."

Fermand looked at Ifir out of the corner of his eye. Another High Lord, Lord Gumbledon, raised a fat hand and stood up once he'd been given permission. He was very large and his skin very greasy. However, it was his demeanor, and the arrogance with which he spoke, which irked those around him and made it so that no one could stand him.

"I have the same problem, my lords…" He said in a high-pitched nasal tone. "Rebels, everywhere, feeding my people and encouraging them to join their ranks. I've even had peasants rise up against me! The nerve of the scum…" His large fingers were adorned with many emerald, ruby and sapphire rings, which seemed awfully small and like they were squeezing the blood out of his hands.

Siegen held up a brightly colored blood-red fan, signaling that he would speak next.

"I will increase the size and strength of your local garrisons, Lord Frederick, as well as send an elite scouting party to patrol your woods. We will find their base of operations, for you so you can then send your forces in and exterminate every last one of them." Siegen nodded to Fermand, signaling him to continue with another subject.

"Ahem… next topic."

"Wait… what about my problem?" Lord Gumbledon objected. "My people won't listen to me! They're running to the woods to join these rebels, and all because I impose a little more of the food tax? Something must be done here! They need to be put in their place—but I need more soldiers for that!"

Ifir was the one who spoke this time.

"We protect you against the Alerian sorcerers, their Night Judges and rebels already, Lord Gumbledon. We protect your trade, lives and lands. If you're not willing to feed your people properly, then that is your problem. However, we still expect you to deal with the rebel recruitment problems your district is facing, or we'll find someone more suited for your position to do so. Do I make myself understood?"

The old lord hung his oiled, blonde head and nodded. "Yes..."

The Songbird rolled her eyes and sat back down. "Good."

"Good. Now, next topic?"

"Next topic," Fermand announced. "Recruitment efforts for the Kollek army." He passed the word to Siegen.

"High Lords... our army needs more soldiers in its service to push back the tide of the Alerians at the frontlines. However, I see that our lieutenants and captains are having a hard time drafting new people up—why is that?"

All the lords looked away from Siegen.

"The Kollek army fights in too many frontlines at the same time. We need more soldiers. We know that most of you have already met and exceeded the draft quotas... but we need you to convince more of your people. Start drafting women, if necessary. We need more able bodies, and expect a more positive response from each of your lands in the upcoming months." He said. The lords silently nodded.

"Next topic: Provisions and Crop Taxation." Fermand said.

The lords all exchanged glances with each other.

"As always, a third of all the crops belong to your High King. The rest will be equally rationed among the people."

"But this year we have so much fewer crops." A lord objected, followed by the others. A howl of complaints covered the room. Fermand tried to hush them, to no avail, as did the court king's steward. The writer found it impossible to keep track of everything they were saying. Ifir then stood up, took a deep breath, looking as calm as the surface of Lake Kellam… and blasted her voice throughout the chamber, as if a hurricane had just appeared inside the room.

"Silence!" Her voice boomed out of her like a blossoming flower, making the room quake and rumble. Because of the way she could focus and control her soundwaves, only the lords heard her screech. Only their clothes and hair flapped wildly, as if in a storm. They all crouched, hands on their ears, wincing in pain. Ulor smiled and looked at Etheria, whose features were set in stone—witnessing the Songbird's power firsthand like that always left a downright sour taste in her mouth.

Witch, she said to herself.

The lords all quieted down, their heads cast down. Some of them still rubbed their ears, grimacing.

"It seems you've all forgotten how to behave in front of your king," Ifir said. "I suggest you all do your best to remember proper court etiquette… or else there'll be harsher consequences to deal with." She announced. The lords stood up, bowed to the royals and sat right back down.

As this happened, a young, well-dressed servant man entered the room and bent next to Lord Franthz, whispering something to his ear. The lord's face paled as the boy walked away. Watching him out of the corner of his eyes, Fermand couldn't help but smile, imaging just what the news were.

"Next topic is taxes." Fermand said. "The kingdom still requires a sacrifice from you, dear lords, as the war continues, and our efforts expand to push the Alerians back. We need to increase the tax rate from last year."

"But… Last year's taxes were so high, we could barely pay them!" Lord Gumbledon said in protest. "I mean, first the food tax… then the coin tax. You can't seriously expect us to keep this up! What's next, giving up our castles and keeps in service of the war effort? King Ulor! You can't be serious, can you?!"

The entire chamber fell into a deep silence, as all eyes fell upon the stocky lord of the southwestern coasts. Etheria looked at Ulor, while the king leaned forward with squinting eyes. Even Ifir showed genuine surprise in her features, staring at the man with her lips slightly parted. The stocky lord looked around him desperately, standing up, and pushed himself a little deeper into the grim hole he'd dug.

"We're all thinking it! Something must simply be done about these unrealistic taxes and sanctions—we'll lose our very way of life if this keeps up! It's madness!"

Now… Gumbledon had always been an arrogant, entitled, miserable little man… but he'd done good work administering his district, and always paid his taxes on time, if begrudgingly. He was a "necessary evil" to Ulor and the other lords—someone to be tolerated, as his numbers had always checked out.

However.

Insubordination at this level was another matter entirely. Gumbledon had proven today, once and for all, that he wasn't only a greedy, odious fool—but also a very stupid one.

The lords all lowered their stares and held their breath in anticipation.

"Tell me… Lord Gumbledon," Ulor began, standing up slowly from his throne. The fat lord seemed to sink down as Ulor's long shadow fell upon him, the sun filtering through the tall, mosaic glass windows at his back. "Is your nephew Siran in good health?"

The greasy, sweaty lord nodded several times, keeping his head down.

"Is he still as accomplished a steward of Westcliff as you'd reported to me in previous years?"

The man nodded again.

"Excellent," Ulor then turned to his own steward. "Roland, send a hawk to Westcliff immediately and inform young Siran Harlan that he's the new lord of the district."

Gumbledon went pale in the face and nearly fainted. "B-b-but… my lord!" He exclaimed, nearly out of breath.

Ulor slowly turned his gaze over to Gumbledon, his expression as fierce and sharp as a cold blade.

"Lord Gumbledon... Do you realize what you've just done here today?"

"I-I-I..."

"You've openly defied... questioned... and *ridiculed* the voice of Aether in this world. The Right Hand of our Holy God, your lord and your king. You've done this openly and without restraint, in front of all the lords of Siran. Do you deny this?"

Gumbledon fell to his knees, his hands spread wide, his face a mess of wrinkles, grease and terror. "My king! I've sinned against you and our Lord! Please, forgive your servant!"

Ulor looked down at the noble for an uncomfortably long time, his gaze fierce, almost like that of a god. The silence in the room was so thick, one could hear a pin drop in the next room. Ifir was savoring every moment. Etheria, on the other hand, looked just as uncomfortable as the lords.

"Aether forgives... Gumbledon." Ulor finally said, and those in the room felt like they could breathe once more, if shallowly.

"My lord... thank you, thank you! I promise that..."

"But I am not Aether." Ulor interrupted him. "I am His Hand—his Judge on this earth. And you are guilty of openly defying me, your king, in open assembly. For this, you must be made an example of."

"No, I... Please, King Ulor, please! I've known you since you were a child—I served your father faithfully, did I not?!"

"For your crime of insolence and insubordination towards your king—towards your GOD... I sentence you to die, Lord Gumbledon. Ifir, if you will?" Ulor said, each word a stone shattering against the ground.

"With pleasure, my king," Ifir slowly whispered, eyes wide, fascinated by how much *fun* today's assembly had suddenly turned out to be.

She stood up slowly from her throne, her glittering green dress sliding around her frame, her green eyes shining bright on her pale, perfect face.

She inhaled a long, deep breath... and everyone in the room cringed, holding their hand to their ears, even Gumbledon.

Yet, when she released her voice, no sound came out. The lords removed their hands from their ears and looked at Ifir. She seemed to be screaming, her eyes and mouth wide open, her arms raised in front of her, palms up, and yet no sound was coming out of her.

Then, the room began to shake.

They all looked at Gumbledon and terror burned itself across their faces, as the round lord shook with the room, the edges of his outline blurring, his eyes wide. He too, seemed to be screaming, red in the face, but without any perceivable sound. They all recoiled back in horror, those next to him knocking some of the chairs over, as the man's ears began to pour blood, as his eyes bugged out of his head, turning red. His entire body trembled and convulsed as if possessed, his eyes rolling back into his head.

Then, there was a sick crunch and the man broke, his neck snapping all the way back.

Etheria looked away, closing her eyes, a hand over her mouth.

Some of the lords shrieked in pure terror, looking at the door—but they knew they wouldn't be allowed out of the room until Ulor gave them his blessing.

"That's enough, Ifir..." Ulor said, a slight smirk on his lips.

The Songbird of the Kollek finished her terrible Songcall, slowly closing her mouth and lowering her arms. She then took a deep breath and sat right back down, looking as content as if she'd just enjoyed a satisfying supper.

"Guards," Ulor said, and two of his royal guard walked forward. "Take Lord Gumbledon's remains and dispose of them in the Direhalls."

"Yes, Sire." They said, and grabbed the man's broken body by his arms and legs, hauling it out of a side door in the chamber which led outside, to the gardens. As they did, the lords stared at the man one last time, noticing the terrified expression on his face, his bloodshot eyes... and the way his head faced the entirely wrong direction.

One of the lords retched, but held his lunch in with every ounce of his body, not wanting to end up like Gumbledon.

"This…" Began Ulor, as calmly as if he'd just served tea to the men before him. "… is what happens when you openly defy the Hand of Your God—the One Who Speaks for Him. This is what happens when you defy *Aether* himself, my children. You think I wanted to do this?" He gestured at the door through which the guards had just exited the room.

"I did not. But Lord Gumbledon left me no choice. For, to rise in such arrogance against me, is to rise against *Aether* himself… And I cannot allow that, as I dare not incur the wrath of our Lord by allowing such insolence. Just as so… all that we ask of you, all that we impose—as unfair as it may seem, is for the ultimate purpose of preserving our kingdom, our *legacy*, as Aether's chosen people. He has blessed us with His own Chosen, my lords—Aether's own warriors, given physical bodies to walk among us. Gifted with power and abilities beyond all the other races. We cannot falter in our stewardship of what our own Lord Himself has seen fit to give us. We must put down everything we have in its defense—our blood, our very lives and even that of our own children, if we must. Until His Sword, the vessel of His power, is revealed to us… Until the Stone is found, and the war is won… No price is too high." He said, finishing in almost in a whisper.

All of the lords fell to their knees and touched the floor with their foreheads, trembling in fear—even Lord Franthz Pentgard.

King Ulor raised his hand over the lords and smiled. "Rise, my children, and let us continue this meeting." He said, then seated himself. The lords did, then sat back at their appointed places, Lord Gumbleton's chair standing noticeably empty among them now.

"Any other questions?" Fermand asked after a moment had passed, as if a man hadn't been brutally executed in front of them. He looked over the lords' pale faces, seeing no one raising their hands, and looked back down to his ledger.

"Good." Fermand said. "Next up is the national census…"

CHAPTER 32

INTO ENEMY LANDS

Urk and his men rode through the Koartiz lands after passing the border line—and the immense Kollek border checkpoint situated there to prevent the enemy from just walking into the Kollek lands.

The brown cloaks they'd worn over their armor hid them almost perfectly in the deep shadows cast by the thick canopy overhead. No one could say they were Chosen from a distance. Urk rode at the front while his men rode behind him, his ears fully on guard for any telltale sounds of enemy presence around them. He stopped occasionally after hearing something out of rhythm with the forest around them, waited until it had passed, then ordered his men forward once more. After riding for about an hour in the dense forest, well into the Koartiz' lands already, they reached the bank of a massive lake, its placid surface glistening under the noonday sun.

"Is this…?" Frain began, in a soft whisper, knowing Urk could hear it perfectly well.

"Lake Foras, yes." Urk replied. All of the Chosen's eyes stared at the empty horizon beyond the calm, blue waters of the lake, which seemed more like an endless ocean than anything else from this side.

"Wow…" Balto said. "Hard to believe Aether created something like this." The others nodded.

"So, the temple we're looking for is on the other side of the lake?" Frain asked.

"If our forward scouts' reports are correct, yes." Urk replied.

"Isn't this the lake of legend?" Hukail asked.

"The very same," replied Urk. "It is said that the sorcerers who could control the power of water used this lake as a way to escape Luden's incoming army, letting the waters carry thousands of them to safety, earning it the name of 'The Living Lake'."

"You think the rumors are true?" Balto asked.

"Which ones?" Asked Hukail.

"The ones that say sorcerers live under the lake? That they come out of the water and pull people into it, never to be seen again?"

"Rumors are just rumors, soldier," Said Urk. "No man can live underwater, much less build a city at the bottom of a lake… not Chosen, nor Koartiz."

The men looked at each other and shrugged.

"Let's keep riding. We've got a long way to go if we hope to reach the other side in time." Urk informed his soldiers.

"What happens if we're spotted, Captain?" Frain asked.

Urk looked back. "If they're just commoners, and they recognize us, we have no choice but to put them down. If they're soldiers, we put them down."

His Chosen nodded, then followed after him into the lakeside path, still thick with trees and large canopies.

After riding silently for about an hour around the lake, they reached the side of the path that curved around the ocean. Lake Foras had actually been a part of the sea once, a great bay, before a magical event caused a massive bridge of land to rise from its depths, and separated it from the ocean. Now, as they rode, they had the lake on their right and the infinite expanse of the sea, waves crashing upon the shore, on their left.

After riding up the seaward side of the lake for another half hour, the group of Chosen eventually came across the ruins of a small fort in the road, its crumbling walls blocking the path forward on either side.

There were Koartiz soldiers on the parapets, holding bows, and two at the entrance.

"How are we doing this, Captain?" Hukail asked Urk.

"Bait and switch, men." Urk replied, still far away enough to not be heard. "We trick them into opening up the gates, then eliminate them efficiently and quickly from the inside. No survivors."

"What if they don't open the gates?" Asked Frain.

"Then you're up, of course." Urk said, smirking at Frain over his shoulder. "Runners are our priority here. We can't allow even one of them to get away. Kill their horses if you have to."

"And if one does?" Asked Balto.

"Chase him down immediately then kill him. We take no prisoners today, men."

The Chosen all nodded and rode forward towards the fort, hoods up, their bodies fully cloaked.

When they reached the tall, wooden gates, one of the sentries on top called out to them in the Koartiz language.

"Hak. Acti veruden ortis?!"

Halt, who goes there?

Urk smirked.

"Yorall, frankta ur de dorsveh. Ami ad drusmah, os kalis dram."

Hail, friends of the scorned. We're just passing through.

As a Chosen raised in Kellum, Urk had received special training in the Alerian language—trained in it almost all his life, then specialized in it upon graduating his basic studies. Ambitious as he was, Urk had determined he wanted every edge he could get on his way up, and that included learning to speak Alerian Koartiz almost as fluently as they did—one of the reasons Ifir had chosen him for this mission.

"Friend of the scorned" was how Koartiz who lived outside the walls of one of the major cities referred to themselves. Few outside the Koartiz lands knew this, but Urk had studied the Koartiz society well, hoping for just such a chance one day: that of seeking a Manuscript and solidifying his legacy.

Into Enemy Lands | 383

Urk's accent, however, would never be as authentic as that of an actual Alerian, and the sentry noticed it.

"Yi kuren ard kaindren… Vri kust drol?"

Your speech-form is not common… from where do you come?

"Yog gral ir kadus fir. Iker drom, mel isan arda vor kest. Bri kardin ust vitori lassaer."

We hail from the enemy lands. We are field agents, heading back home after a long operation. We bring important information.

The sentry stroked his shaved chin thoughtfully. Urk heard the others whispering to him.

"Something doesn't seem right…" One said, still in Alerian.

"But they may have vital information for the war effort!" Another answered back.

The sentry who'd spoken to Urk, the one in charge, shushed the two of them.

"It could be a trap—a group of their *devil soldiers*, masquerading as field agents." He said.

Urk leaned back on his horse and whispered to his Chosen. "They seem to be onto us, men… prepare for plan B at my command."

"Ekka!" Yelled the head sentry. "Ardu vist kord?"

Traveler! Where were you and your men born?

Urk scoured his brain for names of nearby Koartiz settlements—those he'd studied during his formative years at the Chosen academy.

"Farad'ul Stadt," he finally said. In Kollek, it meant *Forgespire City*.

The man stroked his chin again, looking at Urk and his men through squinted eyes.

"Hukail… What do you see?" Urk whispered without turning. The Chosen soldier cast his sight beyond the walls of the fort and onto its interior, noticing how the entire platoon inside the fort was looking up to the sentry, weapons at the ready. He saw what appeared to be traps at the entrance, and men with spears, bows, curved swords and quarterstaffs with bladed ends.

"They're ready for a fight," Hukail whispered barely above a fly's buzz, which Urk heard as clear as thundering rain. "About twenty-five men inside. Traps near the gates. Nothing we can't handle."

Urk nodded. "Relay the information. Be ready," he whispered back.

"Will we open the gates?" Asked one of the sentries.

The head sentry sighed, then shook his head. "They're too big to be Koartiz. Do we have people that big in our scouting forces? Aren't our scouts supposed to be small and quick?"

"You're right. They look more like soldiers than scouts to me." Said another.

Urk sighed. "They know," he told Hukail, who relayed the information. "Do your thing, Frain."

The Chosen nodded and, all of a sudden, his muscles grew larger under his cloak. He dismounted his horse, and the head sentry started calling out to them, holding up a hand.

"Hey, hey, hey!" He said in Alerian. "What do you think you're doing? Stand where you are!"

Urk raised a hand. "He's just reaching for the papers that show our orders."

The sentry frowned. "Papers? What papers? We don't issue…"

"Frain… *now*." Said Urk, and the Musal suddenly shot forward like a bolt of lightning, slamming his shoulder against the wooden doors and blasting them open clean off their hinges.

The Chosen soldiers all moved out of the way as a volley of arrows hit the place where they'd just been standing—one of the automated traps at the entrance. Then, right after the first one, three long "rakes" of sharp wooden stakes shaped like claws, and tipped with iron, swung forward. If any of them had been standing right in front of the gates, or somehow survived the volley of arrows, they'd surely been impaled on the stakes.

The Koartiz soldiers stared in awe for a moment at the speed of the men—and the one who suddenly crashed through their gate like it was made out of straw. Then, the head sentry screamed a blood-curdling cry.

"Jicursnan! Ordil kus drandil ve Kar'Sal, akt! Arkist sidir!"

Invaders! Send a rider to Kar'Sal immediately! Alert the troops!

He raised his bow to shoot the men—but, to his horror, they were no longer outside the fort. The Koartiz sentry looked back inside, and the sight turned his stomach inside out. His men were getting thoroughly butchered by the inhumanly large soldiers, their cloaks now cast aside, armor glistening in the afternoon sun.

Balto was the first inside after Frain, running like the wind. He ran towards four men running at him with swords and spears and threw himself on the ground, sliding past the men on specially designed greaves, and touching the men's legs as he went. The enemy soldiers fell down like sacks of potatoes, as if they'd suddenly fallen unconscious. They were still alive, but their eyes had rolled to the back of their heads, their hands and mouths moving aimlessly, as if they'd been sent into a trance—one of Balto's special powers as a Cauda Chosen, of which there were precious little in Kellum. However, two of the soldiers had managed to jump out of the way in time before Balto touched them. They were clearly sword masters with incredible reaction times. Balto stood up and swung his longsword at them, but they matched him blow for blow. Hukail shot an arrow at one of them from afar, yet the Alerian deflected it with his sword.

Facing actual Koartiz warriors for the first time, Hukail saw how the soldiers' bodies were covered fully in tattoos, like in the stories he'd heard, but their faces weren't. They were also shorter and thinner than most soldiers he knew, but incredibly fast and nimble. The sword masters were moving so fast on their toes that Urk could've sworn they were flying. The element of surprise had given the Chosen an initial edge, where they'd butchered most of the soldiers in the small fort, but soon, ten other men surrounded them. Frain, Urk, Hukail and Balto stood back-to-back, when suddenly, one of the Koartiz mounted a horse and sped through the back gate.

"Damn it!" Urk said. "Frain, on him!" The other Chosen nodded, bulked up, then jumped over the fort walls in a single leap, landing in a small crater outside. He continued to chase after the escaping Koartiz, jumping in massive leaps that closed the distance between him and the man a little more each time.

Back at the fort, Urk and his two other men braced against the remaining Koartiz. The head sentry, clearly the commander of this fort, looked down at them from the walls, his longbow at the ready.

"This is as far as you get, devil-spawn!" He said, in very broken Kollek. He shot an arrow at Urk, who deflected it with his longsword.

"Why don't you come down here and repeat that?" Urk said in Alerian. "I didn't quite catch that."

The Koartiz drew a saber of his own and, enraged, jumped down to join the other ten men.

Urk knew what he had to do. He'd studied the Koartiz and their battle tactics well and thoroughly—knew how they responded to the chain of command in battle... and how to use that to his advantage.

"Face me, heathen!" He told the commander. "Unless your faith in the Five falters today!"

The Koartiz's eyes opened as wide as they'd go at the insult, one of the worst one could throw at an Alerian, and he spat the dirt before him.

"You will regret uttering those words, faithless Kollek."

The man waved his own saber around as his men created a wider circle. Hukail and Balto stayed back, still inside the circle and facing the other soldiers, while Urk met their commander in one-on-one combat.

He smirked, then said. "You're just as faithless as you say we are, heathen. Your Five are as nothing, and you... you're worse than nothing."

There. Urk saw it in his eyes as they went wide, almost feral, with religious zeal and rage. The man howled at the top of his lungs and rushed at Urk with his saber raised to the heavens. Urk simply waited, his own sword at the ready... waited and breathed, listening for the right moment...

Then he simply stepped forward and cut, sheathing his sword with a bloody flourish. He looked back at the commander, who walked a couple of steps further, saber still raised high, then wobbled on his feet. His sword fell from his limp fingers. Then his head, from his shoulders. His body fell on its knees, then crumpled to the side.

Urk turned and spat on his body, and every other soldier around them grew paler than milk—their eyes filled with horror, not just as losing their commander, but also seeing his body desecrated in such an unholy way.

"Kill them all," Urk said to his men, and the other Chosen advanced towards the shocked, panicked soldiers. Even the two sword masters faltered, stepping backwards, shaking, as the Chosen butchered all who stood in their way. Urk himself redrew his blade and cut down three of the soldiers.

In a few seconds, all of the Koartiz were dead. Urk walked over to the two Balto had sent into shock previously and drove his sword into their hearts.

"Everyone alright?" He asked the other two men. Balto had a couple of scratches but was otherwise fine. Hukail was bleeding from a cut on his arm, but he was already bandaging it by the time Urk turned to ask. "Just a flesh wound." He said, as if nothing had happened.

Then, almost as if on cue, Frain landed inside the fort, sending small tremors upon crashing back onto the ground. As he rose, he held up the escaping Koartiz's head for his teammates to see.

"We're in the clear," he announced, then went back to normal.

"Thank Aether," Urk whispered. "Good job, men. All of you. We're officially in Koartiz lands now… be ready for more "welcomes" of this kind from this point onwards."

The men nodded, mounted their horses, then left the massacre scene behind them.

***

Urk and his men rode their horses for hours after that, redonning their cloaks and hoods, and traveling as incognito as they could while still making good time towards their objective. As they rode past the heavily forested roads and paths they encountered a few patrols, which they quickly did away with, and ran into some commoners and peasants from afar, which thankfully didn't recognize them or raise any alarms. (Urk made sure of it, listening closely to each of them long after they'd ridden past them). Urk and his men kept their senses on edge all throughout their ride, passing farmlands, grassy hills and more dense forests than before, riding under warning signs made of bones and what appeared to be skulls of some sort of ape-like creature they'd never seen before.

After riding for the better half of the day, as the sun was starting to set, they rode out into a wide open plain on the other side of the seemingly interminable lake. This plain was unlike anything Urk or his men had ever seen—a blasted heath of dry, yellow grass and brown, cracked land as far as the eye could see.

Incredibly far off in the distance, looking almost like a small molehill from their vantage point, was a rising structure—almost like a pyramid.

"That must be the temple," Urk said. "Hukail?"

The other Chosen cast his sight as far as he could, then nodded. "It's a temple of some sort, alright. I think that's the place our scouts mentioned."

"It's awfully exposed," said Balto.

Urk nodded. There were no trees or cover of any kind for miles and miles around the structure. It'd been built in the middle of a wide-open plain—the kind that could spread for days on horseback. The perfect position to hide something valuable—where none could approach unseen.

"What are we going to do, Captain?" Asked Frain.

Urk weighted his options. "The only thing we can." He said. "We wait for the cover of darkness, then ride our horses towards the tomb. With any luck, we'll slip by unnoticed… however unlikely. If not, the darkness should allow us to approach the tomb as much as we can before we're spotted."

The other men nodded. It really was the only thing they could do under the circumstances. If they'd been given more time for this mission—if they didn't have to be back before the celebrations began, they could've taken a longer, more careful approach… but as it were, they had three days to make it back to Greencrest before the gates shut for a week. And so, they rested in the shadows of the trees until nightfall, away from sight, while Hukail kept a careful watch of their surroundings at all times with his Chosen eyes in preparation for their risky assault. Once darkness had blanketed the night and a pale crescent moon had risen beyond the horizon, the soldiers got back up and mounted their horses, beginning what would be the longest two hours of their lives…

…For two hours they rode their horses in the dry, broken plains, their nerves on edge the whole time, feeling eyes on the backs of their heads. They rode and rode, and Urk could hear the others' hearts thundering inside their chest, but the temple in the distance, a pitch-black silhouette against the night sky, didn't seem to be getting any closer.

Then, about two hours into the ride, the structure in the distance began to grow in size, and the men's hopes lifted. As soon as they had, however, Hukail shouted above the sound of the wind and gallops: "We've got riders incoming! They just burst out of the ground!" He said.

Almost as soon as he did, an arrow struck Balto's horse and the beast tumbled down over itself, spinning across the dry ground. Balto managed to jump over it, almost like he was flying, and continued to run behind Urk's horse. He took his bow and arrows from his back and shot into the darkness, still running, as his Chosen abilities allowed him to *feel* those around him even when he could not see them. With Urk's whistle, all the Chosen soldiers jumped from their horses and landed on their knees, weapons at the ready. While their horses distracted the Koartiz people, they drew their bows and unleashed a rain of quick-fire arrows at them from behind.

Urk picked them out by sound alone. Balto sensed their position and shot his arrows where he instinctively knew they would be. Hukail saw them as clear as day, moving almost in slow motion all around them… and Frain… well, Frain just bulked up to twice his usual size, leapt for tens of meters above the ground, and swung his massive sword wherever he heard a Koartiz coming, his Chosen senses still refined enough to score him some deadly blows.

The Koartiz soldiers seemed like ghosts in their long, brown dresses, pitch-black in the night, flittering around the soldiers with their cloaks flapping in the wind, the scarves covering their necks and faces flowing eerily behind them.

The Chosen continued cutting the Koartiz riders down, pinpointing their exact locations, loosing arrows at them, cutting at their horses when they rode in too close and dodging or deflecting their arrows or blows like the enhanced soldiers that they were—putting up a show of indomitable, near-perfect resistance that would've stricken fear into any regular man or woman watching. Sadly for them, however, the Koartiz were anything *but* normal.

Swords clashed in the night and spears broke against the superior Chosen armor. Arrows bounced back or were deflected, horses toppled over and died, and the Chosen continued their dance of death with the Koartiz riders, hacking the twenty or so men that had ambushed them down to less than ten.

Frain jumped high in the air, covering dozens of meters per jump and crushing riders and horses that tried to get away, using what little light the crescent moon offered them that night to home in towards his targets. Urk cut left and right with Weisor's special sword, slicing Koartiz open like sacks of grain, while Hukail shot his perfectly aimed arrows at the riders, hitting them each time, and Balto continued to jab his opponents hard, moving out of the way of their hits in his complex martial arts style, while sending them to the notorious dream state only him and a few other Cauda Chosen were able to effect on others.

Soon, the hands and faces of the Chosen soldiers were covered with Koartiz blood, and the land hydrated with the blood of its own people. Urk walked next to a dead body and tore his dress open. The dead soldier was wearing regular clothes underneath his covers and lacked the telltale tattoos and marks of a Koartiz warrior… Urk turned the man's neck over and looked at his back. He then threw him angrily back to the ground.

"No tattoos…. Dammit!" Balto walked next to him to look at the corpse, breathing heavily.

"They were villagers?" The young soldier asked, the surprise clear in his voice.

"Yes." Urk answered, clenching his teeth.

"We lost our horses to mere villagers… not even soldiers." Frain said standing next to his own horse's corpse.

"We will walk the rest of the way," Urk said, looking at the pyramid, looming terribly tall before them now. "We're almost there." Urk then looked at Balto and Hukail. "Collect as many arrows as you can find. We'll need them for later."

The soldiers nodded and did as told. Urk cleaned his sword and watched his own reflection on it in the moonlight, looking at his face covered in the enemy's blood.

"Let's go men," he said, starting his march towards the towering tomb. "We've got a Holy Manuscript to collect."

CHAPTER 33

THE LONG-AWAITED ARRIVAL

Axel and Kade rode in silence for a long time.

They'd left the mountains behind and were now down in the Valley of Aether, the heavily forested lowlands just before the great city. Axel had respected Kade's desire to remain silent, fully understanding the confusion the Chosen must've been experiencing. Now, as they slowed down considerably, Axel tried to communicate with the big Chosen for the first time since they'd left camp.

The old man fumbled around with his horse's bridles for a moment, then spoke assertively and with a decisive tone.

"This was the only way, Kade." He told the Chosen. The young man, in turn, looked down at his own horse's mane and sighed deeply.

"It still wasn't right." Kade said.

Axel nodded. "No… it wasn't. But it was exactly what had to be done. They… couldn't have understood, Kade. You were just a prize to them—a means to an end. But to me, you're so much more."

"I really don't understand you—none of you!" Kade suddenly exploded. "You people all lie and cheat each other like it's nothing! How do I know I can trust you, Axel, after you betrayed them like that? I mean, for Aether's sake—Locke's leg is broken! How will they even make it to Kellum before the gates close?"

"It will take them much longer, Kade, but they will still make it by the end of tomorrow before the gates close... if they hurry. They have a solid chance. As for how you know you can trust me... all I can give you is the promise that I know who and where your brother is—and that I can help you find him."

Kade didn't answer, so they just rode in silence for another while. Then, Axel spoke again.

"I understand if you have suspicions of me—I'd have suspicions too, were I in your shoes... but I'm your only hope now, Kade. They would've sold you to your death... and not only that, but the Songbird, your killer, would've then sent people after them too and killed them as well, just for knowing about you. In a way, I saved all of our lives."

Kade shook his head, a deep frown in his eyes. "This is all madness..." He said. "Just what in the seven hells is going on here?!"

"More than you can ever know, my boy... There are powers at play here in the shadows that you can't even begin to understand. Just trust me when I say: you will be reunited with Ellyad soon. It's all part of a greater plan."

"What do you mean?" Kade asked.

"I..." Axel began, and sighed. "I wasn't in Halstead by coincidence, Kade."

Kade frowned. "No... You were there for Merki... which makes what you did all the worse."

Axel sighed and shook his head. "No, dear Kade... I was not. I was there for *you*."

Kade blinked. "Why... how do you..."

"It was all a cover. Merki, her father, the crazy old man act... it was all so that I could be there when you finally arrived... and guide you back to Ellyad."

Kade's face suddenly went pale.

"You mean... I'm not... I didn't make all of that up?"

Axel shook his head, not looking Kade in the eyes. "You didn't. Disassociation sickness doesn't exist. I made it up."

Kade had several emotions flash through his face—confusion, relief, then anger and disbelief.

"You made me think I was mad… that all my memories were fake." He said, almost shocked.

"I'm sorry, Kade. I had to. Merki and Locke… they couldn't know the truth. But I couldn't very well stop you from speaking it once your remembered, so… I had to divert their focus. Give them something else to believe, something more plausible."

Kade stared pure venom at Axel for the better part of a minute as they just trotted their horses down the mountain road they'd been taking for the last few hours, which would eventually join up with the southern main road into Kellum. After the long silence, Kade shifted in his saddle and said: "What else did you lie about?"

Axel didn't say anything—just kept his eyes fixed forward.

Kade eventually gave up and just scoffed. "Of course, you're still hiding secrets. Figures. Was any of it true at all? Your time working at Kellum, tending to Chosen? Your 'tragic' past?"

"Some of it is," Axel said.

"And some of it isn't… But you're not going to tell me, are you?"

"It's for your protection, Kade. The less you know… the better."

"Like Merki and Locke?"

Axel sighed again and nodded. "Like Merki and Locke."

"Are you going to drug me and leave me behind as well once your plans—whatever they are—succeed? Or maybe turn me in yourself to someone worse than Ulor or the Bird?"

"The Songbird."

"WHATEVER!" Kade exploded again. "You're lucky I have this on, Axel," Kade pointed at the new amethyst necklace Axel had made for him a week or so back. "Or else I don't know that I could control what might happen to you right now."

"I want exactly what you want, Kade." Axel said.

"Then why didn't we run away earlier? Why wait until now?"

Axel smirked. "Because despite all my skills, I'm still an old man, Kade. I still needed help getting you here. Merki, Locke… even the other soldiers—they were all necessary… Up to a point. That, and…"

"And?"

The Long-Awaited Arrival

Axel shook his head, and his face turned somber. "Never mind. We're almost there now." The old man nodded towards the faraway sight of travelers, moving down the main road to the city—wagons, caravans, pilgrims from all over and villagers from the nearby hamlets and towns, all journeying for the holiest of celebrations.

Axel stopped his horse a good distance away, out of sight of the droves of people and the soldiers at the gates, and slowly walked it into a nearby copse of trees. Kade did the same, following his lead.

"Why are we stopping?" Kade asked.

"The city gates are just a short ride away. We're nearly there now… but in order for this work, we need to look the part." He procured a fresh set of expensive-looking clothes he'd been hiding on his horse's saddlebags all this time. "These are for you, and these other ones for me. I happen to know there's a small spring nearby with a likewise small waterfall where we can have a quick wash, then change into our new clothes."

Kade looked at the soft, silken clothes on his hands. He'd never seen fabric of that quality before. "Where did you get this?" He asked.

"Back in Orkail. My friend, remember?"

Kade grunted, then looked up again at Axel. "Do we have to?"

The old man shrugged. "If we want to come across as a wealthy travelling lord and his very large nephew, then yes, we have to."

Kade finally sighed and shrugged. "Alright. Lead the way."

Axel then led Kade a few minutes into the forest until they came across the small spring he'd mentioned. They both took their old clothes off and discarded them on some nearby bushes, then got into the cold waters of the spring, washing off all the dirt and grime that had built up on them during the past few days. Despite having bathed in a creek after exiting the Oasis, Kade, especially, had gotten very dirty, and was actually glad to freshen up, washing all the grime away from his well-toned muscles and hair under the very cold waterfall. Axel, on the other hand, just got into the spring behind him, giving him some space, and did his best to wash up as well, silently cursing how cold the water was this time of year. The two men washed up, their backs turned to each other, dried up with some blankets Axel had brought with him, then donned their new, flashy clothes.

As Axel was going through his horse's saddlebags, he suddenly found the clothes he'd found for Merki and Locke's—the ones he'd also purchased in case his plans fell through and he had to enter the city with them.

Pity, he said to himself, then bundled up the dress and suit before Kade could see them and threw them away behind a bunch of bushes. They wouldn't need them where they were going, and they'd just raise questions anyways, so better to get rid of them.

Kade, on his side, was distracted as he tried to style his hair in a less of a wild look, staring at his reflection in the calm waters away from the tiny nearby falls—which were barely more than a trickle but still enough to disturb the water around them—and failed miserably. Axel, seeing the young man struggle, pulled out a wooden comb from among his new clothes and handed it to him.

"A comb. You've been walking around with a comb all this time?" Kade asked.

Axel shrugged. "My beard gets itchy if I don't comb it every now and then. Just use it… then give it back to me. We both need to look our best today."

Kade shrugged, washed off the comb in the spring, looking sidelong at Axel, then passed it over his hair, making it look considerably better. He then passed to comb to Axel who did the same, despite not having that much hair on his head to begin with.

Finally, Axel passed Kade his knife.

"What's this for?"

"That mess of a beard you've been growing." Axel said. "Shave it all off."

Kade grimaced. "Is it that bad?"

Axel nodded, and Kade shrugged. He took the knife and, looking at his reflection on the calm waters, proceeded to shave off the mess of stubble he'd been growing all this time through their journey across the desert. Once he was done, he looked like an entirely new person. That, coupled with the bath and the feel of the new clothes (which Axel had kept surprisingly fresh despite their journey through the desert), made Kade feel like an entirely new man.

Meanwhile Axel looked at the sun, trying to guess the time from his own shadow.

"Come now, Kade," he said. "We don't want to be late." Axel then gave Kade a large robe with a cloak to wear and he donned a similar one. With that, they made their way back to their horses and rode off towards the tall gates in the distance, beyond the trees, leaving their old clothes behind. As soon as they came out of the forest side-road, however, Kade's jaw nearly dropped. They rode out of the trees into a wide-open swath of grassland, and beyond it, previously hidden by the treetops, was the great city of Kellum. Its walls were impossibly huge and the gate they rode towards, even from this distance, looked as if it'd been made for giants, not men. However, instead of riding right for the massive, faraway shape of the city, Axel led Kade to a small wooden building a ways away from the main road—a coach station.

"No matter what they ask, you never talk. I do all the talking, alright?" Axel said. "And keep your hands hidden inside your robe at all times." Kade nodded.

"Greetings!" Axel said to the man at the counter, dismounting.

"Good afternoon, sirs." The man behind it said, sparing a quick look at Kade.

"We require a coach into the city. We have a *special* package to deliver, and must make the utmost haste."

The man behind the counter, a normal-looking Kollek like any other, looked between Axel and Kade… then bowed deeply to Axel from behind the counter.

"We have been awaiting your arrival for over a week, my lord. A special coach is waiting for you in the back."

"Excellent," Axel said, then led Kade around the back of the building.

Kade looked at Axel. "Another favor from your friend at Orkail?"

Axel smirked, but didn't say anything.

They then reached a wooded area behind the station, where a special-looking coach was waiting for them—painted in exquisite red and gold.

The driver bowed just as deeply as the man up front upon seeing Axel. "My lords. This humble Kollek is honored to serve you. Please, get in." The man held the coach's door open for his guests. Axel climbed in first, then Kade, bending over quite a bit to avoid knocking his head on the frame. Once inside, the driver closed the door and got in the front seat.

"Take us into the capital," Axel said, and the driver just nodded. Kade was confused and didn't know what to say or think, but he played along with Axel's game. The carriage began to move, the driver urging the horses forward, and Kade felt his heartbeat quicken.

"Axel... are you sure this will work? What if the guards identify me?"

"Keep your hood up and never let them see your face or hands. Never panic. I have everything under my control, alright? Just trust me." Axel said as he looked into Kade's eyes. Kade nodded. Axel then moved to close the curtains over both doors of the carriage. "You are now my very large nephew, Alistair," he said as he did, "and I am Lord Astor, from the southern districts of the kingdom, near Westcliff. We're visiting the city to enjoy the celebrations and be honored by Aether in person." Kade nodded again.

As the coach shook and trembled, Kade's knee began to shake in anticipation.

This is it. Just wait a little while longer, Ellyad... I'm coming to get you, brother.

The coach got on the road to the King's Gate, passing by scores and scores of people—easily hundreds, as it got closer to the massive city walls. Kade peeked through a slight gap in the curtains, watching as the massive walls got closer and closer, seeming as if they could swallow them whole. He could feel his heart hammering inside him and his hands starting to sweat. To calm himself down, he used the techniques Axel had taught him, taking deep breaths and holding them for few seconds. He closed

The Long-Awaited Arrival | 399

his eyes and counted his each one, and as he did, he could feel the stress gradually leaving his body. Before he knew it, the carriage stopped, and Axel nodded at Kade to reassure him. They listened the conversation between the driver and the gate officer in charge of clearing vehicles into the city.

"Afternoon, officer." The driver kindly said.

"Good afternoon. Who are you escorting today, sir?" The officer sniffed his nose.

"Noble Lord Astor, from the district of Westcliff and his nephew and ward, Lord Alistair."

The officer nodded, filling out a form in his hand, looking quite bored.

"Alright... I have their names down. I'll need to look inside now." The officer said to the driver in a way that made it clear he wasn't asking. The driver simply nodded. "Of course." He said.

Axel and Kade looked at each other, and the old man nodded once more, reassuring the large Chosen. The door next to Axel suddenly opened, and the bright light of the early afternoon spilled into the carriage. Axel looked down at the officer, and when he spoke, Kade could barely recognize him.

"Afternoon, officer." Axel said in the most snobbish (and southern) accent possible. He looked upon the officer as if he were looking at a fly that had landed on his hand, then looked away.

"Good day, Lord Astor. Welcome to the capital city of Kellum. May I see your signet ring, sir?"

Axel showed the guard his hand, without looking at him. Where or how the old man had gotten the forged ring, Kade could not explain—perhaps the driver had given it to him as he'd been getting into the carriage?

"Hmm... never seen that crest before... but then again, there are so many new lords these days you can't keep track of them."

"Yes... quite." Axel said, sounding entirely bored.

The guard pointed at Kade. "Your, uh... nephew. He got a ring as well?"

"I'm afraid not." Axel said.

The officer nodded, satisfied with the answer. He'd seen hundreds of nobles come by during the past few weeks, all with their own rings, papers or stories. He didn't really care as much as he should've. Plus, young lords usually didn't have rings or crests given to them until they'd earned them at a certain age, so it wasn't entirely out of place. Still... the man's nephew was definitely a unique sight... considering how abnormally big he seemed to be under those robes.

"Your nephew... he's quite a large man, isn't he?"

"Quite so, yes. My brother's fault, I'm afraid—he was a giant of a man." Axel said. Then, as if it just occurred to him, he added. "Are we done here, officer? I have *very* important people waiting for me inside the city, and they do so hate waiting."

"Of course, milord. Can I just... Can I see your nephew's face? Or his hands?" The guard cautiously asked, staring at Axel. The old man sighed deeply. "He's just... really big."

"Most certainly not!" Axel said, sounding incredibly offended by the man's impudence. "My nephew is *very* sensitive about his... size. He's not a show pony for others to gawk at." He added the last while looking at the guard as if he were a pile of horse dung left to dry on the side of the road.

"All the same, sir... I'd like to have a look at him before I approve you."

Kade's heart thundered in his chest. He took very deep breaths, but he couldn't see how Axel would be able to get out of this one.

"Hmm, well then... if you want to look at him that badly, I guess it can't be helped." Axel said, then put a hand on his pocket, procuring a rather large, heavy bag of coins. "That said... would you rather look at this instead, officer?" He asked, raising an eyebrow.

The officer grinned from ear to ear. "I'd very much like that, yes."

He extended the bag of gold to the man, but just as he was about to grab it from him, he pulled it away. "You can either look at the bag, or my nephew—not both."

The guard looked at the large bag of coins greedily. Based on its girth, it might well contain several times what he'd make in a month.

"I'd rather look at the bag, sir." He whispered into the carriage.

"Here," Axel said. "Leave my poor nephew be now."

The guard looked at the coin pouch, hefted its considerable weight, his eyes shining… then he nodded. "Sorry to disturb you and your nephew, Lord Astor. Please, go right on in. I hope you have an excellent visit, sir."

Axel nodded, and the man closed the door for them. "Cleared to enter!" They heard him yell to the gate guards from the outside, and the carriage started moving again.

Axel waited for a bit, then said. "You can start breathing again."

Kade audibly exhaled a long breath, and the old man smiled.

"I almost thought that was it," Kade said. "How could that man be so easy to buy off? What if I was a rebel?"

"Welcome to the reality of Kellum, dear Kade, where gold is worth more than faith or duty… regardless of what the people say."

"You mean, he knew I could be a Chosen, and still let us in?"

"He might, he might not. A man in his position is easy to buy, however—especially given the conditions of the city…"

"What if he talks? What if people come after us?"

"We'll be long gone by then. Hidden away where no one can find us. Besides, with the celebrations incoming, I doubt they'll go on manhunts for a single Chosen running around town."

"What do you mean?"

"Let's just say… you're not the only rogue Chosen walking around the streets of Kellum, Kade… and leave it at that."

***

Merki finally managed to stand up without falling down.

She held onto a nearby tree for support, holding her forehead with her free hand as her temples pounded against her skull like a heart.

"Ow…" She groaned, her eyes shut tightly. When she opened them again, she saw the state of the camp—how Axel had spurred their horses away.

"Dammit!" She said, and her world spun for a moment. She held onto the tree, hoping against hope that her legs wouldn't give under her again.

"Locke?" She called out as she waited for the world to stand still once more. "Locke, are you awake?"

No answer.

Merki shut her eyes hard then opened them once more, and the world came into focus again. She turned them towards Locke's bedroll and saw the man, sitting on a log next to the campfire.

"Locke? Are you alright? How long have you been… awake?" She asked him.

The captain simply stared at the scorched remains of last night's fire, his eyes very distant.

"Why aren't you saying anything, Locke?" Merki asked, making her way towards him, grimacing as an invisible lance of pain jabbed her brains. She held onto her forehead as she slowly made her way to one of the logs around the fire and gingerly sat down.

"Locke." She said, one more time. The man seemed to be breathing just fine—he was awake, but something was definitely wrong with him. "Please say something."

The captain slowly rose his gaze from the ashes of the fire and onto hers. Merki stared at them for a few seconds, then felt a knot in the pit of her stomach. The man before him was technically alive… but his eyes looked like those of one who was dead. They were almost closed, and they looked as if they were taking Locke every last bit of his remaining strength to keep open.

"Locke…" Merki began. "It's not over. We can still get to the city in time. The gates don't close until tomorrow in the evening." She said. She looked up at the sky, noticing it was a little past midday. "We can make it before dawn tomorrow if we get going *now*.

Locke said something under his breath, but Merki couldn't hear it.

"What?" She asked.

The man looked at her again, his eyes filled with such emptiness it almost hurt to look at them.

"What's the point?" He finally said.

Merki shook her head. "I… I don't get it." She said. "We can't stay here, Locke! That's the point! Once those gates close…"

Locke shook his head. "What's the point?" He said again. "They're gone. It's... over."

"Locke?" Merki said.

"It's all over," the man repeated, barely above a whisper. "I lost my unit... lost the Chosen... Might lose my leg. I've got nothing left, I lost all in the past few weeks. Nothing left at all."

He spoke in such weak, trembling tone, Merki would've thought he was in his deathbed, saying goodbye to his relatives before slipping away.

"Locke... it's not over. Not yet." She whispered back to him. "We can still find them. Still recover Kade."

He looked up at her, and she saw the slightest glimmer of hope in his eyes.

"How...?"

"We know where they're going, Locke. They're headed for Kellum, same as us."

"How do you know that? They could be running back to Halstead right now for all we know."

Merki smirked. "They can't. They won't make it anywhere else before the gates close. They *have* to go to Kellum, even if they plan to escape for someplace else after—and they'll need to stay there for a full week. We can *find* them, Locke."

A bit of life had returned to the man's eyes now. He looked down at the ashes once more, thinking... then shook his head. "Kellum's such a big place, Merki. They could be hiding in any one hole among thousands in the city."

"Yes... but I'm a huntress and a tracker, remember? I can pick up their trail once we enter the city—they'll likely be traveling incognito if they're there, but someone must've seen a tall, robed man with an old man wandering around. We just have to ask in the right places."

Locke nodded once. His eyes were still half-open and his demeanor still crestfallen, but a bit of life had returned to him now. He took a deep breath, then sighed loud and long. "Ok." He said. "The least we can do is try... I guess."

"Good!" Merki said.

And I've got to get you to a doctor above everything else, she thought. *Once I do...*

"Let's go, then. We have a lot of ground to cover, but we'll make it. Maybe we'll get lucky on the way there and come across one of our horses... Or maybe we'll run into a caravan on the way, or a patrol we can ask for help, seeing as we don't have Kade with us anymore."

The captain sighed deeply again and nodded.

"Until then, I'll support you" Merki said. "We'll make better time that way."

Locke nodded. Merki served them both some breakfast out of what little they had left—which Axel had mercifully left them among all the other things he took, and soon, they were both on their way down the mountain and onto the valley. They moved as fast as they could, leaving most of their belongings behind aside for Locke's armor and weapons, some provisions, and Merki's full hunting kit.

Before continuing, however, the pair stopped near the crest of the road and took one last look back at the empty campsite—at the wagon, the rest of the bags they'd been carrying... and the empty bedrolls that Kade and Axel had been sleeping for weeks. With a deep sigh, they left it all behind and resumed their long walk towards faraway Kellum in the distance.

"If we find those two again..." Locke said. "I'm going to wring the old man's neck with my own hands."

Merki grunted in acknowledgement, but her mind was actually on Kade. She wondered, mostly, whether or not he would be all right in Kellum... traveling with such a lying, deceitful snake at his side.

CHAPTER 34

THE GREAT CITY OF THE KOLLEK

"We're in Freedom Square" Axel said.

He could almost hear Kade's heartbeats. The young man was shaking his right leg and he kept picking at his fingernails without blinking. Axel pulled on his cloak's hood and stood up.

"Come, Kade. We've arrived." He said, and walked out of the carriage. Kade couldn't move for a second, watching the mass of crowds from inside the opened door. To him Kellum seemed like a different world entirely, and the door of the carriage a portal that would transport him out of the only 'safe' space in the whole city.

Axel stood outside the door and beckoned for Kade to come, gesturing with his hand. The Chosen took a deep breath, filling himself with as much courage as he could muster, then stepped out into the harsh sunlight. Now outside, Kade realized the coach had stopped on the corner of a building on a wide main street in the city—full of shops on both sides. The buildings were covered with ivies and flowers everywhere and people entered and left the stores in droves, seeming almost like ants moving through an anthill. Many of the people had other with them carrying their bags and boxes of goods, dressed much more simply than them. Many other carriages moved through the busy thoroughfare, stopping to take or leave their patrons at the different assortment of stores, restaurants and other shops along the incredibly busy street.

Once their own carriage had moved on, Axel grabbed Kade by his arm, leading him away from the street and onto an enclosed square. At the far end of the square, there was a tall wall—once of the inner walls he'd seen as he peeked out his carriage window, covered with colorful ivies and decorated with different engravings of men and figures which didn't make any sense to him. Below the wall was another set of gates, smaller than those he'd first entered the city through, but still very lavish and ornate-looking, a large sign above it reading: "Noble's Row." Right behind the square and gates, way up in the distance on a hill, Kade could see the magnificent sight of Castle Kellum, made out of white, glistening stone, with its many towers, bells and pillars. As he was staring at it in awe, he jumped at the sound of a nearby carriage passing by him.

"Careful now..." Axel warned Kade. "Come." The old man crossed the street as fast as he could before another carriage came through and Kade followed him. They walked towards the end of the square and through the gates at the far end towards this "Noble's Row..." and came out into one of the most impressive views Kade had seen in his life.

"Welcome to Kellum." Axel said in a low voice.

The young man felt a strong chill up his spine, and his chest swelled at the majestic sight spreading in every direction before him. Freedom Square was huge—easily twice the size of Rockpour or Halstead, and decorated with so many manicured trees, rose bushes and ornate arches and statues. At the very center of the square stood a large sculpture of a man, extending his right arm to the sky and holding the sun on his palm. All of the stone roads lead to the statue. There were benches on the sides of the statue where many wealthy-looking people were resting and talking to one another, enjoying the cool atmosphere of the park surrounding the square. Some of the townsfolk sat under the huge trees lining the outer boundaries of the square, while more of the simply dressed people served them fruits and drinks. Children ran around, playing and drinking water from marble fountains set against stone walls, fed by gravity. The scene looked like the perfect picture of happiness to Kade, but Axel, on the other hand, was looking around as if he was in search of something or someone. When he saw Kade's curious looks at the other people, he warned him:

"Don't come eye to eye with anyone. We must hurry. Ahh, come." The old man walked as fast as his old legs allowed him, with Kade following closely behind. They passed through the square and reached another gate, which ushered them into a different part of the city. As they entered this new sector, Kade noticed there weren't any straight roads leading to the magnificent castle at the top of the hill—the roads of Kellum, it seemed, were no different from a labyrinth.

All of a sudden, Axel noticed a group of soldiers coming. He turned Kade around and walked over to the other side of the street. The soldiers were pulling two beggar kids to a place that looked like a flower shop.

"We didn't do anything!" One of the kids screamed.

"Hush, bastard. It is forbidden to beg in sacred days, by order of the king." The soldier pulled the boy as swiftly as he could into the building. Kade snuck a look back at them as he walked away, noticing how the kids' clothes were ragged and they had no shoes on them. Their dirty faces looked like they didn't belong in the same city as the rest of all the other well-dressed people Kade had seen so far. He didn't have much time to think about them, however, as Axel pulled his arm and they walked away.

I guess poverty is everywhere... Kade thought.

After passing a few more streets, Axel stopped under a laurel tree in a small square. His hands and eyes wandered over the tree, looking for something.

"Here it is." He said after a moment. Kade looked at the old man with confused eyes, trying to understand what he was referring to, but his focus was almost entirely distracted by all the beauty and excessive elegance surrounding him.

"Most people seem so happy here." Kade said, almost spellbound.

"Some, yes. Others, not so much." Axel said in a hurry, then added, very chipper: "Ah, there we are. Come on! It's this way."

He walked away towards a market at the end of the street. Kade looked at the tree, hoping to identify what had made the old man so excited, but he couldn't see anything other than a few initials and a strange symbol. There was a very small shape carved onto the trunk of the tree: a sun with six dots around it. Kade looked carefully at it but it didn't ring any bells in his mind, so he shrugged and followed after Axel. The market they were walking onto, he saw with surprise, seemed even more upscale than the one they'd first passed through. Even the people were dressed differently here, wearing clothes of obviously superior quality to those from before—and they had already been almost as well-dressed as Kade.

As they made their way through the throngs of people, Kade noticed a group of men that stood out from all the well-dressed folk. They had long leather overcoats on them with furs on their collars, and they were wearing strange-looking fur hats on their heads. They seemed more at home somewhere else, like Halstead or Rockpour, than here, among all these other pampered rich folks in their fine silks and linens. Kade noticed how well-built they all were, and how loudly they talked and laughed... then he noticed they were all slightly drunk.

At this time of day? Really?

While Kade and Axel passed by them, one of them hit the other one's shoulder as they laughed about something, and the man couldn't keep his balance and stumbled over Kade. Kade held him before he fell and helped him to his feet again. As he was about to walk away, the man held his arm. Axel held his breath in fear.

"Thank you, my friend." The man said, the alcohol in his breath filling the air as he tried to look at Kade's face. Suddenly, a look of recognition flashed past his eyes. He squinted, and said: "Hey... haven't I seen you somewhere before?"

"I, uh..." Kade began.

"No, my good sir—you're mistaken!" Axel came in rushing like a gale and held Kade's arm. "My nephew and I are new in town, so that's highly unlikely. He just has one of those faces." Axel smiled and bowed at the man like a worried grandfather looking after his big, clumsy child.

The drunk man looked at Kade for a moment longer then shrugged, pursing his lips. "That might be it. Aether save you, my friend." He said and waved at Kade as he made his way back to his friends. Kade just smiled sheepishly and nodded, looking sidelong at Axel with very concerned eyes.

"We're ok. He didn't make you out. Come, follow, quickly."

After walking through the throngs of people for a few more minutes, Axel led Kade to a clothing store. The large Chosen noticed that the symbol carved on the laurel tree was also carved on a stone on the ground, in front of the door; so small that it was almost impossible to notice unless one was looking for it. Kade had only managed to see it after he'd followed Axel's own eyes.

The old man then opened the door of the shop, and to Kade's surprise, the inside was full of beautiful ladies. There were at least ten of them that Axel could see: blondes, redheads, brunettes and dark-skinned women—all beautiful and exotic-looking to Kade. They wore colorful dresses with crinolines, and their large bosoms seemed to be having a hard time staying inside their tight tops. Most of the women were also wearing big scoop necks decorated with laceworks, as well as tulle scarves of the same color of their dresses, attached to their head. Their curled hair, a style that seemed very popular in Kellum, shone and fell below the tulle and over their lustrous chests. All in all, the women looked like copies of a singular goddess, if only in dresses of different colors.

Hearing the bell ring as the door opened, they all turned around and looked at the strangers standing at the door. A middle-aged man behind the counter stood on the balls of his feet, trying to get a look at the newcomers from behind the ladies. He finally strode forward and gently pushed the girls aside—but when he saw Kade and Axel, his eyes grew large as an owl's and he gulped very loudly.

"Welcome, men!" A blonde woman with marble-white skin said loudly and with joy. She extended her hand and invited them in. They were as cheerful as whores, yet exuded an air of fanciness like that of noble-born women. They were, without a doubt, more beautiful than anyone either of them had ever seen.

My dear lord. Axel's inner voice said.

"Poly-souled sisters," Axel explained to Kade in a hush. The name didn't mean anything to him, yet it encouraged the women to give them a warmer welcome.

"Indeed we are…" A brunette stepped next to her friend. "Would you be needing our services today, boys? There's *so* much we can teach you…" She blinked sexily at Kade as she spoke.

"No thank you, sister." Axel replied although her eyes were strictly on Kade. "We're only here to buy some new clothes."

"Well enough… what about you, young man?" She stared at Kade.

"N-no… thank you." He shyly said.

"Alright then, whenever you want—you know where to find us." The women shrugged and returned to their shopping as if the men had never come in.

The owner of the shop signaled for Axel to sit at some chairs on the corner of the shop and he did, pulling Kade along. The Chosen did his best not to look at the sisters anymore but failed miserably, hoping to catch their eyes at least one more time.

Kade and Axel waited at the chairs while the women chose the fabrics they liked most. The shop was full of expensive silks and laceworks that could satisfy even the fanciest dreams of a woman. Kade leaned towards Axel and asked in a whisper: "What's a poly-sister?"

"They are… erm… *noble* women, who serve Aether… by, ahh, showing men how to control their desires… or by teaching them how to satisfy their wives or women." Axel blushed while the words coming out of his mouth, which made his inner voice cackle madly. Kade nodded and pursed his lips for a moment… then he got it, and his eyes grew bigger.

Once the women left the shop, the owner ran towards them.

"H-how may I help you, sire?" He asked Axel, with a look that said he already knew exactly how to do so.

"We rested in the shade of the laurel. Our heavy burden got lighter, as it was now shared amongst believers." The old man answered. The man panicked, looking as if he couldn't decide what to do first. Then, he ran to lock the door and closed all of the store's windows. When he came back, Axel stood up to salute him, but the man just knelt in front of Axel, looking firmly at the ground as if he couldn't dare to look at the old man.

"It *is* you! Forgive me, but I had to make sure… You honor your humble servant with your presence, my lord." He said to Axel. Kade was petrified; astonished at seeing such a scene playing out before him.

"Thank you, my son." Axel said and touched the man's shoulder. The man rose.

"Follow me, my lord." Then he looked at Kade, and said: "You as well, sir," as he nodded deeply with his head. Kade nodded back.

The man then pulled a table at the back of the store in a very specific way, and a secret trapdoor leading to a cavernous-looking place below the shop popped open behind them. He burnt a torch, waiting for his guests to come, then closed the hatch behind them. The cave was like a home, possessing everything needed for an extended stay—a well-stocked safehouse, if Kade had ever seen one. There were two beds with a small nightstand between them, a large table for four, a desk with another chair, a sofa on the corner, and boxes with food and provisions, among other things.

"What's… happening?" Kade asked Axel while the shopkeeper ran around tidying the place up.

"He will help us." Axel said, nodding towards the shopkeeper. "If we're to find your brother, we'll need his help, and others'."

"Are you really a 'lord?'" Kade asked him. Axel didn't answer.

"I'm just me, Kade. Let's focus on our mission here—finding your brother. You should be preparing for that."

Kade blinked. "Preparing? How?"

"We'll need to convince him to come back to Norzou with us. He already has a life here, remember? He knows nothing about you… or his own people. You'll need to make him see the truth."

Kade took a very deep breath. "Gods… no pressure, then."

Axel nodded, smiling warmly. "Indeed. Once we find him… everything hinges on you being able to convince him of who you are, and why you're here."

Once the man was done preparing the place, he poured tea on some very nice cups and served them to his guests. Axel and Kade sat on two of the chairs, but the shopkeeper stood by them at first, like a servant. He only sat down once Axel showed him a chair.

"Thank you, my lord." He said. "We have been waiting for you for so long… I couldn't believe in my eyes when I saw you at the door. Please forgive me," he said, bowing his head deeply. "I made you wait, even though you must be so tired from your journey."

"You did the right thing, brother. We don't need the extra attention." Axel said.

The man looked at Kade with astonishment, his eyes shining brighter than the torches around them.

"Is he…?" He started to ask, and Axel nodded.

"He is." He said, and the man gasped, staring at Kade in awe.

Kade was looking at them, trying to grasp just what was happening there. A day ago, Axel had just been a kind old man whom he'd been traveling with—a world-weary traveler aiding them in their journey, and not much more. Now… now Kade had no idea who he was… or *what*.

"Is everything arranged?" The old man asked the shopkeeper after taking a sip from his hot tea.

"Yes, my lord. Everything is set. The only part missing was you…. And *him*." The man sounded so confident. "We knew someone would eventually come looking for your brother," he said, looking at Kade. "It just took longer than we expected."

"You were expecting me? But… that can't be. I… I left my home against the elders' will. It was all on a whim. *I* didn't even know I'd be leaving on this whole, mad journey until I walked out of my home in the middle of the night."

Suddenly, Kade had a clear vision of his home—the sharpest he'd had since he'd started his journey. He saw the temple city clearly, with its domes and spires, high up on its mountain surrounded by even taller mountains and peaks. He saw the fields he'd tended to before leaving Norzou, the streets of his hometown. Saw his home, barely more than a humble stone hut. His mother and sister's faces, smiling back at him. He frowned, and his eyes began to water. Suddenly, he felt a very strong longing for home—for his family. Axel didn't seem to notice, or if he did, he didn't mention it.

"Is that so?" The old man said, and gave the other man a knowing look. Kade saw it.

"What? What are you not telling me?"

"Our paths, young Kade... they're not always as random as one might expect. We might not know the details, the specifics... but there's always a pattern we can predict."

"So... you knew I would one day go out in search of him?"

"You... or another. It doesn't matter. All that matters is that you're here now, and so the final piece of the puzzle has arrived to Kellum. We can now take your brother back home, to your family... with you."

It all sounded so good to Kade. *Too* good. Suddenly, a troubling thought intruded on him, and Kade shook his head. "That all sounds great Axel, but... why do *you* care? Why are you so committed to helping me, even before you knew me? I need Ellyad to save my sister... my family. But why do *you* want him there?"

Axel looked down at his tea. He nodded to himself, realizing this conversation had always been inevitable. "Because we need him to, Kade." He finally said.

"That's not an answer." Kade said. "What's your game here, Axel—if that's even your true name. What are you playing at?" The shopkeeper stared at him in horror, shocked that he would speak to Axel in such a way. He then looked at Axel, nearly trembling, but the old man was just staring placidly at Kade, the look in his eyes almost... sad.

"We need Ellyad to come home... because the world is dying, Kade." Axel finally said, almost in a whisper.

Kade frowned. "What do you mean? How can the world be dying? And what does that have to do with me and my brother?"

Axel took a deep breath. He looked sidelong at the shopkeeper, and the man nodded. Axel sighed.

"I guess you deserve a clear explanation by this point, young one. You know of Luden, of course."

"The Devil. The Cursed King, shame of my people."

Axel nodded. "Indeed. Long ago, he tapped into an unknown power beyond anything this world had ever seen. Something dark and foul, which sapped him of his humanity, turning him into something… else. The Koartiz of that age fought him at every turn, even the Kollek, who were a servant people to the Alerians and the Nor. However, Luden was unstoppable. His new power, whatever it was, gave him control over life and death itself."

"I know the story, Axel. I was raised on warnings surrounding Luden and his darkness, which led to the Nor's downfall and near-extinction. He's the source of the Curse that looms over my people."

"Yes… but what you don't know is that, in order to stop him, to obliterate him and his undying army, and in doing so save the entire world… the Alerians of that time had to do the unthinkable. They'd tried everything else and failed, so The Five Head Sorcerers, leaders of the Alerians, converged at the Cave of Origins—the most powerful magical wellspring in the world where all the magical energies of this planet converged… and they completed the forbidden ritual. The ultimate sacrilege for a Koartiz… in their tongue it was called the *Rahiz Hikarou*. The Wound That Would Not Heal."

Axel paused, looking down at his tea. Kade looked between him and the man—who seemed to be watching them with an almost religious reverence.

Kade looked back towards Axel. "What was the ritual? What happened then?"

The old man took a long, deep breath. "They… called the magic of the world, Kade. They summoned it towards the Cave, through the ritual… draining it from every corner of the planet. They then converged and sealed it all inside a man's body, a sacrifice who would serve as a vessel for all the magical energies of the world. He was… the last Sword of Aether."

The shopkeeper then lowered his eyes and began to quickly mutter something Kade couldn't understand, like a prayer.

"The Sword's body," Axel continued, "could barely hold the unthinkable immensity that was all the magic of the world… and so it changed its form, crystalized, then shrunk… it became the Stone of Eternity, holding not only all the magic of the world, but also all the knowledge of the cosmos with it. Upon its creation, the world was sapped of its life-force, Kade. Of its true essence, its breath. Creating the stone sapped Luden and his army of their dark power, absorbing it along with the rest of the magical energies, sure… but it did so at a great cost."

Kade waited a long time, digesting the information he'd just been given, frowning… then he finally spoke. "So… the world is dying without its magic, then?"

"Correct," Axel said.

"… and we fit into all of this how, exactly?" He asked, dreading the answer.

"The Sword of Aether is the only one who can release the power of the Stone, Kade. Without him the world will keep dying until it can no longer sustain any life. Nature will be thrown into chaos. The seas will rage. The land will become poison, the very air we breathe will choke us and kill us, Kade." Axel said. "And your brother might very well be the next Sword."

Kade flinched, his eyes shooting wide open.

"But in order to unlock your brother's true power—to awaken him, we need him to travel back to where you're from—of his own accord, as it cannot be forced. And to do that…"

"You need me." Kade mouthed the words almost silently.

Axel nodded, almost tragically. "Yes, Kade… we need you. Your brother isn't just the key to saving your sister… he might well be the key to saving *all* of us."

Kade just sat there and breathed, his eyes lost in a foreign dream. He slumped back onto his seat, and another long moment passed until he finally raised his eyes to meet Axel's again.

"Just who are you people? How do you know all of this?" He whispered.

"We're keepers of history," Axel said. "Protectors of life, Kade. Men and women bound by the same mission—to save us all before it's too late. That's all you need to know."

Kade digested the information for a while longer, then finally nodded. "I... I'm not sure I believe you yet, Axel. All of this is... it's just too much. And the only thing you've proven to me so far, without a doubt, is that you're an expert at lying and manipulating others to fulfill your goals."

The shopkeeper slammed his head down against the table again at Kade's words, raised his hands, and began to pray in terror once more.

"But... I don't know why... I feel a... conviction. Not towards you," He said, staring sternly at Axel. "But towards my brother. I feel like you're telling the truth about him... about his destiny."

"And...?" Axel asked.

"I'll convince Ellyad to go back home. Not just for my sister... but for the slightest chance you might be telling the truth here."

Kade sighed, almost shocked at the words he was about to utter.

"I'll do everything I can to help you."

CHAPTER 35

AT LONG LAST

Merki and Locke crested the small hill shortly after dawn and stood in awe at the majesty of the enormous city that suddenly appeared before them.

They were both dirty, sweaty and tired beyond reason. Merki's feet ached with each pulse of her heart and she wanted nothing than to drop in the grass right there and then and sleep the rest of the day away.

Locke wasn't faring much better himself either. They'd kept a constant pace through the mountains and woods the day before, making it into the valley shortly before sunset, then continued walking on the main road for most of the night, taking only very short breaks to eat, catch their breath or rest. They never laid down to sleep, fearful they might not wake up in time to make it to the gates the next day, seeing how utterly exhausted both of them were. To make matters worse, the effect of whatever Axel had used to spike their food hadn't entirely left their bodies. They suffered a constant headache for the final leg of their journey, and Locke even vomited twice during their walk, unable to keep whatever he tried to eat.

They were both, almost quite literally, dead on their feet… But they'd finally made it here, to their ultimate destination.

The capital city of Kellum rose powerfully now before them in the distance, and as they stood there on that hilltop in arms, tears streamed down Merki's cheeks. Her glistening green eyes beheld a sight she'd almost convinced herself she'd never see. Her new start. Her long-yearned-for goal, after so many years.

She was finally here.

Locke, on the other hand, could barely keep his eyes open, barely strong enough to move. And yet, he too felt an incredible sense of relief at the sight of the imposing walls and the respite that hopefully awaited them beyond them.

"Just a little further to go, Locke. You can do it." Merki said to him, smiling.

The young Kollek scoffed, but returned the smile. "I can't believe you're smiling after everything we've gone through in the past couple of weeks."

"Me neither," Merki said. "But we're finally here. *I'm*… finally here." She added the last bit under her breath, staring once more at the city as a fresh gust of cool morning breeze played with her deep-brown hair.

"Who would've thought…" Locke began. "That I'd cross the great King's Gates of Kellum holding onto that spunky lass I met on a village in the middle of nowhere a month ago, begging me to take her along as I sat atop my horse…"

Merki actually laughed. "Who would've thought indeed."

"It's not right. Not right at all," Locke joked, and Merki could hear the relief in his voice. "I should've been the one carrying you through those gates, not the other way around. After all we've been through…"

"And yet here we are." Merki said, still smiling. "Now let's go. We still have a mile or two of walking before we can collapse in the first bed we find for at least a week."

Locke looked up at that and slowly raised an eyebrow. Merki noticed, raised an eyebrow of her own, and said: "Separately, Locke. Before we can collapse in *separate* beds."

The captain actually smiled—a genuine smile this time. "Just my luck of course."

Merki watched him for a moment, then shook him gently across his shoulders. "We'll find you a good doctor first, captain, then we'll look for those two—and find them."

Locke nodded weakly, but determined. "We will."

The two of them then made their way down the hill and onto the main road to Kellum, still quite full of people traveling to the city at the last minute—seeing as the gates would close that very night, and not reopen for a whole month.

It took the pair of Kolleks nearly an hour to make it to the gates. Once they did, Locke showed the gate guards his family crest and emblems, (thankful that his armor had been in the wagon and not on the spurred horse's saddlebags, as most of their other things had). He confirmed his rank of captain, as well as his status as a noble, and the soldiers promptly let the two of them through, even sending a man with them to escort Locke to the city's nearest garrison.

As Merki walked through the great southern gates of Kellum, she couldn't help but notice the walls inside the archway, full of engravings of warriors, Chosen soldiers and patterns dedicated to Aether; such as the sun, the moon and a pair of snakes rising from fire. The street right behind the gate was crowded with so many people, even at this hour, moving from inns to stores and other ornate-looking buildings that catered to a newly arrived clientele. Most of the people here were travelers and pilgrims, Merki saw, fidgeting around to find a cheap place to stay in during the celebrations, hoping against hope to find room and board. It made sense to her that the main street of this part of the city was so filled with inns, eateries and pubs—the perfect welcome to travelers just arriving to perhaps the largest city in the continent.

She also noticed so many stalls and shops, selling provisions and goods for the road: clothes, weapons, tools and ingredients—everything a person could hope to want for a journey, and more. There were also many carriages parked on the sides of the paved-stone streets, waiting for patrons to get in or out. The street stretched so far into the distance, Merki could barely see its end—the inner wall in the distance among the sea of heads and colorful hats.

The soldier that had been assigned to them whistled for a coach and they waited on the side of the road as the driver made his way to them. Once he had, they all got inside, very grateful to be off their feet at long last, and the soldier knocked on the carriage wall, saying: "Take us to the garrison at Hammer's Burg, on the double." The driver said: "Yes sire," and urged the horses along the road. Both Merki and Locke sat back into the plush cushions of the carriage and sighed at the same time, feeling like a lifetime of burden had suddenly been lifted from both of them. Merki couldn't even feel her feet for a time, and felt like she could just pass out right there if she just blinked. She didn't pass out, however, forcing herself to look out the window at the foreign world moving past instead —at the impossibly tall buildings, throngs of vividly colored people, and immaculate gardens and streets.

"If you don't mind me saying, Lord Pentgard," said the soldier, a very young man in his early twenties with light brown eyes and caramel skin. "You two look like hell."

Locke smiled at the soldier. "We feel like hell too, soldier. You have no idea what we've been through to make it here." Then he looked outside his own window, leaning his head to the side. "No idea," he repeated, much softer.

"Did you run into rebels? Where did you travel from?"

Locke smiled. "What's your name, soldier?" He asked the young man.

"Desmond, sir."

"Well, Desmond... if I told you half the things we've seen, the places we've been, you wouldn't believe me." Then he looked at Merki, and offered her a smile. "But somehow, we made it back... despite it all."

Merki returned his smile and nodded, staring into Locke's eyes. She saw something there that made her stomach jump somersaults and her heart flutter... along with a terrible pang of guilt.

They rode the rest of the way in easy silence, resting their aching bodies until they made it to the front of the large garrison. Desmond got out first and helped Locke out of the coach.

"The garrison is nearly empty right now," the young soldier said, "as most guards are spread around the city in preparation for the start of ceremonies tomorrow. The garrison's physician should still be there, though." The soldier began to lead Locke towards the gate of the impressive-looking fort, built right into the walls of the district. Merki followed after them, but was stopped at the entrance.

"No women allowed inside the garrison, ma'am." One of the soldiers said.

"Like hell she's not, soldier!" Said Locke. "I owe her my life many times over—wherever I'm allowed to go, *she's* allowed to go." He said.

The soldier that had spoken looked at his companion, both of them guarding the entrance to the garrison in full armor, holding their spears up brightly in the sun. His companion, an older guard, shook his head.

"Captain, uh…"

"Pentgard," said Locke. "Son of Franthz Pentgard."

"Captain Pentgard… rules are rules, sir. We can't bend them just because of your rank… or your father's. You can come in—but she cannot. Women aren't allowed inside Kollek garrisons unless they're servants. It's our king's law, sir."

Locke looked between the two of them and shook his head. He then looked at Merki.

"It's alright, Locke. I'll find a place to stay nearby and we'll just meet up later. I'll be fine."

Locke looked her in the eyes for a moment, then shook his head. "No," he said. "I'm not going to leave you alone in the city with no money or supplies. If she can't come inside with me, then we'll just find another place to stay."

The soldiers looked between each other and shrugged. "But… what about your wounds, sir?"

"I'll find another physician… or call for the one here once we find a suitable place to stay."

"Locke…" Merki began. "You don't *have* to do this. I'll be fine, really."

"Merki…" Locke began. "You don't know how this city works. You're used to Halstead, but Kellum is nothing like Halstead. This can be a *very* dangerous place for a young woman like you."

Merki took a deep breath. "I'll be fine, Locke. I know how to take care of myself, remember? Plus, I still have my weapons with me." She patted her bow and daggers, but the captain wasn't having it.

"No," He shook his head. "Soldier, Desmond," he called, and the youth stood at attention. "Call the carriage. Take us to one of the local inns."

"Locke!" Merki said. "You need treatment, and I'll be *just fine*, you damn worrywart. Go inside and get treated properly. I'll come around tomorrow to check on you, then we'll… tour the city, like you told me we would."

Locke stared at her for a while longer while the guards exchanged knowing looks between one another. One of them smirked while the other one blew mock kisses at him.

"Sir… should I call the carriage?" Young Desmond asked him.

Locke didn't answer right away. He stared deeply into Merki's eyes and she nodded ever so slightly.

"Fine. Alright." He said, shaking his head. "But take Desmond here with you at least." He looked at the young soldier. "Keep her safe, soldier."

Merki rolled her eyes to high heaven.

"Aye, aye, captain." The young man said, saluting him.

"Make sure she gets the full captain's treatment—she will not pay for board, room or food while she's here. Put anything she wants on my tab." Locke grabbed one of his two family crest emblems from his uniform and tore it off its stitches, pushing it against the soldier's breast. "Anything she wants. Anyone who's someone in town should recognize that crest—and respect it." He said, then to the young huntress: "Be careful, Merki. Once the physician sees to me and gives me something for the pain, we'll… uh… look for those things we talked about together, alright?"

He didn't want to mention Kade or Axel yet, for fear other soldiers might start a city-wide manhunt, hoping to claim the bounty for themselves.

Merki nodded. "We will. I'll come get you. Get better, Locke." She said, then walked away from the captain, who gazed after her as she walked away with the young soldier.

Be safe, Merki... We'll find those two soon... together.

He stared at her back until she disappeared among the crowds, then slowly turned and limped towards the garrison with the help of the other guards.

***

On another part of the city entirely, Ifir sat down on a pew inside a temple. She looked around, thinking about the previous times she'd been here, sitting at exactly that spot, and everything that had changed in her life since then. After sitting there for a while reminiscing, she took a deep breath and walked towards the pulpit in the altar. She trailed her fingers over the golden figure of a man and woman making love on top of the pulpit, which served as the icon of this temple, and then pushed the figure back like a lever. Something *clicked,* then the wooden floor behind the pulpit popped open, revealing a hidden stairway down to the basement. She quickly made her way down, pulling the secret trapdoor shut behind her by a rope.

The torches inside the passageway were all recently lit, offering ample light. At the end of it, Ifir walked out onto what could only be described as a dungeon, its stone walls full of paintings depicting Chosen and Kolleks from another age, while tables of instruments glistened in the firelight, filled with tools and weapons for inflicting pain. The Chosen in the pictures were painted as tall and powerful, lords and rulers, while the Kollek were depicted small and weak, serving them as slaves. Some of the Chosen in the paintings were killing Kollek women, denying them the right of birth, and using their men as slaves in what appeared to be mines.

"This is the real truth behind our history." Ifir spoke, addressing ten Kollek men in the center of the room, hanging from the ceiling by their hands like skinned pigs. Two long feeding troughs had been placed directly beneath their feet, one for each group of five. Two Chosen soldiers stood behind them, waiting at attention for new orders, while another secret passage to the chamber stretched behind them—its stone floors smeared with fresh blood. Ifir walked around the hung men, who were almost entirely naked save for a loincloth at their waist, and addressed one of her Chosen.

"They're all from different camps?" She asked.

"Yes, commander." The man said.

"Good."

Ifir then walked over to one of the men, who were all barely breathing at this point, badly bruised and beaten, and clasped his chin with one of her large, slender hands. She then jerked the soldier's head towards the wall, forcing him to look at the paintings.

"Look carefully... which one is you?" She asked, staring between the man and the painting.

The Kollek soldier was too tired and weak to answer, one of his eyes purple and swollen entirely.

"The slave, of course," she said. "He is you, all of you, and the other one is me, your master. This is a truth that has never changed—despite your lords and masters doing their very best to convince themselves otherwise."

Then she snapped her fingers and one of the Chosen soldiers extended her a glove with very long, sharp nails of steel coming from it.

"It's time to meet with your false god." Ifir said, then placed the claw of her index finger over the first man's stomach—then swiped savagely across it, spilling his guts on the trough underneath. The man shook on his chains, convulsing, bleeding out like a stuck animal, until his eyes rolled to the back of his head and he hung limp. Seeing the savage, grotesque murder, the others started to scream for help—but there was no one nearby to help them.

A few minutes later, Ifir's hand was covered in blood, and the corpses of the soldiers hung on their chains like slaughtered animals—

one with a sliced throat, another with his entire chest split open, etc. The last man had screamed so hard and shook in his binds so savagely, his heart had stopped while Ifir just stood in front of him and watched—literally killed by fear alone.

She'd really enjoyed that one.

"Pack them up and tie each one behind their horses before you release them back to their camps. Make sure their faces remain recognizable." She ordered before washing the blood off her hands, discarding the glove, and walking back out the way she'd come as if nothing had happened.

CHAPTER 36

THE FOX WITH MANY FACES

Merki ditched the young soldier leading her the first chance she got.

As soon as she left Locke in good hands, she'd questioned the soldier about the city, its districts and the upcoming events and parade surrounding the ceremonies, where all of Kellum's major players would be walking *very slowly* towards the Great Aetheliour, or Temple of Aether, in the city.

Desmond, the young soldier, had been more than happy to answer her questions—and clearly, to spend some time away from gate duty showing an attractive young lady around town.

Once she'd gotten all the information she needed, Merki had gotten the young man talking, asking him about his story, family and past—showing great interest in him as he told how he was the eight in a family line of soldiers, proudly serving the king and people of Kellum.

When the man had finished his tale, he'd looked back towards Merki to ask her about her own family only to discover, to his horror, that the woman just wasn't there anymore—swallowed up by the crowds marching up and down the street.

The young guard had panicked, running back the way he'd come… but he never found or saw her again.

Merki, on her end, had taken a sudden turn into the crowd and through a gate leading to an entirely different sector of the city a minute or so prior to the man even realizing she was gone. She'd memorized the man's directions and clearly saw the path she needed to take now, both literally and metaphorically.

She'd finally done it.

She'd made it to the great city of filth and corruption known as Kellum—the center of everything that was wrong with this world, and she now saw the Path clearly illuminated in front of her—her vision focused, her senses suddenly on alert, despite the aching in her body. All the weariness in her mind was suddenly pushed back. She had a mission to fulfill now, the whole reason why she'd traveled this far in the first place, and by Aether, she was going to fulfill it.

She walked through the city streets like a local, confidently and purposefully moving with strong, quick strides. With each step she took, the crowds around her faded more and more into the background, slowly disappearing. So did the buildings, the gardens, flowers and carriages. All the novel splendor of the city slowly disintegrated like sand around her, and she only saw the Path, laid out before her; her every sense attuned to it.

Knowing what she had to do, she traveled into the city district know as Merchant's Way—where the wealthy and middle classes merged and a Kollek could supposedly find anything they could ever want or need. First, she stopped at one of the many public fountains in the city and washed her face, arms, hands and hair, (while also taking the opportunity to drink heavily and greedily from it, parched as she was).

Once she'd done something about her ragged looks, (and the sour smell of the last few days that'd built up around her), she stowed her bow, daggers and arrows in a bush on a little plaza behind some of the buildings next to her, (she kept the knife in her boot, though), then walked out onto the main street of the district, filled with shops of all kinds and sizes. Her eyes then focused like those of an eagle looking for hapless prey, carefully scanning the streets, looking for the perfect mark. It didn't take too long to find it, seeing as the district had folk from both Noble's Row and Hammer's Burg, and was fit to burst with people buying goods at special prices in honor of the celebrations.

He was a well-dressed young man, without a woman or servant near him, carefully watching a group of other women in luscious dresses shopping across the street from him. He stank of money... and a lot of desperation.

Merki perked herself up.

She opened the collar of her cotton shirt, exposing her cleavage quite considerably, as well as her outer leather jacket. She pulled a side of her shirt collar over her shoulder, baring it, then moved forward, shaking her hips and flapping her hair as she went.

She felt absolutely ridiculous. But she knew what she had to do, and if doing so meant she'd had to throw her shame to the side for a bit, then she'd gladly do it.

She walked down the middle of the busy street towards the man, seeming as if she didn't care about him in the least. Her eyes were fixed on the stores behind him, but her feet took her closer and closer to him with each step.... until all of a sudden she "accidentally" bumped into him, her breasts basically pressing hard against his chest.

"Ah! I'm so sorry," she said with a shy smile and wide-open eyes, eyelashes fluttering, leaning forward. "I'm such a klutz... I *absolutely* should've looked where I was going."

"N-no madame—it's my fault! I was the one in the way. I'm sorry." The man said, looking straight into her cleavage.

Merki ran her hand up the man's chest. "Oh, you're such a gentleman. Can you point me towards a reputable inn in the area? I seem to have gone and gotten myself lost."

"O-of course," the man said, and turned to point at an establishment further down the street. "Hal's Rest, over yonder, is a great place to... erm, well, rest." He said.

"Ah... excellent. I can't *wait* to have a bath, you know?" Merki said, then strode away from the man, fluttering her fingers in a goodbye while watching him over her bare shoulder.

The man stared after her, almost slobbering, then a large, stupid grin broke over his features. He slowly raised a hand and waved goodbye as well, until she completely disappeared among the crowds.

Merki waited until she was well out of sight, then pulled the man's coin purse out of her pants. "Oh… how'd that get in there?" She murmured, smirking. She checked the bag and—bingo, the man had been quite well-off indeed. There was more than enough there for at least a room and some of the other provisions she'd be needing.

But not quite enough.

Merki kept walking, six-zagging between the Way and the Burg districts and pocketing more and more money from completely clueless victims—a maid here, carrying her mistress' things, an old man there, another young noble staring more down her shirt than at her hands, etc.

Once she had enough, she turned to the little hidden garden where she'd stashed her weapons and counted the gold. All in all, she had over a hundred gold Kolls between all the bags… more than enough for her needs, she wagered. She stored the bags at different places—inside the soles of her boots, in her pants, on the inner pockets of her vest, and even between her breasts—then made her way around the shops on the other end of the Way, away from most of her victims.

She first bought a new outfit for her stay in town—a gorgeous red dress with a cream-colored vest and some green slippers, as well as a pearl necklace and two silver earrings with small emeralds on them. She then entered a weapon store for hunters that specialized specifically on bows, arrows and crossbows. Perfectly looking the part, she went in, traded her old bow and arrows for more coin, then bought a brand new, long-distance longbow with easily double the power and range of her previous one. She also bought close to thirty brand-new long-distance arrows, and ultimately, a canvas bag to store and hide them all in. The shopkeeper had watched her with very interested eyes as she assessed the weight and draw of the bow like an expert, despite her young looks.

"Planning on doing some hunting in the city, lass?" He'd asked her. "Cuz gates are to be shut for a week after tonight. No place to hunt large game till then." He gestured to the longbow, which was mainly used for such sport.

Merki just turned and smiled from ear to ear, showing her teeth, head titled to the side. "Oh, I know…" she said. "I'm just hoping to present these fine weapons to Aether during the ceremonies, good shopkeeper, so that He might bless all my hunts in the future."

The man nodded deeply. "A sensible thing to do, what with game running scarcer and scarcer every year around here."

Merki nodded, purchased the goods, blessed the man, then hightailed it out of there fast as she could.

She then passed by some stalls and purchased a bag of red elderberries, as well as some other fruits and snacking foods and, finally, a new backpack to store all of her new things in. Then, with her weapons and provisions stowed on the right bags, she traveled to the district known as Edgetown, where the good soldier from before had mentioned things started to get rough and dangerous for "nice ladies like her." She stuck to the main street of the district, however, which was the safest area of town. She didn't want to give some common street trash the opportunity to try and mug her before she'd had a chance to at least bathe properly.

And so, bathe she did. Her first port of call in the new and considerably shiftier-looking district was a moderate-looking inn just outside the bounds of Edgetown's main street, where she was finally able to rent a bath—and a hot one, at that. While she'd stood out quite a bit on the Way and even on the Burg, here on Edgetown she looked not much different than many of the men and women she came across. She still got plenty of looks and more than one comment from guys asking if she was new in town and wanted to have a good time, but she mostly ignored them, or gave them a look that immediately told them she wasn't one to mess with, putting her hand on the hilt of one of her daggers, at her sides. Once she'd finally rented the bath, she locked herself in the room—a private one which had cost her a premium fee, but was still within a very acceptable range. She walked around the room and covered the few peeping holes she knew she would find with arrows, then stripped down completely naked, slowly and gratefully lowering herself into the tub.

The innkeeper's wife, the one apparently in charge of the baths, had left some basic fragrances, soaps and herbs on a small table next to the tub, which was filled to the brim with recently boiling water. An open oven full of hot stones stood by the side on the far side of the small room, in case Merki needed to heat the water further. The young Kollek added some of the infusions to the bath, then lowered herself even further into the water, to where the waterline covered her lips but not her nose. She stayed there like that for a very long time, finally giving herself a long-overdue break after the pure hell she'd lived through in the past couple of weeks. The heat from the water, initially so hot it sent lances of burning pain through her body, now felt like the coziest of blankets, hugging her skin tightly, dissolving the stress, pain and knots from her entire body. Merki enjoyed the moment, not just because of how tired she'd been and how much she thought she deserved it, but because she knew the mission ahead of her would take every ounce of her strength and energy to accomplish. She'd have to eat and sleep well tonight too, or else she could open herself up to mistakes—and those would certainly get her killed, as well as lead her to fail her mission, which was not an option. Not after she'd waited years and years for this, prepared for it, planned out every single detail, made several plans, and then more, in case those fell through.

As she laid there in the hot, steaming waters, her hair streaming lazily around her, Merki suddenly had a brief moment of clarity outside of her Path—one where she thought back to Kade, Axel… and Locke. She thought about him and about those last few hours they'd spent together… the looks and stares they'd shared throughout the last few weeks.

And she grieved.

A part of her, a very small part, wanted that. Something normal and comforting… the possibilities she saw in the young captain's eyes whenever they met when no one else was watching them. A tiny part of her could almost see it all working out.

Him, a captain at a garrison or small town... just like her father. And her, an able and skilled huntress and forester of the region. It'd be perfect.

But she couldn't.

Her mission, her goal, was too important... and she knew that once she fulfilled it, if she even managed to *live* through it, she would close the doors to that kind of life forever.

Unexpectedly, as she was having the thoughts, Merki drew a ragged, sobbing breath and pushed herself further up on the tub, almost sucking some of the hot water up her nose by accident. Her heart suddenly felt very heavy in her chest, and for the first time in her journey—in her life—the tiniest flicker of a doubt flashed past her brain.

Is this the right thing to do?

As soon as she felt it, she pushed it far, far away. She obliterated it, cast it out, never to accommodate it again. It almost felt like sacrilege to have even allowed it for a second.

Of course it is... There is nothing else but the Path.

Refreshed after nearly half an hour in the hot waters, the young Kollek woman gingerly exited the bathtub, her skin quite the wrinkled mess, but feeling like brand new. She wrapped a linen towel around her waist and chest and another around her hair, then put several hot coals into the bathwater, making it boil once more. As soon as the bath was boiling properly, Merki produced the bag of red elderberries she'd purchased before... and threw them all into the bathtub, stirring them gently for a long time. She did this for about another hour, until the water in the tub had turned a deep crimson, eating some of her snacks in the meanwhile... then she lowered her hair into it, letting it soak deeply all the way to the roots of her hair.

Another hour and a half later, Merki emptied the red water in the tub down a nearby grate that led to the city sewers, along with the boiled elderberries, and donned her new clothes—the red dress, green slippers and fuzzy, cream-colored vest. She tied the necklace around her neck and the earrings on her ears, slinging her items on the canvas bag and backpack, then left through a window, not wanting to walk back out the front where the people could make her out.

Free from the dust and grime that had covered her, in her new clothes, and with a sparkling, curling mane of red hair that glistened under the sun like a goddess', Merki walked out of the inn a different woman, almost unrecognizable from the one that'd walked in. The old Merki had essentially disappeared from Kellum, the new woman in the dress taking her place. She then walked out of the shoddy district and towards the Noble's Row, looking for a better place to spend the night with the rest of her ill-begotten money and goods, preferably one closer to the main parade taking place at midday tomorrow… and with a clear line of sight to the temple.

CHAPTER 37

THE MEETING OF KINGS

The members of the royal family were all sitting on their thrones at the end of the massive dining halls of Castle Kellum.

The royal crier announced their guests as they came in:

"King Dlearin of Rekon and his queen and former princess of Kolis, Queen Freana."

The two announced monarchs walked in and greeted High King Ulor and Queen Etheria with a deep bow. Dlearin was a savvy man with a great knack for trade. His golden necklaces and amethyst jewelry, the most coveted gemstone in the world, acted as clear signs of his wealth. Behind him and his wife, two servants carried a well-engraved, gold-lacquered chest of the finest wood.

"Welcome, my dear cousin," King Ulor said with open arms.

"Thank you, my king. Please accept these humble gifts from our lands."

"So kind of you," Ulor said, accepting the chest. His servants carried it away once Dlearin and his wife took their seats at their appointed table.

The crier continued announcing everyone in turn, as there was a long line of kings and queens in attendance for the day's sacred ceremony—the one that was traditionally enacted the day before the celebrations began—apart from all the lords and ladies.

"The king of Kolis, King Suran." The crier said.

A tall, handsome warrior walked in. His athletic body, clad in his lavish silk robes, made a strong impression on everyone in the hall. Both his wealth and talent for war could be seen at a glance, thanks to his massive muscles and splendid attire. Suran's golden hair was tied in a knot behind his head and decorated with a crown of gold, rubies and sapphires, with a large amethyst at its center. He wore the seal to his kingdom on his ring finger, while his other fingers were all decorated with colorful gemstones set upon rings of gold. When he entered, Queen Etheria leaned towards Flora.

"A good husband candidate." She offered to her daughter. The small princess nodded, despite being only twelve, and carefully looked him up and down.

Another announcement was heard: "King Windaq, lord of the island of Touraq."

A huge man walked in then. He had a large cape of fur on his shoulders, which kept him warm in the cold north seas, and possessed little similarities to the other two who'd walked in before him. He knelt in front of the High King all the same.

The crier continued his announcements:

"King Fredrich of the kingdom of Salut."

"Queen Liza from the island of Fretca."

"King Hourak from the island of Jortel."

The last king who walked in was Derkel, king of the island of Marteel and youngest among all the kings, having recently turned twenty-four. His blue eyes, complimenting his black hair and well-shaped face with strong cheekbones, grabbed Flora's attention more than King Suran. She kindly smiled at him, and he smiled back at her too with special interest, despite being literally twice her age.

"Welcome, nephew," King Ulor said, greeting him with less enthusiasm than he had the other kings and queens.

"Thank you, uncle." Derkel said, kneeling. "Please accept my humble gifts." He added, as his servants put the large chest he'd brought on the ground before the high king.

"Thank you, King Derkel." Ulor said.

"Where is Queen Karmen?" Etheria asked Ulor.

"Ifir's bringing her." Ulor replied with his eyes on Derkel, who was being welcomed warmly by the other kings and queens. "Apparently she has some "business" to discuss with her upon her arrival. She'll be her soon."

Once everyone was seated at their tables, Ulor raised his cup of wine, and the room went quiet.

"My dear kings and queens, my lords. As the right hand of our god Aether, I am honored to welcome you here today, in observance of Imperation's Eve, before my soul journeys to the other world to speak with Aether. May He be pleased with our faith and service."

"Long live the High King! May his journey be blessed and true!" The guests said, raising their glasses at the same time.

Etheria raised hers as well, but her mind was somewhere else entirely, wondering at what kind of schemes Ifir could be playing at behind everyone's backs.

***

Back at the harbor, Ifir was waiting for the ship that was about to land, standing confidently and calmly before her escort, a row of about ten Chosen, who were lined up behind her at the pier.

The dark of the night was dispelled by scores of large torches on both sides of the harbor. Soon, the ship anchored, and Queen Karmen stepped out, followed by a small army of Poly-sisters from her islands.

When Karmen saw the Chosen lined up for her, she was surprised. Ifir stepped up, a wide smile in her face, hands clasped together. "Welcome to Kellum, Queen Karmen. High King Ulor is pleased by your arrival."

Karmen paused for a second upon seeing Ifir's confusing smile. Did it mean she was genuinely happy to see her? Or... something else? You could never tell with the woman.

"Thank you, Songbird. I am honored to serve him." She said, then walked with Ifir.

"I hope you had a comfortable trip, my queen."

"I did, thank you. I hope the sisters I sent before me have been enough for your guests?" Karmen said, reminding Ifir of the favor she'd done for her.

"They have, yes," Ifir said. "Commander Siegel's soldiers are so happy to have them in their service, as are our guests."

"They are Aether's druids. They serve all those who seek the joys of life." She calmly said.

"You can be sure that our people will give joy to them as well. Most importantly, however... they would *never* hurt them." Ifir looked at Karmen's face closely after saying that.

"Good. Everyone knows that the punishment of hurting a Polysister is death." Karmen said, sternly.

They reached the coaches waiting for them on the street outside the harbor.

"Quite. Let's ride to the castle now, Queen Karmen. The feast should have already begun." Ifir said, then joined Karmen in the carriage, as her Chosen mounted their horses and surrounded the coach as an escort.

***

"How long will we wait here?" Kade asked Axel, shaking his leg.

"Until they are ready." The old man said, sitting on his chair, watching the entrance to the safehouse.

Kade stood up and walked around the rather spacious room below the tailor shop, taking deep breaths with every step he took. Axel watched his efforts to stay calm.

"What do you think Merki and Locke are doing right now?" Kade asked the old man suddenly, stopping his pacing.

"Most likely looking for us." Axel answered honestly.

"Locke must be besides himself," Kade said. "He sacrificed so much to bring me here." Kade suddenly felt a strong pang of regret in his chest, and his breathing came harder to him.

Axel's expression suddenly turned more serious and he fixed his eyes at young man. "Yes… he did," he said. "But not out of the kindness of his heart, Kade. He wanted only the power and recognition that claiming the King's Bounty would bring him… he didn't care about you, nor about what would happen to you once he turned you in."

Kade took in Axel's words for a moment, then shook his head. "I don't believe that. You said it yourself—they didn't have any idea of what would happen after they 'turned me in.' Not about Ulor's actions, nor that Ifir woman's."

Axel sighed. "He knew enough, Kade. He… knew it wouldn't end well."

The young Chosen continued to pace back and forth across the room.

"Kade… sit down. Breathe. You need to be ready for when the time comes."

Kade stopped, sighing deeply, then made his way to the couch opposite Axel and slumped down on it.

"What about Merki? Do you think she'll be alright?" He asked Axel.

The old man stared into Kade's eyes for a moment, then looked down at the floor. "I hope so. She's a strong one. If anyone here can achieve their goals and dreams… whatever they are… it's someone like her."

Kade nodded several times, thinking about whether he'd ever see her again. "I just… I can't get their last image off my head, Axel. They looked in so much pain and anguish… and I had a hand in causing that."

"What's done is done, young Kade. Let it go. You made the right choice for all involved—they would've been marked for death had you stayed with them, remember?"

Kade nodded, sighed, then looked away. "So you said."

Axel ignored the double meaning behind his words. "Now," the old man began, changing the topic. "Have you thought of what you'll say to Ellyad once you see him?"

The Meeting of Kings | 441

Kade looked at him briefly, then looked away once more. "I'm still working on it."

Axel nodded. "Work fast, Kade. We need him to come with us out of his own accord. We can drag him all the way to Norzou in ropes… but we can't make him cross the threshold of the city outside of his own desire to do so, or else his powers won't manifest."

"How do you know this?"

Axel sighed. "Because it is written as such."

"Written? Where?"

"On one of the Holy Manuscripts, Kade. The records left by the last Sword before he died, telling us how to find and awaken the next Sword of Aether."

"I… I've never heard of…"

"You wouldn't have. It's one of the kingdom's most carefully guarded secrets. We… well, we lost many good men trying to secure the one piece of the Manuscript we got, which revealed enough to us to get to this point."

"How many are there?"

"We don't know. We only know that Ulor and the Koartiz both have at least two more pieces each… but they're beyond our reach by now, as it stands."

Kade nodded. "Might as well be a prophecy about him, with everything else going on." The Chosen man suddenly looked very tired and overwhelmed.

"Relax, Kade… Empty your mind. All of this will be over soon, and you and Ellyad will be reunited and on your way to Kellum. Have faith."

Kade sighed long and deep. He looked up at Axel and met the man's old, gray eyes. "Alright. I'll…" Kade started to say, but his words were interrupted by the sound of the door opening, then that of the shop owner coming down.

Axel stood up slowly from his chair and fixed his eyes on the man. Kade took a sharp breath. "Is it time?" The Chosen asked.

"My lord. Chosen." The shopkeeper said, bowing to Axel and Kade.

"Brother." Axel saluted back.

"Everything has been arranged. They are ready to fulfil their duty." He said to Axel, then cast his eyes away from his. His voice got lower. "They just require that you make the payment. As you know, they don't accept regular…"

Axel cut his speech with a raised hand. "Say no more. Of course he'll have *me* pay them…" Axel sighed. "Very well. Show me the way." The man nodded, then climbed up the ladder to the shop. Axel climbed the ladder after him. As he arrived at the top, he looked down at Kade.

"Stay here, Kade. I'll be back soon, and we'll finally go get your brother. Do not leave this room for any reason whatsoever—understand?"

The young Chosen sighed deeply and nodded, sitting back down on the sofa.

"Take the time to think about what you'll say to Ellyad when you see him." Axel added, then disappeared from view, closing down the secret trapdoor behind him.

Kade sat alone in the room, closed his eyes and breathed deeply. He heard Axel and the shopkeeper's footsteps as they left the shop. The turn of the key as the shopkeeper closed the shop for the night. The sounds of their murmurs as they walked away. Then, the amethysts around his neck reacted to his use of his power and he couldn't hear anymore. He sighed deeply once more.

"*Take the time to think about what you'll say to Ellyad,*" he said, mimicking Axel's voice. "What *am* I supposed to say to him? I've never seen the man in my life!"

He breathed deeply for a couple of seconds, hands clasped together, eyes cast at the floor.

"Hey," he began, speaking to no one in particular. "You don't know me, but I'm your long-lost brother. I've come here to find you, tear you away from everything and everyone you know and love, and drag you halfway across the country to a mythical city in the mountains that your people say doesn't exist anymore—because you're the only one who can cure my sister, and *yours*, who you've never met, from a blood condition that you've never heard of. Oh, and you're also a Nor, not a Chosen or Kollek… and probably the reincarnation of a god-like being, here to save the world before it dies and kills us all. Any questions? No? Great, then let's go!"

Kade hung his head very, very miserably after he finished talking to himself.

"This is going to go *horribly*." He sighed.

CHAPTER 38

THE DEEP DARK

Urk and his men stood before the immensely tall temple in front of them. They'd been on alert since the attack, but for some reason, hadn't encountered any more resistance since then.

"Stay alert, men… Expect another ambush at any moment." Urk had told his Chosen as they looked for an entrance of some sort around the perimeter of the temple—but the weird, pyramid-like structure was completely sealed off… at least superficially. Urk knew there had to be a way in somewhere, though.

Eventually, they decided to climb the structure as a group, seeing as they couldn't find any way to enter it from below.

Urk used his superior hearing and Hukail his sight, hoping to find any cracks or odd-looking seams in the stone—any telltale sounds that didn't belong, which would reveal a way into the temple, all the while fearing another attack at any moment.

After climbing several feet up the structure, Urk finally heard it—the whistling sound of wind slipping through a crack in the seams of a hidden door, somewhere in a flat section of wall.

"Frain," Urk said, and the Chosen walked over to him. "Right there. There's something out of place here. See if you can't give the wall a little push."

Frain looked at the section of wall then back at Urk. "It's going to be loud, captain... Are you sure?"

Urk hesitated, considering their options. While it was true that they'd announce their presence here with this option, (if they hadn't already), they were still on a tight timetable here and they hadn't found any other alternatives after nearly an hour of searching.

"I don't like this, Urk." Said Hukail. "We haven't met any more resistance after that ambush on the plains... and even then, those were civilian Koartiz, not soldiers. What is going on here?"

Urk shook his head. "I'm not sure, men. I don't like it either... but we have a mission to fulfill, and we will not go back home empty-handed. We need to press on."

Hukail hesitantly nodded. The others did as well, then Frain stood before the hidden door. His muscles grew larger and he walked back a couple of steps, turning towards the wall and breaking into a sprint. He then jumped with the force of a lightning strike, tackling the wall with his shoulder, and broke through the stone, opening a wide-enough gap in the rock for everyone to pass through.

He then came out of the hole, rubbing his shoulder, then jerked a thumb over his back. "Door's open." He said.

"Good work," Urk replied. "Hukail, you're up."

The other Chosen nodded, casting his vision through the hole. He stood like that for a moment, staring down at the floor while his true vision flew around inside the hole... then he came back to, blinking.

"What did you see?"

"A deep tunnel... made of rock. This... isn't just a man-made structure, captain. Not fully."

"Then what is it?"

"It's a mountain."

"A... mountain? How can that be?"

"I don't know... but the temple outside... it seems to have been built, or carved, out of an existing mountain. It's all caverns and pits from here on out—almost like a maze."

"That explains why this temple is so damn big." Balto said, and Frain nodded in agreement.

"Hmm…Did you see anything that resembles the outside? Any chambers or passageways that look like they might lead to wherever they're keeping the Manuscript?"

Hukail shook his head. "Just cavern after cavern—and some of the passages are either dead ends, spiked pits or traps."

"Hmm… so they build this massive temple around a mountain and put the only entrance all the way up here… which leads into a maze of some sort." He considered it for a moment, arms crossed, then said: "The true temple is underground, then."

"Sir?" That was Balto.

"That explains it all," added Urk. "Why there are no sentries out here, why we couldn't find any way in below… and why they built this obvious temple in the middle of these wide-open plains. This whole structure is a deathtrap, meant to attract, then defeat any intruders that come looking for the Manuscript—all without losing a single man."

"But that means…" Began Frain, and Urk nodded.

"It means that the true main force of the Koartiz is waiting for us at the bottom of this mountain, ready to pick off anyone who survives the long way down the maze."

The Chosen exchanged looks between each other.

"But how do they get in themselves?" Asked Hukail.

Balto was the one who spoke this time: "They probably have a series of secret entrances all over the plains. Underground, like that hatch they used to ambush us."

"But that didn't lead anywhere—I checked!" Said Hukail again.

"They must have others. It's the only explanation."

"Can't we look for one of those instead?"

Urk shook his head. "We don't have time, men. Even with our powers, I doubt they'll be as easy to find as this one."

"So we'll just… what, walk right into their trap? Play the game on their rules?"

Urk nodded several times. "It's not ideal… but we're more than capable of doing it. We're Chosen, men, not regular soldiers. If their previous defense is any indication, they're not expecting Ulor to

The Deep Dark | 447

sacrifice some of his biggest assets, a full squad of Chosen, by sending them after a Manuscript into enemy lands... no, this was built to deter, confuse and defeat regular men... Not us."

The other Chosen nodded heartily among each other.

"I say we go right in and give them all a surprise they won't soon forget."

The Chosen all nodded and bumped their closed fist over their breasts at the same time.

"Hukail, you take point. Cast your vision ahead and show us the way."

"Aye, aye, captain."

They then went down slowly into the spiraling caverns, stepping carefully, while Hukail led the way with his superior vision and Urk listened for sounds of ambush or traps all around them, holding a single makeshift torch up in the air. It took the men the better part of an hour to descend the entire mountain's interior, occasionally having to stop while a trap sprung mere inches away from them, or move carefully through open chasms full of spike traps underneath—which none of them would've noticed if it hadn't been for Hukail. It almost felt like they were climbing down towards the very center of the earth itself, as the caverns grew more and more ancient and massive stalagmites began to rise like the columns of an ancient temple all around them. The air also got noticeably colder and thinner as they went, and for a moment, Urk and his men had the nagging fear they'd walked into an interminable maze of caverns and chambers, which they would never find their way out of.

Then, after nearly two hours, Hukail stopped and held up a hand. He spoke so softly only Urk heard him.

"I see light up ahead." He said.

Urk gave the signal to the men and they all readied for battle. Urk snuffed the torch as to not give themselves away and they continued the rest of the way towards the light as silently as they could. As they neared the lit chamber beyond their tunnel, the soldiers' hearts began to pound in their chests. They knew they were close to their goal now... but it was something else that gave them the chills down here.

A presence of some sort that none of them could explain. Hukail stopped when they were mere feet from the exit and frowned.

"What's wrong?" Urk asked him, very low, very close to his ears.

"I… can't see anything beyond the opening. I can't explain it."

Urk frowned and tried to Cast his own sense of hearing into the chamber… to the same, strange effect. He couldn't hear anything past the entrance to the room. It was as if the place beyond it just didn't exist.

Hmm… sorcery, it must be… Urk said to himself. *This is definitely not good.*

For a split second, he considered pulling his men back and calling the whole thing off. If there were signs of sorcery here, then that meant… but no, they'd come too far to back out now. They were literally almost to the Manuscript, for Aether's sake! They'd face whatever awaited them beyond the halls… whatever that meant.

Urk took the lead and, following his footsteps, the soldiers walked out onto a massive chamber that almost looked like a cavern itself, so large they couldn't make out the ceiling. The distant walls were full of engravings, as was the stone beneath their feet, and six massive statues heralded their arrival among countless pillars that held a couple of thousand metric tons of earth from caving in on them.

The Chosen were all eyes and ears as they slowly traversed the torch-lit chamber, sticking to the shadows, hoping against hope they could reach the Manuscript unseen. Urk noticed that the symbols on the walls were written in ancient Koartiz, and told the stories of the former Sword of Aether—of his accomplishments, power and prestige… which at least meant they were in the right place, thank Aether.

They saw more tunnels leading into the chamber from the walls—like a massive anthill. They expected a Koartiz savage to jump out at them from the deep shadows within every time they crossed one, and yet they reached the other end of the room unharmed and unseen, encountering absolutely no resistance whatsoever. Urk knew the question on his men's minds because it was also the question on his.

The Deep Dark | 449

Where is everyone? Why haven't we met with a single Koartiz by now? What is going on here?

A very troubling and blood-chilling though entered his mind then—that maybe this had all been a plot of misdirection from the Koartiz in the first place... and that there was no Manuscript here, only death. Maybe they'd close the exits to these inner chambers before the soldiers could even realize it and trap them here to die a slow, agonizing death.

Urk shook the thoughts from his mind. They were already here and would explore the place fully before coming to any conclusions. He couldn't fuss over all the unknowns now, or else he'd miss what was happening right in front of him—and that could cost him his life.

At the other end of the massive chamber, they encountered a set of massive doors—bigger than the gates of Kellum and cast in golden brass. Urk motioned Frain forward and the Musal put all his strength into his back, trying to push one of the doors open only to realize that, just as Urk and Frain, he couldn't summon his power in here. Despite that, the man was still strong enough to open the gate just enough for all of them to squeeze through. Urk was the first one through.

When he looked upon the chamber that awaited them on the other side, his jaw nearly dropped.

The Manuscript chamber, also the burial chamber of the last Sword, was the most glorious thing he'd ever seen in his life—far more than even Ulor's own chambers or the inside of the Great Temple back in Kellum.

Massive columns of gold rose to the ceiling, glittering all over like the surface of a placid lake at night, with diamonds, pearls and sapphires studded into its surfaces. The walls were works of art, depicting the life of the previous Sword, painted with what were undoubtedly paints made out of pulverized gems—emeralds, sapphires, rubies and even amethysts, glittering so fiercely in the light of the long, chamber-wide fire pits on either side of the room, they seemed almost blinding. A massive array of chandeliers hung from the ceiling, all blazing with magical fire the likes of which Urk had never seen, and at the far end, up on an altar, was a podium holding a glowing book. Behind the book, on a raised dais of gold, gems and diamonds stood the casket of the Sword—the saint's final resting place, likely holding his remains too. Each of the Chosen froze on the spot right upon entering the room, completely taken aback by the splendor and majesty inside.

Hukail was the first to recover, and touched Urk's arm as soon as he did, man pointing at the podium holding the Manuscript. Urk nodded, then ordered the other men to follow him in a wide formation as he led them towards the other end of the room. As they stalked through the middle of the room, seeing as there was no other way to approach the altar due to the wide fire pits carved into the floor on either side of them, Urk heard a very troubling sound... The gate Frain had opened suddenly slid back shut.

They all looked back and saw what they'd dreading all along for hours now—around ten of the most elite of Koartiz warriors, the *Hakkari*, as they called themselves, clad in war tattoos all over their skin, even their eyelids, all with weapons held at the ready.

The Chosen soldiers stood ready for battle; weapons raised as well. Without the use of their abilities, this would be an incredibly challenging fight... but it wouldn't be impossible. They still possessed their superior agility, reflexes and strength, so they certainly had a strong chance against the soldiers.

Then, the *Hakkari* lowered their weapons, stepped back a single step and fell to one knee, bowing their heads.

The Chosen looked at each other... then Urk noticed that his sword, Darkness Ripper, had begun to glow golden in his hands. He stared at it, eyes growing wider by the second... then they all turned towards the altar.

An old man was standing before the piece of the Manuscript, clad in a robe as dark as a starless night, with a beard as white as snow. His entire face was tattooed like one of the *Hakkari,* and Urk suddenly gasped in terror, realizing who—and what— he was.

"One of the Five..." He told the others, who stared back at the old man in terror.

"T-the Pentaghast?" Said Balto. "But if he's here, then that means..."

Suddenly, a shadow walked out of the man's silhouette—an exact copy of him, clad in that same midnight-black robe as him. But then the shadow grew to twice the man's size, and it looked at them. Where the eyes should've been, shone instead two blazing rubies, glowing with a fiery red light that stroke an unspeakable terror into the very depths of their souls.

"F-fuck...! It's a Judge!!!" Hukail said.

Urk shut his eyes tightly and regretted not pulling his men back when they had the chance, merely a few minutes ago.

Now, they were all going to die.

The dark entity jumped over the altar and landed right in front of them, easily standing a head taller than Hukail, the tallest among them. The creature looked down at them with those burning coals for eyes, looming like Death itself over the men, daring them to take the first step.

They all seemed to hold their breath in anticipation... then Frain did.

"FOR KELLUM!!!" He shouted at the top of his lungs and ran at the Judge with his sword held high.

He sliced diagonally with amazing speed, but when the sword whistled through the air, the Judge just wasn't there anymore. The dark being had jumped over Frain, spinning the hems of his robe over his head, then landing behind him. It then walked to the side, quietly, and the other Chosen saw as Frain suddenly split vertically in half. The creature's hemline dripped with their comrade's blood, now dyed a crimson red.

Urk howled in pain and rage, followed by the other men.

"BASTARD!!!" The captain yelled as he flashed forward with his glowing blade and swung at the Judge, but the being revealed a ragged sword from its sleeve, as long as a man, and easily parried the blow aside, knocking the blade out of Urk's hands.

Balto, hoping against hope that his powers would somehow work where the others' had failed, closed in on the Judge and grasped its cloak.

The moment he did, a blood-curdling scream tore from his throat, and the man held his head like he'd just gone feral, foaming at the mouth. He began to convulse uncontrollably as blood spilled down his eyes, then he ran towards one of the fire pits and leaped in, shrieking at the top of his lungs as he burnt to death.

"B-balto!" Yelled Hukail in a broken, almost manic voice. Urk had managed to recover his sword in the meanwhile, and joined him.

"Give me an opening, Hou! My sword can kill it!" He said.

"Y-yes, sir, captain!" Hukail said in a high, shaky pitch.

The Chosen moved forward while the dark beast stared down at them, still as the dead, and swung his blade. The Judge parried the blow aside as it had Urk's, but Hukail held onto his weapon, anticipating the disarming force behind the move, then rose just in time to block a cut that would've decapitated him on the spot. The strength of the creature was such, however, that he knelt on one knee, pushed down by the force of its monstrous blade as it got closer and closer to his shoulder. He put every bit of strength he had into deflecting the blow, his entire body shaking, tears of effort filling his eyes, but the Night Judge's strength was beyond even Frain's. The monster continued to push down with seemingly no effort... until it suddenly stopped, to the sound of a groan of pain from the old man behind it.

Hukail looked to his left and saw Urk's blade piercing the creature's stomach, glowing brightly. The horrible stench of burning rotten flesh and bile filled the room, and Hukail literally gagged, as the creature just stared down at Urk, who pushed the blade further into its gut. Then, the Judge rose its blade with blinding speed, sliced Hukail diagonally in half, and did a somersault in the air, kicking Urk several feet into the air and away from it. The entity then grabbed the handle of Urk's sword, pulled it out of its midsection, and threw it into the firepit on its right.

The Chosen captain coughed on the floor, spitting blood, then got up as best as he could, grabbing one of his men's swords in a last-ditch defense. The Judge walked slowly towards him... then it sheathed the sword back inside its sleeve, held the two sides of its cloak and raised them. Urk could see the glow of hundreds of small blades under the cloak's hemline.

Fuck…

The creature jumped over Urk and landed behind him. The captain's eyes barely caught the motion, but his back suddenly flared up with the pain of the cut the monster had opened, his warm blood seeping into his shirt beneath the sliced armor plates. Despite the fire-hot pain, Urk shouted and turned back to attack the monster—but the beast simply moved aside, dodging all of his blows with incredible speed. No matter how hard Urk tried, the monster responded to his every move with ease. Between dodges, it spun in the air and another cut appeared on Urk's flesh. Chunks of his armor were blown away with each blow, until the man was fighting in his bare uniform, which was also nearly torn to tatters. The Judge kept dancing around him, vaulting, spinning, cutting, but not killing him. All of his wounds were superficial—just so enough that he didn't bleed out. Eventually, the captain was so tired, wounded and breathless, he could barely raise his sword. A cut to his forearm sent the blade skittering over the stone floors of the temple and the man simply stood, swaying, receiving cut after cut until his skin was almost entirely coated with his blood. He knelt in the ground before the horrible abomination, wishing for the final blow that would end his horrible pain… but that blow never came.

The creature stared down at him with its ghostly red eyes, then simply moved aside, revealing the High Sorcerer walking towards him from behind. Urk tried to get up, to throttle the man and squeeze the life out of his frail, weak throat… but his legs just wouldn't respond. His arms wouldn't budge, hanging limp at his sides. It was all he could do not to tumble to the side and lay there, motionless, until death came for him.

The Pentaghast knelt before him and looked at the captain's face, noticing how he could barely keep his eyes open. He held a hand under Urk's chin, turning his face while scratching his already torn skin with long, raven-like claws, then released him.

"Good." The man said and rose to his feet, lifting Urk into the air. He placed his old hand on Urk's head and, with the other, he pulled his own hood back, exposing his face and the score of eldritch tattoos covering every inch of his skin. He raised his head to the ceiling, closed his eyes and concentrated for a moment... then suddenly, Urk's head snapped back as well and he groaned, choking, as his whole body began to shake. Blood began to stream out of his nose and ears, and his eyes rolled back into his skull.

Once the old man was finished, he removed his hand from Urk's face and stumbled back, swaying in place, until two of the *Hakkari* ran over to help him, supporting him on their shoulders. The man's face, already old, wrinkled as if he'd aged five more years in the span of a second. One of the other *Hakkari* then took the glowing book from the altar, tore a page from it, rolled it, and put it in one of Urk's pockets, secured safely so it wouldn't fall. He then passed the book to the High Sorcerer, who walked away while holding it tightly in his arms.

"Send him away to his dear king," The sorcerer ordered his men over his shoulder, then left. The Night Judge followed him, then slowly shrunk back to his size, melding with his shadow and disappearing, as the *Hakkari* took a limp, nearly dead Urk away in their arms.

CHAPTER 39

THE DAY OF IMPERATION

The piercing light of dawn shone over the buildings of Kellum, spearing the sky from beyond the faraway mountains in the east, casting the horizon in shades of orange and pink.

Merki had stayed in an affluent inn on Noble's Row the previous night, which was directly across from one of the bell towers surrounding the Street of Kings—the road that led up to Castle Kellum, and though which the entire royal procession would pass during the start of the ceremonies. She now stood at the top of said belltower, the priest who attended to it bound and gagged a just few floors down, fully knocked out.

The young Kollek now stood on the balcony surrounding the bell. For a moment, staring at the rays of bright, golden light shining above Aether's Great Temple, almost framing it in the glow, she felt hypnotized by the beauty she saw. The temple was massive, enough to believe Aether Himself could fit in it. The majestic temple featured colorful glass windows with paintings on them, large marble columns wrapped by ivies on its entryways, and scores of colorful flower gardens that looked as if Aether himself had sent them from the heavens. The huge building was four stories tall, and its most striking feature was the one big dome of pure gold rising from the middle of its roof, surrounded by eleven smaller ones. At its entrance, its massive wooden doors were engraved and inlaid in gold and silver with all the motifs of Aether's religion—suns, moons and stars. Finally, a large glass mosaic with angels of Aether hung powerfully above the doors, built in such a way that the early morning light shone through the building and out of its glass mosaics, casting a beam of multi-colored light on the yard right in front of the entryway.

Merki's new bow and arrows laid on the floor, on top of her open canvas sheath like a set of instruments for a delicate operation, bearing witness to what might well be her last day on this world. She turned her eyes to the early morning sky, watching as the stars slowly flickered out of view while the sun rose higher in the horizon. She gazed longingly up into the heavens, the wind up there playing with her crimson locks and the white robes she was currently wearing over her red dress, giving her an almost ephemeral look.

"Hey dad…" She smiled, weakly and sadly. "Don't know if you can hear me, but… I finally made it. After all these years, I'm finally here. It'll all soon be over… and you'll be able to rest in peace." She looked at the flickering stars, wondering which one was her father.

She stared down at the parade grounds. They've been thoroughly cleaned and prepared for today, decorated with liliums and roses everywhere, while a designated seating area for the nobles and royals visiting had been laid in the gardens around the front yard of the temple. As she looked at the preparations, noticing the ever-present guards keeping careful watch over everything below, Merki noticed how some of the temple nuns were wading into the ponds on either side of the temple entrance, arranging some lotuses which were floating in the cold morning water.

She saw as scores of crowds from all over the city began to arrive at the scene, standing on the sidelines of the wide, majestic street, some carrying baskets of roses, while others were holding flags or banners with the crest of Kellum, Ulor and Aether. Merki hid behind one of the bell tower pillars in a way that exposed very little of her body, not to draw any unwanted attention to herself, despite her disguise. A small army of soldiers took their place along the sides of the street, facing the people and forming two impenetrable "walls" between them and the procession that would soon pass through.

Then, a few moments later, a powerful horn blew from Castle Kellum and the whole city stood still with bated breath. A powerful beat, played to the rhythm of the Rhyme of Aether, began to thunder from atop Castle Hill, and Merki's heart began to thunder inside her chest in response.

The Imperation Day ceremonies had begun.

Merki's hand began to tremble in anticipation and the air got stuck in her throat. She swallowed hard, then remembered her training—all those years she'd spent "hunting" in the woods of Halstead, honing her skills, her senses… and her aim. Hunting bears, boars, wolves and more—whatever she could find in the wild, hoping to achieve the skills necessary to pull off this feat.

Most of all, she remembered her discipline and self-control—the single-minded mental focus that was key to everything else, and which guided her along her Path. She breathed deeply, filling her lungs with the cold morning air, then slowly exhaled from her mouth. Suddenly, the sound of the beats faded to a distant place in the back of her mind. She could still hear it, but her focus was not on it.

The sound of the drums, accompanied by a fanfare of rising trumpets, became almost deafening for everyone else, though. The crowds standing around the long road began to cheer at the top of their lungs, raising their standards and banners, whooping and praying. Some were even kneeling and raising their hands up to Aether in the sky.

The first members of the procession began to walk past—a large group of dozens of young women dressed in white, scattering white petals along the road in preparation for the others. From Merki's vantage point, it looked as if the entire street had suddenly become a glorious path to the heavens, thick with so many white petals one could barely see the cobblestones underneath from up there.

The people all began so sign the Hymn of Aether, as was custom, preparing the king's passing to the temple. The whole city hushed to witness the song, coming from hundreds of thousands of throats, sounding as if the very heavens themselves had parted and their host joined in on the ceremony.

Despite her reasons for being there and her grey disposition towards the Kollek's beliefs, Merki couldn't help but get goosebumps as the entire city began to sign in one voice, joined in solemn reverence to their king and holy herald, and their god, who was supposed to be slowly descending to the temple today the higher the sun rose to the heavens. It was believed that, once the sun was at its zenith, Aether himself would have finally arrived at his Grand Aetheliour, awaiting Ulor for their sacred, week-long audience.

As she listened to the hymn, Merki wondered, just for a second, if Locke was down there among the crowds… and if he was looking for her after she hadn't shown up.

Then she shook her head. She needed to focus. There'd be time to think about that later. Now, she needed to be fully present and alert. And so, the young huntress waited at her spot, watching, her eyes sharp and focused like a hawk's.

Soon, the next members of the procession appeared around the curve of the massive street—the high-ranking Chosen of Kellum (for the lesser ones were serving as guards all around the street). They were all clad in black and gold armor with hints of red, looking like gods among men with their abnormal stature and postures, holding exquisite spears pointed at the heavens. Merki noticed that the Chosen leading the procession wasn't wearing any armor, but a silken emerald dress that glistened like the night sky under the rays of the morning sun. Her long locks of black hair flowed behind her on the breeze, framing her immaculate pale face, and to Merki, it almost seem as if she glided over the petals as she moved. She seemed like a vision from another realm—like a spirit or goddess, completely detached from the physical world around her. Merki didn't know why, but she suddenly felt a cold chill tremble up her spine, and it wasn't because of the late mid-autumn breeze. The woman in green reached the end of the street and stood before the temple, turning to face the rest of the procession. Then, she raised her arms, as if heralding the coming of the king, and opened her mouth.

Merki's breath caught in her throat then once more as the woman's voice joined that of the people's, overpowering it, adding a somber, grave, but beautiful heaviness to it that entranced Merki, sending strange ripples through her skin from the bottoms of her feet to the crown of her hair. It was unnatural, but also perfect, as if Merki had suddenly been thrust out of her mortal shell and was now experiencing the world around her in her true, infinite, ethereal form.

Then, as soon as it began, the startling effect was over. Merki blinked then gasped, realizing that she hadn't done so for a few seconds. Then she fell on her knees, putting a hand over her heart and staring down at the terrifying woman below on the steps to the temple, still singing.

What had just happened? Why had the woman's voice felt like a physical thing, passing through every pore in her body?

Merki trembled again... then, using every last bit of her willpower and training, she recomposed herself, stood back up and resumed her razor-sharp vigil.

***

Down on the street next to the belltower, Axel was standing among the crowds with a hood over his head, draped in an expensive-looking robe of deep red and gold. He stared out into the procession along with some of his "contacts" in Kellum, all dressed as if they were his servants. He scanned the procession, looking for someone, watching as all the Chosen of Kellum marched by after Ifir.

Then, something, Axel wasn't sure what, told him to look at a specific place in the row of soldiers facing his side of the street a few dozen meters down the road. Axel's blood turned cold as ice and he quickly looked away, covering his face with his hood.

Dammit, he said to himself, realizing that one of the guards posted at the perimeter of the parade, just a few dozen meters away from him, was none other than Locke. He was wearing a new uniform, but still leaning on two crutches—new ones too, he noticed. Axel, being far away enough, decided to risk another careful glance... and noticed something was very wrong with the soldier. His eyes seemed empty, and his posture was like that of a man who was dead on his feet. He looked broken as he scanned the faces of the crowds around him, like the weight of the world rested squarely upon his shoulders.

Then, Axel noticed that Merki was nowhere to be seen—not in the crowds around Locke, nor anywhere around him. His senses spiked as, for a moment, he considered she might be hiding in the crowds, looking for him and Kade while Locke scouted the crowds over from his position.

Then, Axel's instincts warned him otherwise. Locke looked burdened by a weight beyond that of just losing the two of them—it was as if something had split him right down the middle.

Merki had deserted him too, then, Axel thought, with immense curiosity and interest. If she'd done that... then the young huntress must've had an agenda of her own all this time too, he considered.

Merki, Merki... he thought. *Always a surprise up your sleeve, eh?*

"Pay attention you old ballsack," Axel's inner voice warned him. *"I think your man is coming up the road soon."*

Axel's eyes grew wide and he came back to the moment, quickly scanning the Chosen marching past him...

... and that's when he saw him.

Riding at the back of the Chosen arm of the procession, sitting astride a mighty white steed dressed in gold and white armor like him, was the man he'd come all this way to collect and convince. The key to it all... and Kade's long-lost brother.

Odmund, the Champion of the Kollek.

***

Merki saw as the champion slowly lit the torches set along the street towards the temple with his own flames, conjuring fire out of nowhere. She stared in awe at the power a Chosen could wield—the power to burn the whole of Kellum down, if they chose.

Then, as the sun rose entirely above the faraway mountains, filling the day with its full glow and splendor, all the bells in the city began to ring loudly and powerfully in order. First, the bell of Aether's Great Temple. Then, those of the other temples surrounding it. Finally, the bell towers circling the Singing Hill of Kellum began to ring in clockwise order, heralding the coming of the king and Aether's descent onto their city… but the rhythm and cadence of the rings stopped suddenly, when one of the towers didn't ring. Merki frowned, then her heart leapt out of her chest when she saw all eyes starting to turn towards her own tower. She swiftly hid behind the pillar, then looked around her desperately for the rope that would ring *her* tower.

"Shit!" she said, breaking out into a cold sweat. Then she saw it, hanging right behind the bell. She ran, threw herself in the air and pulled on it with her full weight. The tower quaked in a blast of deafening sound, the bell ringing three times, then the procession continued, with the next tower over ringing in turn and on time, then the next, and the next…

Merki didn't hear any of them, as her world spun wildly around her while she laid on her back, staring at the temple ceiling. She couldn't hear anything—not even the ringing of her own bell. Then, slowly, painfully, a high-pitch whistle rang in her ears and she covered them with her hands, grimacing and gritting her teeth. The whistle then became a low, steady sound—the drums and music coming from the parade, until at long last, her sense of hearing returned to her. Merki had seen so many cotton balls lying around the lower rooms as she made her way up here, which had puzzled her… Now she knew exactly why the priest had kept so many around. Still grimacing, she made her way over to her viewpoint, panicking, praying to all the gods she knew of that she hadn't missed her chance.

Thankfully, she was just in time.

As she looked up at the curve of the road leading down from the castle—she saw him.

Ulor, the High King of the Kollek, was coming down the road on a large, square platform with wheels, drawn by six horses. The platform

The Day of Imperation | 463

was carpeted, inlaid with gold and jewels and tiered into several levels. Ulor and his queen sat at the very top in two lavish, ornate thrones—most likely replicas of the ones in the castle. Then, below them, their two children sat on smaller thrones, and finally, at the lower level, sat the commander of the Kollek armies, clad in glistening armor, a ferrety looking man next to him dressed in a golden uniform, and the kings and queens of the other Kollek kingdoms and realms beholden to Ulor. The high lords of the Kollek sat in smaller thrones outside the platform, hoisted on the backs of four servants each, and they moved in pace with Ulor's royal platform, surrounding it along with Ulor's royal guard.

Merki grabbed her bow and a couple of arrows and leaned them against the pillar next to her, out of sight, waiting for the perfect moment. She'd have to be quick and her aim perfect, she knew. She'd only get one shot—two at the most, before every soldier and Chosen in the city turned on her vantage point and surrounded the tower. If she managed a perfect shot, she'd have seconds to discard her priest robes, make it downstairs and then blend in with the crowds before the Chosen arrived, no doubt followed by an army of Kollek soldiers.

And if that failed… If she missed, or couldn't make it out in time… Merki wouldn't let them take her alive. She'd climb back to the top of the tower, stare down at her completed work… and jump. She'd ran it all hundreds of times in her mind, taking into account hundreds of different variables… and these were the only options that had made sense to her.

Suddenly, with Ulor's appearance beyond the bend, every sound in the parade hushed. A set of powerful-sounding drums began to beat in a new rhythm, rising and rising in intensity the closer the King of the Kollek got to the temple, and continuing in a steady rhythm like that of a heartbeat, as the lords and ladies reached the front yard of the temple and started to climb down from the platform. First, the lords of the Kollek were placed down onto the grass and they got up and walked towards the first row of chairs placed before the entrance to the temple. Then, the kings and queens of the Kollek followed after them, climbing down a central stairwell built into the platform and walking past the lords in their chairs at the very end of the yard. The monarchs then took their place in their designated thrones, considerably closer to the temple steps than the lords' exquisite, yet small chairs. Every time a monarch sat down at their throne, the flag of their country was raised to the sky by servants dressed in their colors and uniform, signaling to the people where each royal was from. Then, Siegen and Fermand followed after them, along with Flora and Urail, led by the queen; all five of them sat on the closest row of chairs to the temple doors. Once they were all seated, a moment of silence covered the city. Ifir, standing at the steps to the Grand Temple, raised her hands to the sky once again, and began to sing a new melody, different from before. Merki instinctively shut her ears fearing a repeat of the first time, but when Ifir's voice boomed into the city, it was no longer that terrifying clash of breathtaking somberness from before, but a sweet and almost spiritual song that seemed to not be coming from a woman, but from an angel right from Aether's heavenly realms. Her melody was so haunting… but also hopeful and regal, and it rested every soul that heard it. As she sang, and army of white doves suddenly burst from the trees surrounding the temple and Castle Hill and began to fly in diagonally opposite directions over the Street of Kings, forming a complex dance of wings and flutters beginning at the temple, then making its way up towards the king and all the way to the castle.

Even Kade, down in the basement of the tailor's shop, heard the song as clearly as if he was there. He frowned, sitting on the table, and looked in the direction of the ceremonies, his mouth slowly gaping open.

By the gods… what is that? It sounds just like… my mother's voice… but stronger. He thought, using his Chosen senses to pick up every note and inflection in Ifir's lyrically perfect voice.

Once Ifir had finished her aria, she held her arms towards those seated before her and bid them to rise. Once they did, she and very single person in the city; from lords, kings and queens to the lowest commoner in attendance—even the crowds filling the streets for blocks and blocks away from the temple all knelt down, lowering their heads.

Then, and only then, Ulor rose from his throne.

The monarch walked down the steps cautiously, looking around him as he made his way down the carpeted, flower-lined path towards the temple, his gaze focused only on the temple doors…

Merki saw her chance then, as Ulor walked forward, his back to her, and every other head was bowed down. She rose her bow, knocked an arrow and breathed deeply, calming the thunderous beats of her heart.

She breathed, and breathed, until all she saw was the temple yard, Ulor, his lords and monarchs…

…and Siegen, the commander of the Kollek army. The tip of her arrow moved towards the soldier, kneeling in the ground before Ulor. She raised the bow and adjusted the angle to compensate for the distance and the wind. She saw the shot clearly, having practiced with a similar weapon and arrows back in the forests around Halstead for years—having made this exact same shot hundreds, if not thousands of times. She took a deep breath and held it, and the world became only her, the arrow and Siegen—the man who had taken everything away from her… who had ordered her father killed like a dog for no apparent reason all those years ago, leaving her all alone in the world.

"For you, dad…" She whispered.

Her fingers began to slip from the string, less than a second away from loosening the arrow at the commander's head—knowing it would pierce him from temple to temple like the pig that he was.

But then, time stood still for her. Merki couldn't move. She couldn't breathe. She couldn't do anything but watch, as Siegen suddenly turned his head to the side, and his stare moved closer and closer and closer… until it landed squarely on her, piercing her like two fine spears right through her soul. Then, something impossible happened. Merki wasn't in the bell tower anymore. She saw herself in a meadow, with Siegen standing right in front of her. Then, the man dropped to his knees and fell dead to the side as a shadow stood behind him, flaring with black fire. The shadow looked right into her, and past her, and as she blinked, she knew—it was the shadow looking at her from the temple grounds, whatever it was, not the man she was after. Her blood froze and her fingers went limp; the pain and anguish she felt in her heart leaving her motionless. When she came back to herself a second later, the commander had already walked behind the front columns of the temple, waiting for the High King next to the great doors. He was an impossible target now. The young huntress moved around her limited space, trying to get a new angle, but the man was completely out of sight—she would've had to climb down the tower and move across the street, perhaps, to gain a new angle… which was impossible, given her circumstances. Merki bit her arm not to shout, then just fell on her knees with tears in her eyes.

By then, Ulor had already reached the doors to the Great Temple and the lords and royals in the yard had all sat down in their respective chairs—all except Ifir and Siegen, who stood on each side of the door, heralding the way to the inner sanctum. Ulor turned back to face the people one last time before heading inside.

"Proud people of Kellum. Kings and queens of the territories. With Aether's blessing, the days of sacred imperation have begun. As His right hand and your king, I commend myself to learning the wishes of our god and reveal them to you. Soon, the new orders of Aether will be upon us. Pray for me, for the Kollek, and the world, that Aether may finally reveal his Sword to us and deliver us from the profane heathens of the border lands—the hated Koartiz and their dark abominations. Fast in your homes, send your wishes to Aether that we might be free from this cursed war once and for all."

A roar of cheers and applause rose from the hundreds of thousands of voices present in the streets of the city, from the Castle, and all the way to the Silence. The people waved their banners and chanted their approval and their love, hoping against hope that this would be the day Aether would give them the answers they'd all been waiting and praying for—the day they were granted the secrets to their ultimate victory. Ulor climbed the rest of the stairs among the cheers and claps of the people, and the two priests of Aether standing next to Siegen and Ifir promptly opened the doors for him. Because of the way the temple had been built, the sun's light pierced the great dome's glass mosaics perfectly at this precise time, the holy hour, casting a powerful beam of light towards the entrance. Ulor walked into the blinding light, disappearing in its brightness, as the people's cheers grew to a thunderous din that shook the very walls of the city. As the priests closed the doors shut behind him, sealing him inside with Aether, the final sound of the lockdown echoed throughout all of Kellum. A troop of elite Chosen—the King's Own, surrounded the temple and stood in silent guard of their king—as they would in rotating shifts, day and night, throughout the next seven days.

After the doors closed, and the roar of applause and cheers died down somewhat, the other monarchs, lords and nobles accompanied Etheria and her children back towards the castle, all guarded by a whole platoon of Kollek and Chosen soldiers led by Siegen and Ifir, with Odmund riding at the back.

As they were nearing the castle and the people were already dispersing to begin their ritual three hours of prayer in support to the king, a Chosen soldier ran up to Odmund with obvious urgency in his step.

"Captain?" He called to him, bowing. Odmund stopped and looked at him with a raised eyebrow. Efilia, who'd now joined Odmund's side, looked at the soldier warily as well. Neither of them could make his face or voice out very well, seeing as he was wearing a helmet, but Odmund urged him to continue.

"What's wrong soldier?" He asked.

"We caught a conspirator among the people—a rebel Chosen." The soldier informed him in a low voice. "He might be involved with the, um... *disappearances.*" The man said.

Odmund's eyes shot wide open and he looked at Efilia. "Cover for me, Lia. It won't be long." She nodded, then rode towards the castle with the rest of the entourage.

"Where is this Chosen now? Odmund asked in a hurry and pulled the soldier aside from all the rest, dismounting his horse.

"We're holding him in a nearby building, sir—an empty storehouse, away from the people." The soldier said.

"Good. Is he alone?" Odmund asked while already walking out the castle gates with the man.

"Yes sir, but we can't calm him down. He... insists on being your relative, sir."

"My *what*?" Odmund asked, his brow knitting in a deep frown.

"Your... brother, sir. He says he's your brother." The Chosen soldier affirmed, bowing his head slightly. "We think he might be feral, or nearing it, at any rate."

Odmund frowned, a hand on his chin, thinking. Then he looked at the soldier and nodded.

"Alright. Take me to him soldier: on the double."

"Yessir."

The soldier led Odmund down the Street of Kings and then down a side stairway that climbed all the way down to another part of Noble's Row. Once they reached the bottom of the stairway, they found themselves in a secluded backlot filled with trees, fallen leaves and grass—a wooded area that looked more like they'd entered a small forest than a backlot inside the city.

Next to the small woods, nestled against the rising hill, was a dilapidated storehouse. Outside, two other Chosen were standing guard by the door, both wearing the same black, gold and red armor as all the rest, both fully helmeted. They stood at attention, their spears held high, as Odmund walked towards them.

"Sir, Champion, sir!" They both said in unison, and opened the door inside.

Odmund walked into the darkness of the building to meet with the crazed Chosen rebel... but all he found inside was an empty chair in the middle of the room, some rope, and an empty flour sack next to it.

"Wait... what is..." Odmund began, but before he could finish the sentence, something heavy and blunt smacked him hard in the back of the head and his world went completely dark.

CHAPTER 40

MIGHT AND FIRE

Everything was dark.

No matter how much Odmund tried to see, the flour sack over his head only revealed small specks of light, filtering through the fabric in places. A few humming noises made his headache worsen, as his sense of sound slowly came back to him: two men's voices which sounded like roars to his aching eardrums. Odmund could feel his warm breath inside the sack, but his senses were too weak to make out much of what the men were saying yet. He could swear he heard the sound of a river or creek nearby, but the more he tried to focus his senses, the more pain he felt radiating from the back of his skull. As he did, however, he noticed that he was completely bound to a sturdy chair—hands and ankles. A few moments later, he started to make out what the two men were saying.

"Will he be okay?" One of them asked—a young-sounding voice. "You said they wouldn't hurt him!"

"He will be, do not fret." An older voice replied. "He's a Chosen, like you—he'll recover quickly from his wound."

"Do you think he'll believe me?" The young man said, sounding desperate and worried.

"He must, Kade." The old man said. "Did you think of what you'll say to him?"

There was a pause between the two men. "I... I don't know, Axel. I've never met him. What can I say to convince him?"

The old man, the one named Axel, sighed. "Alright, then. We'll have to go with plan B."

"What's plan B?" The one called Kade asked.

"The Mind Link."

Another silence.

"... What's that?"

"Just... touch your forehead to his, Kade—and your thoughts will merge. All of your memories and secrets. You will know each other intimately."

"Like a customary Nor greeting? How can such a thing be possible?"

"Just do it, Kade. We don't have much time. We need to get you both out of here before they start a manhunt for him... if they haven't already."

Od heard the two men walk closer to him until they were standing right beside him. He tried to conjure up a small flame in his hands to burn through the rope, but discovered that he couldn't. Something was blocking his powers.

"Gently now, Kade... I'll remove the bag and then you touch your forehead to his. The process will be... uncomfortable, but it will work. You will both immediately recognize each other."

Kade nodded and put both hands on the back of the chair, over Odmund's shoulders, then started to lean down towards him. The man looked to be completely knocked out, his head hanging limp over his chest. Axel removed the sack from Odmund's head and, the moment he did, the Chosen champion looked up with his eyes in a fierce scowl.

Kade didn't have time to react. Odmund leaned forward, rocking the chair on his feet, then pushed himself up—headbutting Kade so hard in the nose with the crown of his head that he broke it. Kade staggered back, holding his nose with a yelp as Od fell back to the floor with a crash. Other men came out of the shadows of the dimly lit room and pulled Od back up, holding him against the chair once more.

"Rebel scum!" Odmund growled, spitting at their feet.

"Hold him steady!" Axel said. "Champion Odmund, control yourself!" Meanwhile, Kade was trying to stop his bleeding by squeezing his nose and bending his head backwards.

"Who are you?!" Odmund's voice was raucous and dazed, but still fierce.

"We are your friends and allies, Champion." Axel calmly answered, hoping to calm Odmund down. "And we are here to help you."

"Liar!!!" Odmund yelled.

"You have to believe us, Odmund—we're here to help you!"

"Help me? By smashing me in the head and dragging me to Aether knows where? You need to work on your lying, old man!" Odmund shouted while trying to conjure up flames in his palms. Kade and Axel exchanged a sidelong glance at each other.

Seeing as he still wasn't getting any results, Odmund began to struggle against the hands holding him in the chair, hoping to break free somehow.

"Odmund..." Kade began, but Axel cut him off with a hand gesture.

"We don't mean you any harm, Champion," Axel began. "I specifically told the men not to hurt you... but given the circumstances, we *had* to bring you here at all costs."

"If you don't mean me any harm, then prove it! Untie me!" Od spat out.

Axel grimaced. "We... can't do that."

"Why not?!"

"Because you'll burn us all to a crisp before we've had a chance to talk."

Odmund's chest heaved as he frowned pure venom at the old man.

"If you won't free me... then at least answer my questions. Where are we? Who are you?"

Axel nodded, then sat on a chair opposite to Odmund. "I am Axel. He is Kade. We're not rebels. We've travelled long and far to find you—to speak with you. There is something very important you need to hear."

"What is it? Come out with it, then."

Axel sighed, then beckoned Kade forward. The young Chosen had already gotten his nosebleed under control and he nodded, taking a seat next to Axel.

"This man… Look at him carefully, Champion."

Odmund did… and now that his eyes had focused properly, he was horrified at what he saw. Aside from the man's hair looking different and his skin a bit tanner—he was an exact copy of him.

"What… what is this?" Odmund asked. "What is going on here? Who is this man?" He looked between Axel and Kade, eyes wide.

"This man, Lord Odmund… is your brother."

Odmund looked into the man's eyes once more… then he started shaking his head. "No, he isn't. This is all a trick—a plot to get me to do something for you; to confuse me! I don't have a brother, and I don't know this man!"

"There is no plot here, Champion…" Axel said. "This man wants to show you something—just let him touch his forehead to yours and you'll understand everything."

Odmund scanned the room carefully. They seemed to be in an old barn somewhere—not the same storehouse he'd walked into before all this. He could hear birds outside, and that same creek or brook. Could they be outside the gates…?

"We're sorry for all of this, Odmund," Axel said. "For putting you in such dire circumstances and binding you up like this. If we had any other way of doing this, trust me—we would've." Axel said, then urged Kade forward once more. He looked between Axel and Odmund warily, not wanting to get his nose broken a second time. Seeing Axel's nod of approval, he took a single, tentative step towards Odmund.

"Don't touch me!" The Chosen growled. Kade stopped in his tracks, looking at Axel.

"We don't have much time, Champion. Please… if you'd only let him touch his brow to yours—you'll understand everything, far better than any of us can explain it."

"Oh, you'd like that, wouldn't you?" Odmund said. Then he looked Kade from head to toe and stared venom at him too. "What are you, then? A Cauda? Are you casting an illusion right now? Making me see myself in your face? You're trying to absorb all my thoughts so you can supplant me as the champion, aren't you?"

Kade looked at Axel again, grimacing and looking completely clueless.

"Calm down, Captain Odmund, please." Axel calmly said.

"You lying traitors! I'll not fall for your lies so easily! I'd killed many of your kind before, and I'm onto your tricks!" Odmund said, feeling the heat rising in his blood. He struggled once more against the ropes, rocking the chair left and right while the other men held him. He felt one of the legs give slightly, and smirked to himself—his previous fall must've damaged it.

"Untie me now, you filth—and I'll make your deaths quick and painless!" Odmund said again, rocking the chair again, feeling the leg give more and more, just about to break.

"We are not in the best place for you to lose control now, Captain…." Axel warned Odmund. "If you light this place up… we all die."

"I don't need my fire to take you and your dogs down, old man." Od angrily said. He looked at Kade as he said the word "dogs." "Just untie me and you'll see…"

"I am not his dog!" Kade scowled.

"Then what are you?! What do you want with me?"

"I am your brother—and your true name is Ellyad, not Odmund!" He said, stepping forward. "We are Nor from Norzou—and our mother is waiting for you to come back home! Our sister's life depends on it!"

The rush of mad senselessness the Chosen had started spouting all of a sudden shocked Odmund and he stopped struggling for a second, visibly stunned.

"Kade, now!" Axel said, and the young Chosen strode forward, grabbed Odmund by the shoulders and was about to slam his head against his when the champion jerked the chair's leg free, dodging

Kade's moves and falling to the floor. Instantly, he freed his legs from the limp ropes at his feet, then rolled on his back, freeing his hands from the backrest as well. Despite his hands still being bound—with amethysts bindings no less, he held one of the chair's legs like a club between them, ready to defend himself. He stepped back, facing the men around him one after the other.

The men around them, regular Kolleks as Od saw, all drew their weapons, but Axel stopped them. "At ease, men! Do not harm him!" He said, standing up and holding up a hand.

"Ellyad, calm down, please!" Kade said, reaching out a hand towards him. "I don't mean you any harm—none of us do! I know this is all shocking and hard to believe, but… I really am your brother… and I just want you to come home with me! Our mom and sister need you!" Kade said.

"Oh… there's a sister now? Waiting at home… in Norzou? Where we're both from?" Odmund asked, staring Kade right in the eyes.

"Yes!" Kade said, excitedly. "Do you remember it now?"

"Yes…" Odmund said. "I think I do. Why don't you come a little closer and we can talk about it more, then?"

Kade frowned. "I'm being serious!"

Odmund frowned. "You're mad, Chosen. Feral even. Either that, or you've clearly been deceived by these crooks."

"I'm not!" Kade said, clearly at the end of his wits now.

"You are… and you're all a bunch of traitors! You will all hang for this treason, and for spouting such nonsense! I don't have a mother in Norzou, nor a brother, nor a sister! My only family are the Chosen, back at the castle!"

Just then, Odmund grimaced and gritted his teeth, groaning as his face turned deep red. The veins in his neck popped out and steam started coming out from his skin. The amethysts on his bindings began to dim, growing darker and darker, until they became as black as coal.

Axel gasped and stepped back, pressing himself against the wall. "Impossible!" He said. "Those were brand new amethysts!"

I told you they wouldn't hold, you old shit! Now we're all going to die! The voice inside him said in a panic.

Odmund's bindings shattered and his hands became two balls of fire.

The men all looked between Odmund and Axel. Seeing the look of fear on the old man's eyes, they advanced on the champion with their weapons.

"Wait... no!" Axel said, but it was too late.

The three men moved against Odmund, swords raised high, hoping to do something before he could burn them all to cinders... but they didn't move as fast as Kade. The Chosen, heartbroken over his brother's attitude and insults after he'd spent so much time and effort looking for him, had torn his amethyst necklace off. Before any of them could realize it, his body had swollen up to twice its size, his silken shirt all but exploding around his torso, and he'd moved forward with the speed of a gale, bashing them all aside with his bare hands like pesky flies. He then rounded on Odmund, who stood looking up at him, his two palms glowing with flames, eyes wide.

"So, you were a Musal all along... Not a Cauda. Well... shit."

Kade blasted forward with insane speed, grabbed Odmund's arms and flung him clear across the barn like a stack of hay, smashing him through the weak walls.

"Kade, no!" Yelled Axel. "Control, Kade! Control! We need Odmund alive, remember?!"

But the Chosen was now entirely out of it—fully given into his powers. He jumped outside through the hole he'd made and found Odmund getting up in the grass. They were outside the barn, in the middle of a forest outside the city walls. How they'd gotten out here with the lockdown, Od had no idea, but he knew they must've been close to the city.

If I start a fire here, they'll see the smoke from the walls... and send soldiers.

He looked around at all the trees around him... then started to blast plumes of bright fire all around him, setting them all ablaze. Kade saw the brightness of the flames, felt their heat, and the flames inside him roared all the louder. He jumped next to Od in a heartbeat and swung his arm over his head. The champion ducked just in time and put his hand over Kade's stomach, blasting a gout of fire at him point-blank.

The large Chosen staggered backwards, almost roaring in pain, looking at the badly charred flesh over his stomach muscles.

Odmund stared at the wound as well, eyes wide, heart thumping inside him, remembering the last time he'd lost control while using his powers… and an innocent life had paid for it.

Hugo… He thought.

In that moment of hesitation, Kade tackled him with blinding speed and pinned him against the grass with his arms and knees. Odmund tried to break free, but it was like having an ox sitting on him. He shot two plumes of flames from his open palms, burning the grass around them, but Kade squeezed his wrists so hard that the flames died out and Odmund felt like his bones could shatter at any moment.

"I will take you back home, no matter the cost."

Kade's narrowed eyes and clenched teeth had no sign of sympathy or love anymore. He breathed deeply over Odmund as the champion grimaced in pain.

"Only my dead body!" He said with effort, then spat Kade in the face. The giant leaned so close to Odmund's face, scowling, that for a moment they could feel each other's breath in their faces. Then, Kade smashed his head against Od's, and both of them shook, convulsed, then passed out—their eyes rolling to the backs of their heads. Kade's body went back to normal and he fell limp on top of Odmund.

Axel had already exited the barn by then and rushed over to them.

"Finally," he sighed, pushing Kade's body away from Odmund's, not to leave the champion breathless under him. Both Kade and Odmund laid motionless on the grass, and both their bodies suddenly got as cold as if they were on ice.

The old man looked at the flames around them, burning and spreading through the trees, and cursed under his breath. He knew the soldiers would see the inferno… and some might be brave enough to break rules and come check it out, despite the lockdown. The other men he'd hired for this job walked out of the hole in the barn's wall then, rubbing their heads and sides after being smacked away by Kade, and Axel immediately gave them orders to load Kade and Odmund's limp bodies onto a nearby carriage.

As soon as they had, Axel got inside and gave the order for the driver to get them as far away from there, and Kellum, as possible.

CHAPTER 41

A SECOND CHANCE

The moon slowly appeared on the sky as the day turned into night.

Queen Etheria was resting in her chambers atop the royal tower, watching Aether's Great Temple from her balcony as the cool, crisp autumn wind caressed her face.

Her maids were standing next to the chamber doors, standing at attention, ready to serve. Suddenly, as Etheria looked out over a starlit Kellum, someone knocked on her door. One of the maids opened it, and lo and behold, Loure entered the queen's room. She knelt on the floor before her.

"My queen," she said. "You requested to see me?"

"Welcome, dear Loure. Please, sit." Etheria waved her arm over the sofa next to hers. Then, to her maids: "Wait outside... Ah, except you, Kareen. You stay for a little longer." The maids did as told, closing the doors behind them while Loure sat on the couch Etheria had indicated. Kareen, her head maid, stood by the side of her couch, waiting for further orders.

"Tea." Etheria said, and the maid promptly rushed to serve them. "Thank you dear. *Now* you may go." Kareen bowed and left.

"How are you, my dear?" Etheria asked Loure as she took a sip of the hot, fragrant tea, her eyes looking her up and down. Loure kept her stare cast at the floor, unsure as to how to act or behave in front of the queen of the Kollek, or why she was there in the first place.

"I am… well, my queen." She said, voice trembling.

"Good. I heard all about your accident in the kitchens and felt so sorry for you." Etheria put her hand gingerly over Loure's as she spoke. "But… as tragic as it is, beauty isn't everything in life, dear. In fact, your situation could open doors that were previously shut for you… if you know to seek them." Loure raised her eyes to meet Etheria's, and the queen smiled warmly at her. She didn't look fazed in the least as she stared at the side of Loure's burnt, melted face. If anything, her eyes were appreciative, calculating, thoughtful.

"As your high queen, I can help you to step into these new opportunities." She smiled at her again. "You'll have power and prestige here in the castle beyond any that a man can give you."

Loure's good eye opened wide. She bowed deeply to Etheria in her seat.

"M-my Queen…! Your servant would be honored. W-what would you have me do?"

Etheria gently raised Loure's head by her chin, then produced a black leather mask from behind her. She put the glistening mask on the wounded side of her face, covering it entirely, then adjusted the strap holding it in place behind Loure's hair.

Loure stared at the queen with her good eye—the burnt half of her face covered by the expensive-looking mask. Etheria held up a hand mirror and Loure gasped as she looked at her reflection, barely recognizing the woman that stared back at her.

She was beautiful again. The mask complimented her face perfectly, hiding the scars as if they'd never been there to begin with. The material was comfortable and supple—almost like a second skin, and when Loure looked at her reflection, she saw only her youth and beauty on display once more.

"M-my Queen," she muttered, staring at Etheria. "What has your servant done to earn such mercy and honor from you?"

Etheria titled her head to the side and caressed Loure's golden hair as she looked at her, appreciating her own handiwork. "It's not what you have done, dear... but what you can do."

Loure blinked, not sure as to what the queen was referring to.

"The mask is yours to keep, whether you accept my offer or not. I will not force it upon you. However... if you do accept, know that there will be many more rewards in store for you."

Loure blinked again, shocked, then bowed once more at the waist. "What would my queen have me do?"

"The job is quite simple, dear Loure. Here... come closer... let me tell you what I require of you."

Loure did as told, and the queen shared her task with her in a whisper.

"Easy... no?" Etheria asked.

Loure's face was pale and she was close to shaking, but she swallowed hard, composed herself, and nodded.

"You will do it, then?"

Loure considered for a moment... Longer than she wanted to. Could she really go through with something like this? What would happen to her if she failed? And yet... this was the opportunity she'd been looking for all along—her chance to finally climb the ranks of power in Kellum and make a very powerful ally in the process. Loure finally nodded. "I will." She said, in a confident voice.

Etheria smiled a very pleased smile. "Excellent. I knew you'd make the right call. I'll send you the specific instructions for the job later."

Loure bowed deeply to Etheria, then, upon her command, left the room.

A smile played upon her lips as she walked down to her chambers. Her one hand was on her new mask. She felt like she didn't need to hide anymore.

Loure stood in front of the door to her and Mere's room and opened it slowly.

The old maid was still serving up at Ifir's chambers, so Loure sat on the side of her bed and touched the soft leather fabric of the mask, wondering how much her life would change after tonight. Fate had dealt her a cruel hand, but now... maybe she'd finally gotten the chance she'd been waiting for all along.

"Loure... where did you get that mask?" Mere asked in amazement, standing at the door.

Loure hadn't even heard her come in, lost in her thoughts.

"Oh... Hello to you too, aunt. You really have no manners. The mask is a... gift."

"From whom?" Mere asked, tilting her head to the side, squinting. She saw the fine make of the fabric—knew that whoever had given it to her had had it custom-made to fit her face... and was definitely rich.

I've been with my lady Ifir all day, so it couldn't have been her... so then who?

"Quit stalling," Mere said. "Where did you get it? Why would someone give you such an expensive gift?" Mere extended her hand to touch her mask, but Loure stepped back.

She gave Mere an aloof smirk.

"Just a friend who really cares about me and feels bad about what happened to me, aunt. They just wanted to help me." Loure stared at Mere's eyes with that same aloof smile, which told her there was so much more to this than what she was letting on. Although Loure seemed so calm and composed, the old maid could see the hate and blame in her one good eye, which reflected her feelings as plainly as an open book.

"Don't worry about me, aunt. Everything's alright. It's just a very kind favor from a new friend I made at work." Loure said, then hugged her aunt. The old lady hugged her back and caressed her hair. "Ok Loure... ok... I just want you to be well and safe. This castle's a dangerous place for someone like you, and I... I feel I was wrong to bring you here at all in the first place." Mere's eyes stared into space. "I just want to protect you."

Mere's old arms held Loure tight while her eyes shone with fear and worry for her... and more than a little guilt.

"Don't worry aunt Mere. I learned my lesson after last time. I know my place in the castle now..." Loure said as she held her in her arms, but the kindness of her words did not reach the deadly serious expression on her face.

"I really hope so, my Loure." Mere sighed. "There are games at play here that you can't even imagine… and they swallow those who get mixed in them whole. I just don't want that to happen to you."

The young maid smiled. "I know. Don't worry, aunt… it won't."

She stared deep into space for a moment too, before letting Mere go, then said:

"Everything's going to be perfectly fine."

***

The dinning chamber at the keep's ground floor was almost ready for tonight's feast.

All the tables had wide selections of food on them: from deer, to rabbit, fish and mince pie, while small hills of fruits topped the center of most tables in elegant arrays. The castle maids ran to and fro, setting down the silverware and giving the banquet the last finishing touches before the nobles and monarchs arrived for dinner.

"Hurry up, girls! Hurry up!" The head maid ordered while walking around, clapping her hands.

All of a sudden, the doors of the chamber opened wide and all the maids turned to look at the door. A Chosen soldier was standing there, all business. He looked carefully around for a moment, then walked away as fast as he came. The maids looked at each other after they'd left, shrugged, and kept on working.

The Chosen, on his part, strode towards Efilia, who was talking with some other Chosen at the center of the keep's foyer.

"Is he in the dining hall?" Efilia asked the young man as he reached her.

The Chosen shook his head. "I'm afraid not, ma'am."

"Damn! Check everywhere. Everywhere!" Efilia ordered the young Chosen soldiers under her command. A full group of young, recently graduated Chosen and a few other lieutenants were walking around nervously, checking every corner of the castle after the lords, nobles and queens had retired to their rooms before dinner… and Siegen had left the grounds for the night.

"Lieutenant, he isn't in his chambers." A young soldier reported back to her.

"Okay, you three keep searching the castle. If you find him, come get me immediately. You five—come with me. We're going out to the Row." The young soldiers nodded and left with her.

Efilia grabbed a torch, got on her horse, then left the castle with the five other Chosen, riding down the hill towards Noble's Row.

"Where did you see him last, lieutenant?" One of the Chosen asked her.

"Right by the castle gates. He left with another Chosen who reported a captured rebel inside the city."

"Rebels? Did he bring any backup?"

"No... he went alone with the soldier."

And I should've gone with him. Stupid, Efilia! Stupid!

"Did you hear where he was going?" Another of the Chosen asked her.

"I think I heard the man mention a warehouse... but I'm not sure." She said.

The Chosen all trotted their horses behind hers, looking at each other.

"With all due respect, ma'am... there are a lot of warehouses in the city."

Efilia shook her head. "It must've been nearby. The man was on foot."

"That's still a lot of warehouses... many nobles buy them to store whatever they can't fit in their homes, and..." One of the other Chosen, a young man, began... but then Lia cut him off, turning back on her horse.

"We'll search *every damn one* if we have to, Liam! Even if it takes us all night, then the rest of tomorrow too! This is the Champion of Kellum we're talking about here—and he's missing!"

The young Chosen all looked away from Efilia's dire stare, looking very embarrassed and chastised.

"Yes, ma'am!" They all said in unison at attention.

Efilia looked at them for a moment longer, then continued leading her horse down the lamp-lit Street of Kings, still full of petals from the morning ceremonies.

"Now, do any of you know where the nearest warehouses are?"

The Chosen all looked at each other. They were granted precious little time off from their training at the castle and never allowed past Hammer's Burg unless on a mission to the other parts of the city. Despite that, one of them spoke up.

"I recently patrolled Noble's Row as part of a scouting exercise, ma'am. Our group leader took us through every street and alleyway… and I remember seeing some, yes."

"Excellent. Take us to each one you remember, starting with the closest. You two—" She pointed at two of the other Chosen. "Knock on every door from here to the Way—wake up our dear nobles if you have to, but ask around for every warehouse in this part of town and the next over. Once you have a sizable list, rejoin me and the others."

The two Chosen she'd selected nodded and broke away from the group. One of them was a Veruter, who could cast his voice over long distances like her, and the other an Acris, who could locate them quickly with her superior sense of hearing.

Efilia and the Chosen then began their search in Noble's Row, hoping to pick up Odmund's trail from earlier that morning. They searched the first warehouse, right next to one of the nobles' manors, but the Scal in her group found nothing. They moved onto another one, next to a high-end store that catered only to the elite of the city, but like the first, there were no signs of a feral Chosen, Odmund or any rebels being there. No blood, ropes, signs of struggle, hair—nothing.

They'd searched the district for nearly an hour when the other two Chosen rejoined them. One of them mentioned an old warehouse in an overgrown backlot behind a row of shops—one with direct access to the Street of Kings. They all rode there in haste and Efilia dismounted her horse the moment they broke into the small forest, drawing her sword. "On me, Chosen!" She said. Then, to the Scal: "Make sure there's no one around but us."

The young Chosen cast his vision around them for a few dozen meters, as he was still in training, but didn't report any enemy presence. Satisfied, Efilia blasted the warehouse door with a focused surge of her voice, sending it flying clear across the warehouse interior and they all went inside, torches in hand. Efilia's Scal immediately found traces of a struggle. He saw a few drops of blood near the entrance, almost invisible among the dust, dirt and dry grass covering the floorboards, as well as the impression on the floor left by a large body.

Efilia knelt down and touched the dried blood, then ordered the other Chosen to conduct a thorough search of the building.

They all came back to her shortly after.

"Well?" She asked, standing up.

"Ma'am…" That was the Scal again. "I'm afraid there are signs of a struggle here. Those responsible tried to hide it… but someone was definitely hit in the back of the head here with something hard—by the way the blood fell by the entrance. Then they fell here, across the floor. The assailants tried to cover it up, but my eyes can see the impression left by the victim's body in the dust as it hit the floor. He or she… they were as tall as a Chosen."

A cold hand of fear gripped Efilia's heart then and there. "Od…" She said under her breath. "Dear Aether… no…" Her eyes began to water… but she put every ounce of her strength into it and composed herself in front of her soldiers. She then remembered the weird forest fire just outside the city's south gate in the afternoon—which the guards at the castle had just dismissed as bandits and thugs making a scene, as they usually did outside city walls during the Imperation Day celebrations.

"Report this back to Ifir on the double," she told three of the Chosen. "We need to get a search party going outside the walls as soon as possible."

She considered whether to say the next words out loud—whether she could speak them without breaking down. Finally, she spoke, her voice quivering.

"Let her know that… Champion of the Kollek is missing… and presumed captured by the enemy."

***

A few kilometers away from the walls of Kellum, the carriage carrying Kade and Odmund continued to drive fast, away from the city.

It's been hours. Let's wake them up. Axel's inner voice said.

"We can't yet. It's too dangerous," Axel silently said to himself. "It's their first time experiencing the meld, so it's normal that it's taking so long."

I still think something's wrong, you old sack... Look at them! They look pale as death itself. And I know death! The voice replied.

Both Kade and Odmund looked like they were moments away from dying, Axel had to admit, and they seemed to be in pain or anguish as if they were both experiencing horrible nightmares. They were also sweating as if a deadly fever were consuming them from the inside. Still, he remained calm.

"Again... it is only natural," Axel reassured his inner voice. "They have many, many memories to share after more than twenty years apart, after all. Then there's the fact that they're both very special Chosen... The process might be even more violent for them."

What's special about Kade? His inner voice asked him. *I mean, Odmund is an Odon... but Kade's just a simple country bumpkin, no?*

Axel smirked to himself. "Have you ever seen a Chosen with two abilities? Kade is both an Acris and a Musal... or haven't you been paying attention?"

His inner voice hesitated for a second.

I knew that.

"Of course."

But wait... doesn't that mean that he might then be...

"We don't know for sure yet. All we know is that they're both special... and that they might be both integral to what is to come. All we can do is ensure they both get back to Kellum—and see what happens then."

Axel stared at the two Chosen, sitting side by side in the carriage, and hoped their torment would be over soon. Then, all of a sudden, Odmund woke up with a jerk, eyes wide, gasping like he'd just ran a mile. He looked at Axel, bewildered, and the old man nodded sadly, reassuring him. Kade was still unconscious.

A Second Chance

"Where are… what is…" Odmund said, looking around him like a madman.

"Easy now, Champion… You're safe. We're in a carriage that's taking us somewhere safe. You just had a very strong experience—allow yourself to process it."

"I…" He looked at Kade, still unconscious beside him. "He… He is… Stop the carriage! Stop!"

Axel knocked twice and the driver started to slow down. Before the carriage had completely stopped, however, Odmund burst through the door closest to him, ran a few meters into the grass, and vomited.

Axel promptly climbed out of the carriage after him and put a hand on his back. Odmund looked at the old man's face again, eyes wide, but Axel just shook his head.

"First time is always the hardest." The old man said, looking into Odmund's eyes.

"What in the seven hells *was* that?!" Odmund's voice trembled. "I saw… I saw his entire life!" He said, pointing back at the carriage. "What kind of sorcery is this?!"

"No sorcery, Champion Odmund. What you saw were your brother's memories—through your unique connection. This is something only Chosen can do. Haven't you ever wondered why they forbid you to touch each other's foreheads back at the Nest?"

Odmund stared at Axel, blinking. "It's forbidden by Aether himself—a sacrilege before His eyes. It muddles the souls of the Chosen."

But Axel was already shaking his head before he'd finished. "Not quite. It only works on siblings that have both drank from their mother's milk… but if just one of you were to accidentally touch your foreheads together, and meld minds with a sibling back in Kellum, the secret would be out."

"W-what secret?"

Axel breathed deeply. "…that the Chosen are not Kollek… but Nor. Taken from their home soon after birth in those odious black carriages, to be raised as elite, holy soldiers of the kingdom."

Odmund took a couple of steps back away from Axel, pointing an accusing finger at him. "You... you're lying! You poisoned me! Did something to me... This... this isn't real! Any of it!"

Axel frowned sadly. "I know it's a lot to take in, Champion... But I promised you the truth. And this is it. I'm here to help you—to awaken you to your true nature and purpose... and guide you the rest of your way."

But Odmund was shaking his head madly, still stepping away and stumbling, looking like a man who'd drank five cups too many.

"No... NO! This is some sort of rebel trick... it has to be."

Then, Kade exited the carriage as well and fell to his knees, throwing up, much closer to the carriage.

"Kade!" Axel said. "Easy my boy, easy..."

"A-axel..." Kade stammered after emptying his stomach. "W-what was that?"

"Your brother's memories, Kade. You saw his life through your eyes."

"He's... he's a murderer!" Kade said, staring at Odmund in horror. The champion also stared back at him with the same look of horror on his face.

"You..." Odmund began, his eyes full of pain.

Kade pointed a hand at him. "He burnt a child to death, Axel! He's a killer!"

"That was an accident!" Odmund yelled. "And I've spent every waking hour since then hoping I could take it back! Who are you to judge, anyways?" Odmund continued, waving his arm around. "You've torn more men to pieces in the last month alone than I've killed in my entire life!"

Axel smirked. "You saw that, did you?" Odmund looked at him. "Did you see who those men were?"

"They were..." Odmund said, squinting, blinking, forcing the memory back to the forefront of his mind. "They were rebels... I think. At least one of them—the big one. It's all a little foggy."

Axel nodded. "Why would we kill rebels if we were working with them, Champion?"

Odmund stared at him, then at Kade, who was still staring pure venom at him.

"Just... who are you, people?"

"We already told you who we are. You've seen it for yourself now as well. Do you still deny what you already know?"

"I... I know you're a liar, old man. You manipulate with your words, fool others to follow your whims. And he's a gullible child who doesn't know black from white!" He spat at Kade, who just sat on the grass, frowning at him.

Kade opened his mouth to say something, but Axel beat him to it.

"I... am someone who knows the true fate of this world, Champion, and what has to be done to save it. I have been waiting years for this precise moment, to find you and take you back to where you truly belong. The fate of the entire world depends on it." Axel raised his head with pride and honor. Then he continued: "And *he*, is your brother, who was travelled very far to find you and bring you back home—despite the wishes and laws of his people. Your people."

Odmund continued to look between Kade and Axel, his face a storm of conflicting feelings.

"What fate? What are you talking about?" He finally asked, realizing that he already did have answers to most of the other things Axel had mentioned, as he'd seen Kade's entire journey with Axel and the others during the past month and change.

"That of the world dying, Champion Odmund... and you being the only one who can save it."

"Because I might be the Sword of Aether? I am not the Sword, and I am *not* going anywhere with you. My place is at my king's side, and... Oh..." He suddenly looked like he'd seen a ghost. "Lia. She doesn't know where I am..." Then he looked up at Axel. "I need to get back to her! Right now! Where in Kellum are we?" He looked around himself, seeing only trees, the carriage and the road.

Axel's inner voice whistled. *Damn... he's really out of it, isn't he? He doesn't even remember his fight with the bumpkin, apparently.*

"We are many leagues away from Kellum by now, Champion." Axel said, ignoring his other self. "The city isn't safe for you anymore, and neither is the road back there. Please, Champion… you must stay with us." Axel said.

"I don't care," Odmund said. "I'm going back to serve Aether and my king… back to my Lia, who must be worried sick about me right now…" Odmund said, frowning, wondering why he was explaining himself to these people. Then he began to walk, or more accurately, limp, away.

"Captain…" Axel spoke after him. He didn't respond. "Captain," Axel said again. This time, Odmund did stop. He raised his head to the high heavens and sighed.

"What?"

"Give us one more day. Just one. If we can't convince you by then, we'll take you back to Kellum ourselves and leave you right at the gates."

Odmund looked between the two of them sternly. "And why should I believe you? Why would you take a risk like that, after 'all the effort' you've gone through to find me?"

Axel stared him down with a wise, knowing look. "Because I know that, when the time comes, you'll choose to stay on your own."

CHAPTER 42

THE SCREAM

"Songbird," the servant boy of around seventeen said, bowing.

"Speak." Ifir ordered.

"Lieutenant Efilia searches for the champion everywhere. Her soldiers are looking for him as we speak. She's causing quite a stir throughout the castle."

"Stupid girl..." Ifir said, getting angrier. Ifir turned to Captain Fergison, one of the many Chosen under her command who outranked Efilia and commanded the Chosen Corps. "Stop her, captain... and send a troop to secretly search for him. Stop every soldier that has heard of this, every single person, and have one of our Cauda erase their memories... No one other than us can know Odmund is missing. Understand? The official story must be that he's on a special retreat mirroring Ulor's, in hopes of communing with Aether." Ifir stared into space and her voice was very calm as she spoke—something Captain Fergison knew wasn't a good sign.

"Yes, madame." He said, and marched out of her chamber fast, signaling to the boy to do the same.

"Find him!" She shouted again as they left.

She walked into her study, looking around as if she were trying to put so many thoughts in order. She drummed her fingers over the surface of her work desk, biting a finger from her other hand, then paced on her study, arms under her shoulders. While passing in front of her desk again, her eyes caught a piece of parchment with many numbers on it. Her hand reached for it, touched it for a short while… then she crumpled it and threw to the ground behind the desk and a nearby bookshelf. Her eyes filled with twin flames that seemed like they could burn the whole continent. Standing by a window, she turned her gaze over to Aether's Great Temple and clenched her hands and teeth, watching as both the upper galleries and large, golden dome both shone brightly in the moonlight. She took a deep breath, puffing out her chest, then tried to calm herself down.

Feeling more composed, she walked out her study and towards the dining hall on the first floor of the castle.

She heard raised voices the closer she came to the corridor leading to the hall; everyone was there tonight enjoying the feast, and many of the guests were already drunk. King Derkel, Ulor's cousin, was one of them, drinking and laughing with them. When Ifir appeared at the door, the men around it hushed and stared at her beauty. Once more, she had managed to draw the attention of all the royal men in her presence, as she often did. Ifir walked past them and over to the royal table, where Etheria and her children were sitting and enjoying their food. She bowed to them out of respect and etiquette, ignoring Etheria's stern gaze, then walked over to Fermand. She whispered into his ear.

"Odmund is missing… I've sent my men to find him, but the people *cannot* know. Not even Etheria. He's in a special spiritual retreat somewhere in the city if anyone asks." The smile on Fermand's face hung on for a while. Ifir left him, still smiling, but visibly starting to sweat, and sat next to Queen Liza, joining the cheerful conversations among her and her cohorts. Soon, the hall filled with vibrant energy and joy, ushered by the music and drinking.

A few hours later, most of the nobles and kings, including the royal family, had retired from the feast and into their assigned chambers. Ifir, however, still sat at her table, waiting for news from her people.

On the other side of the hall, a few high lords sat with poly-sisters on their laps, still enjoying both their company and the wine. King Derkel was among them—clearly having a great time. He raised a glass of wine in Ifir's direction when he saw her looking, and cheered, clearly drunk: "For the most beautiful lady in this entire city!"

***

Loure walked past the large doors to the dining hall and saw Ifir still occupied by her guests.

Good... she said to herself.

She walked up the stairs to the royal suites, fast, then stopped when she got to the third floor. There was no one on these floors except for the soldiers on duty, standing watch at the doors—most of which led to the chambers that had been prepared for the kings and queens, with those for the high lords a floor below. Loure looked around nervously from the archway leading into the floor's main hallway, then took a few steps down the stairs and listened for anyone coming up or down. Satisfied, she took out a candle from her pocket with shaking hands and lit it up, using one of the torches hanging on the wall. She stopped at the seventh step down from the third floor, then counted the stones on the wall from floor to ceiling. Her fingers pushed on the thirteenth one, just like Etheria's instructions had told her to. She pushed it in with a satisfying click as fast as she could, and a very small door popped open. She rushed in and closed it before someone else saw her.

The small light in her hand was barely enough to light her way inside the cramped, pitch-black corridor full of dust and cobwebs—a second and very tight-fitting spiral stairway climbing around the walls of the first.

Damn it, Loure said to herself, as she tried to focus on just putting one foot in front of the other.

At the end of the tight, cramped stairs was another likewise cramped corridor moving along the walls of the royal suite. Loure nearly held her breath as she made her way through it, as much for the smell of damp and mildew as for fear of being heard, as she could hear the noises the lords and royals were making on the other side of the walls... and those of their whores. At the end of the tunnel, she turned right and counted her steps up to forty. Once there, she stopped, then bent and took a deep breath.

Aether be with me...

She pushed the right stone on the wall and another hidden door swiveled open. Loure walked through and found herself in a large, spacious chamber lit by moonlight and fire coming from a large, ornate fireplace. There was a desk and a small library on her right, while the door was on her left. Loure assessed her surroundings quickly, her heart beating so hard she thought the sound of it might give her away. She quickly found what she was here for—a desk, close to the secret door she'd come out of, and she rushed towards it. She pulled the drawers, trying to read everything she saw with her little candle as fast as she could. She searched and searched, then put the documents back as she'd found them, but she couldn't seem to find the one she was looking for—the one Etheria had asked her to find.

Panic built in her chest and her blood turned to ice as she turned the whole desk over, then searched another, then an armoire next to them—but still found no trace of the thing she sought.

Numbers... numbers! Where is it?!

Suddenly, as she finished searching the last desk in the study, she heard noises from outside.

"Songbird." One of the soldiers outside said in greeting.

Loure panicked, closed the armoire and ran towards the slim stone door she'd come from. In her haste and panic, however, she bumped against the door and heard, with pure horror, as it *clicked* back shut—with no apparent way to open it from this side.

"You're dismissed, Mere!" Ifir said beyond the door. Loure panicked even more, her heart beating faster than the drums of Aether.

Damn it! Have to hide—now! But where?!

She looked at one of Ifir's huge wardrobes. Seeing as she was out of time, she pulled the door open, pushed furs and dresses aside, and jumped in.

"I do *not* want to be disturbed. No matter what." Ifir informed the soldiers and Mere, then walked into the room. Loure pushed herself to the very back of the wardrobe and held her breath, listening.

***

Ifir closed the door of her chamber, locked the bolts in place and poured a glass of wine for herself. Then, she sat at her favorite chair, looking out her wide balcony and onto the sleeping city of Kellum. She tapped her index finger in anticipation, taking slow sips of the very expensive and flavorful wine, thinking of Odmund and a million other things. Then, the sound of stone scrapping against stone was heard, and Ifir looked back into her room. King Derkel stood by another secret door into her chambers—the same Derum had used before a few weeks back. He walked in with a bottle of wine in his hand, then frowned upon seeing Ifir already holding a glass. He moved towards her, doing his best to seem sober and walk in a straight line. His young and extravagant head of full hair glistened under the light of the fireplace as he walked towards her, a cool smile playing on his features.

"Oh… fancy meeting you here," he said to Ifir.

"Be quiet… and close the door." Ifir said nodding towards the open secret door into the room.

Derkel closed the door as told, then walked next to Ifir. "So… here we are, at long last…" He said.

"Shhhh…" Ifir shushed him, a brazen smile on her lips.

"Welcome, King Derkel." Ifir stood up and ran her hands up his chest.

"Oh… how I've missed you," the young king said. His eyes were so full of lust, they made Ifir smile. He left the bottle on a nearby desk and held her abdomen, then pulled the Chosen woman, a head or so taller than him, against his body.

"You truly are a talented poet, Derkel… I enjoyed the little notes you sent to me." Ifir said, then slipped from his hands, walking to the balcony.

"A single night with you can make any man a poet, my dear Ifir." He slowly walked behind her and kissed her neck.

"That's very kind of you... Now, about that ship you sent to my men...?" Ifir stopped halfway, waiting for an answer.

"Just a small gift... to show you how sincere my feelings are. I am not like my father or uncle, Ifir. I won't leave you in the sidelines... and I won't stop fighting for you. I know we can bring everyone to heel... together." He said, while his eyes burnt with desire and his fingers slid over her soft skin.

He pulled her body to himself once more. "Honor me with your love." He whispered, staring right into her eyes as his hands wandered all over her dress.

"To be loved... you have to prove you're truly worthy, Derkel... My heart has been broken enough times." Ifir softly said, returning the same lustful stare, while carefully pronouncing each word.

"Let me prove myself, then." He said, and passionately kissed her. With no resistance from her, he swiftly slid off her dress and his pants. Soon, Ifir was naked on her desk, as Derkel made love to her; his young body full of passion and desire. Ifir moaned and acted as if she were enjoying his love and touches... but her eyes were upon Aether's Temple down below, shining in the night.

Among Derkel's passionate moans and breaths, Ifir suddenly noticed another sound... it almost sounded like heavy breathing... coming from somewhere close. She stopped him, then put a finger to her lips. She listened closely at the room, hearing nothing but the crackling of the fire... She got off from the desk and walked around her chambers. Derkel felt even more turned on as he looked at Ifir stalking through her room, entirely naked. The young king moved aside, crossed his arms and waited for her, staring at her from top to bottom in the firelight, wondering what kind of game she was playing now.

Ifir walked past one of her desks... her wardrobe... an armoire, then stood in front of the fireplace. She listened, and heard the almost imperceptible sound of labored breathing again... mixed with the sound of the crackling fire.

She sighed deeply.

"Come out." She ordered.

Derkel frowned. "Ifir... what are you... I'm right here." But Ifir held a finger in his direction to shush him.

"You... the one in the wardrobe. Out. Now."

Derkel's eyes grew wide, looking between Ifir and her large wardrobe, then he pulled up his pants in a rush. The doors to the wardrobe opened slowly and a trembling, pale Loure walked out, looking like a dark ghost in her black dress.

"Oh... well damn..." Derkel said. Loure never raised her eye from the floor, too afraid to look at anyone, her hands laced under her belly.

Ifir recognized her the moment she saw her face. "Alright... what's your name, girl?"

"L-Loure, my lady..." The young maid said, trembling, almost choking on her own words.

Derkel took a sip from the wine and watched the scene with joy.

Seeing her shaking body, Ifir walked next to her, held her chin and raised her head. She looked into her good eye.

"Mere's niece..." She said, almost in a whisper. "Tell me... Why are you here, little girl? How did you get in?" Her voice was so calm and composed, it gave Loure shivers.

"I... I used the secret passage." Loure said, suddenly unable to help herself. There was something in Ifir's voice... something alluring, yet terrifying at the same time.

"Good... and who ordered you to come here? What were you hoping to find?"

"I was... I was..." Loure tried to fight Ifir's deep, rich voice, her velvety tones and pitch... but she couldn't. "I was looking for a special document... numbers."

Ifir's eyes grew wide.

"For whom...?" She said, in the same sing-song tone that made even Derkel a little sleepy.

"I..." Loure said, resisting Ifir's voice with every single fiber of her being. "For... for no one." She finally said, then perked up a little.

King Derkel and Ifir came eye to eye. Ifir's voice was soft and compelling again. "I'm only going to ask you one more time, my dear Loure… why did you come here? Who sent you on this quest of yours…? Was it Mere?"

Loure's eyes opened as wide as the room, and she shook her head. "N-no, my lady! My aunt had nothing to do with this… she doesn't even know I'm here right now."

"Then who? Come now… I'm not mad at you, sweetie. You're just a tool here. A pawn. Just tell me who put you up to this, and I'll let you go… free as a bird." Ifir whispered gently to her, caressing the good side of her face.

"I… really?"

Ifir nodded, blinking. "Really… I'll even keep whoever sent you from retaliating against you." She put a hand on Loure's shoulder. Every time Ifir spoke, Loure felt the same strong feeling conquering her soul and pulling all the strength out of her.

"I… it was… it was…" She tried resisting it again, but Ifir had broken her will by now, made her doubt her conviction. Suddenly, the words spilled out of her.

"It was the queen, my lady…" Loure said, almost in a trance.

"The queen…" Ifir said, nodding. "Of course."

Ifir looked at Derkel with a smile that did not reach her eyes. The young man rolled his eyes and shook his head. "Leave it to Etheria to play at being you, sending little spies around as if she knew what she was doing." He grumbled, then took a sip of the wine.

Loure stayed silent, her eye cast at her feet. Ifir could see the tears falling from her cheek. Her body was frozen and her soul trapped in limbo.

"Don't worry, little girl. This is not about you. You're free to go."

Loure slowly raised her head and looked at Ifir, having a hard time believing her. However, the Songbird's attention wasn't on her anymore. She stared at her balcony, frowning thoughtfully.

"I'll make sure to send our dear queen a message she won't soon forget… You fly away now, little bird." She ordered.

"T-thank you, my lady. Thank you! You are so graceful and merciful..." Loure bowed as low as she could and hurried towards the door.

Derkel was watching everything carefully. Ifir beckoned him close to her and he joined her by the fireplace. Loure stood in front of the door, looking at all the bolts and locks with a confused look in her eye. She looked back at Ifir, and the naked woman suddenly grinned from ear to ear—a grin that would even give a Koartiz chills down his spine.

"M-my Lady?" Loure asked, her voice weak and trembling.

"I said you could leave, little bird..." Ifir said, still grinning like a serpent. "But not through the door." Hearing her words, Loure froze at her spot, eyes wide. She barely had time to register the implications of the words before Ifir walked towards her, took a deep breath and opened her mouth.

Suddenly, Loure lifted off the ground. She was in midair, hovering, while a horrible wail like that of a hundred dying women pierced every inch of her body. Her whole body was in pain as the pressure around her crushed her. She couldn't breathe, couldn't speak, couldn't scream... all she could do was stare in horror as her world started to suddenly turn black.

Then she broke.

Her arms snapped the wrong way and her legs bent sideways with a crunch. And still, she couldn't scream. Ifir continued her terrible wail, audible only to Loure, piercing her eardrums, stabbing a thousand tiny knives into every part of her being. Loure floated as if in water, moving closer and closer to the balcony, until she was hovering over the edge, barely conscious now from the pain and lack of air.

Then, as if in an act of mercy, Ifir blasted her out into the night sky like a puppet... and the young girl flew free for a weightless, fleeting moment. She was still awake enough to feel the wind at her hair, whistling past her ears as she fell from what felt like the very heavens... then she hit the hard stone ground below with a loud *splat*, shattering into a million tiny pieces, and all the pain and suffering stopped.

Derkel walked over to the balcony and looked down at the front yard of the castle keep below—at the guards already scrambling over the body that'd just fallen in front of them. He could make out the girl's silhouette—twisted and broken, a dark pool of blood spreading all around her. Her head was smashed open like a porcelain vase—part of its contents spilled over the cobblestones.

Derkel whistled. "Damn…" Then he turned to Ifir, looking her up and down, smirking. The Songbird looked out of the balcony, seeming a million miles away. Derkel walked over to her and slowly, carefully, put his hand over her bare back. Ifir flinched as if she'd suddenly been pulled back from a dream and looked at Derkel, a little dazed.

"That… was hot." He said, then kissed her in the mouth again, resuming their previous business right where they'd left it off. However, just as before, Ifir's mind wasn't truly there. For Etheria to have gotten so bold as to send a spy to her chambers looking for dirt on her… things were moving too fast. Faster than she'd previously thought.

Ifir looked out the window at the night sky while Derkel kissed her stomach in bed. Despite the moon being high in the sky, she could tell a new day was dawning. A new status quo. She knew she'd have to make some very important moves in the upcoming days… and that after tonight, nothing would ever be the same.

With those thoughts, Ifir closed her eyes and gave herself to Derkel's affections. She could deal with the queen and all the other moving pieces in her game tomorrow…

Tonight should really be just about her and her pleasure, after all.

CHAPTER 43

THE ARROW

Odmund had begrudgingly agreed to spend one more night with Axel and Kade, seeing as the way back to Kellum was long and the roads incredibly dangerous this time of year.

If it came to it and Axel went back on his promise, Odmund knew he could probably take the carriage from them at some point and just drive it back. It definitely beat walking all the way back and exposing himself to all the rebels and thugs on the roads.

They'd made their way to and made camp for the night at a place known as the King's Ascent; a clifftop hidden away from sight, yet with a sprawling view of the entire Valley of Streams several dozen kilometers southwest of God's River.

During camp, Odmund helped light the fire with a snap of his fingers and they all sat down to eat. The atmosphere had been tense since they'd all gotten back in the carriage and little words had been spoken. Now, however, over a warm, satisfying meal next to a cozy fire, Od was the first one to break the silence—to the surprise of everyone.

"So…" He began, addressing Kade. "The redheaded woman in the vision. Your mother…"

"Our mother." Kade said, sipping his tea.

"… What's her name? I saw her face… her suffering. She seemed to have gone through a lot."

"Her name is Lilian. And yes… she has." Kade said, looking down at his wooden cup. "First, she lost you when we were just babies… Thought you dead. Then she lost our father when he went out to look for you, after he learned you might still be alive."

"And then your sister fell ill, right?" Odmund said, not looking at Kade.

Kade nodded gravely. "Right."

Odmund sipped his own tea. "Sounds like her life's been nothing but suffering…" He said, and Kade nodded. "And your sister…. What kind of sickness does she have?" Odmund recalled seeing the young girl's face in his vision, about ten years old, lying in a simple bed with a terrible fever, her skin pale as the dead.

Kade took a deep breath. "Bloodrot," he said. "It's an affliction of our people… extremely rare and thought to be incurable, except with a blood transfusion from a healthy sibling. She needs your blood to get better."

Odmund frowned. "Why mine? You're the elder brother, aren't you?"

Kade nodded. "But mine didn't work. One of our greatest healers—a friend of our family and a respected priest… he assured me your blood was the only one that could save her."

"What about your mother?"

Kade shook his head. "We all tried to give her some of our blood, but none of it worked. It has to be yours."

Odmund nodded, nursing his cup of tea. "And you say your father left to find me…"

"Our father, yes." Kade nodded. "But he never came back. We… we think he must've died out in the wilds. I barely made it out alive myself. Norzou is very hard to get in and out of. Very hidden."

Odmund sighed deeply. He looked at Axel, who ate the rest of his meal silently, occasionally sipping his own tea. The old man caught his eye and nodded, almost sadly. These people, Odmund thought: if they were lying to him, they were doing a damn fine job of it. They seemed very committed to playing their parts.

And yet... the more time that passed after Odmund had had the visions, the clearer and stronger the impressions became. It was as if his brain was slowly waking up to them, slowly accepting them not as visions... but as memories.

"You said I was... sacrificed?

"To Aether, yes. We didn't think you were alive. My father kept digging for the truth, however, seeking out after the black carriages that carried our children away from the city. He eventually discovered the children might not actually be sacrificed... but taken somewhere as slaves. He broke Nor law to do that... and when it was clear he'd failed, I decided to follow his path."

"Why?" Odmund asked, probing the consistency in Kade's story, seeing if he could poke a crack through it.

"Because my sister wasn't getting any better... and I fear losing her might kill my mother. Agnes doesn't have long." The older brother said, sighing deeply. "I felt useless. I couldn't do anything for her back home, so I decided to set out myself and do whatever I could out here—no matter the risk."

"... I see." Odmund flatly said, looking at the fire.

Kade smirked, a little sadly. "And all the while, here I was, thinking you might've been sold to a wealthy family to work their farm or mines... and yet, you turned out to be one of the most powerful men in the land. Growing in the kind of privilege a Nor can only dream about."

Odmund gave him a sidelong look. "It's not all dresses and feasts."

Kade nodded. "I know. I saw. Sounds like they put Nor children through the seven hells and back before they earn their stripes."

"Chosen," Odmund corrected him, and Kade just sighed.

"Sure... Chosen." He said.

"You two must rest," said Axel, hoping to stop them before they broke out into another fight. "Tomorrow we will have a long way to travel..." Then to Odmund. "And if at the end of that journey you still don't believe us, then we'll just double back and take you home."

Odmund held Axel's gaze for a while, then nodded.

"I'll be on guard duty tonight," the old man said. "You have both been through a lot lately and need your rest. I'll take turns with the driver."

Odmund looked at the man, sitting inside his carriage, eating some of the soup from their pot. Axel had invited him to join them, but he'd refused.

"Are you sure we can trust him?" Odmund nodded towards the carriage, and Axel followed his gaze, then nodded.

"He might not say much… but like all my acquaintances in the city, his loyalty is without question."

Satisfied with the answer, both of the Chosen laid down to sleep in their fresh bedrolls after Kade had put the fire out.

"He might try to run tonight." Axel's inner voice said to him as he sat, watching over the two Chosen after they'd laid down.

Maybe, Axel replied to him wordlessly.

"He will." His inner voice said, very sure of himself.

"Good night." Kade said, closing his eyes, forcing himself to sleep.

Odmund didn't reply. He heard the Chosen sigh then turn his back to him on his bedroll.

***

Odmund laid on his back, looking at the stars, considering his situation. He'd been kidnapped by an old man and a raving Chosen who spoke of conspiracies, hidden truths and madness; all of which could easily be considered treason enough to hang a man over back in Kellum. He could easily run away from them without even having to kill them if he wanted to, as they seemed to have lowered their guard by now… Plus, they were just an untrained Chosen, an old man and the driver, who was also old… and reminded him of Radolf a little. However, the visions in his mind continued interrupting his thoughts. He saw the Temple City, getting clearer and clearer as if emerging from a fog. Saw Kade's mom and sister. Faint impressions of their father. The people of 'Norzou,' or wherever Kade was really from.

They were all Chosen, like him. And yet, they existed as commoners, completely unaware of their special birthright… or even their powers. A whole city of domesticated Chosen, living like peasants. Odmund shuddered at the thought.

Then he realized he wasn't just observing the visions from a distance anymore—as something that had been done to him, but recalling them as his own truth. He stared at Kade's back as the young man clearly just pretended to be sleeping, and sighed.

Just what the hell is going on here, anyways…?

***

Odmund woke to the smell of eggs, ham and greens being cooked over an iron cast skillet.

"Morning!" Said Axel, hunching over the fire. "I'm making breakfast before we set out."

Shit…it wasn't just a dream. Odmund thought, then shook his head. He'd spent all night dreaming of Norzou; of the Nor and Kade's family… dreaming someone else's dreams. Today, however, they felt oddly personal—as if they'd happened to him, if just in another life. He noticed that Kade was already up, sitting on the ground a few meters away, drinking from a cup. He looked at Odmund with squinted eyes.

"How will we get back to Norzou?" Kade asked, mostly to himself. "I didn't see a way back when I left. The earth around the forest is torn—a massive fissure we call the Edge."

"We'll figure it out once we get there. One day at a time, I always say." Axel replied. Then he saw the looks the two Chosen were giving each other and nodded towards the carriage.

"There's a small apple orchard back the way we came. Do you mind gathering a few for the road?" The old man then pointed to an empty cloth sack next to his things.

"… Alright." Odmund said, standing up, and grabbed the bag. Kade followed him and passed him a cup of water with some mint leaves in it. Odmund took a gulp, gargled the water, then spat it on the grass, handing the cup back. As they were walking down the slope, Odmund turned to him, giving him a sidelong look.

"I dreamt about Norzou all night," he said.

Kade nodded. "And I about Kellum."

Both men sighed at the same time, and for a moment, they almost looked like the same man in different clothes, wearing slightly different hairstyles. Even their voices sounded similar.

"How…" Odmund began. "How much did you see?"

Kade was the one giving him a sidelong look now. "… Enough."

Odmund stared at him and blinked. "Did you see me and… Lia?"

Kade looked at him again and, to his surprise, the young Chosen grimaced in embarrassment, getting as red as the apples they were supposed to be getting.

"Ahh…" Odmund said. "So you did."

Kade looked away. "She's… very pretty. Seems to really love you."

Odmund sighed. "She is… and she does."

"You must really be looking forward to getting back to her."

Odmund gave him a suspicious look.

Then, Kade added: "I know if I were in your shoes, I would."

"Yeah… I do. And I will—once the day's up and your old chaperone there takes us back to Kellum."

Kade sighed again, exactly like Odmund. "Still not convinced?"

Odmund didn't say anything.

"There's… more at stake here than just our sister, Ellyad."

"The name is…" Odmund began, but got cut off.

"The world itself is apparently dying. And you, the awakened Sword, are the only one who can heal it before it's too late."

"So the old man says," Odmund said, then frowned. "Do you trust him? He doesn't seem all that right in the head, you know?"

Kade actually smirked at that. "I'm… not sure. I think he's got more of an agenda than he lets on. He's been lying to me—to those who journeyed here with us, from the moment we set out. And yet…"

"You feel he has good intentions?"

Kade nodded. "I don't think he's a bad person. Just…"

"Complicated." Odmund finished. Then to himself: "Fuck... I'm actually finishing your sentences." He frowned at himself, visibly conflicted.

Kade smiled as he stopped below one of the apple trees. "Listen..." he told Odmund, turning to face him. "I don't know what Axel's end-goal is... or what is happening in the world right now, and how we fit into it. And to tell you the truth, I don't really care that much. All I know is that you *are* my brother... that I set out to find you, and I finally *have*." He put a hand on Odmund's shoulder and smiled.

"Just come back with us, Od. Come back, see our mother, heal our sister—then go right back to Kellum if you want to. Axel believes that by entering Norzou and reuniting with our family, you will awaken as the Sword. I... just want our family to be whole again. For my sister to live. That's all."

Odmund stared at him. He felt, deep inside, that the man was being entirely genuine with him now, despite all previous evidence to the contrary. He couldn't explain it, but... he trusted him. He felt like he'd known him his entire life.

"Will you come back with us?" Kade asked.

Despite that, he looked away. "I... I don't know, Kade... This is all too sudden. I mean, how do I know this isn't all a... spell, or something? That Axel or his chauffeur aren't sorcerers and just cast some sort of mind spell on me? How do *you* know? Maybe they tampered with your memories as well. Made you think you are something you aren't."

That gave Kade some pause, and the young Chosen frowned, looking away, remembering how Axel had played with his memories before, making him think he was mad. Then he shook his head.

"No. I know who I am." He said, in a tone that brooked no further argument. "I don't know who nor what Axel truly is—but I know our purposes align, and that he's been nothing but good to me... and for now, that's good enough."

"Good enough might get you killed," Odmund said, smirking.

"Maybe," Kade said, smiling back.

Then he frowned, and Odmund staggered back in shock as droplets of blood sprayed all over his face. Kade stood beneath the apple tree, frowning, looking very confused. He looked down at his chest and saw an arrow the size of a javelin coming out of him. He stared at Odmund, eyes wide... then fell on his knees.

"Kade..." Odmund said, almost in disbelief. "Kade!" The size of the arrow coming out of the poor man's torso was unlike anything he'd ever seen in his life. He looked at the trees from the direction the arrow had come, loosening a massive plume of roaring flame into the trees and setting them all ablaze, hoping to flush out the archer. He saw the shadow of a man fleeing through the tops of the trees, almost like a bird, disappearing into the forest.

Odmund held Kade in his arms. "Kade! Stay with me! AXEL!" Odmund shouted, looking back towards the camp. "HELP!"

The old man and the coach driver both ran down the slope towards the orchard. As they did, Kade grabbed Odmund's arm, blood pooling out of his mouth. "Od... brother... save her." He croaked with immense effort.

"Don't speak, Kade! Save your strength! AXEL!!!"

The old man reached then and, upon seeing Kade in Odmund's arms, and the massive arrow coming out of his chest, he howled.

"AHHHH!!!" He knelt next to them and looked at Kade running his hands over him, as if hoping he could somehow heal the wound. "What happened?!" He asked Odmund.

"The arrow—there was someone in the trees!"

Axel looked at the burning line of trees, eyes wide. "Did you see him?" He asked Od.

"Just his silhouette as he ran away—Axel, he's dying! What do we do?"

The old man moved closer to Kade's head and looked deeply into his eyes. Tears began to fill his own eyes.

"Kade... my boy. No..."

Kade looked up at Axel weakly... and smiled. "Y-you... reunited me... with my brother... Thank you."

"Hush boy," Axel said, gently combing his hand through Kade's hair. "Hush, now."

"M-make sure he gets… back to… her."

Then his eyes stared up into the sky… and stayed there. Fixed. Frozen. His skin went pale, and his head hung to the side in Odmund's arms. The Champion of the Kollek stared at Axel, horror in his eyes, tears streaming from them as if he'd known Kade all his life. An indescribable pain clutched his chest.

Axel stared down at the dead man in Odmund's arms. He blinked his tears away and smiled. "Aether receive you, my boy… Rest now…" He said, and closed Kade's eyes shut.

"Your work is now done."

CHAPTER 44

THE LAST FAREWELL

Odmund and Axel stood before Kade's body, back at the top of King's Ascent.

They'd laid Kade's body in the grass under a lone oak tree that grew from the overlook, near the edge of the cliff. Odmund stared at the shaft of the arrow that had killed the young Chosen, having split and removed it from him with great effort. The massive arrow had been fitted with an equally massive amethyst arrowhead, sharp as any sword Od had ever seen.

"I can't place it," he said to Axel, as the man looked at Kade's prone, pale body. "I've never seen an arrow like this in my life. It's clear it must've been a Chosen—as no other man or woman can draw a bow powerful enough to shoot something like this."

Axel looked at the arrow. "Let me take a closer look," he said, and Odmund handed him the split half of the shaft. Axel looked the bloodied arrow over, then sniffed at it thoughtfully for a while. Odmund watched him as they stood silently beneath the oak.

"It's wood from an Ascendant Birch." The old man finally said.

"A... what?"

"It's a powerful, magical tree that only grows in the old places where magic gathers… like the keeps of the Five Head Sorcerer. And Castle Kellum."

Odmund frowned. "The Castle? I've never seen such a tree there."

"You have," Axel told him. "It's a white, spotted tree. Massive in size."

A look of recognition flashed over Odmund's face. "You mean… the Kingtree?" He asked.

Axel nodded.

"But… what does that mean? Who would've wanted to kill Kade? I mean, no one but you and the others should've known about him, right? And why him, when I was standing right next to him?" Then he frowned, thinking. "It must've been the Sons. Who else has Chosen that can draw and shoot arrows like these in their service?"

Axel sighed and shook his head. "I don't know, dear Champion." He put the arrow on a bag, then turned back to Kade. They stared at the body in silence for a while longer, as the breeze made the grass dance around the body and the oak ruffled overhead, sighing, as if sharing in their sorrow.

"He… really wasn't a bad sort, was he?"

Axel nodded. "He was a good man. A very special man."

It wasn't supposed to be his time yet, was it? Axel's inner voice told him.

No… it wasn't. He replied to it.

Odmund took a deep breath, looking at Kade's body, then turned to Axel.

"I'm in," was all he said.

Axel looked at him, a quizzical look in his eyes, then understanding dawned on him. "You mean…"

Odmund nodded. "I'll travel with you to Norzou. I'll meet up with our… *his*, mother. Save his sister, if I really can."

Axel's features contorted into an old, sad, weary smile—but a genuine one all the same. "You have no idea how much it relieves me to hear those words, Champion."

Odmund nodded, still looking at Kade—basically a reflection of him.

"I'll honor his last wish and save his family... then I'll find his murderers and bring them to justice, as is my duty as the Champion of the Kollek. He was a Chosen, and no Chosen should die such a meager death."

Axel nodded. "Agreed."

"But once I've done this—I'm heading back home. I have friends and loved ones waiting for me back in Kellum, Axel. I won't abandon them."

"Of course," Axel said, heaving a deep sigh of relief to himself.

"Now... we need to do something about him," Odmund said. "And about me."

Axel raised an eyebrow. "What do you mean?"

Odmund sighed. "Ifir," he said. "She must've sent her people after me by now. Knowing her, they must've already picked up our trail. We can't outrun them. However..." He nodded towards Kade.

"He looks just like you."

"Indeed," Odmund said.

My dear Lia... please forgive me for this.

"If we dress Kade in my ceremonial clothes... and leave him my signet ring, as well as the necklace Lia gave me... Yes, that'll work."

Axel nodded, then asked: "And when we come back? How will they know it's you and not an impostor?"

Odmund looked at Axel and smirked. He held up a hand and summoned a tongue of dancing fire.

"I'm the only Odon in the kingdom."

"Ah, of course," Axel said, smiling to himself.

"He's quick, this one. I like him," his inner voice said.

Indeed, Axel silently replied to himself.

"Right. Then let's get to work. We have a long road ahead of us, as you said, and Ifir's agents must be getting closer by the minute."

With that, Odmund and Axel took Kade's clothes off his body and dressed him, with great effort, in Odmund's own clothes—the same he was wearing during the ceremony. They then left him his ring and Efilia's necklace. Finally, they tied him to the oak—making it look as if Od had been bound here before his assailants executed him... then stood back and watched.

"It looks very convincing," Axel said.

"It does. There's just one thing left to do..." Odmund said, now wearing a fresh change of clothes Axel had brought for Kade on the carriage. Axel looked at him.

"We need to burn his body." The champion said.

"... burn his body? But... the ring and the necklace! They'll melt!"

Odmund shook his head. "They're both made from a special blend of alloys, as are all of the signet rings given to royals in Kellum. They can only melt under incredibly hot fires—the kind that can only be produced in a large smelter or furnace. Not even I can produce flames that hot."

"And the clothes?"

Odmund shrugged. "Their shape and outline will give them away... even if they're charred. They're treated to withstand burning to a point as well, given that... well. I'm literally a walking torch."

Axel nodded. "Well... if you feel like it'll make it look more believable."

"I do. If I were a rebel, and I captured the only Odon in the kingdom... fire would send a very clear message, don't you think?"

Axel nodded, despite a part of him not wanting to go through with it. Kade had already been through so much. "Before you do, may I say some words to him?" Axel asked him.

Odmund nodded. "Of course."

Axel nodded sadly then walked towards Kade. He knelt before the young man's body and put a hand to his shoulder. "I'm so sorry, my boy... This wasn't the way it was meant to happen... May you rest in Aether's Garden today." He whispered softly, then stood up and walked away from the body. He nodded at Odmund as he passed him by, and the Chosen champion approached the corpse.

Odmund knelt before Kade's body, sleeping peacefully, a look of contentment on his face, and put a hand to his shoulder as well.

"Rest in Aether's Garden, brave Chosen." He whispered. "And may we meet there again one day." Then, as soon as he'd said the words, Od's palm shone brightly and Kade's body just caught on fire, the flames just igniting all around him as if he'd chosen to alight on his own accord.

Odmund stood up and stared down at the man's body and, again, despite having just met him, a tear rolled down his cheek. Once he was ready, he turned around and nodded at Axel.

Axel nodded back. "Let's go then, Champion."

Odmund walked over to him and, together, they walked towards the coach.

"Call me Odmund, Axel," Od said, and the old man smiled.

"Alright… Odmund."

As the champion got into the carriage, Axel glanced back at Kade's body, sitting by the roots of the tree, legs spread towards him in Od's royal ceremonial attire, covered in glorious, blazing flames which were now slowly climbing up the trunk of the tree, all but ensuring that the body would soon be found.

Farewell, young Kade. Axel said, then got into the carriage.

Till we meet again.

The End.

Printed in Great Britain
by Amazon

Printed in Great Britain
by Amazon